To Pet Lai
and Yam Lai

from

John

J.L.Sears

2077

KNIGHTS OF PEACE

J. L. SEARS

BALBOA
PRESS

A DIVISION OF HAY HOUSE

Balboa Press books may be ordered through booksellers or by contacting:

Balboa Press
A Division of Hay House
1663 Liberty Drive
Bloomington, IN 47403
www.balboapress.com
1 (877) 407-4847

Because of the dynamic nature of the Internet, any web addresses or
links contained in this book may have changed since publication and
may no longer be valid. The views expressed in this work are solely those
of the author and do not necessarily reflect the views of the publisher,
and the publisher hereby disclaims any responsibility for them.

The author of this book does not dispense medical advice or prescribe the use
of any technique as a form of treatment for physical, emotional, or medical
problems without the advice of a physician, either directly or indirectly. The
intent of the author is only to offer information of a general nature to help
you in your quest for emotional and spiritual well-being. In the event you use
any of the information in this book for yourself, which is your constitutional
right, the author and the publisher assume no responsibility for your actions.

Any people depicted in stock imagery provided by Thinkstock are
models, and such images are being used for illustrative purposes only.
Certain stock imagery © Thinkstock.

Printed in the United States of America.

ISBN: 978-1-4525-2017-9 (sc)
ISBN: 978-1-4525-2018-6 (e)

Balboa Press rev. date: 09/18/2014

To the memory of my dear wife
Pamela Jane Sears
1951-2013

And they shall beat their swords into ploughshares, and their spears into pruning hooks: nation shall not lift up sword against nation, neither shall they learn war any more.

Isaiah 2:4

A new commandment I give to you, that you love one another as I have loved you; even as I have loved you, that you also love one another. By this all men will know that you are my disciples, if you have loved one another.

John 13:34-35

To give light to them that sit in darkness and in the shadow of death, to guide our feet into the way of peace.

Luke 1:79

For with thee is the fountain of life: in thy light shall we see light.

Psalm 36:9

Contents

CHAPTER 1

THE TRIAL

The path wound down into the early morning mist. He was going downhill without any load instead of uphill carrying stone slabs. Only part of one wall had been built and completing the hut was going to stretch his endurance, as it was meant to. At this moment he was exhilarated and was enjoying the sense of making progress with nothing to carry and with gravity working in his favour, although he knew that before the day was finished he would be sore and exhausted.

The triangular form of a transpod softly hummed into view out of the mist, moved towards him and hovered above.

He could of course end the Trial at any time. It would be so easy to make a signal to the transpod, be picked up and whisked away to the exit camp. That was the point – to make it easy to quit. If he did not have the will and stamina to complete the task, to build the stone hut, he would be lacking two of the qualities which a Knight needed. He would have to abandon the Trial and all hope of entering the Order. Such tests for entry into military forces, or advancement within them, had been used since ancient times.

The Order was not a military one yet some of its techniques and culture derived in part from the fighting forces of the past.

As he descended into the mist he reflected that he was being tested only for endurance and the will to succeed, not for physical strength. The hut building exercise was geared to individuals and took into account the candidate's innate muscular power. The more muscular the person the bigger the hut they had to build and the heavier would be its component materials. Knights needed to have quickness of mind and body, empathy, ultra-alertness and humility to be effective. When physical strength was needed they had bionic technology to assist them. Unaided physical strength was sometimes useful but the proportion of Knights having powerful muscles could be left to chance; the other qualities were in general more important to the completion of missions and only the most frail of applicants would be rejected on grounds of insufficient muscular strength.

The transpod tilted slightly, glinting in the sun as it broke through the mist, and sped off across the valley, at a level just above the lingering layer of white fog, then lowered itself to where another stone hut was being built. This one was at the critical three walls stage. He had heard that if you got that far you would likely be on the verge of giving up; but if you started on the fourth wall you would probably finish.

This was the last of the tests that made up the Trial. Previously there had been mental ordeals to test reaction times, empathy, lateral thinking, logic and mental speed. These he had been able to prepare for and he felt fairly certain that he had reached the required standard. The neuronic coaching and stimulation games worked well.

Suddenly the transpod on the other side of the valley ascended. Earlier he had been able to make out the shape of a person near the two walls that had already been constructed and on the previous day he had seen a figure traversing a path leading down from it. Now he could see no such figure and suspected the candidate had been taken away in the transpod after giving up and he felt a pang of sympathy.

The remaining mist was dissolving into filaments across the valley as the sun climbed. The descending path ended by a large pile of thin stone slabs which had been deposited by a roboworker. He heaved one onto his shoulder and started back up towards the hut site. All the candidates had been taught by the invigilator the correct way to lift, carry and set down a stone slab. He had also taught them how to build the walls of the hut, fit pre-cut beams into the pre-drilled holes and screw on the wooden roof.

It was not only for the Trial that the huts were constructed. They were meant to serve as places of retreat where a Knight could meditate between missions and were becoming a familiar sight in many parts of the world to pilgrim trekkers who could use them for shelter or prayer.

He almost staggered up the path and felt like having a rest half way but knew from the previous days of lugging stones that this would only make the job harder. Once he stopped he would find it very difficult to start again, especially if he sat down. Besides, there would be the extra energy expended in lifting the slab to shoulder height after the rest. The best way was to keep on and fall into a rhythm. That was how he had managed on the previous days. Yet it did not seem to be getting any easier. The sun was feeling hotter than yesterday, the sweat was seeping from his body and he was becoming dehydrated. He would have to stop for a drink from one of the bottles placed on platforms at intervals along the path.

After drinking the water he began to feel slightly faint and knew that he would not be able to pick up the load again. He would have to have a proper rest and cool off or he would collapse. The only shade was on the north facing slope opposite; so he made his way down to the stream flowing along the valley floor and moved up towards a rock overhang where he could rest.

Another transpod appeared; or was it the same one he had seen earlier? It had been patrolling the valley and as he half expected had spotted him. It landed near the overhang and the driver, a girl with auburn hair he recognised as being part of the selection staff who had met him on arrival, got out and walked gracefully towards him. She had an air of strict professionalism combined with caring sympathy.

'How are you?' She was bending over to feel his brow and a strand of her hair touched his face.

'Just having a rest from the sun.'

'Are you sure you don't want to give up? You look very tired.'

'I'll be OK in an hour or two. Thanks.'

'Well, just flexcom me if you need help.' She smiled and returned to the transpod.

If he gave up now he would be treated sympathetically, allowed to rest in comfort and gently told that he was not suitable for the Order. Alternatively, he could persevere and in doing so subject himself to days of suffering made worse by the possibility that he could still fail the Trial. He had chosen the latter. Why?

Youth throughout history had been more susceptible to fashion than were adults and there had always been a tendency to idealism and adventure. Since its recent formation, the Order of the Knights of Peace had been very much in fashion. Its objectives of world disarmament by force but without violence, including often visually arresting live coverage of commando raids on the telepresnet, both appealed to the young and had the approval of their elders. You could join the Order and immediately feel respected, if not admired, in whatever capacity you entered, whether as a frontline Knight or as a support worker.

Yet it was more than fashion or peer pressure. In the decades leading up to and following the Cataclysm the world had changed in both a material and a spiritual way; and the Knights were part of this transformation in both senses.

He decided to eat his sustenance pack and rest for the next two hours. By then he would have recovered some energy and be ready for further lifting, carrying and building until dusk, when he would move down into the shelter of the valley and switch his smartsuit to 'night' mode for sleeping comfort.

Exhausted though he was he did not immediately sink into sleep that evening. He was comfortable enough as his smartsuit shaped itself to match posture and he put his head down onto a pillow which the suit had formed and ejected. It was a warm night and parts of the smartsuit adjusted themselves to be sufficiently thin for him to sense the bracken. The feel of the bracken was somehow soothing, like sleeping on a sack of straw, and gave a sense of being at one with the earth, while the spray of stars above reminded him of the immensity of the universe.

It was a kind of exhilaration and in this state he always found it difficult to avoid his mind racing. What were his chances of passing the Trial? He felt confident about all the other tests he had been set, so all depended on the hut building exercise. Did he have the will to complete this? Then he rather childishly imagined himself as a Knight on a mission to capture a target – perhaps a gang leader or a dominophile - surrounded by armed guards; the approach behind an invisibility shield, the projection of holographic images to startle and confuse the guards, the ultra fast manual overpowering of the target as the invisibility field collapsed and the rapid summoning of an escape pod in which to take away the target.

He began to feel drowsy and as he faded into sleep he fleetingly remembered the girl from the transpod and the touch of her hair on his face.

* * * *

The Exit Space, designed to blend into the side of a mountain, had been constructed for candidates who had finished the Trial. Here they would be interviewed by the Selector, told their results and either formally invited to join the Order or informed of their failure.

Failure was unlikely now that he had successfully completed the hut building. The other tests had not really been a problem. Not that they were easy but they were mostly testing abilities which, unlike strength of will, could be improved fairly reliably with practice and bio-enhancement where one's natural aptitude was not high enough. He had undergone augmentation exercises in areas where practice could have a significant effect - reaction times, lateral thinking, logic and thought velocity. Empathy was the only area where techniques for improvement were of doubtful efficacy and he suspected that this component of the selection was given a relatively low weighting. As for neuronic enhancements these were not widely available, although the Knights were thought to use them regularly and they were an integral part of the Enlightenment procedure conducted by the Monastery.

He wondered how many of the others sitting at tables or cyberbays in the candidates' waiting area would be successful. The pass rate was low, about one in ten, but did this include those who had gone back to retake specific tests? He had never found out.

To pass the time he went to sit at a cyberbay where he could play Knight Attack. He activated the input scanner and went through a series of motions. Within seconds his small avatar hologram appeared beside him together with the game setting. The face, black hair and slight stature were fairly accurate representations of him but he was dressed in the chain mail and cylindrical helmets sometimes worn by the Knights of Peace when on non-covert attack missions designed to be high profile. As always, the Knight had no weapons capable of inflicting permanent injury, although he did have disabling devices. The object of the game was to use a virtual shield which made you intermittently invisible, with a cumulative invisibility lifetime of only twelve seconds to penetrate a labyrinth in which were placed seven armed guards and to overpower a lethally equipped dominophile at the centre. Points would be lost if the dominophile was harmed as you abducted him to a waiting transpod. In real life a Knight would face penalties, even dismissal from the Order, for deliberately harming an enemy. It was this which made their tasks all the more challenging. Part of the game involved reading the facial expressions and bodily stance of each guard and guessing the next move. This was the part he found most difficult.

The game absorbed him so much that it took his mind off the interview which awaited him. Then he became aware that a female voice was calling out his name with a questioning intonation and that this was happening in the real world.

'Mr Roscoe Finley?' The voice was familiar.

He looked up and saw the girl who had stepped out of the transpod during the hut building exercise. She must be doubling as the Selector's assistant. 'Hi. Sorry to keep you waiting. The Selector is ready to see you now.' As she ushered him in to meet the Selector he felt a warm, attractive presence. He had met and interacted with a large number of women in his adolescence and early maturity, especially while studying philosophy at Cambridge, but never had he been so stirred. It was only for a moment and he had not even caught her eye; but it was unmistakable. He could not help wondering whether this was a moment of destiny. If it was it seemed strange that it should coincide with a meeting which would be so pivotal in deciding his vocational destiny.

The Selector welcomed him into the room. It was very simple – four walls, a table and two chairs. 'Good morning, Mr Finley.' He signalled Roscoe to sit down. 'Good morning, Knightmaster.' It was well known among applicants that the Selector was in fact Knightmaster Franklin.

The Knightmaster's smartsuit assumed the form of a civilian tunic. Roscoe realised that he must be at least ninety years old and recalled that he had been one of the founders of the Order. He had seen a lot of action, both in the Order and in his previous military career with the United Nations, the predecessor of the Global Federation. Although his skin was ripening and his hair beginning to grey he was physically and mentally agile, and had an upright military posture.

'You must be relieved to have finished the Trial.' The Knightmaster seemed both severe and kind and spoke with a precise eloquence. 'We are honoured that young people like you are so keen to join us, although there are many other ways of serving the Divine Light.'

Roscoe respectfully acknowledged this.

'You have done well in reaction times, lateral thinking, logic and thought velocity. You have also shown your resolve by completing the hut building exercise.' Roscoe's pulse began to thud as he anticipated a proviso. 'Yet one area – empathy – does not seem to be your strong point, according to our tests. Your Countenance Cognition coefficient was sixty one per cent, which is above average for the general population but significantly short of what we expect of a Knight and unfortunately this brought down your overall empathy score.'

Roscoe felt a wave of faintness engulfing him 'So I've failed the Trial?'

The Knightmaster was sympathetic. 'I'm sorry to have to tell you this but I know you will understand. Reading facial characteristics and expressions is fundamental to your operational effectiveness in certain situations and many candidates are unaware of this. Because a Knight is in a sense handicapped by his lack of weapons, at least in the old sense of injury-inflicting weapons, he has to compensate with every means at his disposal, and this includes the ability to guess a person's likely next move by picking up every nuance and subtlety of his or her countenance. Similarly with the body. You did better on Body Cognition than Countenance Cognition, but the two work together and both are needed in times of action.'

Roscoe sat in silence. Deep down he had been so sure of passing that it was a shock to discover that a person he greatly respected was telling him that this certainty had been founded on an illusion. 'Is there a way I can retake the Countenance Cognition on its own? Or do I have to go through the whole Trial again?'

'Not at all; but I am afraid that few candidates are able to improve on their CC score by more than a few percentage points. You would need to reach seventy percent, that's nine points higher than you were able to achieve this time. I don't want to put you off, Mr Finley, but retaking the CC successfully will not be a trivial task. It could be an impossible one.'

Suddenly, Roscoe's respect for the General was eclipsed, though not dissolved, by resentment and deflation at his rejection. Nobody could have tried harder and be more fervent in his desire to join the Order. Yet according to the Knightmaster his best efforts to re-apply could come to nothing for the sake of one part of one test.

The Knightmaster looked genuinely concerned. 'I'm sorry, Mr Finley. This has clearly been a big disappointment. There are training courses out there which might help - I wouldn't like you to go away devoid of hope.'

'Can you recommend one?'

'Sorry. Even if I was in touch with the latest training in this area I would not be at liberty to advise you. Not directly, that is. What I can do is suggest you have a word with Ms Hanson on the way out. She is actually here as part of an assignment to study the Knight selection method, although that's not her main subject. She is currently doing a multilayer course on quantum computing at the Cambridge Cavendish Lab.'

'Thanks, Knightmaster. I will do that.' He had been studying philosophy at King's College. He guessed they must have been at Cambridge at the same time but he had never seen her.

'I can see you won't give up easily, Mr Finley, which is admirable. However, keep in the back of your mind the awareness that there are other, equally worthwhile careers that our Creator may have you marked out for. I see you have Life Extension so you have plenty of time to decide.' They rose, clasped each other's arms and Roscoe was shown out by Ms Hanson. As they left the room the

Knightmaster called out to her: 'Isla, Mr Finley is looking for a good CC course. Could you help him out?'

She smiled but there was a slight tension. 'I'm actually quite busy now, Mr Finley, and we will need time to discuss this. Could you meet me in the Candidates' Bar?'

'Should I just go in and wait for you …?'

'Yes. I'll see you in there, probably within the next ten minutes. Is that alright?'

*   *   *   *

The ClearSpin could only be described as pleasantly refreshing. It tasted of spiced apple and strong ginger, had a kick and an indefinable elating effect akin to the alcohol that had been drunk up to a few decades ago, without being toxic, and was imbued with health giving trace elements. It distracted him from an overwhelming sense of failure and disappointment but the effect disappeared after a few minutes. He felt he had worked as hard as anyone could to pass the Trial, driven by the promise of a glittering future of adventure, worthwhile achievement, a secure income and, it had to be admitted, a certain amount of glory. Yet the promise of entry into the Knights had suddenly vanished, as if a dark curtain had dropped.

As he tried to will himself into a positive frame of mind Roscoe noticed another applicant, a fair haired youth not much younger than him and stockier in build, emerge into the bar area. Despite his efforts to disguise it there was an unmistakeable look of triumph and elation on his face as he made his way across the bar towards the exit door. Roscoe recognised him as someone he had spoken to shortly after arrival at the entry camp. There had been an instant mutual respect between them, although they were obviously very different in character. They had both been full of expectation and trepidation and had wished each other well. Now a gulf separated them.

The applicant spotted Roscoe and walked over to him. 'Hi, Roscoe, do you remember me?'

He had almost forgotten the name but it came back to him. 'Yes, Eric Reed isn't it?' Roscoe was reluctant to ask him if he had passed; it seemed unnecessary. It was obvious from his demeanour but he asked in any case.

'Yes, I did.'

'Congratulations.'

'And you?'

'Not so well. I failed the countenance cognition.'

'That's bad news. Can you retake it? Did you pass the rest?'

'I did. I'm going to book some CC training but the impression I get is that the chances of success on a second attempt are abysmal.' He tried to treat the whole thing light heartedly, but his nature was too transparent. He knew this and wondered whether this was acceptable for someone who would need to be adept at deception when fighting evil.

'If you'll excuse my saying so that is not a positive attitude.' Reed spoke almost jovially.

Roscoe hoped that Reed would not want to talk for too long. He wanted to be alone or, better, to start discussing his future with the Knightmaster's assistant rather than pretending to be pleased at another's success. Not that he was displeased; but it made his own failure all the more difficult to deal with. Just as he managed to offer congratulations and explain that he was waiting for the Knightmaster's assistant to come back, she appeared at the bar entrance. Reed wished Roscoe a successful retake and resumed his walk towards the exit.

He sensed that had he been accepted into the Order Reed would have become a friend and they would even now be on first name terms.

'Sorry to have kept you waiting, Mr Finley.' Ms Hanson sat down next to him on the bench seat. Her smartsuit assumed the form of an olive green top and a black skirt. He was not normally sensitive to matters of dress, so why did he notice this? He found himself wondering whether she had chosen the colours and clothes to match her auburn hair or the smartsuit had done this automatically from its large library of clothing forms. 'There are at least three CC courses on offer but the only one which appears to have a chance of getting you through the test is rather expensive - 500 GMUs. My guess is that if you were successful the KOP would refund the fees but I can't guarantee that.'

'Thanks. Do you have the details? I'm prepared to risk it.' Even if he failed it would not be difficult to repay over ten years or so, a very short period for someone with Life Extension.

'Yes. I've transferred them to your flexcom. The claim is that they can increase your CC by around 15%. If that happened in your case you should pass the retake.' Although his countenance cognition was not great he saw a lot of sympathy in the girl's smile and again became aware of her charged presence, enough to temporarily eclipse the dejection of failure. 'I can really recommend this course. It is run by the Monastery of Divine Light. Some engineer monks have invented a new way of utilising the latest neuronic research. A friend of mine went on the course and increased her score from 64 to 75%.'

Roscoe was encouraged. He had learnt a lot about the Monastery since a fellow student at university had applied for entry and could well believe they had made real progress. Maybe the Knightmaster really was a bit out of touch with the latest developments.

'Well, I have to go now, Mr Finley. Good luck – we will see you again if you reapply.'

'Goodbye; and thanks again.'

He watched her as she moved away, then drank the rest of his ClearSpin and made for the exit.

The transpod he had hired was only a short walk away so he remotely activated the start-up system. It was getting dark so he could see the cabin glowing and he heard the gentle but powerful hum of the magnetronic lifting engine as its photonic drive came to life. Transpods were a new form of transport, and as with the vehicles of previous ages – the steam locomotive, the automobile, the aeroplane – the designers and builders of the earlier models, of which this was one, had been rich with inspiration, achieving a degree of engineering and aesthetic excellence which was never to be quite matched in the later models.

Roscoe climbed into the cabin then spoke in the coordinates of a transpod park in Cambridge. A route plotted itself on the holodisplay as the transpod lifted and positioned itself automatically three hundred metres above a roadline.

He could remember how, when he was a boy, roadlines had been roads for wheeled vehicles. Now they were just compulsory guidance lines for transpods, only necessary to prevent the potential chaos of innumerable flying machines moving in all directions over town and country and occasionally he could see buildings on the old tarmac.

Today had been one of emotional turmoil: the excited anticipation of his successful entry into the Knights of Peace, the crushing negation of this, the hope of salvation through a retake of the CC test and the girl who had moved him in a way which was disturbing, but only disturbing in that it was totally new to him. The hovering transpod accelerated forward as its almost silent fusion powered photon thruster came into play and the vertically acting magnetronic drive held it at a steady height. Now he felt positive as he raced above the roadlines of Snowdonia in the afterglow of the recently set sun, with the slim crescent of the moon hanging just above the mountains to the west and Venus shining brightly beside it. At this moment anything was possible.

CHAPTER 2

OVOSKOTIA BRIEFING

He had kept a handwritten diary since late childhood and all through his time at King's College. It was a pleasant, therapeutic and solitary, not lonely, process. The physical action of controlling a pen and setting down the words on paper in some strange way had a calming influence while at the same time eliciting a creative flow of words. He could work creatively in a digital medium but for some reason it took longer to get started.

It was neither a reflective nor an event-recording diary but a mixture of both. The ritual of writing something every evening in the large battered notebook was important to him and if he missed an entry he would always complete it later.

He fingered back through the pages, scanning the entries at random. Many concerned the retaking of his entry tests. Then there was the intensive training he had been put through in the last year. Soon it would be over and he would embark on his first proper mission. Today he had twice had to correct himself for the wrong attitude, once for excessive interpersonal competitiveness during combat and once for feeling hatred and contempt while reviewing recent periods of ethnic conflict:

5 May 2077, Cambridge, East Anglia Province, Britlandia

While in the forest exercise zone Eric and I were timed individually as we took it in turns to cocoon a dummy victim. He did it five seconds more quickly than me and I demanded a chance to try again because I was sure I could beat him. My face must have revealed meanness. Tutor Knight Wang looked at me and said I had the wrong attitude. Competition was important but it should be against oneself and one should never be satisfied. One could compete with others in order to see what can be achieved by those competing but one should not compete against others in order to demonstrate your superior worth as a person. It is not in the spirit of a Knight. Try your hardest to please Yahweh by the act of trying, not to gain prestige.

This afternoon I studied the results of the sociodynamic model of Ovoskotia. I could see the probability of mass ethnic conflict as mutual resentments mounted, as failure to recognise humanity in people of a competing culture became rife and as charismatic dominophiles began to appear on either side, ready to urge their ethnic brothers and sisters to new depths of barbarism . I felt disgust and loathing for the ethnic groups involved, seeing each side as a wretched, collective personification

of hatred and ignorance. I wanted to kill them. Again,
to feel such loathing is not in the spirit of a Knight.

Adopting the right mental and spiritual attitude was much more central to a Knight's development than he had ever suspected. Tutor Wang said it was the foundation on which all else depended. The whole aim of the Knights of Peace was to abolish war for all time and that meant abolishing the hatred and contempt for others which made people prepared, even eager, to kill. Ridding the world of ordnance was a worthy cause in itself but if it generated hate in the process, nothing was solved in the long term. The physical action had to go hand in hand with the spiritual healing and not all of that could be left to the Monastery.

The holocom lit up in response to his present state of mind and emitted the gentle and sedate adagio of the Telemann concerto for trumpet and strings in D major. He let it continue for its two minutes, filling the room with its stately splendour. There was no urgency but someone would like to contact him when he was ready. He was ready now so he blinked each eye alternately to signal this and a small avatar image appeared on the desk in front of the holocom. It was Reed, who he had befriended during the selection process.

'Ros, are you ready to go to the Knightmaster's briefing?'

Roscoe was slightly irritated. There was no hurry – the Knightmaster had been flexible, saying that any time after four would be acceptable - and he wanted to write some more in his diary. He normally got on well with Reed but wished they could go separately. On the other hand he didn't want to appear unsociable and if they were briefed together they might find it easier to compare notes afterwards. 'Look, Eric, I was planning on going around six thirty. It's only three now. Any particular hurry?'

'Well, the pre-mission dance starts around eight and I wanted to get there at the start – more chances of meeting the ladies; I've seen precious few since our training started. So I would say we need to get to the briefing by four thirty. That is, if you want to arrive in time for the Dance of Life.'

He had forgotten about the Dance of Life, having become so totally engrossed in his training and he felt the same about the absence of females. Few girls joined for active service; not because of the danger but because the power of opposite sex attraction was so strong it caused operational problems. Mixing the sexes would be a bad idea and since males were physically stronger on average and had an innate preference for attack work it was logical to select in favour of males. Nevertheless, some of the Observer Knights were female and covert operations occasionally needed to have both genders in the field.

The very fact that he longed for feminine company made him wary. He feared the distraction on the eve of the mission but nevertheless decided to compromise. 'I've got something to finish. Shall we meet outside the Mission Room at, say, five thirty? The briefing should be over by not much after seven and it won't matter if we don't get to the ball until around eight thirty.'

'Just the song, Ros. See you at five thirty.'

He closed his diary, planning to resume today's entry after the ball, although he was not expecting there would be much to add. For the time being he would need to remind himself of the steps and movements of the pavane, so he chose a neuro-adaptive fuzzy set on the computer and stuck receptors to his wrists. The motion hologram of the figures projected in front of the screen as the Elizabethan music played and he sensed the pulsations as they coaxed his nervous system into the mode needed to perform the sedate steps, sweeps and gyrations of the updated pavane, a dance form from sixteenth and seventeenth century England which had become favoured by younger people in the last decade over large parts of the world. He would be expected to know at least some of the popular pavanes; but having avoided dancing events since adolescence and having no natural inclination for dancing, he felt that even with the aid of the fuzzy set he had reached a barely acceptable standard.

Defiantly he thought that as long as he did not make a fool of himself he did not really care much. He wanted to be a Knight, not a dancing maestro, although a pavane made an aesthetically appealing spectacle and seemed somehow to reflect the aspirations of the young for a gently ordered world in which love, honour, humility and chivalry prevailed alongside adventure and freedom. Such an aspiration would have been hopelessly unrealistic at any previous time in history. Now, this envisaged world was the only one that could survive when technology had unleashed potential destruction in a category that could render ordered and humane society powerless to resist a collapse into chaos. Humanity was being faced with an increasingly stark choice: create a harmonious, pleasurable, dignified way of living for the whole world or resign itself to a hell on earth. Letting affairs continue to steer between the two extremes was no longer an option.

There was still an hour before he had to set off for the briefing, time enough to go over the notes.

Objectives of the Ovoskotia Mission

In the short term: to destroy all ordnance manufacturing in Tripsino and surrounding areas.
In the long term: to permanently prevent conflict in Ovoskotia.

Preliminary mission

Impregnate local flour supplies with heat resistant nanometric Q-wave transmitter chips (QTCs). Centrally monitor the Q-wave spectra and positions of the groups of people who have ingested QTCs. The monitoring of Q-wave spectra is central to identifying dominophiles and will continue indefinitely.

Short term mission

Deploy incognito Knights with sensor insects to locate explosives. Impregnate explosives with nanometric identification chips and neutralise the explosives with chemicals released by genetically modified bacteria. Track explosives to weapon manufacturing sites and use QTC data to identify dominophiles near or on the site. Dispatch Combat Knights to arrest the

22

dominophiles and take them to Shanghai for trial at the International Court of Justice.

Long term mission

Examine sociodynamic models of the Ovoskotia community and combine with QTC data to identify dominophiles active in instability zones. Dispatch Commando Knights to impound (not arrest) the dominophiles and transport them to Shanghai, for handover to the MDL. (Some of the dominophiles active in instability zones will be the same individuals associated with weapons manufacture.)

He remembered what the Knightmaster had said about quantum computers and how crucial these would be to the overall success of this operation, the Ovoskotia Mission, and those which were scheduled to follow. Destroying weapons and ammunition was only a secondary objective, as was the arrest of arms dealers or manufacturers. The primary aim was to first locate a geographic area where sociodynamic instability was likely to break out, then identify and capture without injury those who would otherwise push societies into violent conflict. Quantum computers alone had the data processing power to enable such fine selection of individuals likely to cause death or misery for a large number of people. Once captured they would be handed on to the Monastery of Divine Light who would also make use of quantum computers, this time to complement the spiritual guidance of a Hermit Sage, the overall aim being to recover or discover the humanity that resides, albeit sometimes deeply hidden, in every living person.

Q-wave spectroscopy was another pre-requisite for identifying such people. He looked at the footnote:

> Q-wave energy was mathematically predicted by physicists, then detected and measured in controlled experiments with simulated neuronic circuits around 2050. It is now possible to measure the Q-waves emitted from a person's neural network and represent these graphically as a spectrum, with intensity plotted against wavelength. Labelled bar shapes at certain positions on the plot were caused by their state of mind at the time of the measurement. Somebody with a strong H bar in their Q spectrum is experiencing hate. Similarly, a strong Sp bar indicates that the person has formed a strong stereotype perception– a racial stereotype, for instance. And a heavy Cp bar indicates a strong will to control people. When all three spectral bars – H, Sp and Cp – are present a person is likely to give rise to catastrophic effects in certain sociodynamic situations.

Roscoe decided to use the remaining time before the briefing resting on his bed. He thought of the missions being planned for the next decade. They were so critical they made his spine shiver. The Knights of Peace and the Monastery of Divine Light had to succeed with these missions before the technology which was at present in their exclusive control - Q-waves, invisibility technology and nanobotics - percolated to the wider world. In the wrong hands, the hands of those who wished to dominate others for maleficent purposes, such technology would reduce the civilised world to chaos. All order and security would vanish and with it all true freedom, pleasure and achievement in life. The malevolent minority, be they sociopathic extremists or criminals, who had always been a problem for the decent majority, would have power to wreak havoc out of all proportion to their numbers.

He suspected that this afternoon's meeting with the Knightmaster would amount to a detailed assignment of duties for the next phase of the mission after the preliminary one in which molecular machines to detect and relay Q-waves had been inserted into mounds of flour stored in mills throughout Ovoskotia. By now most of the population would have absorbed these transponders into their bodies by eating bread made from the impregnated flour. The Q-waves from these had already been monitored and the whereabouts of potentially dangerous dominos were known to the Knightmaster and his team in the Operations Room.

So he would be assigned either to deploy explosive detecting insects from locations around Tripsino, and other parts of Ovoskotia, an undercover operation, or to assist in the impounding of dominos, which would be done openly in the name of the Knights. Impoundment or arrest was done openly because it avoided each of the opposing factions assuming that the other side had abducted the person concerned, thereby possibly sparking off or adding to conflict rather than preventing it. The public, almost theatrical nature of the capture also helped to promote the cause of the Order and inspired young people witnessing the capture, which was often networked worldwide.

Roscoe would prefer the explosives neutralisation mission. He would be part of a small group and able to share with only two or three others the satisfaction of eliminating a centre of explosives manufacture and arresting the prime culprits. An opportunity to test his combat skills and learn directly from experienced Knights in action.

It would be an honour to be part of the impoundment mission, the first in the world to prevent a major conflict in which thousands could die or have their lives ruined as a result of a few dominophiles. Yet he would be part of a larger group and would feel less personally responsible for its success. Not that the success of either mission was a foregone conclusion; but however it turned out he would no doubt find excitement and gain valuable experience.

The holocom came to life, stimulating a subtle but unmistakable awareness in his sensory system. It was Eric. 'Ready to go, Ros? See you outside the Ops Room in five minutes.'

*   *   *   *

As they entered the Operations Room Knightmaster Franklin was standing with an air of proud fascination by a large illuminated floor map of Ovoskotia on which grey areas indicated places of social instability, as identified by sociodynamic models. Ethereal tubes of light in three different colours projected up from the map. The tubes of light indicated Q waves emanating from residents in the place they originated from. Blue tubes indicated feelings of hate (H bars in the Q- spectrum), red tubes were associated with a tendency to form stereotype perceptions of people (Sp bars) and yellow tubes revealed a strong will to control others (Cp bars). Not surprisingly, most of the tubes came up from the heavily populated town of Tripsino.

'You are both familiar with this projection. As you can see there are some regions from which all three Q-wave tubes emanate and each coloured tube is quite high. At this scale we cannot of course locate individuals but by magnifying the map to street level we can at least find parts of a street, or even large buildings, where there are dominos with strong hate and stereotype perception levels.' He pointed to small areas from which tubes of red, blue and yellow projected to high levels above the map. 'With that information the ground team can home in and impound the dominos.'

Eric interjected with what Roscoe thought was a rather shallow point. 'Knightmaster, there are more dominos than we can possibly impound. There just aren't enough Knights available, surely.'

'Cadet Reed, I'm afraid you've overlooked other information we have derived from the sociodynamic model. Let me give you a clue: "social instability." Does that suggest anything to you?'

Eric cleared his throat with embarrassment as he realised that what he had thought was a perceptive remark in fact appeared to reveal a lack of understanding of the whole mission. He realised his mistake and Roscoe sympathised. 'Eh, yes sir. My apologies. We only have to impound those dominos who coincide with socially unstable situations.'

'As identified by the model. Exactly so. Not all dominos will precipitate conflict. They may make a few people's lives unpleasant but they won't set off violence on a large scale. Some could even use their charisma to prevent it. That narrows the field considerably.' He blinked his eyes to switch off the display. 'Now to get to the point, which is to brief you on your specific missions. I'll do it in alphabetical order, so if you would come this way Cadet Finley, into the briefing office…and Cadet Reed, please wait here. You can experiment with the model while we are talking.'

Roscoe moved into the briefing office behind Knightmaster Franklin, who then showed him to a chair on one side of a table. 'Well, Cadet Finley, you've come a long way in the year since the selection interview. How have you found the training? Were you happy with it?'

'I found it fulfilling, sir, but would have preferred more time to prepare for tomorrow's operation.'

Franklin sat down opposite. 'I can well understand that. The problem is that we can't work out the details of an operation until quite close to the time. So much depends on the exact locations of the dominos who not only have strong hate and stereotype perception bars in their Q spectra, but are linked to potential mass conflict situations. The Q-wave transmitter chips – QTCs we call them, as I expect you know - only remain active in the body for about twenty days. This also means we have to act fast to get Knights on the ground so that they can locate the individuals while their ingested QTCs are still transmitting.'

'How long ago were the QTCs planted in the flour supplies?'

'This begs an associated question: "which flour supplies?". We had to choose sources of flour close to the food production sites throughout the area.'

'Why is that?' He realised the answer almost as he spoke but decided to let the Knightmaster continue.

'The whole operation has to be completed within a short time span with as few uncertainties as possible. If the QTCs had been buried in mounds around flour mills some would have been transported outside the region while others would have taken anything up to six months or more to get into bread or other flour-based foods. So we chose flour supplies on bakery sites or warehouses close to them. It takes only about fifteen days, on average, to get into the bodies of those eating the bread or rolls or cakes or pies with imbedded QTCs.' The Knightmaster signalled to a stainless steel kettle on the table. A portable gas stove stood next to an earthenware teapot and a small bowl of fresh tea leaves. 'These are from the Afghan plantation. A great improvement on opium.'

'Thank you, sir. Can I ask how old is the tea making equipment?'

The Knightmaster switched to a pleasant and informal mode of talking. 'Nineteen fifties Britain, except for the stove, which was sold for camping in the 1970s. I like to keep old technology alive.' He paused as he reflected on this and became more serious in tone. 'I am far from alone in this. The world is full of virtual experiences and possibilities for illusion, one needs to be anchored down occasionally; it is good for the soul.'

He filled the kettle at a sink in the corner of the room and lit the stove with a match. The way it suddenly ignited with a hiss of gas and settled down to a steady flicker of faint blue flame lapping around the base of the kettle was fascinating in a way which motion holographs and simulations could never be.

'So... your mission details are in your flexcom. Scan through them while I finish making the tea. Then we can talk about it.'

He pulled out the flexcom from his smartsuit – set to the mode of a standard Knight's chain-mail tunic with black trousers. The screen, rolled up into a cylinder, unscrolled to full size and his pulse raced as he read the file name: 'Tripsino insects'. So he would not be involved in an impounding operation. Although he had previously decided that he would prefer the explosives destruction to the dominophile impoundment operation some part of him would like to have been part of the latter and he could not really identify why.

'You look disappointed.' Knightmaster Franklin seemed genuinely concerned and softened his normally austere manner. 'Detecting and destroying explosives, then arresting the key figures involved, has always been our core business.'

'Admittedly that is what attracted me to the Order but I had hoped to be taking part in one of the new impounding missions mentioned during the induction.'

'Why? Explosives destruction also involves capturing dominos. Capturing for arrest is every bit as honourable and dangerous as capturing for impoundment. And on the explosives mission you have the added task of finding and neutralising the explosives.' He sat back in his chair, inviting Roscoe to respond.

'But impoundment is something new. The result of a successful mission is more far reaching. It can save thousands of lives and prevent generations of hate.'

'It will indeed be a momentous development, for the Order and for the world, if it proves successful. But much depends on the game designed to enhance the miniscule compassion which dominos seem to have along with their distinguishing Q-wave spectra. Pride must also be removed. Dominos usually lack the humility to recognise that all their mental and physical attributes come from a Creator. This distorts their view of reality.' The water came to the boil and the Knightmaster resumed the tea making, treating it almost as a ritual. It was the first time Roscoe had seen tea being made in this elemental way, rather than synthesised.

'How can pride be removed, sir? Would this not be coercion, an infringement of human rights under Global Federation law?'

'Not at all. They will simply be taught that submission to the Creator wins a greater victory. As Father James will tell you, defeat of the ego brings new life, one that lasts for ever. The Resurrection showed that. Once the captive recognises this he will gladly submit to the will of God. It will be a free decision.'

'But how can pride be eliminated without force?'

'By recognition of reality. They will be taught cosmology and taken into space- normally to the Monastery of Divine Light on Mars. A hermit sage shows them that the Creator is real, that God's presence permeates all aspects of reality. When confronted with the lifeless extraterrestrial world they can't fail to recognise how precious is our planet and the gift of temporal life. It makes them immensely grateful and want to worship the giver of the gift rather than themselves.'

The Knightmaster paused. 'But you must understand that we cannot afford to use many novices on such missions. And from your point of view the explosives assignment will test and enhance a wider range of skills.'

'But some Cadets will be used.'

'It is a new type of operation for us and so new skills not possessed by our longer serving Knights will be required. However, these will be primarily technical – analysing QTC data and matching it to sociodynamic models, the actual process of identifying dominos likely to precipitate major conflict and bloodshed by their influence on those around them.' He poured out two cups of tea. 'The Knights concerned will be working with university research teams as assistants and considerably divorced from the action on the ground.'

'I understand, sir.' Roscoe picked up the large, shallow porcelain cup and sipped the tea. The temperature was perfect – hot enough to sooth yet not scalding. It had a freshness and indefinable dimension of taste which, together with the sensation of drinking from a porcelain china cup, relaxed him and lifted his spirits. As he drank he realised why he had been disappointed. It was because he knew that impounding was the only thing that could make a real long term difference to the amount of suffering in the world; although it would be some time before Knights were released from their vows of secrecy on this new class of mission.

He began to scan through the briefing notes. 'May I suggest you close the file; you can look at the details in your own time. I can tell you the main points now.'

A holographic image of a mountain range appeared over the table. A small encampment of tents was nestled in one of the high pastures.

'This is Mount Apeksia, about eighty klicks fromTripsino, and this is where you will be sleeping tomorrow night. From this base you and three experienced Knights will be transported at dawn to the town centre, just a few minutes away by transpod. There will be twenty groups like yours spaced around the town and other parts of Ovoskotia.'

The holograph changed to the town centre, near a large park.

'You will have your smartsuit adjusted to incognito and hide in the park while the microcam is deployed to monitor the dress of the locals. Your smartsuit will then adjust itself to blend in on the basis of the pictures it gets from the microcam. Then each of you will travel to various places around the city and deploy sensor insects – GM bees in this case - and set up a monitoring station, probably behind a tree, for the sensor bees to return to after locating any explosives. The monitoring station will register movements of the bees and decode these to determine the direction of the explosives and transmit this information back to the base camp on Apeksia over several days.'

'So there will be eighty monitoring stations and eighty bee swarms dispersed over the Ovoskotia Reservation, mainly in the Tripsino area.'

'Yes. Once the sites of explosive manufacture or handling are determined we can move in to implant the NICs, that is nanometric identification chips, in case you've forgotten, although I've no doubt your memory is better than mine.'

'Why are the NICs needed, given that the locations of the explosives have already been discovered by the bees?'

'The NICs are for tracking in case the explosives are moved over the days that follow. You will simultaneously impregnate the explosive chemicals with neutralising bacteria excreted by rats to render them increasingly inactive, until after several months they will be totally inert. Of course, this phase can't be planned until the explosives sites are found by the bees. We don't even know if there are any but given the amount of ethnic hatred revealed by the QTC spectra I find that unlikely. Have you heard Ovoskotia called the Hate Reservation? There is also little attempt to prevent ordnance activity there.'

'One question. Why do the neutralisers take so long to work? Is it a technical problem or is this deliberate?'

'Deliberate. Once people discover that the explosives are inert they won't continue to use them in weapons. The longer the explosives take to de-activate the more people will become associated with them and susceptible to surveillance.'

'But the explosives may be used in weapons that are fired or detonated before they de-activate. Lives could be lost.'

'True and that is regrettable, but remember our overall objective, which is to eliminate all ordnance from the face of the planet and that means finding the people involved, otherwise they will replace it as fast as we can destroy it.'

Knightmaster Franklin leaned back in his chair. 'I am sure you will enjoy this mission, Cadet Finley. You will be joining an experienced Combat Knight on this first phase – that is, locating the explosives then introducing the NICs for tracking purposes and neutralising them. All this will be done incognito.'

'How long will this take, sir?'

'A few days.'

'And the next phase?'

'That depends on how the first phase proceeds and how closely the location of the tracked NICs coincides with domino locations. If no such juxtapositions occur there will be no next phase, no arrests or impoundments.'

'So the mission would be a failure.'

'Not at all. The explosives will have been de-activated, at least.' Franklin got up and they clasped arms. 'Good luck, Cadet Finley.' He followed Roscoe out of the briefing room and beckoned to Reed, who was walking around the large illuminated map of Ovoskotia which covered the floor of the Operations Room.

Sitting in a corner of the room was Isla.

CHAPTER 3

THE DANCE OF LIFE

A wall of coldness greeted him as he entered into the darkness of the pavane arena. Stars and a crescent moon shone from the holospace sky above, faintly but distinctly illuminating a small frozen lake which formed a white ribbon across the frosty grass of the arena where the mathematical elegance of the dancing would later express itself to the music.

His smartsuit took the form of a coat and this kept him warm as he waited for more people to arrive, but the air felt like ice on his face and hands. He could just make out a small elevated stage beside the lake of ice and the musicians were beginning to position themselves and tune up. Gradually he became aware that the dance ground was beginning to fill. Most of the males were, like himself, recently trained Knights on the eve of their first mission, while the females were either non-combat members of the Order or girls from the Cambridge Institute of Technology, only a kilometre or so from the Knights' training school. The Knights had smartsuits formed into greatcoats while the girls' smartsuits were finely, personally tuned to be both warm and attractive.

From more than a few metres away the entrance was invisible, hidden by a silvery bush in the moonlight, and it was difficult to guess how many people had arrived; but there appeared to be a big enough crowd for the first dance.

The ensemble - a pianonium, flute, cello, violin and viola - began to play a slow melodious, rhythmically complex piece not intended for dancing and Roscoe enjoyed just listening and absorbing the scene around him. He could not quite place the music. It was reminiscent of Bach at his most sedate but could have been by any one of a number of modern composers whose work rested on the deeply spiritual foundation which Bach had created. As the rhythms and melodies periodically overlapped, separated and coalesced, he began to forget the surroundings and lose himself in the music.

His reverie was broken by a tap on the shoulder. It was Reed. 'How long before the physical contact starts? It may be dark but I've brushed close by some of the girls and ...'

Suddenly the quintet produced a flourish of sound to signal the first dance. Roscoe was mildly irritated by Eric's juvenile anticipation of sensual contact and disregard for the aesthetic aspects of the event; while Eric resented what seemed close to a kind of pomposity in Roscoe.

There were a few moments of silence as a luminous number appeared on each person's coat and they began to find their partners. If a male had the same number as a female they would join hands, the number would vanish and they would remain as partners for the duration of the dance. The lunar image, which had been a crescent, now became full and it was possible to see clearly not only the people but the frozen ribbon of lake and the frosted turf on which they were now waiting for the music to start. Roscoe could see that his partner was nervous and wished he could be a calming influence. Although his feel for music was good he had no natural sense of bodily rhythm and was so uncertain of the steps he would have to rely on following the choreographic symbols that would be programmed to show up on his partner's coat: symbols for holding hands, letting go, gyrating, turning, walking away from or towards her and joining with others to form a circle.

The ensemble began to play a courtly adagio in early Renaissance style and it was clear they would have to start the dance. Holding her hand he sensed her tension as they joined the two-abreast line of dancers. At times, when she was in the right position, the moonlight illuminated her face and it looked anxious. Once he nearly stumbled while concentrating on the choreograph symbol. Neither of them seemed able to relax and he had the impression she just wanted it to be over as soon as possible, seemingly a reflection on his own inadequacy.

Fortunately they would not have to be together for the next dance since their partner numbers would change. Yet it would probably be just the same unless he happened to be paired with someone experienced in pavanes. He had heard that a new dance had been programmed and that it involved a prop. Was this for professionals or would he be expected to do it, even if, as he suspected, it would be complex? The title, 'Dance of Life', intrigued him.

The number changed and he was paired to another girl. She was less nervous but certainly did not seem overjoyed to have Roscoe as a partner. During this dance he noticed that the moon was sinking low on the horizon but it was getting lighter as the simulated dawn progressed and this made him feel all the more visible and vulnerable to making a fool of himself. The ensemble stopped playing at this point. The mock sun was high and the trees, plants and flower borders were now clearly illuminated.

After a few more uncomfortable sessions in the brightening sun he noticed it had got noticeably warmer and the ice on the lake had melted. The grass underfoot was no longer frozen but since it was not real grass it was not wet or muddy. The smartsuits had turned from coats to indoor wear and this gave the girls and some of the more flamboyant men the chance to show off their dress sense. He wished he could stop dancing and just watch what would no doubt be an impressive spectacle but as long as partner numbers kept coming up on his smartsuit this would mean leaving a girl stranded.

Now it was lighter he caught a glimpse of Eric looking cheerful and confident, the girl smiling and relaxed. He could not help feeling resentful. This was the first pavane ball he had gone to and in fact he had attended very few dance functions of any sort.

Once again the music stopped and new partner numbers flashed up. Just as he was about to pair up he saw Isla moving up to her partner who had been standing nearby. She smiled recognition at him briefly before settling into dance mode. Roscoe periodically was taken fairly close to Isla as the dance proceeded. Her auburn hair alternately shone and darkened as she gracefully moved into and out of the direct sunlight. Again he nearly tripped as his attention was diverted not only by having to study the choreoglyphs but by the image of Isla stepping and turning in her undulating green smartdress.

As the pavane came to an end a voice announced that the Dance of Life would begin in a few minutes and that everyone should sit to watch because it was going to be performed by professionals. Not only was this a considerable relief but it gave him a chance to enjoy what promised to be a fine spectacle and if at the same time he could sit with Isla his fortune would have turned indeed.

He saw her moving towards some tables that had not yet been occupied and with studied casualness came along side her. He decided not to speak at this stage in case she replied or responded in a way to put him off; but instead just sat down next to her at a small round table, such that they were both facing the arena. After a few moments of silence he asked if she knew anything about the theme or background of the performance.

'I do as a matter of fact. It's supposed to reflect the teleo-evolutionary model of life.'

'You mean the theory that evolution proceeds not just by natural selection but predominantly by hierarchically guided information transfer?'

'Yes. At the molecular level. Gene swapping and editing, for instance. And a whole host of epigenetic processes. A far cry from neo-Darwinism.'

Roscoe suddenly became aware that something was happening to the grass. Large silver rings were beginning to emerge. Each horizontal circle, as it rose, was revealed to be the top of a double helix, like a DNA molecule, unscrewing itself upwards from the ground but stopping after only one twist. Then the music started, a strange, unearthly Sino-western fusion. It was a blend of the plucked strings of a pipa, the ethereal soaring and diving of a flute, the meandering of a violin and madrigals sung by two young men who had joined the musicians. The entire surface of the arena was covered in the helixes, all shimmering and changing colour as they were illuminated in laser light and as the music took on the feel of the most holy of medieval chants in a cathedral.

The spectators were transfixed, although the actual performance had not even started. The music built up in a series of crescendos then abruptly stopped and the performers slowly and with a kind of rhythmic deliberation walked to the helixes in pairs, each pair stepping onto the platform on top of a helix. The girl dancers wore smartdresses in four different colours and the smartsuits of the males were in the same four colours.

As the music resumed in a sedate pulsating rhythm the helixes rose up several twists and the figures on each disc moved around each other, pirouetted and gyrated in every conceivable way as the helixes continued to rise, rotating slowly. The grace with which they did this chimed in an uncanny way with the rhythm and melody coming from the ensemble. Then the music dissolved into a kind of chaos but with an underlying order and one person from each couple, sometimes a male, sometimes a female, appeared to float upwards and then descend onto another disc and after the new distribution had settled down the music returned to a more sedate and structured form but with a markedly different rhythm and melody.

When the performance ended the applause was loud and long and Roscoe turned to see Isla smiling ecstatically. As he caught her eye he could not help hoping that he might be responsible for some small part of her elation; but this hope rapidly dissolved. When the applause finally subsided and the partner numbers flashed onto their dance clothes she immediately moved off to find her partner and was obviously looking forward to resuming the dancing.

He went off in search of his own partner and this time, as the music started, he was relieved to find her very experienced, so although he still regretted not being able to take the lead he at least did not have to risk further embarrassment.

After this dance it was time for everyone to dine. He had agreed with Eric that they would sit together at the first vacant table and leave to chance the choice of dining companions. Then at least they would be able to compare notes about their mission assignments and their impressions of the pavane ball.

Eric seemed relaxed as he glanced around and was obviously relishing the whole event. 'This must be the best one I've been to. What do you think?' He asked this in a loaded way, implying that Roscoe was not so keen.

'It would be better if I could just watch. The Dance of Life was the high point for me.'

'It was great for me but so was the rest.'

'I don't have the rhythm. Anyway, I didn't join the Knights to dance except as a confusion tactic during a capture mission.'

'You ought to take lessons if you want to meet girls.'

'There are other ways but you may have a point.' Roscoe decided to change the subject. 'What assignment did you get for Ovoskotia?'

'It's good news and bad news. The bad news is that I won't be in the field for the first part of the mission. Just analysing data at the HQ.'

'And the good news is you will be using the latest sociodynamic models and Q-wave data to identify dominos for arrest or impoundment. This is a first for the KOP, or the whole world for that matter. You will be helping to make history.'

Roscoe was astonished to be interrupted by the voice of Isla. 'Who's making history?' She had sat down at the round table opposite him and Eric, smiling almost mischievously. Roscoe felt sure it was Eric she wanted to be with.

'We were talking about our assignments for the Ovoskotia mission,' said Eric. 'The first part of mine is data analysis. You can hardly call that making history, although Ros thinks it is. I'll be stuck at the Apeksia mountain base camp.'

Isla considered this for a moment. 'That depends what data you are analysing and by what method. Are you dealing with spectra from Q-wave transmission chips and the output of sociodynamic models?'

'So Knightmaster Franklin tells me. But my second assignment will be field action. Domino arrest or impoundment, depending on what comes up. If we find a domino who has actually broken the laws on ordnance it will be an arrest. If it is one who is a substantial danger, regardless of any laws broken, it will be impoundment and an involuntary trip to Shanghai or more probably Mars.'

'In what sense a danger?' asked Isla.

A robotrolley carrying their meals drew up to the table, transformed itself into a vaguely anthropomorphic waiter and started to serve.

Roscoe took this opportunity to join in. 'It has to be a big danger to justify an impoundment. The dominophile, identified by his Q-wave spectra, has to be linked to a high probability of serious large scale conflict or destruction. The sociodynamic models used store so much data and need so much processing power that only state-of-the-art quantum computers, modelled on certain parts of the brain, can manage it.'

She laughed good naturedly. 'You're telling me?'

'I think I remember now. Knightmaster Franklin told me. You are studying quantum computation at the Cavendish.'

'The Cavendish? Where's that?' asked Eric.

Roscoe was frequently surprised by the gaps in Eric's knowledge. 'It's part of the Cambridge Institute of Technology – it was inherited from the old university. I finished philosophy at King's last year, also a remnant from the university.'

Isla looked surprised. 'And our paths didn't cross? Didn't you go into the town or to any of the social events?'

He was embarrassed. He had led a rather isolated life at Cambridge, to the extent that he sometimes felt socially inadequate. He had an image of Isla bubbling up all over the town and university institutions while he sat reading philosophy in his study. She had lived life to the full while he just reflected on it.

Eric interjected. 'Ros is not exactly one for the social life.'

She looked sympathetically at Roscoe. 'Well, that's how the world keeps turning; we're all different.' There was a brief pause and Roscoe's spirits leapt momentarily as a flash of her eyes suggested an interest in him. 'You've not told me about your own assignment.'

'I'm restricted to the short term mission. Planting nanometric identification chips and microcrawler neutralising agents in explosives. We use genetically modified rats which burrow into the explosives and eject the NICs and microcrawlers in their excreta.'

'But what if a domino-type Q-wave spectrum coincides with the location of explosives. Would you be sent on an arrest mission?'

'Probably. But it would not have the same significance as an impoundment.'

'Why? What's the difference?'

'Impounding is the only way to prevent conflict in the long term. Wars happen when dominos are present in certain sociodynamic situations. Remove the dominos and correct their Q-wave spectra by sending them to the Monastery of Divine Light on Mars and you are on the way to ridding the world of armed conflict. Providing the Enlightenment works.'

'But if you arrest a domino for his connection with explosives you are also on the way to stopping conflict.'

'Arrested dominos are only sent to Shanghai. They don't get the same treatment. They just serve time in captivity and are then released. True, attempts are made to reform them and sometimes this works better than before the Divine Light, but more often they just go back into the world and again get involved with ordnance in some way.'

The robotrolley returned with the dessert and the conversation was paused for a while. Isla helped distribute the food but continued to show an interest. Eric gave the impression of feeling left out as Roscoe continued. 'Just destroying weapons and explosives and slowly reducing the number of people who organise or instigate the manufacture, distribution, sale or use of them will never stop wars. You have to stop the demand for military technology by preventing conflict situations arising in the first place and that means stopping dominos turning potential conflict into war.'

'How to stop people stirring up hatred for fun. That sounds like a spiritual problem,' said Isla, looking quizzical.

'Primarily it is. Dominos need to control people, almost for the sake of power alone. Others only want to do it to achieve something worthwhile; once the goal is reached they back off and disengage, possibly moving on to some other undertaking. The dangerous ones are those who want power at any cost and use their empathy for control purposes. They are drawn to destructive tasks and seem almost to thrive on hate, deceit and the suffering they cause.'

'So this is where the Monastery of Divine Light comes in,' she suggested.

'The MDL has a monastery built into the side of the Valles Marineris, a canyon on Mars that dwarfs the Grand Canyon. Father James told me about it. A Hermit Sage, or even Father James himself, will engage impounded dominos in a dialogue and attempt to guide them towards spiritual renewal. But it's not entirely a spiritual process. There will be a new computer game connected to their neuronic circuits to provide feedback from victims and stimulate awareness of the consequences of evil actions to inform the spirit.'

'I think I've heard of it,' she interjected. 'I've picked up some things this summer while working for Knightmaster Franklin. In fact it's relevant to my Cavendish course because it uses quantum computing. It must be some game to need that amount of processing power.'

There was a flourish from the quintet and Roscoe was dismayed by the speed with which Isla got up, obviously looking forward to the next dance. Dancing meant a lot to her. He hoped he would not have to be her partner and was relieved that his number was different from the one which flashed onto her smartdress. So far he thought he had made a good impression but if he had been paired with her she would have found him a great disappointment. He hoped he would escape being discovered for the rest of the ball. There were bound to be other ways of meeting her.

Once again he was paired to a girl who expected to be led firmly and every so often, as he struggled awkwardly through the courtly movements with his eyes fixed on the choreographic instruction symbols, he caught site of Eric confidently leading his beaming partner round the arena. He had got used to this by now and no longer resented it. Reed was his friend. Why should he not enjoy using his natural penchant for dancing to good effect? It was just a matter of accepting this.

The next two girls happened to be naturals who could effortlessly enact the steps and so take some of the pressure away. This put him in a better frame of mind. Then, just as the ball was coming to an end and a feeling of relief was beginning to engulf him, fortune turned. There was Isla swirling round the arena with Eric, an unmistakable look of admiration on her lovely face.

*   *   *   *

Roscoe lay awake with his mind and body in turmoil. What were these sensations evoked in him by Isla? Lust? No. He was sure it was not based purely on sexual attraction – that made no sense. He had encountered numerous highly attractive women at college and had desired them, talked about them with other male students at meal times. Neither was it pheromones. This theory of attraction was now regarded as superficial, with pheromones merely being a symptom of something much deeper and defying scientific investigation. Or was this what love was like? But it could not be love; this needed mutual understanding, kindness and commitment over time. He had felt this way about her almost at first sight – not during the hut building trial, when she had stepped out of the transpod to check that he was alright, but when she had brushed past him in Knightmaster Franklin's office. But perhaps love was not always something that grew from a chance encounter; perhaps it was sometimes, even always, a matter of providence or destiny.

How did she feel about him? He made an effort to be analytical and objective. She had voluntarily sat opposite him at the pavane dinner but she had also been opposite Eric. She had taken a considerable interest in his assignment for the Ovoskotia project and listened to his descriptions of how the Knights intended to eliminate from the world both ordnance and the will to use it. Then she had seemed to assert in one swift move away from the table how much she preferred dancing to his company and later had appeared to admire Eric's polish as a partner.

The image of her auburn hair curling up softly against her cheek in profile came into his mind, put an end to this brief interval of analysis and set him off twisting and turning, his hormones intermittently surging. He got up and fixed an electrode to his neck. He walked over to the neuronic interface on his desk, then plugged one end of a cable into the electrode, the other into a port on the interface. Hopefully, the sublimation programme would calm him physically and allow him to think creatively or logically or to meditate; or get some much needed sleep before tomorrow, the first day of the Ovoskotia mission.

Although Eric occasionally irritated him he was, overall, a good friend. How did Isla feel about him? Was it just his prowess in the pavane arena that she liked?

He remembered seeing them together in the Operations Room after the briefing with Knightmaster Franklin. They had not been physically close and it was only a fleeting impression but he sensed there was some rapport between them. Or was he imagining it?

He at last began to feel sleepy, and so disconnected himself from the sublimation port, then removed the electrode from his neck and went back to bed.

CHAPTER 4

OVOSKOTIA: FIRST PHASE

Eric joined him at breakfast in the refectory where most of the Knights assigned to the Ovoskotia mission were dining. This would be the last time they were together before they went their different ways. They talked about how well they had slept but no reference was made to last night's ball.

'Ros, I keep hearing about the "Divine Light". Do you know where this comes from?'

'The expression was first used by Plotinus, the Neo-Platonist, around 250 BC. As for the Divine Light as we know it today.... you would have to ask Father James.'

'Why did they set up a DL monastery on Mars? They already have one in Shanghai.'

'Good question. Maybe the culture shock helps with the Enlightenment.'

'Anyhow, I have to leave. The Apeksia camp is a couple of thousand kilometres away and the transpod will take hours. I have to be there before three and haven't finished packing yet.'

'My assigned senior is taking me in his transglobal, presumably so we can spend some time practising before tomorrow.'

'A transglobal! You should get there before me even if you take your time starting.' Eric quickly finished his breakfast and got up from the table. 'Not sure when I'll see you again but good luck.' They clasped forearms and Eric walked briskly out of the restaurant.

Roscoe felt a touch of sympathy for Eric after envying, if not slightly resenting, his success with the ladies, including Isla, the night before. He knew he would like to have gone on an attack mission rather than spend the next few weeks at HQ analysing data. Yet he would gladly have changed places because he knew that Eric's mission, though comparatively dull in its initial phase, was of historical importance. If a domino with a dangerous Q-wave spectrum was matched to a sociodynamic instability node an impoundment would be justified and although this would probably not be any more difficult or dangerous than an arrest, Eric would undoubtedly gain status. He chastised himself for giving in to thoughts of prestige and envy.

Just as he was finishing his second cup of coffee a large, thick-set senior Knight with a weathered face came into the restaurant and approached Roscoe's table. 'Cadet Finley?' He had a loud rough voice and a good humoured, if slightly ironic, expression.

'That's me.'

'Combat Knight Davies. Call me Harry. What do I call you?'

'Ros.'

'Looks like we've got a job to do in a Hate Reserve, otherwise known as Ovoskotia. Ros, can you be ready in, shall we say, thirty minutes? Just stand at the entrance to the parking zone.'

*   *   *   *

The transglobal was now some twenty five kilometres above the Alps, visible through the lower front window. Roscoe had not been this close to space before and had not travelled at more than the usual few hundred kilometres per hour maximum of a transpod. He was now making perhaps five times that speed and was sitting in a shirt sleeve cabin on the boundary between the atmosphere and the vacuum above it.

Davies had been cross examining him. He needed to know as much as possible about this novice before being thrown into action with him. Both their lives depended on it.

'It says on my notes that you can cocoon a resisting opponent without injury in three seconds. In an actual combat situation how realistic is that?' He looked askance at Roscoe in a way which suggested he did not really expect an answer. 'Just have to try you out this afternoon. Have you much experience with a refraction shield?'

'I can maintain invisibility cover for up to twelve seconds.'

Davies gave him a mocking but good natured look. 'Up to? I need to know the minimum. That's what our lives depend on.' Again he did not really expect an answer. He just wanted to get Roscoe prepared for the real world of capturing dominos without injuring them even when they were surrounded by armed guards. 'We make arrests by teamwork by the way – no individual heroics. I hope you're used to teamwork – it's usually more important than technical skill.'

'I spent a lot of time practising with Cadet Knight Reed, my fellow trainee. I understand from Knightmaster Franklin that our synergy was high.'

'Well, that's good to hear, but you have to work with strangers.' He started paying attention to the view below. 'Still, there has to be a first time. By the way, I hear you're a philosopher.'

'I got a degree in philosophy from King's.'

'London or Cambridge?'

'Cambridge.'

'What made you move into a life of action?' Davies became jovial. 'As a philosopher you could have spent a long life just thinking in comfort and safety instead of risking a short and dangerous one.'

'Three hundred years of just thinking sounds too long, Harry, even for me.'

Ovoskotia was now on the gently curving horizon, partly in cloud but with the Apeksia mountain complex clearly visible, some of its peaks capped in snow. It was difficult to believe the amount of hatred that was down there. He wondered how it would seem when he was walking around Tripsino, its capital. Would it be written in people's faces or as electronic wall graffiti? Or would it be subtly pervasive in the atmosphere of human interactions, a poisonous presence? All these probably. Yet this place, at this time, was one of many places through human history that had been gripped by such evil for no reason knowable by any mortal man.

The transglobal began a steep descent but stayed horizontal by coordinating the horizontal fusion thruster with the vertical photon drive. Apeksia gradually revealed more of its relief and soon they could see the small high plateau of pasture on which had been erected temporary huts to form the KOP base for the duration of the Ovoskotia mission. Many transglobals were already parked but it would be several hours before the transpods arrived.

Davies looked around as they stepped onto the grass. 'Plenty of places to practise. But first let's get some lunch.'

*　　*　　*　　*

Roscoe was put under considerable pressure that afternoon as they went through various manoeuvres taught over the last six months. Many of the techniques were dismissed by Combat Knight Davies as not likely to be needed in practice on this mission and they concentrated on the few which would most likely be useful and which Davies had found by experience were most effective in confusing or distracting or surprising their opponents or rendering them immobile without harming them. Basics such as erecting a refractor shield to make you invisible for a few seconds, deploying holofigures in all directions and cocooning a captor all had to be completed ultra-fast to ensure that the defenders were overcome and the captor removed before anyone realised what was happening.

Tomorrow there would probably be more time to practise after they had completed the first phase, which was to locate explosives in Tripsino using GM bees and release the GM rats near the explosives. This would be an incognito operation and relatively straightforward. They could be back by early afternoon.

At supper he parted company with Davies and sat with a group of cadets exchanging stories, observations and humour. When talk turned to their assigned Combat Knight mentors one of the cadets said he had heard that Davies was referred to by his mentor as the Pied Piper. No one had any idea how he had earned such a sobriquet.

It was clear that Davies had great technical skill and judgement. Roscoe wondered whether his commitment to the moral principles of respecting and not harming one's opponent was equally strong. He had certainly not said anything to indicate this one way or the other but his general character seemed highly individualistic; if he had absorbed the Knights' ethos it must be after deep thought, not simply through reciting oaths at the initiation ceremony.

*   *   *   *

It was quite cold, and the first hint of dawn showed above the Apeksia peaks, as the Knights, with smartsuits adjusted to blend in approximately with local civilian attire, boarded their designated stealthcarriers. Within minutes an almost invisible swarm of dark machines was heading over the mountain range towards Tripsino, silently transporting its cleverly equipped human cargo.

Roscoe and Davies were set down on a patch of waste ground near the centre of the city, still predominantly in darkness. It was almost as quiet here as it had been in the mountains since there was no engine powered traffic in Tripsino: transpods were banned under international law and the last road vehicles had almost gone as both gas supplies and repair skills ceased to be renewed. Only pedestrians, bicycles and rickshaws populated the roads and there were few even of these at this hour.

'Hand me the beepack, Ros. Let's get our little friends working.'

Roscoe put down his bag, picked out a small box and tossed it over. He sensed that Davies was not impressed by this. Such dedicated living organisms should be treated with respect, although he was sure no damage was done.

'The first thing we have to do is send these fellows on their way. With any luck the first messengers will return here within a couple of hours and we can start walking in the right direction. Meanwhile, we can scout around here and make ourselves more inconspicuous.' He knelt down and opened the box. After what seemed like a long wait the first bees crawled out and flew off in various directions. Soon there were myriads buzzing off to all corners of a metropolis that was becoming increasingly decrepit.

'How likely is it they won't find any explosives?' asked Roscoe.

'Almost zero. They are genetically programmed to sniff out all kinds, from dangerous mixtures of common substances to the most deadly. And in this city you can be sure that some group will have something nasty stashed away.'

After watching the last of the bees depart Roscoe packed the box into his backpack, the type a local trader might use to carry small goods to a market stall. They set off to join a main thoroughfare where local Ovoskotians were walking towards stalls set across a wide avenue of partially crumbling tarmac which had once been a main road for motor traffic. The smell of freshly baked bread seemed somehow incongruous with the signs of urban decay which were becoming apparent. Later, however, he saw that the bread was being sold from a stall by an old woman whose creased face shone with a rare kindness that seemed to belie this town's reputation for endemic hatred. He pictured the nanometric Q-wave transmitters that would be in the bread, after Knights had previously embedded them in the Ovoskotian flour supplies, ready to be taken into the body of whoever ate it and so enable their Q-wave spectra to be monitored for signs of hatred, racial stereotype perception and the will to dominate. For this woman, he knew, there would be none of these signs. Father James had once mentioned how divine love sometimes reveals itself when you are least expecting it. Somehow he felt sure this old lady was such a revelation, one truly filled with the Holy Spirit.

Once among a suitably large sample of locals their smartsuits fine tuned themselves to become as unlikely as possible to attract attention. It was of course true that neither of them had the racial features that most typified this part of the world but it was a fact that interbreeding with foreign racial groups and even, much more rarely, between Krosnians and Ovoskotians, had made exceptions sufficiently common that physical appearance was no guide to ethnicity unless your features and skin tone were pronounced.

They walked more or less at random among the pedestrians, cyclists and rickshaws to get the feel and layout of the wide, unfriendly streets. The town being predominantly Ovoskotian it was rare for Krosnian racial stereotypes to be visible except in ghettoes of the latter. Anyone of obvious Krosnian origin walking the streets among Ovoskotians would probably be treated with superficial politeness or some degree of animosity or spat at, such was the memory of atrocities committed by ancestors of Krosnians against Ovoskotians, memories kept alive by endless anecdotes, often exaggerated. Inevitably, the Krosnians had similarly wicked memories of the Ovoskotians, to ensure that they did their share in keeping the mutual resentment and acrimony as alive as it had been for centuries.

If anything, Roscoe and Davies would be suspected of being Krosnians because their skins were fairly light; so they had taken the precaution of learning some Ovoskotian and were able to stop at an Ovoskotian pavement café without attracting attention. They found an empty table and ordered two coffees. Caffrosia was almost unknown in reservations outside the Global Federation.

The waiter seemed cheerful but they felt that if they spoke Krosnian his mood would change instantly. Roscoe recognised a different kind of smile from that of the old lady selling bread, something much shallower and with a subtle hint of meanness.

'The bees should be back at the monitoring station in about an hour, ready to point us to the explosives,' said Davies. 'There is likely to be more than one target.'

'How accurate?'

'Not very. We just get direction and approximate distance but as long as we get to within fifty metres of a charge and providing there is a way in the rats will find it. Once a rat gets into the explosive it starts excreting droppings which contain the NICs and the neutralising bacteria.'

'Suppose the explosives are encased in metal shells, bullets or cartridges. How can the rats get inside?'

'These are not really the target. It's the raw materials for making ammunition and bombs we are after. Fully encased explosives will not have been located reliably by the GM bees and the rats wouldn't be able to get inside them even if the bees detected them. A large bulk of explosives not too soundly encased- this is the ideal target for the rats.'

'But isn't it difficult to release the rats without people noticing? If we have to be within fifty metres that limits our choice of release point.'

Davies suddenly warned him to lower his voice when speaking English as the waiter came up to remove the cups and give them the bill. They were dressed to look like Ovoskotians and would be expected to speak accordingly. Roscoe was surprised to find that the cafe did not require cash and was equipped to receive Global

Federation barter points electronically. He seemed to take a long time to complete the transaction and it was a relief when they could resume talking.

'As I was about to say, it is the trickiest part of this phase. But we have something else to do before getting close to the explosives, which is to set up a transponder station somewhere it won't be spotted. Otherwise the efforts of our rat and bee friends will be to no avail.'

'There is a park nearby.'

'That would be ideal if we can get the transponder module into a tree top, among the foliage. It would be hidden from view and have a good enough transmission range to reach the Apeksia camp. And receiving signals from the NICs in the explosives for relay to the Apeksia base should be no problem.'

They walked off in the direction of the park. In most parts of the city, including the park, there were still few people around at this early hour. When they got there Davies spotted a suitable tree and asked Roscoe to keep watch while he clambered up into the upper foliage with the transponder station and clamped it to a large branch.

'Hold on, Harry, some people are coming.' He walked on towards a nearby park bench and used the transcom without taking it out of his smartsuit. 'I'm sitting on the bench about fifty metres away and can see several people near you. I'll tell you when it's clear.' He pretended to be sleepy, half closing his eyes, and held the backpack on his lap. 'It's clear now; but hurry, I suspect there will be more people soon. Things seem to be getting busier generally.'

Davies quickly climbed down the tree and they met up by the bench. It was quite light by this time and Roscoe realised he could distinguish facial features. He recognised one of the passers by as the waiter from the Ovoskotian café where they had just had coffee but there did not appear to be any reciprocal recognition.

After sitting on the bench for a while it was time to return to the waste ground from which the bees had been released. By now they should have located any charges lurking in the city and returned to their release point. As they approached the waste ground Roscoe took off his backpack and removed the beepack, placing it on the ground. Within a few minutes returning insects landed on the top face of the box and began to move in a pattern which the flexcom was able to decode. Some indicated directions and others distances. Soon it became apparent that just two caches had been found. The main one was in the deserted buildings of the Global Federation Head Quarters in Kolniko Street. Further bees from there suggested two types of explosive at the same address – gunpowder for making ammunition and, of more concern in the short term, a large bulk of Oxytek explosive, probably for a rickshaw bomb.

The other cache was much smaller, probably used in a detonator device, but its location was a surprise - it appeared to be in the very café they had been at only a couple of hours ago. This was not really a suitable target for rats but it was useful to know it was there. They could send some spyflies to patrol the area as well as the old GF building to see if there was suspicious activity.

'Well, it looks like next stop is GF HQ, Kolniko Street,' said Davies. 'Agreed?'

'Yes. And presumably we won't be releasing rats near the café.'

'Which is just as well given that it might attract the attention of our waiter friend.'

They moved off towards the purportedly deserted Global Federation offices, only a few hundred metres away. They had been vacated when the GF pulled out of Ovoskotia in exasperation at its inability to get the two ethnic groups to coexist peacefully and at least acknowledge each other's humanity, despite a large peace keeping force and massive investment. Whenever the peace force had acted to quell violence or ethnic cleansing by one side, that side would react with violent indignation and question its impartiality. The area had been ringed off and isolated from the rest of the world, so that it became stagnant economically. Power now resided with the Krosnians since Ovoskotia, with a mainly Ovoskotian population, had been returned to Krosnia, of which Ovoskotia was part. Predictably, the Ovoskotians were fiercely opposed to this.

The hope now was that eventually the leaders responsible for stirring up and perpetuating ethnic conflict could be impounded and transported to the Valles Marineris on Mars for Enlightenment at the monastery there. But for now the Knights would continue their efforts to remove or deactivate all ordnance and arrest those responsible for making, selling or using it.

Some way along Kolniko Street they came across the semi-derelict GF building and walked up and down the front separately, looking for signs of recent access as unobtrusively as possible. Davies noticed a door in the basement which did not seem to be in the same state of dereliction as the rest of the structure. He released a tracker bee from a small pocket container.

'Detects scent to parts in billions.'

'What scent? How does it know what to look for?'

'Human-type scent – the whole range. If anyone has walked through that door in the past twelve hours the bee will tell us.'

After a few minutes the bee returned and, by its coded pattern of movements, indicated that the door was still serving as a human thoroughfare. They moved further along the street, past the GF building, and stopped by a fence about thirty metres from the door. Somehow they had to release the rats here without inviting question or suspicion.

Fortunately, the cage could be made invisible for a few seconds since it was configured to act as an optical refractor shield, causing light to travel around it. The shield was similar in principle to the ones which Knights used in combat, although these were rather too big and cumbersome to be useful in most covert situations.

'You do this bit, Ros. Make sure it's invisible when you pull it out. I'll distract the passers by.'

Roscoe knelt down to open the backpack which he had placed on the pavement and Davies produced from his pocket a small flute on which he started to play a simple Krosnian folk tune. As people walking by began to show interest he edged away from Roscoe, who was then able to release the rats without drawing too much attention. Some noticed as they became visible ten centimetres from the middle of the cage and thought this must be a kind of illusion, part of a street show, an impression reinforced by Davies having placed a collection tin on the pavement.

Davies read the expression on Roscoe's face as he finished playing and the small group of spectators dispersed, some looking understandably perplexed. 'Ah – you've heard. Yes, that's why they call me the pied piper, after the old fairy tale, the Pied Piper of Hamelin. Now the rest is up to the rats. They should be able to home in on the explosives from this position.'

They headed back to the waste ground where they had landed at dawn. While waiting for the stealthcarrier they stared high into the mainly clear sky and noticed a small glint of light moving in a wide circle above the town. 'Dronepod,' said Davies. 'Which reminds me that we have to release some spyflies to monitor activity in and around the GF building and also the café.'

'Do the spyflies work with the dronepod?'

'There is a two way data stream between them. And another one between the dronepod and the Apeksia base camp.' He felt into the backpack and drew out a small bag containing several metallic, arthropodal devices and activated their launch program, causing them to fly off instantly.

'So – your first day of active service. What happens next depends on what the spyflies tell us.'

'Have you gleaned anything so far?'

'I would guess the Ovoskotians are planning a rickshaw bomb in a Krosnian ghetto, probably using Oxytek.'

'Why would that be – pure hatred?'

'Hatred plus resentment. The Ovoskotians have been seething with resentment ever since the Global Federation pulled out of Ovoskotia and handed control back to the Krosnian government in Helegrad. It's been brewing for five years.'

A faint but insistent series of bleeps seemed to come out of the surrounding air. Davies looked round. 'Here's our transport. Time to go home.' The stealthcarrier became visible, silently hovering close to ground level, and they climbed aboard.

* * * *

As they were called into the Field Operations Room at the Apeksia mountain camp by Knightmaster Franklin he looked uncomfortable with what he was obviously about to tell them. He pointed to a holodisplay of data already gathered by the spyflies deployed in yesterday's mission, including an image of the café owner entering the basement of the old GF HQ via the door they had identified the day before as still being in use. 'Looks like there's a link between the Oxytek hoard in the GF basement and the detonating device somewhere in the café.'

'That's quite a revelation, sir. And Oxytek is powerful medicine – 1 kg is enough to reduce a multi-storey block to dust. Did the rats succeed in planting the NICs?' Combat Knight Davies was deferential without being subservient.

'It appears so. The signals were picked up yesterday evening. This is another alarming sign – they indicate that the explosives are being moved around.'

Roscoe began to see where this was leading. 'Does this mean that a major explosion is imminent?'

'Possibly, if not probably. It could still be planned long enough into the future for the neutralising bacteria to take effect and stop it happening. If, however, we can establish that the detonator has been moved to the same location as the Oxytek we will have to assume that a terror attack on the Krosnian population of Tripsino is indeed imminent. Also, we need to be sure it is Oxytek since you were using general purpose detector bees and they are not always reliable in identifying particular types of explosive. The loss of life and the amount of hatred that would be generated by an Oxytek explosion must be prevented, otherwise our long term aim of bringing the Ovoskotians and Krosnians together in peace will be all the more difficult. We could fail the way the GF failed in the past; but hopefully this is not a fantasy.'

'So does this mean another expedition?' asked Davies.

'As soon as possible. We need to know whether the detonator has been moved and, if so, where. How would you go about that?'

'First I would release GM bees from the park. This is closer to both the café and the GF HQ than is the waste ground we used yesterday. But it's also busier. The stealth will have to put us down carefully, where there are few people about, to avoid us being noticed as we step out of the invisibility shield.'

'How soon would you get data from the bees?'

'Within an hour of their release.'

'A two man stealthpod is parked outside with a box of bees - some for finding detonators, some for Oxytech. I'm told they're very effective. Good luck.'

CHAPTER 5

OVOSKOTIA: SECOND PHASE

Roscoe looked down and saw that the park was busier than they had expected.

'No chance of putting down there without attracting attention. Someone would walk straight into the invisibility shield and hit the hull. Any suggestions, Ros?'

He felt he was being assessed by a rhetorical question and was relieved that he had an answer. 'Kolniko Street was not at all busy, it was wide and it had some large trees near the curbs.'

'We could get quite close to the GF building if we landed there – not so far for the bees to go. That's assuming it's still quiet there. Let's find out.' Davies was controlling the stealthpod manually and raised it fifty metres before nudging it in the direction of Kolniko Street. 'We still have to release some detonator hunters near the café if we want to get sure signs that there is no detonator there; in other words confirm that it's been moved.'

'If it was busy on the park it will probably be busy in the streets near the café; they are not that far apart,' ventured Roscoe. 'But I did notice an old pedestrian sidewalk off the main street that passes the café.'

'Apart from bicycles and rickshaws all roads in Ovoskotia are for pedestrians now. Sorry, just reflecting on how things have changed. More to the point, were there houses or shops near the sidewalk?'

'I'm not certain but I believe there was a square with trees all round, about twenty metres in from the main street.'

'Could be ideal. We'll have to try it at least. But first let's put down on Kolniko Street. There's a tree near the UN HQ which could partially hide us as we step clear of the pod's refractor field.'

Davies steered them slowly over the roughly maintained streets of Tripsino. The invisibility field around the stealthpod was not complete except when landing or parked on the ground. It worked by refracting light around the craft and this meant that images coming in from outside could not reach the small windows. To be able to see through the windows you either had to turn off the refractor field or configure it to leave a space in front of the windows, a technique, he recalled, that was noted for its unreliability.

A rickshaw loaded with heavy sacks, its driver pedalling wearily, a beggar, a prideful striding youth, a mother with two children, one on each hand, occasional rows of market stalls. Roscoe watched the small figures, some purposeful in their gait or stance, others non-committal. He felt himself at an interface between two worlds. A human sitting in the latest form of transport, silent and invisible, a product of thousands of years of creative, intellectually driven evolution, belonging to a society which, intermittently at least, strove to advance materially, intellectually and spiritually, observing biologically similar humans, poorly educated and unable to develop new technology or even maintain the infrastructure they had inherited from the Global Federation, blinded by prejudice, each living in an ethnic group bonded by a common hatred of another group, wedded to a past coloured by true, exaggerated and false stories of atrocities committed by their ethnic foes. He was filled with contempt for both the Krosnians and the Ovoskotians. Yet was this worthy of a Knight? He wondered if Davies felt the same. How could he not? Yet he knew there were Spirit-filled Knights who had conquered such feelings.

As they hovered over Kolniko Street Davies pointed to a tree only a hundred metres from the derelict GF block and took the stealthpod down towards it. 'If we land here we'll be hidden by the tree in one direction as we emerge. Nobody approaching from the GF would see a thing; so it's just a matter of waiting until the road beyond the tree and the pavement immediately opposite are clear.'

When it was safe to do so they both walked out onto the cracked pavement in the hot sun and Roscoe put the box down beside the tree. Oxytek and detonator hunting bees were soon crawling out of the opening in the side and flying off towards the door in the basement of the GF building. They decided to strap the box to the side of the tree, well above ground level and out of sight, and get back into the pod until the bees returned with their information.

Davies poured himself a small glass of ClearSpin. 'The trouble with this machine being in total invisibility mode is we can't see out. We'll just have to guess when the bees have come back and configure the field for window visibility for a couple of seconds.'

'Not much chance of being detected.'

'No. Just two small transparent ovals. Even if we are unlucky and passers by see the windows suspended in the air they probably won't believe their eyes.' He took a sip of ClearSpin in a contemplative way. 'Nevertheless, we have to be careful. Keeping this stealth technology secret gives us a strategic advantage over – what shall I call it? Let's not mince words: evil.'

Roscoe remembered that the Knights' knowledge of technology gave them another strategic advantage and this reminded him of Isla. His mind suddenly became filled with her and the potent memory of her electrically charged presence stirred him biologically. Knightmaster Franklin had mentioned that she was studying quantum computing at Cambridge. Perhaps he could use this as a pretext for meeting her again when he returned to the Knights of Peace HQ there. As he had discovered from Father James quantum computing was proving to be invaluable in the struggle for a peaceful world and it would be a good pretext for meeting her again. Yet if he did meet her she may not allow it to lead to anything more than cold conversation after his dismal display of dancing incompetence at the pre-mission ball.

'I sometimes wonder, Ros. Why do these people want to kill each other? Most are already dead spiritually.'

He did not want to start a philosophical discussion. Davies was just expressing his exasperation and in any case it was true in a sense, for some of the population at least.

Davies put down his glass of ClearSpin. 'I think it's time we tried cancelling the invisibility field in front of the windows. So let's peel our eyes for the return of our apian friends.'

They went over to the oval frames and peered out as Davies touched the invisibility shield controls. Gradually the scene outside the pod became visible and they looked hard at the box, just in view above them. No people were in sight so they let the windows show for slightly longer as they tried to make out how many detonator and Oxytek hunters had returned to the bee box.

'Looks like enough messengers to me, Ros. What do you think?' They checked all directions for pedestrians and left the stealthpod.

*   *   *   *

The smell of freshly baked bread reminded him of the old lady who had emanated kindness and who he had seen the day before. Then he realised that the aroma was coming from the very stall from which she had served the bread. He had been walking and stopping for two hours, fairly systematically, carrying, releasing and analysing tracker flies to trace the trail of the detonator explosive after it had left the café.

It was much easier to release GM flies than bees or rats without being noticed and you got the results more quickly. As he moved through the local districts, from Ovoskotian to Krosnian to

Ovoskotian, he could see much less hatred in people's eyes than he had expected. It reminded him that most people, even in parts of the world like this, just wanted to get on with their lives peacefully, and that it was in dominophiles that so much misery originated.

The main street past the café had indeed been too busy to risk a disembarkment so they had parked the stealthpod in the tree-lined square in a sidewalk and released the detonator hunting bees. The ones which had returned suggested that, as they had feared, the detonator had been removed from the café.

Davies had taken the stealthpod back to the Apeksia mountain base. Only experienced Knights of proven trustworthiness and soundness of judgement were authorised to handle stealthpods, mainly to avoid any possibility of refractor field technology getting into dangerous hands; so it had fallen to Roscoe to try to track the path of the detonator after its removal from the café. He and Davies had already established that a detonator from somewhere had been united with the Oxytek in the GF basement but there was still the possibility that this was not the one from the café, which would mean the one from the cafe was being moved to another hoard of explosive.

The bees had indicated that the structure of the detonating device was sufficiently leaky for it to shed a molecular trail traceable by GM flies providing it was carried on foot or in a rickshaw, and since motorised vehicles and transpod technology were not available within the Ovoskotia borders there was every chance that a systematic patrolling of the streets would trace the detonator's route.

Which it had done. As he approached the GF building it was clear that this wretched, primitive piece of destructive equipment was indeed to be used with the Oxytek to lethal effect. Roscoe contacted Davies on his flexcom and asked him to bring the stealthpod to the agreed position, which was by the tree on Kolniko Street where they had parked the stealthpod that morning.

Then Roscoe's world changed so suddenly that his consciousness of what happened could not keep up. Broken glass showered much of the street and pavement as the windows of the GF block - those which were not already minus their glass - imploded and he realised, after the event, that he had experienced a percussive blast.

But it was not from the block: the source was clearly from some distance. It must be some parallel minor attack, perhaps used as a decoy to divert attention from the planned destruction of the GF building.

He ran down a side alley in the direction the blast had seemed to come from; then slowed his pace at the sound of screaming and wailing from the road parallel to Kolniko Street. He did not want to go any further. Was it necessary? He did not feel ready to face the carnage of scattered limbs, writhing bodies and pools of blood which would be waiting to assault him around the corner. Subconsciously he feared that it could fracture his belief in the reality of the Divine Light. Yet what was this belief worth if it cracked at the first stark sign of man's brutality to man?

*　　*　　*　　*

Knightmaster Franklin greeted them kindly as they entered the Field Operations Room. 'Well done. We now have firm evidence that a detonator and main explosive charge are located in the basement of what was the Global Federation HQ.'

Davies interjected. 'And we know that the detonator at the GF building is the same one that was previously at the café, thanks to Cadet Finley's trek through the streets, which means the café detonator did not go somewhere else. The rickshaw explosion must have been planned some time ago, before the Ovoskotia operation.'

'Quite so.' The Knightmaster looked sympathetically at Roscoe. 'And I'm sorry you had to witness the Krosnian attack. Had the Ovoskotia operation started sooner we would probably have stopped that one. Knights rarely encounter such slaughter so early in their career. Hopefully by the end of it this kind of wretchedness will finally have ceased for good.'

'Thank you, sir. Is there any more evidence to indicate that we should attack at once?'

'The evidence is what you were unfortunate enough to witness yesterday, Cadet Finley. The sociodynamic model at Cambridge picked up the Q-wave spectrum of a potential suicide bomber in the Krosnian ghetto which grew up near the GF HQ. The spectrum stopped being transmitted at the time of the explosion. Our sociodynamic advisers say this small blast was probably a precursor to the main attack we are trying to forestall.'

'So the likelihood of an imminent Ovoskotian attack on a Krosnian ghetto using the Oxytek bomb has increased. Does that mean an immediate arrest raid?'

'It certainly looks that way, Harry. But there has been another development which complicates matters and also presents the Knights with their first opportunity to try an impoundment.'

Roscoe and Davies looked surprised, then puzzled.

'As you know, impoundment of a domino is appropriate when we have evidence that he or she is closely associated with a major sociodynamic instability. The computer models of the region indicate that the domino associated with the impending rickshaw explosion is also at the centre of a sociodynamic configuration which could spark major ethnic cleansing throughout the whole of Ovoskotia. So in addition to arresting all those involved in preparing this particular attack we need to impound the domino.'

Davies was thoughtful. 'Why not just arrest him along with the others? Wouldn't that be simpler?'

'It would; but if he were just arrested he would eventually be released and liable to offend again. If we impound him we can send him to the Monastery at Shanghai, or even Valles Marineris on Mars. True, the domino would have to be released eventually, but only after six months, and, hopefully, Enlightened. Even if they don't achieve Enlightenment at least the sociodynamics is likely to have changed. This would be the first ever real trial of the procedure for an impounded domino.'

'Has the technique not been proved to work, sir?' asked Roscoe.

'As far as possible; but only volunteers have been used. So I am proposing two raids more or less simultaneously – one to arrest all those involved with the Oxytek plot and another to impound the domino who is associated not only with this plot but a probable large scale ethnic cleansing.'

'Have we got their movements and speech well monitored?' asked Davies. 'The attack will have to be well timed.'

'There are spyflies everywhere in the building and around the entrance. I propose two teams: one for the arrest and one for the impoundment. It is a matter of waiting for the domino to separate from the rest. We will probably have to encourage this.'

'Sir, who will be doing the impoundment?' asked Roscoe.

'Harry and you. The arrest will be done by two experienced Combat Knights and two cadets.'

'Me?' He was astonished that he was to be on this, the very first impoundment raid, having been assigned primarily to an arrest operation.

'There are two reasons for this. First, you and Harry seem to work together well. Secondly, you have fast reaction times.' He hesitated before resuming. 'And there is a third reason. As you know, whenever the Knights conduct a non-covert raid, they are also projected in virtual space before a world audience on the telepresnet. This is a key part of our unarmed struggle and is the reason that the raiders wear full regalia and make no attempt to disguise themselves. In particular, we want to attract the coming generation and our feeling is that you are the right person to do that, as I am sure Harry agrees.'

'I see the argument,' said Harry, 'but this could be seen as too theatrical. Our job is to arrest or, in future, impound, not to entertain.'

'What do you think, Cadet Finley?'

Roscoe did not want to contradict someone of Davies's experience and obvious competence. 'I'm not sure, sir.'

'It's not an easy question. Some could indeed see this as reckless exhibitionism, since it puts you at greater risk than if the raid was done incognito. The policy has been heavily debated by the KOP Council. The conclusion reached, and it wasn't unanimous, was that by making each attack as public as possible we engender a strong feeling of sympathy with our objective. The young in particular like to see people of violence outwitted and out manoeuvred in an exciting way. The entire world population will witness non-covert raids as they happen, because the broadcast breaks into all telepres sessions. It also makes a vivid impression on those witnessing the attack directly; and these are normally the very people we want to steer away from the kind of internecine activity we are determined to eliminate, along with the mental and spiritual states which go with it.'

Davies responded light heartedly and with mock resignation. 'We'll do our best to put on a good show.'

'Successfully complete the mission – that's the first priority. If you concentrate on that the show will be good anyway.'

*　　*　　*　　*

All but one of the arrest party had climbed aboard the stealthcarrier: two Combat Knights and a cadet who he had seen only fleetingly before, during training. Roscoe and Davies constituted the impoundment duo, so they were waiting for an additional cadet to join the arrest group. This gave them all time to sort out their hologenerator packs, which in action would be fixed to the backs of their armoured mirror suit, but which during transit had to be stowed in the luggage bays around the edge.

Roscoe realised that his mirror suit was the only one switched to reflection mode. It was normal practice to keep the suit black and opaque when not in combat because it was disorienting to see yourself, your fellow Knights and surroundings reflected so vividly, which was the very reason why reflectivity was made a feature. He quickly switched the reflectivity to zero and sat down, placing his baton on the round table at which Davies and the other two Combat Knights sat together with one of the arrestor cadets.

'Any idea what's keeping him?' asked the Combat Knight.

'I don't know him, sir.'

Davies could not resist a quip. 'Well, he can't be polishing his mirrors,' a reference to the fact that unlike medieval shining armour their smartsuits required no such arduous maintenance.

'Ah, ha…. here he comes,' said one of the arrest Knights, Ryder, the tall and lean one who had got up and was peering out of the window. A few seconds later Eric strolled in and calmly sat between Roscoe and the other cadet.

'Hi. Are we ready to go?' Roscoe could not understand how Eric could be so self-assured given the obvious irritation and inconvenience he was causing. Yet there was much about his friend he could not understand.

'Ready? We were ready ten minutes ago,' said Hull, the shorter and more muscular colleague of Ryder. He took the controls and soon they were a hundred metres up heading for Tripsino. As the three experienced Knights fell into conversation and the latecomer started tending to his flexcom Roscoe was able to talk more or less privately to Eric.

'How did you get onto this mission? I thought you'd be back at base analysing data.'

'That was the plan. Then things changed – namely the location of an imminent attack in Tripsino, complete with a domino suitable for impoundment, at a time when Knights are being deployed all over Ovoskotia, causing a shortage of cadets for this op. Not that I'm assigned to the impoundment; instead I have to help with the arrest of the explosion plotters.'

'Congratulations – that's what you wanted wasn't it?'

'Well, it's better than data analysis. But you've got the best job, surely– the first impoundment in history. Also, you have only got to work with one Combat Knight; I have to work with two and another cadet.' Eric tapped the shoulder of the other cadet who had been assigned to his mission and smiled briefly. 'No offence. What's your name?'

'Johnson, Rick Johnson.' Eric reached over and they clasped arms.

The three Combat Knights suddenly brought their own conversation to an end and Davies moved next to Roscoe, obviously intending to get down to business. 'We need to look at the GF basement.' He triggered a virtual display above the table, fed with live data from spyflies in the vicinity of the explosive devices. They had to gauge their attack according to how the conspirators moved. Surprise was even more important than for most attacks. The impoundment of the domino had to immediately follow the arrest of the other conspirators but be kept separate.

Davies spoke generally to the arrest party. 'We need to find a time when as many conspirators as possible, including the domino, are close together, then pounce in a blaze of glory. Everyone except Hamazu – Denis Hamazu, our local domino – must be arrested. Hamazu will then, we hope, try to escape.'

It was clear that Davies had been designated as the main commander for the two attacks. He switched his attention to Roscoe. 'Then it's up to Ros and me to see that he doesn't.'

As they approached the city it was suggested by Hull that he put them down in Kolniko Street, close to the derelict GF building. This would allow them to move in with minimum delay once the spyflies showed the conspirators to be in a suitable position, preferably in one place. Davies looked at Ryder and they tacitly agreed this was the only way.

It was obvious from the present images that the five were spread among different rooms and the translated conversation indicated that they intended to meet in what had been a conference room in the basement, close to the entrance door, on the opposite side of the corridor from the store room where the rickshaw bomb had been placed and the detonator added. This would be an ideal opportunity to storm in. But how long they would have to wait no one knew.

The faces of the Ovoskotians showed up on the display, enough to reveal their expressions. Hamazu was cold and calculating most of the time, but occasionally he would smile or frown or ridicule to motivate or crush one of the four people whose minds had been gradually warped to the point where killing and maiming innocent Krosnian civilians was not only acceptable but exciting and for the good of the Ovoskotian people. Hamazu had come to regard the Krosnians as less than human and therefore any action against them was justifiable; and he had controlled others to the degree that they felt the same and would willingly follow whatever wretched scheme no matter how lacking in humanity or human decency. Besides malice there was crass brutality and manic joy in their faces. Roscoe had never seen such expressions, except in a milder form on the faces of some of the inhabitants of Tripsino, both Ovoskotians and Krosnians, as he had walked through the streets the day before. He realised that Father James had been right when he had once told him that evil was a very real phenomenon in the world and that no theory of the mind could explain it and how it could manifest itself in any population at any time if not guarded against. That the Divine Light was a real spiritual entity he had long ago accepted. Now he felt the same about evil.

'Difficult to put into words isn't it? Definitely not a pretty sight. But just remember, almost everyone in the world is with us,' remarked Davies, catching the patterns of bitterness, disgust and puzzlement that animated Roscoe's face. The stealthcarrier had by now landed on Kolniko Street. 'Hey, they are already moving towards the conference room.' He turned to address Combat Knights Ryder and Hull, then cadets Reed and Johnson. 'Time to take up our batons.'

They moved to the luggage bays around the edge of the cabin and clipped on their hologen packs, then returned to the table to pick up their batons. Hull waved his hand in the coded motion which activated the door opening mechanism and they quickly emerged onto the street. The few passers by stood intensely curious and uneasy as the four Knights materialised, apparently stepping into the real world from out of nowhere in their mirror armour, each with a small backpack and wielding a long matt black baton.

Davies held his baton vertically and high up, then gripped the cylindrical banner control, turning it clockwise. A large rectangular plume of fine particles rapidly ejected from the baton and floated along the street towards the GF building. Then words were projected onto the aerosol.

KNIGHTS OF PEACE
WAR ON WAR

Intermittently the words changed first into Ovoskotian, then Krosnian, so that as many local people as possible could read and ponder the message. But sight of the floating banner was not restricted to direct eyewitnesses: users of the world telepres network would experience the attack as it interrupted whatever session was running on their connected devices. Even the large number of people who still used the ultra broadband internet had it displayed in the standard GF videoframe which came up by default whenever a Knight attack was in progress. These telepres and internet live viewings were made possible by the hovering camspheres, much larger than spyflies, which Ryder had sent into the air as they alighted from the stealthcarrier.

The metal door in the basement was bolted from the inside; so Hull set up a small fusion gun on a tripod and silently vaporised the door in a few seconds. The arrest party of four Knights – Ryder, Hull, and Johnson as well as Eric - entered the corridor and stood outside the conference room. Roscoe and Davies waited outside the building.

Ryder set his hologen pack to standby and blinked three times, instructing it to emit his deceptively solid avatar into the corridor. It positioned itself to guard the way into the interior, wielding with menace a curved sword of steel showing the intricate patterns of Damascus steel in its polished blade, so that when Hamazu rushed out of the conference room to escape arrest he would feel he had no choice but to make for the exit, where Davies and Roscoe would be waiting for him, rather than run through the corridor into the labyrinth of passages that pervaded the building.

Hull spoke to Cadet Knights Hull and Johnson. 'The door's not locked. Get ready to storm – ultra fast – when I drop my fist at the count of five. Remember, you have five friends: hologens, cocoons and batons; speed and surprise.' He raised his arm and clenched his fist. 'One, two, three, four...five!' The instant his fist dropped Ryder kicked open the door and shot his avatar to the far side of the room and waited for the startled Ovoskotians to turn their eyes from the door to the solid looking hologram of a Knight in mirror armour and cylindrical helmet wielding a lethal looking scimitar. Hamazu pulled out a gun from inside his black leather jacket and fired at the avatar. The bullet passed through, revealing its lack of solidity and Hamazu, after a brief moment of bewilderment, turned back towards the door; but as he did so Hull jumped in, thrust a hood over his head, tied it tight and forced him into the corridor.

Hull could see Roscoe and Davies at the entrance to the building and shouted to them. 'Here's your man, all present and correct and awaiting impoundment.' They moved in towards him and Davies released from his baton a cloud of fine white cobweb-like thread which floated near the hooded man. He twisted and rotated the baton to control the motion of the cloud, manoeuvring it to engulf him. The cocoon tightened itself around Hamazu as Roscoe removed the hood and as it did so the cobweb strands thickened then hardened, until they formed a cylindrical encasement which nevertheless gave him sufficient room to walk.

'That was incredibly easy, thanks to Combat Knight Hull' said Davies. 'Now we have to read out the impoundment statement while our colleagues inside arrest his four friends.' Roscoe wondered what use he was going to be on this mission. Hull and Eric had already done the work.

Inside, Ryder and the two cadets had stormed the conference room with the usual combination of shock tactics and hooding; but as Hull returned Ryder shouted to him. 'The storeroom! One of them managed to put the rickshaw bomb on a short timer. We need to scoot...*shit f***ing fast.*'

Davies had to make a snap decision. Keeping the captives secure would slow them down. Yet to abandon them, especially with the whole world watching, would do no good for the KOP and its mission, because they needed to convey the message that their target of achieving peace without violence was realistic. Only when a large proportion of people felt this would it in fact be achievable.

'OK, but don't let these people go.'

Hamazu was neatly immobilised in his cocoon so Roscoe and Davies ran into the building to help the others get the hooded figures out onto the street and away from the building before the bomb exploded – which could be any time. As they got to the door they saw the remaining four figures, hooded, and being led out by Ryder and Johnson.

'Where's Reed?' asked Roscoe.

Ryder looked peeved. 'He shot off into the storeroom before I could stop him.'

Roscoe half attempted to justify his friend's action. 'I know he studied bomb disposal'.

'This is real life –get him out of there, faster than light.'

Roscoe burst into the storeroom to find him peering around the large contraption strapped to an old rickshaw. 'Eric, for the sake of all that's holy let's get out of here. Ryder is livid and we are all shit scared.' Roscoe's mouth was dry and his forehead sweated.

'Wait, I think I've found the timer.' He peered at a small primitive looking clockwork dial. 'It's the timer and it says … time to go. We've got two minutes.'

They bolted into the corridor and out on to the street before they even thought of doing it. The rest were heading smartly for where the stealthcarrier, still invisible, was parked, forcibly guiding both the arrestees and the cocooned Hamazu. Roscoe and Eric, some fifty metres behind, were exerting themselves to the limit as they ran, when Roscoe lost his footing on the curb and his ankle collapsed. He tried putting pressure on the ankle but it was impossible. 'If you stay to help we are both dead. Move!'

Eric was physically powerful but in this situation his strength verged on the miraculous as he bent down, hoisted Roscoe onto his shoulder and ran like a demon towards the stealthcarrier, now switched into visible mode.

He almost threw Roscoe into the cabin, then about turned and headed back towards the basement door before Davies, Ryder or Hull could stop him. He could hear Ryder calling out: ' Reed.

Come back . Cut the heroics. We want our Knights alive - not vaporised. You know what an Oxytek explosion does. I have to get this ship out of here with or without you.'

Eric managed to shout back 'Get out now, sir. There is only a minute left.'

Roscoe reluctantly reinforced this. It was too late to pick up his friend unless he managed to prevent the explosion.

Hull did not wait for confirmation but closed the door and took the craft up to a hundred metres and sped off to hover far enough away from any blast to be safe. Roscoe could see Ryder's expression, a grim shifting compound of anger, shame and hope that somehow Eric would pull it off. He looked at his watch. If Eric was right it would go off in around twenty seconds but all on board would live - despite the carnage on the ground, and the certain death of Eric, if the whole GF building was blasted away by Oxytek.

But no explosion happened. Either Eric had defused the bomb or he had misread the timer, and from the faces of the five captives, especially Hamazu, the former seemed most likely. Roscoe knew that Eric would not have misread the timing by more than a few seconds so he told Ryder he thought it was safe to go back for him because he had disarmed the bomb.

After a few minutes Davies made the decision. 'OK Mr Hull, take us down to where we were.' Then just as they started to move towards Kolniko Street the whole craft shuddered and they all knew what had happened. Roscoe, in particular, was devastated as he realised the implications.

Hull stopped the descent and hovered around while they absorbed what had happened. Eric would be dead along with any civilians, mostly Ovoskotians, in the vicinity of the GF building. There was a smirk and an inane pride on the face of Hamazu. Two of his subordinates reflected this while the others turned away as the Knights stared in disbelief. Roscoe knew that both ethnic groups were religious. How could they have so separated themselves from God as to rejoice in the suffering of others, some of whom could even have been Krosnians?

Davies was now angry with himself for not guessing that the captives might have a secondary timer. They descended to near the rubble of the building, with dust still rising in the gentle breeze. They cocooned all the captives, apart from Hamazu, who was already encased, and strapped them to small perches around the edge of the cabin, then alighted from the stealthcraft without bothering to make it invisible and went off to look for casualties. Roscoe had to stay behind, still unable to put the slightest weight on his fractured ankle.

Roscoe recalled that they had the medical technology on board to deal with his ankle; but more important there would be injured civilians being brought into the cabin. He decided to tend to his ankle himself so that he could at least move around enough to help with the triage aid. This would also ensure that the medical carousel, which was next to the table on the far side from where he was sitting, was opened and ready for the intensive use that could shortly be expected. He carefully worked his way round the table.

Before opening the carousel he switched on the outside viewer. There was desolation; but as yet he could see no casualties. Had the plans to detonate the Oxytek in a Krosnian market materialised there would have been mass carnage.

It was strange how little he was thinking about Eric. He felt guilty at treating what was likely to be his death in an almost matter-of-fact way. Then he remembered that this was a common phenomenon: a refusal to accept that something really dreadful has happened. Or was it that deep down he believed that, against all odds, his friend was so much a survivor that he would have escaped and that he would be able to enjoy his three centuries granted by God via the biotechnology that God had created through the human mind.

The holocom lit up and made a functional buzz. A surge of joy flushed through him as Isla's face and shoulders appeared. 'Hi Ros. What's wrong with your ankle?'

'Just a small fracture I think.'

'Can you deal with it?'

'Yes. We get plenty of training.' He was concerned about the way the conversation was going to go in the next few minutes. What had happened made him feel incompetent both as an individual and as part of the team.

'Where are the others? Gone for a picnic?' She laughed, touching her hair.

'Isla. Things haven't worked out well here.'

'But you seem to have your captives there...'

'Yes, although they've not been arrested yet. The old Global Federation building has blown up and the others are going to look for casualties.'

'You mean the Rickshaw bomb went off?'

'Yes. At least we thwarted the plan to suicide drive it into the Krosnian market.'

He was ashamed that he could not bring himself to mention Eric's role in all this and his probable death. Was it because he was afraid of how much she cared for Eric, how little for him? She appeared stunned and concerned. Next she would be asking about him. It would all come out. Eric's bravery. Roscoe's stupidity. Eric's death?

'But how did it go off?'

'One of the captives had double primed it. The first primer was disabled but another captive initiated the second fuse after capture.'

'How was the first one disabled?'

Then the stealthcarrier door opened and Eric walked in.

CHAPTER 6

ISLA

It was getting dark as he crossed the bridge over the Cam. Fronds and layers of November mist were forming over the river and the grass in front of King's College chapel. The mist seemed to work in consort with the light effects on the building as a visual metaphor to show how thin was the membrane which separates the material from the spiritual. The material world itself, he recalled, was highly ethereal according to 21st century physics, consisting entirely of energy configurations in space. And since it all came from outside of space-time, in the Big Bang, was not everything spiritual?

He wondered how the fifteenth century architects of the chapel, with their deep faith and holy inspiration, would have used such optical engineering to enhance their design. Yet the contemporary architects were also inspired by the Holy Spirit.

Roscoe had an affinity with autumn. It engendered a sense that change was inherent in the natural order as it faded, died and was reborn. Reality was death and regeneration, each embedded in the other. Father James had reflected in conversation how a thread of continuity connected the seasons. The natural order in any seasonal state had within it the power to proceed to the next state, to perpetuate itself.

The view from the green expanse between the river and the chapel was familiar to him, having spent three years at the Cambridge Institute. Yet this long, exquisitely proportioned rectangular building, with its soaring turret and spire at each corner and its two longer walls each having twelve stained glass windows, always touched something within him. As with many other pivotal events in life he was not always aware of this as it happened – often he realised only a long time after that it had left an impression deep within him.

As usual he entered through the north door and craned his neck to look at the geometrically elegant vaulted ceiling, its twelve bays stretching away to the far end of the building. Then his neck relaxed as he focused on the lower points of interest. Every structure, every carving, all twelve windows, the organ pipes, seemed mathematically inspired, constructed according to some divine scheme that the architects, masons, carpenters and sculptors could not discern but knew existed.

A small rectangular area of synthetic limestone was set into a wall near the entrance. A gold inset disc in the centre beckoned to be touched and he knew this would activate a holoplaque, so before joining those praying and meditating in the pews he viewed a short history of the chapel. The foundation stone had been laid on St James's day, July 25 1446. This was seven years before the ending of the Hundred Years War, which would be followed immediately by the Wars of the Roses. It was difficult to believe how this great monument to Christ's message of eternal life through grace and divine love had all been largely conceived and built during a long period of 15th century warfare.

Yet was this surprising? War then involved only a small fraction of the population, two armies of not more than a few thousand facing each other on a battlefield, with civilians largely unaffected. Over the centuries combat had been transformed by ever more destructive and accessible technology, so that the world was approaching a time of almost limitless destructive power being in the hands of individuals or small groups.

The widespread availability of catastrophic technology was not the only problem. The internet and telepresnet gave any small, resolved group of people the power to spread destructive ideas and organise violence by exchanging coded information. Multiple conspiracy theories fermenting in the early twenty first century prevented the majority of people becoming aware of real conspiracies and undermined people's trust in the prevailing political systems, so that transactions of all kinds were impaired – social, business, political, even spiritual. And on top of this was the spreading of a hedonistic lifestyle which became almost an ideology, sapping the will to innovate and progress, even the capacity for sustained thought.

His father thought that humankind was doomed to destroy itself. Roscoe disagreed, believing that Father James had the answer: human nature itself had to change. Yet until the Divine Light manifested itself in people of all nations there would be no transformation. Human nature would not change until there was widespread recognition of reality, of which human nature was a part.

He had always had a tendency to think about macro-issues and forget his own role in the scheme of things. Now, in this holy place, was the time to reflect on his own life and how to live it. He remembered the Ovoskotia mission earlier in the year. For the Knights of Peace it had been a success: six dominophiles in the region had been captured and sent to the Shanghai Monastery, although as yet it was too early to know the outcome of the Enlightenment treatment. A major outbreak of ethnic cleansing had been prevented and no lives had been lost.

Measured against Eric's achievements his own looked dismal. Eric had distinguished himself with quick thinking and bravery not only in delaying a bomb explosion but in warning, at personal risk, the people in the vicinity to get clear only minutes before it went off and in rescuing Roscoe from his own clumsiness in tripping over.

He had been a competent assistant to Davies, apart from spraining his ankle on a critical mission, and had enjoyed working with him, but had not really engaged in proper action or distinguished himself in any way. He felt ashamed that he resented Eric's success not only in peace combat but in winning the attention, possibly the admiration, of Isla, both as a Knight and as a natural dancer at the pre-mission ball. In contrast, he was not even able to reach a passable standard and Isla could hardly have failed to notice.

Suppose Isla and Eric became romantically entangled. How could he avoid conflict with his friend? Two men loving the same woman, or vice versa. It was an age-old problem that still existed in this era where spiritual evolution was moving towards the ending of conflict between nations, ethnic groups and religions, albeit having some way to go. There did not seem to be any sign that the love triangle would become soluble, even with the inspiration of the Divine Light.

Part of him knew it was too early to be thinking about an Oath of Bonding to Isla. Yet he also knew that he did not want to lose any chance of a developing engagement as she became enamoured with Eric.

He knew it was quite likely that, with Life Extension, he would live three hundred years, as would Isla. Fortunately, his feeling for Isla, having received no obvious encouragement, had not progressed to such a depth and intensity that he would feel unable to live without her. Yet he sensed that his life would be so much more if he could be bonded to her; although at the same time he was aware that no romantic coupling in all history had needed to last for three centuries. Perhaps, with so many decades of life ahead, he would find another woman who would mean this much to him but somehow he could not conceive of it. Isla seemed like his destiny.

Was there a destiny? It certainly seemed so when you looked at the extraordinary interconnected systems of the ecosphere, where every virus, bacterium, plant and animal seemed to have a role. So why not with people? Was destiny to force him to make an enemy of his friend?

A choir began to chant a Christian canticle. Small holographic icons floated above the organ pipes: the Christian cross, Islamic crescent, the Buddha, the Tao and symbols of other religions he did not recognise. Occasionally they would all merge into the cross which then brightened and exploded. He closed his eyes after one such refulgent moment and prayed that the Holy Spirit would illuminate his soul and give him the wisdom to deal with the dilemmas of life. He decided that what he should do now was to force himself to stop being obsessed with Isla and to let events take their course. Perhaps Isla or Eric would make the next move and if this was not in his favour it would not be too late for him to disengage and live meaningfully without her.

The tall, elegantly narrow windows indicated a darkening sky behind the translucent stained glass. It was getting late and he was feeling hungry so he got up, bowed and respectfully retreated from the chapel. Once outside he walked towards the King's Parade, where the mist from the river was thickening. There were several places to eat along this road and he was making for the Wheel of Life, a combined café and meeting place reminiscent of an old fairground Ferris wheel. The five pods which hung at equal intervals around the wheel were small, each seating no more than four people, and made of heavy synthetic limestone with a relief pattern, colour and texture matching the medieval architecture that dominated much of the city.

As he approached only part of the Wheel was visible, so that most of the time one pod was rising out of the mist, one descending into it and the lowest three were obscured. Roscoe entered the transfer tunnel and climbed the steps to the entry platform, waiting for the next compartment with a vacant table. The first one to come into view out of the mist below had three people deep in animated conversation as they ate and drank. He decided to let this pass by and wait for the next. As this came into view he saw that it was empty and activated the entry control. The compartment stopped by the platform and a door slid open.

Inside he sat at the oval table and relaxed as the menu lit up. It was not a choice for gastrophiles. The Wheel of Life was a place for discussion and human interaction, the food and drink being offered as a facilitating backdrop rather than a topic of conversation. One of the graphics on the menu denoted a small snack containing a savoury concoction of noodles, protoveg globes and sauce in an edible cone together with a sweet cake and a beaker of ClearSpin. As he touched the image it pulsated to confirm that the order had been registered and was on its way.

The view outside showed various college buildings, all subtly illuminated and yet not in a way to spoil the view of the sky, now bedecked with stars since much of the time the compartment was above the level of the mist. Roscoe spoke in his details to the menu screen: 'philosophy, Cam Inst Tech; peace combat, KOP'.

A small tray carrying his order slowly ejected from the side of the table. As he reached to pick it up a gentle musical bleep indicated that someone was on the entry platform. He felt in need of company and welcomed the request to join him. There was a message on the menu screen: 'quantum cryptography, Cavendish Lab'. After touching the confirmation icon he became aware that there was something significant in these words. Then he realised that Isla fitted the profile. He remembered what the Knightmaster had said during his selection interview – that Isla was studying this very subject at the Cavendish. The fact that in all his time at the Cambridge Institute he had not encountered her was not surprising, given his tendency to value solitude more than most people of his age, although since that time he had often walked around the town when not on KOP duty hoping for a chance encounter. Was destiny about to take a new turn?

Then his hopes faded a little as he faced the fact that she was not the only person at the Cavendish learning quantum cryptography. Even if it was her it might only confirm that she had no feelings for him. Nevertheless, if it was her...

The revolving entry door opened behind him and he looked round gingerly, trying to quench his hope to avoid disappointment.

'Oh, Roscoe, hello.' Like him, she was surprised but not startled by the encounter. He even wondered whether she was being slightly guarded as she sat down diagonally rather than immediately opposite. Then her face became more friendly 'Wonderful to meet up. I thought I'd come here to finish my decoding assignment and get some food at the same time.' She unfurled her flexcom but to his relief did not yet begin working with it.

He watched her delicately touch the menu. 'I've just ordered the same as you.'

'I can recommend it. What's your assignment? Are you decoding something real or is at an exercise?'

'It's a project set by my tutor.' She adopted an ironic tone. 'I'm doing it now because I spent too much time earlier on doing something real.'

Isla's food tray slid out of her part of the table. He watched her manipulate it into position and delicately pick up her fork. Every move she made exuded vitality and occasionally her hand would rise to touch her auburn hair, and her eyes would close for slightly longer than usual.

'Where did you live before coming to Cambridge?'

'Not too far actually. Burnham Thorpe.'

'Is that in Norfolk?'

'Yes. Not far from the north coast. But I grew up in Brancaster, which was near the sea. We had to move when the sea level rose. Where do you come from?'

'Hertford. A long way from any sea.'

They fell into a temporary silence as they started to eat.

What did he feel for Isla? There was no denying the physical dimension. But why her in particular, out of all the others, many of whom would have been classed as more explicitly alluring in a sexual sense? He had met many such girls and had noticed that some, superficially attractive, lost their beauty quickly because of their behaviour or speech or facial expression. What was it that made her so vital to him? Up to a decade or so ago, prior to the revelation of the Divine Light to Father James, the relationship of male to female was seen by most as a simple animal bonding, little more than a part of a meaningless cycle of birth, mating and death. Many still saw it that way, abandoning all pretence of a spiritual dimension. The movements and mannerisms which captivated him were just biological stratagems thrown up by chance in a cosmic machine without purpose. He knew this to be untrue. The Light had revealed this through logic: how could the products of a pointless machine even know the concept of pointlessness? Yet if he felt love for her then according to the Light he should feel none of the jealousy which seemed to be growing within him. How could there be any kind of spiritual peace for those who, like Roscoe, had chosen life expectancies of hundreds of years? There would be innumerable encounters and potential relationships. Even if she did turn out to reciprocate his feelings, and they could not form an Oath of Bonding if either wanted to possess, rather than give themselves, to the other.

Isla paused in her eating and looked up at him, smiling. 'It's about three months since the Ovoskotia mission. How did you like it?'

Roscoe hesitated. Not only did he feel the need to impress her but to make himself appear superior to Eric. He resisted. The fact that he felt this way was wrong and was no basis for love – only desire and possession. And to compare himself favourably to his friend would go against his devotion to truth and be morally wrong.

'It was experience but I had no chance to distinguish myself.'

'To distinguish yourself is not the point of being a Knight, is it?'

'Well, to be more precise, I had hoped to get an opportunity to exercise my combat skills.'

'You gained experience in subterfuge and the way missions are conducted, surely?' She looked concerned and sympathetic. 'And there will be plenty of chances in the future.'

'True; but as you know I tripped over while escaping from the GF basement and sprained my ankle. Eric helped me back to the stealthcarrier; otherwise I could have died.'

'But there was no explosion until later, was there?'

'Only because Eric had returned to disarm the first detonator fuse, at considerable risk. He had also warned the passers by to scatter when he realised the second detonator had been primed. He saved many lives and risked his own. He had also captured an armed domino, something which should have been done by Harry – Combat Knight Davies - or me.'

'Do I detect resentment?'

'No. Just disappointment at my own performance.' Roscoe then remembered the pre-mission ball and realised that there was indeed resentment that Eric would compare so well with himself in Isla's eyes.

'You performed competently according to Harry's report. It just happened that the right situations presented themselves to Eric, situations which enabled him to use his skills to greater effect. In different circumstances you could have used your own skills just as well.'

Roscoe felt encouraged by her reaction. She seemed to like him, at least at some level. He decided to bring up the subject of the pre-mission ball and see if he could ascertain her reaction to his ineptitude at dancing.

'It was terrific. I love all dancing; although my own efforts paled alongside the Dance of Life.'

'They were professionals. I suppose you enjoyed dancing with Eric'

'Yes. He certainly knows how to keep time and make me feel confident. I'd say he's a natural.'

'And me?'

She teased him lightly. 'You didn't ask to dance with me, so I can't tell.'

'Isla, there was a reason for that. I am totally without the neurological equipment you need to dance. I can't coordinate my feet with the music. I'm sure you will have noticed.'

'Ros – you elected for Life Extension. You mustn't keep comparing yourself with others. You have to be spiritual. Three hundred years of life will be hell otherwise. And I mean good spiritual, of course, not bad spiritual.'

'Sorry. Did you also have Life Extension? You are certainly sounding more spiritual than me at this moment.'

'Yes, although I have not made a formal application for Enlightenment. It's easier for me to lecture you about spirituality than for me to practise it.' She moved to signal a change of subject and activated her flexcom. 'I must complete this decoding job.'

'Can you tell me about the real life assignment you mentioned earlier?'

Isla looked thoughtful for a few moments, and then smiled. 'As a matter of fact I've been wanting to talk to someone about it for a while.'

'I'm listening.'

'Has Eric told you I have a brother called Damien?'

The words hit him between the eyes. Eric and Isla must have been meeting alone and Eric had not mentioned this. He felt almost faint and was not good at hiding his feelings, but tried to look unperturbed. 'No.'

'He's got himself involved with some strange people. Have you heard of the SSS?'

'No.'

'It's a kind of religious cult which believes that the world will end within the next decade.'

'A familiar story.'

'Exactly. Only this one is different. The SSS thinks that its role is to help fulfil the prophesy.'

'Let me guess. They got this from the book of Revelation?'

'They have a leader who claims to have talked with God shortly after reading Revelation and he is convinced that his mission, the SSS's mission, is to make this happen.'

'It appears I am not the only one the Divine Light has failed to reach.' He was afraid his tone sounded sarcastic, dismissive and disgruntled. He felt both revulsion at the idea of maligning God by using his holy book as a reason for destroying his creation, and resentment that Isla must have been meeting Eric secretly, or at least without his knowledge. He tried to sound more sympathetic. 'SSS? What does that stand for?'

'The name sounds a bit scary to me. Servants of the Seven Seals. The leader styles himself "Pastor Wayne". Damien met one of their recruiters at a university social event and later was invited to a meeting in Wayne's house.'

She made it clear she needed to get on with her work and he knew she expected him to leave. He felt crushed. He didn't seem to count in her scheme of things.

Then she looked up. 'Eric, I have to do this work now but could we meet tomorrow?'

'Yes.' His spirits lifted. 'Where?'

'I talk best when I'm walking.'

'How about alongside the Cam? We could walk out towards Grantchester.'

'Right. King's Bridge at ten tomorrow?'

'I'll be there.'

* * * *

He stood watching the river slowly flowing under the bridge. He felt happy that she had actually asked to see him again; but checked himself in case it meant nothing. At least she did not find him ridiculous. More non-spiritual thoughts. He hoped that when he had completed his spiritual renewal sessions with Father James he would no longer feel so negative, although it was true that he was being severely tested in what could easily become an old fashioned love triangle.

It was gone ten. He looked across the grass in front of King's College, expecting to see her distant diminutive figure walking towards him.

'Good morning, Ros.' Startled, he turned round to see her standing on the bridge in her exquisitely shaped green coat. 'I went out for a warm-up walk and to clear my mind. Sorry I'm late.' Her face, framed by curls of auburn hair, looked flushed by the chilled air and autumn leaves stirred gently round her ankles. He wanted to put his arm round her waist but knew this was out of the question. Even to hold her hand would be a presumption.

They set off on the path towards Grantchester. Nanowood walkways over the river had been erected where the footpath stopped because of waterside buildings and soon they were out into the meadows.

She started to talk. It was about her brother. 'Remember I mentioned Damien? Well, as you might guess from his involvement with the SSS, he is worrying me.'

'How did he get involved?' It was difficult to imagine how a brother of Isla could be drawn into such a weird sect.

'One of their female recruiters met him at a university social function and, I suspect, more or less lured him to the SSS HQ in Burnham Thorpe, where he met the leader.'

'Pastor Wayne?'

'That's what he's known as. I often go home at weekends or outside term times. Initially we had long conversations about the SSS and I tried to dissuade him from getting sucked in.'

'Are they harmless? I mean, they might want to wipe out the human race but hopefully they wouldn't know how.'

'Initially he talked about their aims but there was never any mention of plans to bring them about. Like you, I had the feeling that there weren't any, that they were just a bunch of harmless cranks.'

'Initially? What made you change your mind?'

'Well, after he had been going to their meetings for a couple of months he became quiet. He started to work alone in his room for long periods and grew increasingly withdrawn. I felt uneasy about what was happening.'

'A lady's intuition?'

'You could call it that. One day he went out and left his study door open. As I walked past I noticed his flexcom unfolded on his desk. I flicked it on and as the screen lit up there was an icon portraying the SSS logo. It seemed likely that he was networking and I took it on myself to find out more about the organisation.'

'Was it encrypted?'

'Yes. Which was when I started to worry.'

'But you are studying quantum cryptography.'

'Yes, but to decode messages I need access to a quantum engine. Somehow I had to transfer his coded SSS exchanges and pages into my Cavendish Quantum Engine. This was the risky bit because the only way I could do it was to physically take Damien's flexcom into my lab and pick up the data via the interceptor device installed there. Not that this was the only thing worrying me.'

'What else worried you?'

'Damien had fallen silent about the SSS and had become uncommunicative in general. Maybe he was being brainwashed.'

'So did you get the flexcom into the lab?'

'I took quite a risk. I was only away from his study for about an hour, because I used a transpod to get me to the Cavendish, but he could have returned at any time. I photostreamed the coded flexcom data to the interceptor and transferred these into the

QE set-up, then raced back home in the transpod to return the flexcom.'

Roscoe knew a little about quantum computing and could not resist showing this to Isla, although at the same time he was aware that it would not impress her. 'How many qubits does your Cavendish QE use?'

'Two hundred and fifty.'

'That's two hundred and fifty superpositioned quantum states. Does that mean you can do two raised to the power of two hundred and fifty calculations simultaneously?'

'Well done. Not many people outside the field know that.'

He felt gratified that she even pretended to be impressed. 'It must be quite a number.'

'It is staggering, actually. It works out as more than all the atoms in the observable universe. So with that processing power we can decode any message encoded by any system, unless of course it is encoded using a quantum engine.'

'So did you manage to decode the messages?'

'I did and it's ….frightening is the only word.' She stopped walking and looked at him, almost pleadingly. For the first time he thought she looked frail and vulnerable.

'What is it, Isla?'

'In fact I'm not sure what to do. Maybe you can help.'

'Probably not; but tell me anyway.'

'Well, it seems that the idea of bringing the world to an end is more than just an idea. This Pastor Wayne is almost certainly a domino and a powerful one at that.'

'Has someone managed to get his Q-wave spectrum?'

'Nobody can get near him except his guards and close followers; so no one can plant QTCs in his food. But from the messages I have decoded there isn't much doubt about his Q-waves. He is what used to be known colloquially as a control freak and has gathered around him a group of people who seem to thrive on being controlled, seek certainty and yet are of high intelligence.'

'A dangerous combination.'

'An understatement. They have a world network of devoted followers working in all aspects of society and the inner circle has access to nanobot technology. They have their own research facility and appear to have developed a nanobot swarm which can be deployed destructively.'

'How do they get scientists to work for them? They need intellectual freedom, surely.'

'It's done on some kind of contract basis with the research kept at arm's length. As long as the scientists get their funding most don't ask too many questions. Those who do find themselves without funding fairly quickly.'

'But there must be an inner clique of engineers who turn scientific discoveries into actual destructive technology.'

Isla became slightly uneasy, as though she had not thought of this. 'Presumably, but I could not find any direct evidence.'

'I suppose that's not too surprising, Isla. The secrecy around such teams would be doubly secure. But did you get any idea of their overall objectives?'

'They are planning to destroy directly and indirectly. Directly they want to disable an orbital antenna, part of the asteroid defence network – the ADN. Once destroyed it would take at least six months to replace it.'

'The indirect result would certainly be the end times. Bete Noire is scheduled to hit earth in March seventy eight. If it did, and if the ADN didn't stop it, then life would be wiped out. But the SSS would have to get their nanobots into orbit.'

'Well, that appears to be the weak link.'

They had come to The Orchard, a former pub fairly close to the river, now converted into a studonium where students, tutors or anyone else could work, meet or eat without payment. Roscoe suggested they have a drink and Isla agreed. He was feeling slightly emboldened and took the initiative in choosing the drink from the menu. Although the style of the studonium was traditional and in keeping with the pub it had once been, the menu was set into the table, as it was in most culinary establishments. He pulled out a chair for her and sensed her presence stirring him as she gracefully seated herself. The Afghan tea which Knightmaster Franklin sometimes drank was on the menu. He suggested they try it and, almost to his surprise, she readily agreed. Could she really be getting closer to him?

Roscoe touched the menu and as they waited for the tea to arrive he restarted the conversation. 'Isla, when you first spoke about your brother this morning you seemed more distressed than I would expect you to be given that, even if they have the means of deploying the nanobot swarms, they can't get anywhere near the ADN antenna. They don't have the surface-to-orbit technology.'

'I feel I've missed something. They fully intend to use those bots and yet I can't prove it and have no idea how. Is there any way you can get the KOP to help?'

'It's difficult, Isla. The KOP has to have its bureaucratic procedures, like any other organisation. They will need proof.'

'Proof in what sense?' She seemed slightly irritated.

'Proof that the SSS are more than just a harmless cult. If we could demonstrate that they have the technology ready and the means to disable the ADN then the KOP would do something.' He felt inadequate because he wanted to give a positive answer. A waitress arrived and placed a pot of Afghan tea on the table together with two porcelain cups and saucers. Isla ignored them.

'I suppose I was hoping you might be able to get your father's friend, Father James, to support you. He has considerable influence.'

'He would do his best but the KOP would still need hard evidence.'

'Look, Ros, this is important.' She started to pour out two cups of tea. 'Suppose you or Eric secured a case with a nanobot swarm package. Would that be evidence enough?'

The mention of Eric felt like a challenge. It appeared she was suggesting that if Roscoe could not help her then Eric might. After all, he had demonstrated his abilities both in peace combat and dancing as well as his courage in disarming the rickshaw bomb.

'Have you mentioned this to Eric?'

'No. I only found out the day before we met in the Wheel.'

'Have you mentioned it to anyone at all?'

'No, of course not.'

'Do you have any idea where one might be able to get hold of a swarm package?'

'Next time Damien leaves his flexcom unattended I intend to risk another data transfer. I think I may be able to help.'

A feeling of recklessness was beginning to well up inside him. He wanted to impress her, to do something for her at all costs.

CHAPTER 7

THE AQUATHEATRE

Lulworth Cove was still and blue. The cliffs had been converted into terraces seating a thousand spectators, so that the cove became an arena. Ramps and hoops had been placed in the water, which was now near to its deepest as the tide rose.

He listened to the live choral music celebrating and thanking the Creator through the ocean ecosystem; but now this was fading into silence as the ocean performers approached. Projected into a space above the entrance to the cove were luminous holographic images of the whales, dolphins and flying fish filmed by robotic aquacams as they headed for the arena. Another aerial screen showed whirling visual renderings of the voices emitted by the approaching artists and as the choral music faded it gave way to the sound of their voices, electronically converted into the audible range and relayed to the audience.

The attention of the audience temporarily moved to a stone platform near the entrance to the cove. A group of dancers walked on to it and behind them stood three singers, one brightly dressed girl and two soberly attired men, blending their voices with those of the marine artists to create a unique sound, suggesting, he thought, a kind of fusion between a Gregorian chant and a Rossini opera, to which the multicoloured troupe of dancers moved in sedately gyrating waves as the stage ascended and floated airborne around the arena.

He remembered a very different kind of arena. His fingers had bled as he struck the metal strings of a bass guitar, almost lost in a trance, forcing complex but primeval rhythmic melodies into the huge space of the Shanghai Stadium amid intermittent waves of exhilarated applause. He had been touring with Baroqo, which produced a huge range of baroque-influenced music, sometimes filling the auditorium space with a transcendental presence, partly choral, partly instrumental, sometimes shattering it with loud but intricate melodies riding on a powerful heavy metal beat of varying time signature. The musicians, the choir and the solo singers of Baroqo entertained not only the youth of the day but people of all ages. They frequently performed at the disarmament and anti-war demonstrations which had arisen in most cities around the world; and they always finished their performance with the age-old protest anthem We Shall Overcome performed in a traditional style but with new words and with the massive audiences joining in.

A sparkling sunlit splash far out to sea was spotted by some people in the cliff- side audience and a loud cheer ascended as knowledge of this quickly spread. He realised that this was the much talked about greeting of the approaching marine performers.

It all changed after the two nuclear explosions, one in Tehran and one in Riyadh. These had had a far greater impact than the Hiroshima and Nagasaki explosions of World War II. Not only were they bigger but the media network carried the images and information about them to the whole world rapidly and pervasively. The fact that they were free of radioactive fallout only made people more terrified since this raised the probability that there would be more nuclear strikes. It, together with the HIV plague which followed, became known globally as the Cataclysm. One third of the world population had died.

The demos had taken on a new urgency. Previously they had been wholly passive and peaceful but now they had an air of desperation which seemed to generate an electric atmosphere of impending violence which struck fear into political leaders. Action to disarm was being demanded not requested. Yet to use violence would mean using weapons which would defeat the objective of the violence. The idea of a war to end all wars had arisen after the carnage of World War I in the early twentieth century; yet World War II had followed two decades later.

A kind of mass psychosis was born out of a sense of despair and the feeling that something could be done, but nothing would be done, to bring about the end of the killing and maiming technology which man continued to use, produce and develop. The evolution of HIV into a strain spreadable by droplet infection defied all attempts to fight it with drugs and condoms. There was a pervading sense of being lost. The music of Baroqo seemed to act as a catharsis and an escape from the immediate question of what to do next to stop mankind from creating an anarchic hell on earth, if not obliterating itself. The audience always came away from a Baroqo concert feeling uplifted and hopeful; but the next day reality descended on them once again like a black cloud.

Because of his popularity as a musician with Baroqo and because he frequently made public statements against the arms trade Jameson became a kind of focus for the protest movement. Balancing his life as a popular musician against his anti-war activities was hard and led to nervous exhaustion. His doctor advised him to rest in a mountain retreat and for the group to cancel the remainder of its tour. Drugs, other than a few which had been found to ameliorate certain symptoms of mental illness, were strictly taboo for Baroqo, as they were for a growing proportion of the world's peoples.

After he had recovered and felt relaxed and was ready for more touring, he had the vision. It was not a chemically induced hallucination. Nor did it come from wishful thinking or a predisposition to believe that such phenomena were more than states of mind induced by material phenomena. He knew the difference between a hallucination and an experience and he had not followed or adhered to any religion, though logic had led to a belief in some kind of creator. James saw religion largely as a problem for the world. Yet what he experienced sitting on his hotel veranda, overlooking a pine forested valley in the Swiss Alps, was a revelation of a spiritual truth and an illumination of his inner being. The images were still vivid in his memory and so was the message per se. He had no idea what Jesus Christ had looked like in the flesh, nor Mohammed, nor Moses, nor the Buddha, nor Confucius; yet the image had conveyed to him that it/he/she was all of these, sometimes alternately, sometimes all at once – yet somehow the Christ had been present in all of them.

Father James watched transfixed as three pilot whales and five dolphins chased each other in and out of the cove in a perfect figure of eight formation. Periodically they swapped places, changing the sequence of whale and dolphin, and each time they swapped a shoal of flying fish glided over the whole formation in a new direction, glinting in the late afternoon sun.

The being in the vision had flickered between masculine, feminine and neutral forms, all with a type of beauty and mystery he could not define.

All three manifestations appeared to have humanity in common but could not be reduced to gender. Each form shone with a light which he could only describe as infinitely loving and merciful; to call it bright or dazzling or by any adjective pertaining to the material world would not do it justice. Had it spoken? Not really. It was not a voice but a meaning that had formed in his mind and which he knew had somehow derived from what later became known as the Divine Light, although more accurately it was really the source from which the Divine Light emanated.

After the vision James had been filled with awe at what he had witnessed and his life transformed. Some commentators in the media, as well as many viewers, listeners and readers, were cynical, thinking it was a publicity stunt, so he gave up his entire wealth, lived simply and retired from Baroqo.

The show in the cove was approaching the climax. The dolphins and whales swam in concentric circles while the flying fish gathered at the centre, then leapt up and flew out radially in all directions, forming the spokes of a wheel. As the crowd applauded, Father James reflected on how reverse engineering in marine communication and bioneuronics had advanced sufficiently rapidly in just the last five years to make such displays possible. There appeared to be no limits to the technology that the Lord had imbedded in the natural world and given us the power to imitate.

The performers were now returning to the open sea, heading back to their natural habitats and the audience was slowly vacating the cliff-side terraces.

He paused and gazed towards the sun setting over the ocean.

So much had been discovered in so short a time. Advances in physics had made the finely controlled fusion engine and the vertical photon drive possible, two inventions which had revolutionised transport and pollution-free energy production. Using these power sources it was now possible for people to travel flexibly around the earth in transpods, or transglobals, their larger cousins. Interplanetary craft powered by dark energy drives enabled travel to any planet in the solar system in only weeks instead of months or years. The rapid growth in quantum computing had permitted information processing to be increased many billion fold, allowing the kind of interaction between humankind and the animal kingdom he had just been witnessing.

He walked along with the departing audience up the wide cobbled path with cottages on either side that led from the cove arena. Further up the path he came to the transpod park with tethered, silently hovering vehicles for hire stacked in three layers and boarded the most conveniently placed one. It took only a few seconds for his biometrics to be verified and for him to voice his destination; then he was flying above the grass-carpeted folds of the Purbeck Hills. The roadlines were barely visible in the dusk as he headed north towards Wells.

As the Cathedral came majestically into view he took over the manual controls and guided the transpod around and down towards the small chapel in its grounds which had been built as an outpost of the Monastery of Divine Light. He landed just outside the chapel and climbed down from the cabin onto the lawn next to the moat. He watched the empty transpod ascend and automatically begin to head for the nearest hire station, where it would dock itself into a parking stack.

It was a warm clear evening and the Cathedral looked almost ethereal in the subdued, modulated lighting specially designed to give a sense of an interface between the material and the spiritual world, while the stars reminded one of the magnificence of the material world which had somehow emerged, together with space and time, from the same immaterial source as the vision which had inspired him over thirty years ago.

The chapel was not much more than a hut in which to meditate and living quarters were attached. There were many of them in holy places around the world, all built by the religious institutions which had previously competed, each chapel devoted to the Divine Light. The Monastery had only two actual communities, one near Shanghai and one on Mars. It seemed difficult to believe that the planet which now hung as a far off red lamp in the night sky housed a small community built on the edge of the deepest widest valley in the solar system, the Valles Marineris. The mathematician in him pictured the relative positions of Earth and Mars and calculated that a dark energy powered spacecraft could reach it in only six weeks.

He went inside, prayed modestly and contemplatively in the manner of a Benedictine monk, then retired to his living quarters to rest. Tomorrow would be a demanding day.

*   *   *   *

Dawn broke. Father James switched his smartsuit into normal daytime mode: a plain collarless black shirt and jacket. After a light breakfast and an hour of *Lectio Divina*, he activated his secretron. It reminded him that a novice from the Knights of Peace was due to visit tomorrow.

As he scanned through the details he became aware that the cadet was known to him as the son of Paul Finley, an old fellow member of Baroqo, with whom he had maintained occasional contact over the years. Roscoe Finley had obtained a degree in philosophy at King's College, Cambridge. He had failed the Trial initially because of just one of the tests but later retook it and passed, then went on the Ovoskotia mission. He was the product of an old-style nuclear family: mother, father and children.

He reflected that Paul had always been cynical about the Knights of Peace and the Monastery, right from their inception, not long after Jamie Jameson's vision, so there was perhaps an element of the candidate rebelling against his father.

CHAPTER 8

WELLS

The narrow street between medieval houses, winding its way towards the Cathedral, had not altered much over the centuries, but the traffic through it had changed. Up to the twentieth century it had been horses, carts and pedestrians, then it had become choked with cars until they were replaced by transpods by the middle of the twenty first century, and since these did not require roads pedestrians now ruled the street.

The sun was hot on his face and Roscoe felt conspicuous, as his smartsuit had automatically assumed the standard form of a simulated chain mail tunic, usually reserved for non-combat roles and with Arthurian overtones. He could not help noticing some admiring looks from girls, which made him feel slightly awkward and unsettled as well as proud and elated.

He would be meeting Father James in only ten minutes. Why 'Father'? It was a title usually reserved for Catholic priests. But he was not a Catholic or a member of any denomination, any more than Julian of Norwich after her revelation of Divine Love in the 14th century. Probably it just seemed appropriate and no-one really knew why.

Roscoe wondered what would be likely to crop up in this interview. It was well known that Father James, after the vision that thirty years ago had diverted him from a life of fame and fortune, was a man of humility, kindness and wisdom. What did unsettle Roscoe was the thought that he might want to talk about things he had not even considered or just knew nothing about.

After walking around the moat, which surrounded what had been the palace of a medieval bishop, the small chapel building came into view. It seemed so small a place to house the founder of the Monastery of Divine Light. Yet it was the very modesty of his material existence, his complete denial of the trappings of power, the total abnegation of status, which made the peoples of the world, the secular as well as the divinely inspired from all the classic faiths, listen to him.

Roscoe's father was deeply sceptical about all matters of faith and mistrusted the motives of all those who styled themselves 'holy', despite his long association with Father James. Paul also thought that the Order of the Knights of Peace was on a fool's errand and he had tried to steer his son away from it. In fact it was partly because of his father's attitude that Roscoe had been attracted to the Order as a career, a common adolescent reaction to a parent's wishes; but something much deeper than a slight rebelliousness – it could only be called a sense of destiny – was also driving him.

Father James was standing in the doorway as he approached the chapel. He had never actually met Roscoe before: most of his meetings with Roscoe's father had been on neutral territory or at his home while he was away at school or university. His father had, however, occasionally talked about his old friend from the

Baroqo days. They clasped each other's right arm and Roscoe saw both humour and a penetrating wisdom in his eyes. There was also kindness and modesty in his every nuance of expression and movement as he motioned Roscoe to sit on one of the two parallel pine benches spaced a metre apart.

'Mr Roscoe Finley I understand.' Father James sat down on the bench opposite.

'Yes, Father.'

'Congratulations on entering the Order. Shall we use first names?' Roscoe nodded, glad that this was a rhetorical question and that he was not expected to answer. Although he felt at ease he knew he would be unable to address him as anything other than 'Father'. 'Paul and I have known each other since we were fellow band members.'

'Was that Baroqo? I assumed you just went your separate ways after you left the band.'

'We have only occasionally met since; but we always have plenty to say to when we do. How did you get here?'

'I took the public carrier from Cambridge. It landed only a kilometre from the Cathedral.'

'A pleasant morning for a walk. Do you know why you're here?'

'Not really. All I know is that it's standard procedure for a KOP novice to be interviewed by you or a Hermit Sage.'

'So let me start by asking what made you apply for the Knights after getting your philosophy degree?'

'I wanted a challenge and an adventure in a worthy cause.' He felt this was too glib and juvenile an answer. It was true as far as it went but he felt he needed to say more. 'Well, part of it was I wanted a change from just thinking about the world. I wanted to participate in it. And I have to admit the glamour was a factor.'

'And the girls it attracts? It would be understandable at your age.'

'I suppose – no, I didn't expect that or even think of it. But I have noticed it since setting the smartsuit to chain mail.'

'And your parents, how did they react when you announced your intention to apply. After all, the missions can be dangerous, as you no doubt discovered in Ovoskotia.'

'They were both against it. My mother was concerned mostly about the danger but in my father's case there were additional objections.' Roscoe wondered whether he should avoid going into more detail, not because his father would mind but because it might seem offensive.

'Could you say what those objections are? Don't worry about offending me. I know your father well enough not to be surprised by anything he says.'

'He feels strongly that trying to divest the human race of weapons after tens of thousands of years of using them is foolishly unrealistic and will do more harm than good. Human beings will always resort to violence when they are desperate or just greedy. He says that even if by magic we could make all weapons vanish in an instant people would soon make new ones. And taking arms away from just parts of the world, which is what we have to do in practice, only leaves those parts vulnerable.'

'And does he not have a point?'

'He does, or would, if disarmament per se was the whole story. But it's not. Most people in the world want universal disarmament and are right behind the Knights. Their disarmament raids together with social pressure will eventually win, even if it takes decades.'

'But are these really enough?'

'There is also the rising standard of living to stop people resorting to violence out of economic desperation.' Then, embarrassingly, he became aware that he had missed out the cause for hope that the Father might think most important of all. 'And conflict aided or instigated by religious differences is on the wane because of the healing power of the Divine light.'

'Even with all these factors it may not be enough.' Father James paused and his face became reflectively sad. 'It is so much easier to destroy than to create, to injure than to heal, to hate than to love, to seek vengeance than to forgive.'

Roscoe looked and felt puzzled. 'So you think my father may be right?'

'Possibly; but the missions of the Knights will in any case reduce the death and destruction even if they do not eliminate them. The Ovoskotia mission showed the power of quantum computing and nanotechnology in identifying dominophiles and centres of sociodynamic instability – a new departure for the Knights. Yet as long as there are people who of their own free will desire to dominate others for evil purposes there will be violence and disorder which grows as destructive technology advances.'

'So are you saying there is no ultimate solution?'

'Not necessarily. It all depends on Enlightenment; but as a philosopher you may have reservations about free will.'

'Because the process overrides the free will of the dominophile? Yes. I feel this has to be weighed against the damage the dominophile may do to other people but that any change of worldview by the domino must be done freely in communion with the Lord. If the Enlightenment is forced it will not be as God wishes. Is it forced?' Roscoe had asked himself and other Knights this same question and never got a good answer.

'No. Not in any way. We give complete freedom to the domino and allow him to reach his decisions without coercion.'

'But how then do they change so radically?'

'The Ovoskotia mission yielded us Hamazu, our first impounded domino. We hope he will redeem himself voluntarily. But he may not. If he hasn't done so in six months he will have to be released under GF law. Nevertheless he will be arrested for normal imprisonment if he endangers others. Impounding a second time would be pointless. We just have to hope that the Enlightenment process will have a delayed effect and bring him to the Lord.'

'So, Father, the ones who do change; how is this brought about?'

'I will come to this shortly but first...what do you know about quantum computing?'

'We learned something about them during my philosophy studies. They are typically a hundred billion times more powerful than the old silicon chip computers. They utilise superpositioned multiple quantum states for parallel processing, although I never fully understood what that meant.'

'Fortunately, computers of this power remain only in the hands of the Global Federation. Strict measures are taken to keep them away from those who intend harm. Quantum computing as a possible tool for achieving the removal of all ordnance from the world has been investigated by the GF labs in Shanghai. These are affiliated to the Monastery and so I have had a first hand glimpse of the work that has been going on.

'The Monastery labs at Shanghai have developed a way of simulating a spiritual process in a game which encourages the player to grow spiritually in the Lord. It is obviously part of God's plan and ultimately the creative journey that culminated in the Enlightenment game comes from our Lord. The player is constantly presented with moral choices and is compelled to make decisions throughout. When he chooses to do evil he is, in a sense, affected the way God is. Each sin in a simulated moral scenario evokes pain in the player. It is not the simulated neurological consequence of an action, such as would result from hitting a person in the stomach, but it is the actual act of deciding to sin that hurts the player. This is of course the crudest shadow of how God is pained by sin but is nevertheless enough to bring out a heightened moral awareness in the player.'

Father James folded his arms and his face became serene.

'Father, the vision you had, thirty years ago, did a voice instruct you?'

'No. There were images which seemed to convey the need for love, mercy and humility in all man's affairs. The reality and necessity of their opposites – hate, vengeance and pride – were also portrayed. I realised vividly that the former would be meaningless without the latter. They all come from the Creator – but why remains a mystery. The Divine Light is a kind of metaphor for something very real but which comes from the same source of being, beyond space and time, beyond logic, and cannot be understood other than by metaphor.

'Each religion is a metaphor, a different way of communicating with the divine agent of all being. The metaphors advance and evolve, just like the ones in science. Einstein's theory of relativity is a metaphor which superseded Newton's laws of motion - superseded in the sense that it was more powerful, covered a greater variety of situations.'

'Metaphor? But the Resurrection was not a metaphor.'

'It was in a sense a metaphor.' He saw a look of dismay forming on Roscoe's face. 'But it was also real. Like the healing miracles, such as giving sight to the blind. They really, physically happened - the evidence grows ever stronger as more methods of historical investigation are applied. but they were God's metaphors for a deeper spiritual truth about people seeing the light of God. Similarly, the Resurrection, the most real event in human history was also the most powerful metaphor for the conquest of spiritual death and the triumph of hope over despair, of optimism over pessimism.'

Roscoe was struck with a sense of reverence. Then Father James returned to more practical matters.

'The impounded dominophiles would be passed on to the care of a Hermit Sage from the Monastery of Divine Light.'

'Dominophiles? They cropped up on my first mission but I'm not entirely sure what the word means.'

'They used to be known colloquially as "control freaks". They enjoy exerting power over others and have the charisma, intelligence and even empathy - but without compassion - needed to do this. So when it comes to preventing an unstable sociodynamic situation escalating into violence it is especially important to capture such people. The real use of quantum computing would be as an aid to their Enlightenment. They would begin to understand how the very decision to commit evil is hurtful to God.

Roscoe was full of doubt. How could the Global Federation ever agree to such a process? There would be questions of infringement of the rights of dominophiles. Father James sensed his concerns.

'Let me reiterate, Roscoe. The Enlightenment Team will not be forcing people to change against their will and the game will be part of a programme of meditation and spiritual dialogue with a Hermit Sage. The object of the game is to assist the Hermit Sage in nurturing the growth of an awareness of God in the soul of the domino.'

'Earlier, Father, you mentioned software modelling social systems and identifying problem points, situations which without correction would lead to widespread disruption. This might make it possible to design a scenario which shows the player the wider social effects of what he does in the game. Do you know if this is being pursued?'

'You are one step ahead of me. That also is to be presented to the player and will probably be integrated into the same simulation of social cause-effect chains. The *Confucius* has such a simulation on board. It is planned to use this on dominos as they are transported to the Monastery on Mars.'

Father James paused. 'While you are here is there anything else you would like to ask or discuss? There is plenty of time.'

'I have heard a lot of talk about the Divine Light by people who had previously been sceptical about anything religious or spiritual. How does it guide you and the Hermit Sages in dealing with, for instance, a complex problem of morality?'

'We have first to submit ourselves to it, then let it into our being, then pray for guidance and reflect deeply on the problem until a morally acceptable way is revealed. Humility is paramount throughout.'

'How do you know when you have found the right answer?'

'The Divine Light forms a realisation of this in the mind. It is in fact another word for the Holy Spirit. It comes from our Creator.'

'Can anyone consult the Divine Light?'

'In principle they can, but it takes time, patience and practice. As a Knight you will of course be taken through Enlightenment.'

'But the vision you had was sudden and unexpected.'

'It was and that is a mystery. For some reason it was the right time in the evolution of humankind. Perhaps because I was in the public eye Yahweh used me as an intermediary. Who knows?'

'The Divine Light. Is this from God or Christ or Allah or some other deity?'

'It is from our Lord Jesus Christ, as described in the New Testament. But all the non-Christian faiths emanate from the same God, a single divine source of being which underlies all existence. In Christianity the Light is recognised as a magnified Holy Spirit, and belongs to the Holy Trinity – three persons in one Creator having personhood.'

Father James stood up and gazed out at the placid surface of the moat, with the wall of the bishop's palace on the far side. Swallows were flying low over the water, scooping insects from the air. 'The Divine Light is here to prevent conflict between religions, transform them and yet magnify their power and bring them to convergence. It dispels darkness, inspires love and generates awe at the Almighty who created us.'

They reflected on this together, silently, still looking out at the moat.

CHAPTER 9

FATHER JAMES CONTINUES

Again Roscoe felt he was being invited to ask more, to fill the silence, to put forward anything which was troubling him, and again he felt nothing could offend this man who had made the journey from a hedonistic idol of a heavy metal baroque band to a kind of saint.

'Since religion is so dangerous when mixed with politics would not the world be better without it?'

'We have no choice. There is so much mystery. The first humans wondered about the sun, moon, planets and stars, how they moved in cycles, about claps of thunder and bolts of lightning, how the world around them came into existence, what it was for, what was their place in it, how they should behave towards each other and to the living world around them, about sexual union, birth, death, about love and friendship and much more. Most of all about where life comes from and what happens after physical death. Religion is a metaphorical way of living with the mystery and it is as natural to the soul as breathing is to biological life.'

'But do we not have a choice today? Surely science has removed much of the mystery.'

'Science has solved some mysteries but each discovery uncovers new ones. The more we understand about the workings of the natural world the more miraculous it becomes. For over a century it was believed by many that the theory of evolution by random change and natural selection explained the living world. Then from microbiological and biomolecular phenomena it became clear that evolution proceeded in a much more sophisticated way involving cooperation according to mathematical laws of chaos and order, and biomolecular information exchange, transcription, translation, epigenetic editing, non-random mutations, virus transfer and cross fertilisation. Competition is only part of an unfathomable infrastructure. It now looks as though life came into being as a natural consequence of intelligence built into the universe and that this intelligence guides evolution.'

'You mean God guides it?'

'No, Roscoe.' He was gentle in his tone, in no way dogmatic. 'Intelligence is a property of God's universe. When a new species is needed to fit into an ecological niche natural selection is indeed involved. But for any living system to be viable even as a contestant in the natural world, it has to be intelligently put together, as when a new invention is tested in human society. It is at this stage that somehow, we still don't know, a source of intelligence is drawn upon to develop a number of new organisms to see by experiment which is most fitted to the eco-system. This is probably how the first bacterial life forms started.'

'So the universe gets increasingly strange, Father.'

'Yes. Then there is quantum physics in which one has to accept that energy can take on the properties of a wave and a particle simultaneously. I believe there are other quantum phenomena that have been changing out perception of reality. Perhaps you could remind me, Roscoe.'

'Two ways I can think of. One is quantum entanglement, by which certain atomic phenomena affect each other instantaneously across the entire universe i.e. in no time, so that time and space do not exist for these phenomena. There is also the principle of nonlocality which shows that observer and system observed form just one system. They are not separate.'

'That last part means that the dualistic view of the last few hundred years has had its time. Mind and material world are not separate- they form one system. And the way we perceive the world of the senses has become almost terrifyingly mysterious. We have learned that the everyday world around us is not solid and filled with matter. It is all space. Only energy conspires to make parts of it look and feel solid. So now we ask why we humans are constructed to give us the illusion that we live in a solid world. The idea that we are purely material beings that have evolved by chance becomes increasingly untenable.'

'Yet today there are still Atheists. Were you not an Atheist before the Divine Light vision?'

Father James sat down again and smiled as though in pity and incomprehension at his own past self. 'It is sad. I lived in superficial denial, although deep down I always knew that there must be something behind it all. I used to perform with Baroqo in front of audiences of hundreds of thousands – hundreds of millions if you include the telepresnet. Occasionally there was a strange rapport; energy of some kind seemed to come from nowhere. I could never explain it and never even tried.'

'I doubt whether anyone could explain it, Father.' A feeling of silliness came over Roscoe, that he should patronise a man recognised as holy by all the religious leaders of the world. Yet it was largely humility which made him holy.

'Yes. There are some questions which science has not only failed to answer, but never will, because of the nature of the questions. From where does the idea of unconditional love originate, or justice, or truth, or our sense of beauty and the sanctity of life? Where does logic itself come from? Someone once asked: "are we human beings who have spiritual experiences; or spiritual beings who have human experiences?" Modern physics makes it increasingly easy to believe the latter. The material world is shown to be so ephemeral and illusory.'

'Yet can any religion connect to the transcendental? They all seem to disagree. How do we know which one is right, if any? There can only be one truth. To say there is more than one truth is logically self contradicting, because that very statement claims to be the absolute truth.'

'You are right. There can be only one.'

'So how do the Moslem and the Christian both relate to it?'

'The Divine Light vision I had makes it clear that there is a place for the concepts and spiritual methods of all the classic religions – their scriptures, rituals, mystical practices, cosmologies and application to normal life.'

'I remember someone saying no one religion is big enough for God.'

'I think he was right. Our efforts to relate to and revere the Creator are all inadequate but I think that the one which reveals the human attribute of God is the one which has brought us closest to God by revealing the Holy Trinity. Although at times I fear its followers have failed to revere the godhead with sufficient awe. Many Christians still fail to recognise the omnipotence, omnipresence and omniscience of the godhead from whom space, energy, time, love, morality, justice, truth, beauty and logic originate.'

'Father, do you think the world has become a better place since the nuclear bombs of 2045, the Plague which followed it and your vision in 2048?'

'It has in a material sense. Even spirituality is improving in important ways. Organisations like the Knights of Peace, dedicated to the removal of war and violence from human affairs; and the Monastery of Divine Light, a bringing together of the world's religions at a deep level under the influence of the Divine Light, which is part of the Trinity, and a special form of the Holy Spirit. This is real progress. But there is danger.'

'From Bete Noire?'

'Bete Noire can be technically dealt with by the Asteroid Defence Network, although if anything went wrong with that the consequences would be dire. No, the danger is spiritual.'

'But I thought there had been spiritual progress.'

'It is often overlooked that not all spirituality is good. A spiritual dimension to reality is beyond question. It is built in and has pervaded every society through all of history. Mostly the spiritual aspect of life is aligned with the source of goodness as manifest in the classic religions and the Divine Light.'

He stood up again, walking over to the window. A luminous hologram of a Crucifix was projected in front of the wall of the old bishop's palace on the other side of the moat.

'Goodness manifests itself in most places at most times and in most people, religious or otherwise. Unfortunately, that is not the whole story, because there is also a transcendental source of badness that sometimes descends on people. Whole nations can be affected - war or an ethnic purge or religious persecution. Inhumanity rather than humanity reigns, hate rather than love, cruelty rather than kindness, death rather than life, injury rather than healing, destruction rather than creation, pride rather than humility, retribution rather than mercy, ugliness rather than beauty, disorder rather than order.

'Evil breaks out when people lose faith in goodness, when the spirit of goodness is allowed to die, so that we become spiritually empty. Then the seed of evil is planted. It happened in Nazi Germany, in the Reign of Terror after the French Revolution, in

Stalin's Russia and in Mao's China. It also happens at times in the religions of the world.'

'How does this happen, Father? Do the religious followers become spiritually empty?' Roscoe hoped he was getting near to dealing with the question his father had raised repeatedly and cynically.

'Yes. Religious followers can lose their true faith and so become spiritually empty. Faith has to be practised daily, reinforced and lived by studying, reflecting upon, or putting into practice the teachings of the Christ or Mohammed, for example, in a spirit of humility. They have to be filled with the spirit and truth which transcends all the classic faiths. Without this they become empty vessels in danger of being filled with the spirit of evil.'

'Are such people more dangerous, more evil than Atheists?'

'Once their faith in the divine truth is replaced by lust for power or material gain, then the rituals and props simply aid them in their selfish zeal. Yes, they can be worse than Atheists because they are reinforced in their selfishness. Diabolical acts can be committed with an illusory sense of righteousness, without guilt. The good Atheist is unknowingly subject to a divine influence via his conscience. Remember Hebrews 10:15-17. It tells us that God has planted a conscience in all his people, regardless of belief. The principle of evil sometimes eclipses it and this is likely to happen when a believer in the one true God believes in a surrogate, man-made god.'

'So is my father right to denigrate religion?'

'Bad religion is worse than no religion. But good religion provides reminders of the spiritual reality we all have to relate to, because it is always there. The trappings of faith are needed because few are so naturally blessed with a sense of union with goodness that we need no prompting or reinforcement. It is only when these accoutrements become ends in themselves or bound up with political power that they can be dangerous. What cannot be denied is the existence of God and Jesus Christ. They are reality and accepting them might not always be telling us what we want to hear; but if we depart from truth it is bound to bring suffering, self-inflicted suffering. In the last analysis, it comes from God, because the self comes from God. This, I think, is what the scriptures meant by judgement.'

They both had a sense that the dialogue had come to a natural end. They walked slowly towards the meditation aisle of the chapel. 'Will you join me in a short prayer, Roscoe?' Father James stood with head bowed in concentrated thought and Roscoe emulated this.

'Almighty Creator, source of all that is Divine, may you illuminate our souls with wisdom and compassion as we walk the journey of life. Amen.'

As he departed, and they clasped arms, Father James made an observation. 'You have asked pertinent questions, Roscoe. Your education in philosophy shows. I hope my attempts to answer them were adequate and may God guide you in your career.'

Roscoe walked out into the noon sun and made his way across the lawn beside the moat. This day would always be with him.

CHAPTER 10

BURNHAM THORPE FAIR

Roscoe moved slowly amongst the colour, music and stalls of the fair where the world of the early twentieth century had been carefully reproduced.

Burnham Thorpe had become a tourist attraction as well as a part of life for the population of the village, which had expanded rapidly following the migration from Brancaster, Blakeney, Cromer and similar coastal towns forced by the rise in sea level along the Norfolk coast.

The fair had been created only a decade ago as a reproduction of the travelling fairs which had prevailed in England up to the early twentieth century and had originated in the age of steam, when engines had become available to work the exuberantly decorated swings, merry-go-rounds and Ferris wheels, all enjoyed to the pervasive accompaniment of the steam powered organ.

There had since the Dark Ages been fairs associated with feast days, holidays and celebrations: acrobats, clowns, exotic foods;

143

story tellers and magicians would perform among the stalls where crowds would wander and linger to buy trinkets, play hook-the-duck, throw coconuts or consult fortune tellers. In crueller times, when people were less spiritually developed, freak shows would allow visitors, for a few coins, to gawp at the deformed. As the steam driven rides appeared in the nineteenth century these gradually usurped such attractions, partly because western societies were spiritually evolving, until these rides were themselves replaced by diesel or electrically powered fun machines ever larger and more extreme, with electrically driven beat music replacing organs and neurological stimulators enhancing the visceral experience of roller coasters.

Then the fairgrounds declined as people began to tire of the extremes which they presented to the senses and seek new forms of amusement offered by the virtual world, undersea exploration and space tourism. But change has always occurred in cycles. In the last decade people had begun to hanker not for the recent, overly sensational extravaganzas of thrill seeking, but for the experience of the fairgrounds of the early twentieth century, minus the freak shows.

Roscoe wished he could enjoy it more, that he had not committed himself to this self-appointed mission. Yet what else was he to do? He wanted Isla to love him, but she was showing clear signs of having feelings for Eric, who was showing himself to be both more capable and more courageous than he was. The information she had decoded from Damien's communications with fellow SSS cult members, including Pastor Wayne, almost certainly a domino with apocalyptic plans, meant it would be cowardice not to act.

Yet he felt uneasy. He was not concerned about his safety but about the fact that he was being selfish in not revealing to Eric the mission he had decided upon. In this respect he was acting not as a Knight but as a selfish suitor of the pre-Light world. If the mission to retrieve the nanobots was to have the maximum chance of success he must cast aside all concerns about his own feelings and either ask Eric to make the raid or at least invite him to cooperate with him in a two man operation.

Perhaps his worry that Isla felt him more than Eric despite all that had happened? Did she want to give him a chance to prove himself, knowing that the Ovoskotia mission had not given him such an opportunity? In any case, was it not true that a woman could love more than one man? He found this difficult to believe.

Roscoe tried to focus on the task in hand. Isla had found out something which made the whole idea of stealing the nanobots more urgent: the SSS had access to a private scoopship, normally used for gathering orbital debris. Given this they would be able to get the nanobot swarm into position near an ADN orbital antenna. It was possible that with this extra intelligence they could persuade the KOP of the need to act quickly but the stakes were too high and the KOP's response too uncertain. Hard evidence had to be found and the chance that the nanobot package would be in such a vulnerable position again before it was ferried into orbit was small. Which made him feel all the more foolish in not trying to get Eric to help.

Yet there was logic in this. Tension over Isla might have arisen between them and together they might be less flexible and more visible as they tried to reconnoitre and move in. Nevertheless, deep down he felt the chances of success would be higher if they had worked as a pair. In any case, it was too late now. The whole outcome, in a sense the future of the race and all life on earth, might depend on him stealing the nanobots.

He did not have much information to go on. Isla had said that the SSS was using a nineteenth century style wooden gypsy caravan as a front for some of their activities. A man was due to arrive at the caravan around two p.m. and hand the packet of nanobots over to a group meeting inside. Where was the caravan? How would he recognise the person? How would he snatch the package without breaking the Knight's code of non-violence? If what Isla appeared to have found out was true then getting the package was more important than the Knight's code and once he had used it to help reveal the SSS's plan he would only be mildly chastised while at the same time being honoured, unless he had caused serious injury. Yet if she were wrong and the SSS were harmless then he would be disciplined, possibly discharged, for conducting an unauthorised raid.

After walking around the fairground systematically for an hour he decided it was time to change tactics. He needed to get a vantage point and one way of doing this would be to ride on the Ferris wheel which he had passed a few minutes ago. So he doubled back and waited for it to stop and allow him to climb into an empty seat. Within a minute he was riding sufficiently high to have a panoramic view of the whole fair but the wheel was moving so fast it was not easy to pick out individual features unless they were some distance away. In fact this was the area he needed to concentrate on because he had already walked around all of the central part. Then, as the ride came to an end and the wheel slowed down, he saw it, standing next to a field on the outskirts, a bright red, showily decorated caravan, a horse drawn one, but with no horses connected to the wooden shafts at the front.

It took only a few minutes to get near it. On the other side of the small field was the edge of a forest and he thought this would be a good place to keep hidden, hopefully while viewing the arrival of the man with the nanobot package and his entry into the caravan. Roscoe had a backpack on so it would seem natural for him to walk across the field as though about to go on a trek.

The forest was quite thick. It had once been a pine forest but over the decades of global warming had diversified into scots pines, ash, walnut and sweet chestnut. A short way in from the grassy perimeter was a tall shrub with an adjacent tree stump serving as a seat. He decided to sit here to observe the caravan and wait for the arrival of the carrier, taking off his backpack and relaxing, ready for a long wait. He pulled out a small transceiver from the backpack and connected this to his flexcom. A map, on which his position was marked by a blip, appeared on the screen and he used eye movements to move the blip to a clearing in the wood, then transmitted a coded message to a transpod parking lot.

There was definitely some activity around the caravan but the information he had from Isla was that the agent with the nanobots would not be arriving until around three in the afternoon. It was early December so by that time the light would be fading rapidly.

Two men came out of the door at the front of the caravan and walked in towards the centre of the fair. Hopefully this was not a change of plan. Why would they go into the centre only an hour before the rendezvous time? Were they planning to collect the nanobots there instead of at the caravan itself? It was quite conceivable. If they did and got back after dark, how would he know whether or not they had the package or what it looked like unless he was very lucky and got a nightscope focus on it? It would be folly to risk an attack without a good chance of success. They might not even come back but go somewhere else entirely. Or suppose the agent did not arrive before dark. Again he would not be able to reliably identify the target he needed to snatch. His pulse began to race as he sensed failure and the likely consequences: Isla's disappointment, dismissal from the Knights and the end of intelligent life as Bete Noire flashed past the Asteroid Defence Network on its way to obliterate the biosphere.

The two men at last came back into view walking towards the caravan and they were carrying something. He put on his remote vision scope and focused his eyes on each of the two people in turn and discovered they were carrying old bottles of beer of the type that might have been bought at fairs near the end of the nineteenth century. Of course, even members of death cults like the SSS had their moments of humanity. Probably they were intending to celebrate their procurement of the nanobots.

He looked at his flexcom screen and saw that it was now close to three. The sky was completely clear, the blueness beginning to take on a dark metallic quality, hinting that night was not far off. He could see the crescent Moon beginning to brighten and a thin layer of mist was forming over the field. It was going to be an unusually cold night, more typical of the December nights his grandparents had known much earlier in the century.

Then he became aware of a violet glow in the sky approaching from the far distance and moving steadily towards the caravan. It was still light enough to see that it was a transpod and as soon as it had gently touched down a figure emerged and moved towards the door, which was being opened from inside. With his RVS fully focused he just had time to see a package being carried in before the door closed.

At last a target.

Roscoe strapped his hologen to his back and hurried across the field. There was no window facing his direction so this part of the operation at least should be safe. Once along side he crouched down by the front axle behind the horse shafts and below the level of the door, then pulled out a miniature plasma knife.

It cut quickly through the wood and he flung himself clear as the whole structure lurched downwards towards the corner where he was standing. His training as a KOP Knight now came into use and his whole being focused intensively on the task in hand. He scrambled almost instantaneously under the caravan and listened for activity. The sound of footsteps transmitted through the floor indicated that someone was making for the door. It was imperative that when the door was opened the person emerging should be distracted and all the remaining occupants should leave. He fired a KOP nanogrenade under the vehicle out to the other side where it exploded with a brilliant flash and a blast that violently shook the whole caravan but caused no injury.

Just before the occupants climbed down from the door Roscoe ejected a luminous avatar from his hologen and set it to lope off in the direction of the fairground, then moved to the back of the caravan. Hopefully the shock caused by the breaking axle and the explosion would blot out a rational assessment of what might be happening. It certainly seemed so as three SSS people together with the deliverer of the nanobot ran after the escaping avatar.

This gave him his chance. He was fairly certain that no one was left inside and so scrambled up the damaged steps and went in. The lights were still working. There was a table with spilt drinks all over it and a wall-mounted SSS emblem had been knocked awry. Five chairs were chaotically positioned. But there was no sign of the package. If he could not find the nanobots the whole raid would have done more harm than good.

He returned to the doorway and saw that one of the SSS figures was running back towards him carrying a parcel, presumably containing the nanobots. This was not the plan. To get the package by force without causing lasting injury was a challenge he had hoped not to be confronted with.

The hologen had a large database of holofigs. The fewer you released in one go the more solid and realistic they appeared. He hid behind the opened door and the SSS man entered cautiously, placing the package on the table then moving to the far end of the room as an Arthurian armoured Knight, wearing his metal helmet and vigorously wielding a sword, approached him from behind. As the SSS man turned he was startled by this threatening apparition and was barely aware that Roscoe was standing at the other end of the room.

Roscoe lunged forward, picked up the package, exited the caravan and ran across the field towards the wood. It was getting ever darker and he had to be careful not to stumble on one of the mole hills which were scattered across the field.

The Arthurian holofig would only last another few seconds before vanishing and the SSS would be on his trail very soon. As he entered the gloom of the darkening forest he stopped to get his breath and look back in the direction of the fairground as its coloured lights began to twinkle into life and its strange, jaunty but ethereal organ music drifted intermittently in his direction. There was no sign of anyone moving onto the open grassland and for the time being he felt safe. A picture came into his mind: millions of people around the world sleeping, working, playing, fighting, courting, mating or thinking. The absurdity of the situation struck him. A planet full of people all depending on him and, apart from Isla, wholly unaware of the fact. Not only that. The whole of human destiny could be balanced on a razor's edge between survival and oblivion and the way it tipped depended on his actions. Or did his actions depend on a destiny which had already been decided?

His heart thudded with exhilaration and excitement as he moved further into the forest. The air was cold, the sky was clear, the crescent moon had almost set. Darkness was absolute except for patches of stars packed between the tree canopies. The beating fairground music was getting fainter. Twigs crackled and creatures rustled and in between the sounds there was black silence. Frightening but reassuring.

Then the barking of dogs shattered the stillness. The sound seemed to be getting closer. Did they have sniffer dogs? At least they did not appear to have cyber trackers.

Now it was his turn to be jolted. A brilliant light showed through from the edge of the wood, drowning the darkness of the forest and he guessed that a candleball had been deployed by the SSS. The barking got closer. He moved faster but tripped on a stump and fell headlong, fortunately falling onto a cushion of leaves. Instead of getting up at once he feverishly pulled out his flexcom and connected it to the transceiver, taking advantage of the light provided by his enemy. The display clearly showed the direction of the transpod which he had parked earlier that day, the map showing it to be only half a kilometre off.

The barking was now dangerously near. Dogs had always scared him and the thought of a snarling hound ripping into his leg was so terrifying that he forgot the implications of whatever happened in the next few minutes for mankind's destiny. He stopped and picked up a long heavy stick, part of a tree branch that had fallen on the forest floor. It was becoming increasingly likely that it might be needed for defence against his canine pursuers as he heard them padding over the fallen leaves, panting and sniffing frantically between barks. There was no other option than to stop and use violence. The KOP code did not cover treatment of animals, although unnecessary injury of any kind would in practice be reprimanded or frowned upon.

He stopped and turned to see two hounds vaulting towards him over a fallen tree trunk. No trick of illusion or distraction would work on these creatures. As they sprang to attack him he swiped the stick vigorously in front of him then encouraged them to bite it. One did. The other lunged for his smartsuit trousers and started to bite through. He should not have got the first dog to grip the stick because he now needed it to fend off the dog which had attached itself to his leg.

In his shirt pocket was the plasma torch he had used to cut through the axle of the caravan and, given that so much depended on his escape with the nanobot package, he considered using it directly on the dog, but decided that would be gratuitous cruelty. Wincing with pain he let go of the stick which was in the grip of the hound's teeth. He then snatched the plasma torch from his pocket, grabbed a small branch hanging near his head and burnt through it.

One swipe on the nose with the branch was enough to stop the tenacious biting of his leg and send the attacking animal away whimpering. Then the other, looking startled, decided not to risk the same fate and joined its companion.

As he began to relax slightly he became more aware of the pain. The next overriding priority was to get to the transpod before the rest of the SSS party caught up with him. There was still nearly half a kilometre to go. Voices were closing in and running at full speed was impossible, partly because of obstacles and partly because his injured leg protested when he put weight on it.

There was still the hologen. Before they got within sight he released three holofigs in different directions, one of them on a path through the wood at right angles to his. The other two glided through the trees and their ethereal nature would soon be detected. Nevertheless, overall, he felt he had created enough confusion to keep them off his trail as he almost limped in the direction of the transpod which his flexcom showed was parked in the clearing, now only a couple of hundred metres away.

The triangular form of the transpod, his sanctuary and salvation, showed through the trees. Behind, the sound of feet disturbing the thick carpet of leaves indicated that the pursuing party was getting uncomfortably close; so despite the wounded leg he gathered pace, scratching his hand on the brambles that surrounded the clearing. A long time seemed to elapse between activating the door from his flexcom and the ramp actually lowering to the point where he could gain entry. He climbed on and gripped hard before it touched the ground and began to slide and clamber down into the cabin. As he reached the inside he turned round to see one of the party with a foot on the ramp. How could he stop him without causing lasting injury? Then he realised that his baton was on one of the seats in the cabin and picked it up, wincing as his leg grazed against the side of the seat. With one quick sweep and a twist of the handle a white cocoon ejected lengthwise from the baton, spun towards the pursuer in the form of a ball and, once making contact, enfolded him in a matter of a few seconds as he staggered towards the door. Roscoe then grabbed the enwrapped attacker and pulled him down to the ground just as his companions reached the clearing. He got inside and raised the ramp barely in time to prevent another intrusion.

As the transpod rose clear of the wood exhilaration eclipsed the sight of blood and the pain in his leg and his scratched hand. The sea, a misty grey layer below a brilliant canopy of stars, was in front, and he let the machine coast forward for a minute, for no other reason than to exhilarate in the experience, then turned back to head for Cambridge, the Knights of Peace and Isla.

*   *   *   *

It was hard to accept that he was being disciplined. Isla had been overjoyed at his success at what amounted to no less than saving the world, difficult though it was for either of them to really take this in. Yet he was here in front of what amounted to a tribunal. Knightmaster Franklin looked severe, while the two senior officers, one either side of him, looked merely serious.

'Cadet Knight Finley, you are aware that you have broken the KOP rules?'

'Yes.'

'In what way have you broken them?'

'By not informing the KOP, not getting authorisation, sir, before attacking the SSS to obtain the nanobots.'

'Precisely. And why did you not seek permission?'

'There was no time.'

'According to the information obtained by Ms Isla Hanson the planned nanobot offensive on the ADN antenna was not scheduled to take place for months; that is, until about a week before the ADN missiles were scheduled to be fired, by which time it would be too late for the damage to be repaired before Bete Noire struck our planet. Surely there would have been enough time to present us with the evidence and request a formally sanctioned attack with the help of experienced Knights. Instead you chose to plunge in alone with minimal experience and with no support or backup of any kind.'

'I was afraid that the claims being made by Ms Hanson would not be believed. There was also the danger that another opportunity to retrieve the nanobots would not present itself.'

'Do you have so little faith in our organisation? Why did you join it and take the oath if that's the way you feel?'

'Sir, it was no criticism against the KOP. I was just being realistic. Delays of this kind are intrinsic to any large organisation. There was nothing to lose. If the heist had failed, and I admit it could very easily have done so, the situation would have been no worse than if no attack had occurred.'

'Cadet Knight Finley, you know that is not true. You took a great risk. The SSS would have been alerted and on their guard against all future attempts to thwart their plans to attack an ADN antenna, with or without vacuum nanobots.'

'But I honestly thought that there was a distinct chance that the KOP would not have listened to me, and taken the SSS seriously, without this example of the kind of technology they now have.'

Knightmaster Franklin looked sternly at him without answering. 'I am surprised and disappointed in you. It dismays me that one I thought so promising should fail to uphold the code of a Knight so soon after his admission to the Order. Go into the reception please. I have to consult my colleagues before continuing this conversation.'

Roscoe gave the slight bow of a Knight to one of different rank and retreated from the room. In the reception area he was surprised to find Isla approaching. She must have been doing some KOP support work during her December vacation from the Cavendish Lab. They sat side by side.

'Did he compliment you?' she asked.

'Far from it.'

'Was he at least sympathetic?'

'Not even that. All the emphasis was on what would have happened if I'd failed.'

'Well, I suppose from his point of view he has to be careful not to allow procedures and codes of behaviour to be undermined. On the other hand I can't see how they can fail to realise that you had no choice.'

'He seemed to think that if I had merely alerted him with the information you obtained via Damien they could have taken official action against the SSS.'

'But we agreed that was too improbable. How could we have got them to believe us without the evidence? Roscoe, if this has seriously affected your career with the Knights. I am so sorry.'

Despite Isla's sympathy, and there was no doubting it was a consolation, Roscoe's mood was dark. He felt a long way from the Divine Light. He had tried to use human initiative, as the Knights were meant to, and he had been crushed. How could such an organisation succeed? Perhaps his father had been right. The Knights of Peace was in the last analysis nonsense and its mission to rid the world of war and all violence against human life was hopelessly quixotic. Yet what choice was there? Technology had presented man with a terrible choice: live peacefully together or not at all. Maybe it was humanity's destiny to exterminate itself. Maybe it would not really matter if the SSS just speeded up the process slightly.

Isla sensed his desolation and felt it herself to some extent. She moved closer to him and gently touched his hand then moved away as the door opened and the two officers who had accompanied the Knightmaster walked out of the room and across the reception area to the exit. The Knightmaster himself appeared, looking less severe.

'Cadet Finley, could you come back in now?'

He sat down on the bench opposite the desk. 'I'm not going to apologise for chastising you. It would not have cost much to have at least tried to alert us. If we hadn't responded quickly enough then you could have taken the action you did.' Roscoe suddenly realised that in this the Knightmaster was right. He had been afraid that the KOP would indeed take it on officially and he would have missed his chance to demonstrate his prowess, both to Isla and the KOP. Was that what mattered to him more than the future of humanity? His vanity? His wish to impress Isla?

Knightmaster Franklin then relaxed. 'I'm sorry it turned out this way.' He got up and gazed absently out of the window at the Grantchester Meadows. From his manner he appeared to be about to say something significant. Was Roscoe going to be punished or even dismissed? Somehow that was not the impression conveyed although exactly what the expression on his face denoted was impossible to read even for one trained in empathic techniques.

'Cadet Knight, there are some things I can now divulge to you. First, I do owe you congratulations.'

Roscoe looked puzzled.

'You broke some rules and took unnecessary risks, yes. However, you also achieved a result for which you deserve considerable credit and I would have tempered my previous rebuke with well earned praise had I not been restricted in what I could disclose. First, I must be able to trust you to keep totally to yourself what I am about to say. Do you understand?'

'Yes sir.' Roscoe was mystified by this sudden turn.

'The Servants of the Seven Seals was already recognised as a serious threat by the KOP over a year ago.'

'Before I stole the nanobots, then.'

'About a year ago we had heard about them having vacuum nanobots for release in orbit and their access to the scoopship. Your raid has thwarted their short term plan to disable the Global Federation's ADN defence against Bete Noire.'

'Their short term plan – so they plan something worse? Something worse than human extinction?'

'No; but what concerns us is that they have developed a knowledge base. We had hoped that the destructive technology they are acquiring was being purchased or stolen. Recently, only a few months ago, a KOP undercover team found evidence of laboratories and a number of scientists ideologically committed to the SSS. This makes them a long term problem. Take away the weapons they have now and they will make more. If they don't succeed in disabling the ADN they will find some other way of exterminating humanity.'

'Does the KOP know where their research labs are?'

'Unfortunately no. What we do know is that they are due to have a major conference in three months. Pastor Wayne, the inner circle and several of their senior scientists are scheduled to attend.'

Roscoe realised where this was leading. He could see now why the KOP leaders had been so fazed by his heisting of the nanobots. 'Is the KOP planning an impoundment, sir?'

'Logic dictates that we should. Impounding the leaders and putting them through the Enlightenment is the only way to eliminate the long term threat.'

'Can I ask where they are holding the conference?'

'This has to remain strictly secret for the present but I can divulge to you that it will be in England, although even that must remain in confidence. It is vital that the SSS get no inkling that we are on their trail.'

'Which raises the question of my raid at Burnham Thorpe. Presumably that will have suggested to them that some of their messages are being intercepted.'

'That was my initial fear; but after contacting our undercover people it seems that the information about the conference and the research operation was encoded at a much higher level of security than the nanobot delivery to Burnham Thorpe. Ms Hanson did very well to decrypt what she did with the quantum computing facilities she has access to at the Cavendish. But the fact is that the KOP decoders are using a much more powerful system developed in Beijing. According to what they have found the SSS have no idea that we are on to them.'

'That is a great relief to me, sir.'

The Knightmaster paused and he appeared to be mulling over something. 'How heavily is Damien Hanson involved with these people? And why are they so keen to recruit him?'

'Isla, Ms Hanson, should be able to help us there but I believe Damien has trained as a scoopship pilot. Perhaps they wanted him to take the nanobots into orbit near the time of the Bete Noire intercept. Of course, now the cat is out of the bag, thanks to my efforts, they won't require him; in fact they might want to dispose of him.'

'Ideally, we need to get him on our side, even to the extent of helping us with the impoundment.'

Roscoe remembered that Father James had been his father's friend since the days of Baroqo and the first glimmer of a plan began to form in his mind. 'Sir, could we call Ms Hanson in? I think I know a way of persuading Damien to join us.'

CHAPTER 11

GRASMERE

The invitation was enigmatic. His sister wanted him to join her in Grasmere to meet some friends of hers yet she knew he was not fond of company in general. He had until recently been depressed, feeling that life was pointless, so pointless that it was difficult to summon up the energy or the will to do anything, although he had kept his job as a scoopship pilot and maintenance engineer for Orbital Technologies Inc.

Now he was actually enjoying flying the transpod over the spring landscape much more than he ever did taking the scoopship into and out of orbit.

It was unusual for a ground-to-orbit pilot to feel like he had. Usually the sight of the Earth from orbit and the sense of mystery which it engendered conspired to expand a person's awareness of the world, in fact of the universe, and keep the sense of a material self in the background, so that one felt spiritually alive and in contact with God and with those around you. Even Atheists felt a kind of mystical awareness of the cosmic expanse. Many people, of all faiths, including former Atheists, had become illuminated by the Divine Light partly as a result of such experience. It was the reason dominophiles were taken to Mars, rather than Shanghai, for Enlightenment.

Yet he was unable to feel this way. While he was small his parents had become followers of the Divine Light through the Ecumenical Church of Christ, and, seeing that their son showed unhealthy signs of self preoccupation, had hoped that he would follow their example, finding peace in liberation from the tyranny of earthly distraction and desire. Yet this did not happen. Their disappointment descended almost into despair when even the flights into orbit during his scoopship apprenticeship failed to transform him. How he could be so different from his younger and only sister, who was so vivacious and sympathised with almost everyone on a first meeting, was both perplexing and frustrating.

Compounded with his depression had been a sense of bitterness. People, he thought, were either deluded into thinking there was a Creator which they thought gave them some kind of immortality; or they just enjoyed living for the day and saw the pursuit of pleasure as the only rationale for existing. Except perhaps for the Knights of Peace. They did have a goal which amounted to saving civilisation from extinction, although he had even then wondered whether such a goal was really worthwhile.

Then Pastor Wayne had come into his life and transformed it by giving him a sense of purpose while reinforcing his feeling that human existence was futile, though not meaningless. He had shown him that the world was in a state of sin beyond redemption and that God needed to punish it. One day this would happen and it would be destroyed, as would everyone on Earth, except those who 'helped' God, although Hanson had not yet discovered what was meant by 'helped' in this context. Wayne had allegedly received a vision which modified the wording and the interpretation of the book of Revelation and had, he claimed, newly decoded its imagery, including the seven seals and the blowing of the seven trumpets. Wayne was charismatic and confident, conferring on his followers, including Hanson, a sense of direction in the scheme of things. He now felt content that he was part of a cosmic plan and he was honoured that Pastor Wayne obviously had a role for him, one that had not yet been divulged.

Looking below he could see the fells, crags and wide ribbons of water radiating out from the centre of the mountain complex and realised the transpod had already taken him close to his destination, the village of Grasmere, situated by a small lake, where his sister was staying with her 'friends'. She had been enigmatic about them but he supposed they would be a gaggle of females among whom she hoped he would find one with whom he could form some kind of relationship. It was ridiculous. Like a Jane Austen novel. No girl had ever felt any affection towards him after a few sentences of stilted conversation. Physically, they were initially attracted to him but then his speech and manner revealed a coldness, almost a weakness, which either mildly repelled them or left them indifferent. Had he not felt more confident than usual, almost cheerful, he would have refused Isla's request. Perhaps it would not be so bad; he would at least be able to talk with some enthusiasm about the Servants of the Seven Seals, although he hardly expected any girl that Isla had as a friend would show much interest.

He had talked with Isla about his intended entry into the SSS and she had not been impressed. She had called it a crazy sect, as had his parents. Why could he not find a purpose by working for the KOP or by setting up as a scoopship charter pilot?

The transpod dropped rapidly out of the sky and Hanson could see what must be the lakeside village rushing up at him before the machine levelled out. He took control and landed on the shore opposite a house built out on almost invisible supports over the water with an arched bridge connecting it to the grassland where sheep grazed.

Isla came towards him over the bridge, which gave the impression of being fashioned out of blown glass, smiling and waving. 'Hi there Dami.'

'Isla,' he said, touching her hand, 'where are your friends?'

'Come over to the seat and I'll explain.' They sat on a bench overlooking the lake. The tranquil silence was prominent. She pointed out the small tree covered island where Wordsworth and Coleridge had lit a fire one night and made tea. He was, of course, unimpressed. 'Had they nothing better to do?'

'Some people enjoy life, including some who write timeless poetry.'

'Poetry is a diversion from God's purpose for us, a diversion from his plan.'

Isla almost winced but ignored what he had said. This was no doubt a view he had picked up from Pastor Wayne. Except that because he had stated the view it was the iron truth, not the view of a dangerous eccentric, probably a domino, who, like numerous oddballs before him had tried to decode Revelation in order to determine God's plan for mankind.

'Dami, you asked about my friends here. They are inside the house. You need to listen to them. They know things about the SSS you don't, things the Pastor and his followers don't want you to know.'

'What do you know about the SSS that I don't? You have never shown any interest. When I talk about them you just shut your mind.'

'They sounded dangerous, creepy, not to say blasphemous, just from your descriptions. But I'm not going by intuition only. I have hard evidence.'

'Hard evidence? How?'

'This is difficult. As you know I've always had my doubts about the SSS. You didn't even believe in God yet you suddenly started talking about his judgement for mankind and listening to the claims of someone who thinks he has a direct line and can understand Revelation, or rather the modified version he claims has been dictated to him by God. Theologians and biblical scholars have been puzzling over Revelation and disagreeing on it for two thousand years.'

'So?'

'So…you are my brother and it worried me that you should get involved.'

'What's new?'

'What's new is that I acted on my worries without your consent.'

'How?'

Isla paused as she worked up the will to incur his indignation, if not his anger. 'Well, as you know I'm studying quantum cryptology at the Cavendish. This gives me access to a quantum engine for use in both encryption and decryption. I had a terrible suspicion, based only on intuition, that you were being drawn into something evil.'

'Thanks for your confidence.'

'I borrowed your flexcom and photostreamed the files into my QE space, then read the messages.'

'That was inexcusable Isla. In any case it was heavily encrypted. Much of it was not intelligible even to me.'

She could see that he was hurt. 'But the QE software I'm using allowed me to decode it. I'm sorry Dami.' She put a hand on his shoulder. 'They are planning to use vacuum nanobots to disable one of the antennas of the ADN when Bete Noire approaches. This could mean a direct hit. Life would be wiped out.'

Hanson went silent. He got up and walked back towards the transpod, then stopped and turned round. 'Is that why you called me here? Why couldn't you have told me over the flexcom?'

He continued walking away. Isla signalled Roscoe and Eric to come out of the house. 'Dami, we can't let you go back. Not yet, anyway. A Knight has stolen the nanobots they were going to use and they may connect you with this. It could be dangerous.'

He stopped as the two Knights gently prevented him from boarding the transpod. Eric prepared to deploy a cocoon if necessary, but it was not. Hanson looked shocked.

'How could you do this?' He became angry.

'I broke into the SSS computer system because I was suspicious and Roscoe stole the vacuum nanobots to stop them sabotaging the Earth's defence against an incoming asteroid. We invited you up here for your own protection, although the evidence points to them not connecting you with Roscoe's attack. Are they not good reasons?'

'If you hadn't broken into my flexcom I would not have been in danger.'

Roscoe interjected. 'But the ADN would probably have been destroyed. You know what that would mean. Did you know what the SSS was planning? Do you really want to be part of those plans? If Isla had not decoded their messages they would still have had the means to destroy our planet.'

Isla held her brother's arm to calm him and his anger subsided. 'Dami, I know you are not a bad person. You have been misled by Pastor Wayne. He himself has been misled, by himself, and because of his power over people he has been able to mislead others; he has probably allowed himself to be misled so that he can have a reason for dominating others and, in a sense, dominating humankind itself. You have to separate yourself from him and the SSS.'

It was clear that Hanson had not known how the SSS were intending to use him. Wayne had said nothing about using nanobots to sabotage the asteroid defence or even intimated anything along those lines. He became morose and withdrawn. Isla showed him to a room in the house where Roscoe had lived with his parents until only three years ago.

Eric sauntered over to Hanson's transpod, opened a panel on the side and disconnected the finely controlled fusion unit that powered the thruster. 'Can't afford to take chances.'

'I think he's got the message,' said Isla, returning from showing her brother to his room.

Roscoe explained. 'I know the sabotage has been prevented but we must not let the SSS know that Damien is involved. When the time is right he can help us plan to prevent future attacks. When he does return it must be to help us, not the SSS.'

Eric felt awkward. 'Ros, I think I'll go for a row on the lake. See you later.'

*   *   *   *

The Battle of Agincourt had taken place in 1415 during the Hundred Years War. The English had beaten the French although much outnumbered, largely as a result of their skilled use of the longbow. An alternative version of the conflict, miniaturised, but complete with the sound of rushing arrows and the smell of horses was now taking place in the main room overlooking the lake with Roscoe's father in control of the battlesim. He was re-enacting it with the odds changed. The French side had been allocated some skilled longbow men and with his father's experienced manipulation of the battle parameters the outcome had been reversed.

Roscoe settled down by the window on a seat overlooking the lake, just outside the battle arena that occupied much of the room. He could hear his mother's voice calling from the kitchen. 'Paul, you've been playing that game since breakfast. You know Ros and his friends won't be able to stay long. Why can't you make an effort?' Tina obviously had not realised that Roscoe was actually in the room. If she had she would have been even more angry but would not have said anything.

Paul had not seen his son enter the room but noticed him as he turned his head to shout an answer, trying to suppress his irritation. 'Ros is here now.' He smiled and moved across the room to join his son on the window seat.

Roscoe asked him about the battle and who was winning, although he was not really interested. The very idea of war bored and depressed him. Computer simulations were not in his view harmless. They made it seem exciting and kept the whole concept alive, so that real ones were more likely than they need be.

What military forces remained in the world trained soldiers to overcome an inbuilt natural reluctance to kill by using violent virtual games, although it had to be admitted that the creators of Battle Pro and most other simulations now accepted that real social and spiritual damage could be done by introducing gratuitous violence.

'This is how to stop real wars – give people an outlet for the natural impulse to fight.'

'I'm not sure it is a natural impulse. If it is it should hardly be encouraged.'

'Do you think I'm going to go out and start fighting people? This is just fun and the strategic aspects stretch the mind. You should try it. And you need to learn to enjoy yourself, Ros, relax and stop being so serious.'

Roscoe knew that his father had not been pleased when he had joined the Knights. He had not taken seriously Father James's vision initiated by the Divine Light and the world-wide monastery which had followed it, or the Knights of Peace which had been inspired by a Hermit Sage from the monastery. He was a committed Atheist and did not entertain the idea that anything was divine. The universe and everything in it, including the mind, was the outcome of meaningless interactions between elementary particles and it was just self delusion to consider it anything else. He loved his wife, his son and his friends and appreciated beauty and yet when Roscoe had asked him where he thought love and beauty came from he simply dismissed this as a pointless question – it was just an illusion thrown up by the random events of evolution.

'I can enjoy life as a Knight. I know that I am part of a great historical change moves towards a world free of war and the misery that goes with it. The cosmic Christ is an aspect of the Triune God and he is transforming the whole universe. The actual process of changing things in this world is itself a challenge and gives me satisfaction.'

'I thought Christians were waiting for the "Second Coming". Why should they bother to improve the world?'

'They are; but meanwhile God expects us to work towards heaven on earth. Maybe that is so we can participate in creating the new heaven and new earth at the end of the age.'

'How do you think you will attract a girl if you stay so serious?'

He hesitated. To mention Isla as a girl he was becoming romantically involved with would also mean admitting his doubts about whether she felt anything for him. In some respects his father was right. He must seem dull to her alongside Eric and he had always tended to be too preoccupied to be at ease socially. He pictured his father as a young man in Baroqo, the same band that Father James had played in before the Divine Light vision. They had both been single and must have had numerous opportunities for relationships with girls.

'Dad, you know I opted to take the Life Extension treatment. I could have three centuries to make relationships with women.'

'I hope so. But why did you opt for Life Extension then go and join the Knights? What could be more dangerous than confronting potentially violent individuals without being allowed to use weapons?'

'War is a scourge that needs to be stopped by radical measures and you can't stop it by violence without causing more wars in the long term. It is only what Christ said two thousand years ago.'

'Well, you know my views on the Knights and their crazy quixotic mission.'

At this point Tina came into the room. 'Paul, you aren't still trying to talk Roscoe out of the Knights? He worked hard to get in and the least we can do is give him some encouragement.'

He knew his parents meant well but he felt like a child as they talked about him. He was thirty years old and even for one expecting to live to three hundred he was regarded by the rest of the world as an adult. Looking out of the window he could see Eric rowing on the lake in the distance, his freedom and assured independence making him feel even more like a child.

'But Tina, you are no more in favour of him having entered the Order than I am?'

'Only because it's dangerous, not because I don't think it's a noble cause. Now he is in we should give him every support; not try to undermine his chosen vocation. Can't you see that?'

'I respect his sincerity and applaud his success in getting in; but he is my son as well as yours and I think he has made the wrong decision. He will be getting plenty of support from James, I mean Father James, when he arrives here. When is he due?'

'I'm not sure. Do you know Ros?'

'Thanks for acknowledging my presence.' He could not resist the sarcastic quip. 'About dusk. That's as accurate as you can tie him down.'

The quarrel came to an end and they went into the kitchen for a cup of Afghan tea. Tina asked Roscoe if he wanted to call Isla in but he wanted to see her alone, before Eric returned, so he drank his tea quickly and went upstairs to find her. She had left Damien's room and was now sitting alone in her own with the door open. She had reconfigured her smartsuit into the form of a loose multicoloured skirt and looked relaxed.

'Isla, can I come in?'

'Of course. Was this the room you slept in as a boy?'

They sat opposite in two chairs by the window with a view of the lake.

'I was lucky to be brought up in such a place. It must have cost my father a lot but he certainly had the money then, when he was playing in Baroqo. He didn't follow James's example and renounce all his worldly possessions.'

'You must not hold that against him. James only did it because of his spiritual experience. He had been an Atheist before that.'

'How is Damien? Does he still feel betrayed?'

'Not really. I don't think so. He is just desperately unhappy at having lost something he was beginning to enjoy – a sense of purpose. Wayne had given him this without mentioning why he wanted him as a scoopship pilot or what the SSS had in mind for the world.'

'Presumably he is not one for the Divine Light. Do you know why? Has he considered it? You must have talked to him about it when you were going through your introductory sessions with a Hermit Sage.'

'I tried but he seemed against it on principle. Probably because I'm his younger sister. If he had come across it himself it might have been a different story.'

'Maybe if Father James approached Damien. He is due to arrive in the next hour or so. He could at least persuade him to see a Hermit Sage.'

'Is there one near here?'

'The MDL have erected a stone hut high in the fells, several kilometres from here. It is used by a lady Hermit Sage for meditation and prayer and as far as I know she is still there. If Father James could persuade him to spend a couple of days up there his whole life could be transformed.'

'But he can be obstinate, Ros.'

'Possibly. But the Hermit Sage has software to inspire submission to the Holy Spirit, or Divine Light, which is one form of the Spirit.'

It was getting close to dusk and the lake was very still. There was no sign of Eric and they could see a boat tied up by the landing stage. The room was getting dark and a wave of strong physical desire swept through him. He wanted to move close to her, feel her electricity, and touch her hair. It was so tempting to reduce her to an object of lust where the Divine Light would, he knew, reveal her as something much greater once he had properly let it into his being. Isla turned her head towards him and smiled knowingly, then got up and put on the lights.

What did the smile mean? Was she just amused by him? Or did she really feel something like he felt for her? Or was she just pleased that he was offering a possible way of filling the spiritual vacuum in her brother?

'I think you're right. Shall we go downstairs and see if Father James has arrived? And Eric should be in the house by now.'

*   *   *   *

He sat on the lakeside bench as the February sun rose, clearing the distant mountains to the south west. It all seemed as bleak and soulless as he felt within. A month ago he had started, almost for the first time in his life, to feel alive as Pastor Wayne had begun to introduce him to the belief system of the Servants of the Seven Seals. Yet Wayne had only wanted him because his expertise as a near-space pilot and lack of social contact fitted into his scheme to destroy an antenna in the Asteroid Defence Network as it attempted to intercept Bete Noire, a scheme which had been intended to be secret.

Why had he been so easily taken in? Or perhaps Isla was wrong and there had been no such plan to use him in this way. Yet he had confidence both in Isla's good intentions and in her technical expertise in quantum cryptography.

He thought of the Divine Light. He had heard Isla talk about it many times and knew she believed in it; but to him it meant nothing. It was just wishful thinking and illusion, just one more belief system for people to disagree on. Yet he had almost been drawn into a belief system himself: the SSS. This only showed how dangerous and ridiculous was all religion, including even the Monastery of Divine Light, although at least its aims were laudable.

Thinking of Wayne and his followers depressed him even more. They seemed to derive certainty and direction from their secret belief system. Yet it was either total delusion or the God from which it came was irrational in demanding the destruction of life on Earth, the life which he had himself created as the culmination of a long evolutionary process. In the depths of his mind somewhere he had hoped that one day he might become absorbed in a spiritual movement; but this attempt by the SSS to exploit him had made Damien afraid ever to commit himself again to any cause or ethos or faith. All hope had been dissolved away and he felt more empty inside than he had ever done. He had always been told that self pity was dangerously self fulfilling and believed it to be so. Yet this was overwhelming, incapacitating despair, not self pity.

His reverie was interrupted by the sound of someone approaching on the gravel path up to the bench seat and he looked round. A man in a plain black tunic stood facing him, a small haversack on his back. An understanding and searching look passed over his face as he stepped forward. 'Mr Hanson?'

'Yes.'

'I'm Father James. Your sister may have mentioned me. I arrived last night by transpod.' He cast his eyes around the lake and the surrounding fells. 'A wonderful morning, cold and clear.'

Despite his lowness of spirit, which made him weak, there was an air about this man that demanded an effort. The demand came not from the man but from within Damien himself. 'Yes, Isla had told me you were coming.' He could scarcely believe that such a man could once have enthralled arenas full of people with his music and stage performance, that he had preached Atheism and courted celebrity.

'How long have you been up, Mr Hanson? Have you had any breakfast?'

'Only a few minutes. I came straight out here. I couldn't eat any breakfast.'

'I'm going for a walk along the hill behind the opposite shore of the lake and plan to cook a bit of breakfast on the way. Would you like to join me?' Father James noticed his hesitation. 'Forgive my intrusion, but I think there are things which you want to talk about.'

He did not ask how he knew this. 'How long would the walk be?'

'Only as long as it takes to get to the Rydal Cave and back, as well as have some breakfast. We should return here by lunch. Is that OK?'

'Yes, I suppose it is.'

'Don't be downcast, sir. There is nothing in this world that can destroy you. I hope to make that clear as we walk.'

They set off across the damp grass to the end of the elongated lake, crossed a wooden bridge and climbed up onto a track that led parallel to what had been the far side and as they walked along this Father James began to speak. 'I'll stop along here somewhere and get the stove out.' A few more steps, then he began to get to what they both felt was the point. 'You must think Pastor Wayne a particularly evil man. Is that so?'

'It is. He deceived me while pretending to be holy.'

'How much has your sister told you about the Light?'

'Very little. She has tried but I have always made it clear that spiritual matters don't interest me. I thought it all fantasy – a waste of time. Then the SSS came along. After that experience I feel even less inclined to talk about religion or anything spiritual. I am sure you will understand that, Father.'

'I do indeed. This is a good place to light the stove and shelter its flame from the breeze.' He unpacked the haversack, placing the small gas stove between two slabs of volcanic rock, then lit it with a match from an old box which Knightmaster Franklin had given him. They shared a liking for primitive tea making paraphernalia but unlike the Knightmaster his interest was confined to its outdoor use.

Father James pulled out a small pan and began to fry pre-cooked pancakes. 'You may not have noticed but it is Shrove Tuesday.'

'That's a Christian tradition isn't it? Pancake Day. I thought you were a follower of the Divine Light.'

'We are already talking about religion. I am both a Christian and a follower of the Divine Light. In fact the Light is a manifestation of the Holy Spirit, from the same Trinity as God the Father and God the Son. I have a Moslem friend, a Sufi, who also submits to the Light. Strictly, that means he is a Moslem in name only.' Father James scooped out two pancakes and put them on their worn enamel plates. Then he looked into the flames of the stove licking around the base of the kettle. 'The Light illuminates all who submit themselves to God. It is the healer of divisions and ultimately will bring us all under Jesus Christ. The vision I had thirty years ago revealed that the Creator relates to us through different faiths, according to laws beyond our understanding.' He looked up. 'You have a question, sir.'

'The SSS profess to be part of God's plan. Are they not illuminated by the Divine Light?'

'They can't be; they do not submit themselves to the Creator. Pastor Wayne pretends submission to God, claims he understands this Creator, and knows his plan, just by reading, even altering, our Christian bible. He believes he is right, can do no wrong, that his way is the only way, because he is on God's level. He feels justified in manipulating all around him to bring about the end of mankind, knowing, as he thinks he knows, that humankind's destiny is to die – except, of course, for him and his followers. Pride is by far the biggest sin.'

'If you are a Christian or a Moslem or a Jew or a Zoroastrian... how can you all be right?'

'All are in some way relating to a deity, a real being from which our reality emanates. I believe that Jesus Christ gets us closest and uniquely embraces the fullness of God; because God cannot be fully reached other than through the Resurrected Christ, the Holy Spirit and the Father. What is certain is that all agree on a monotheistic Creator who cares about God's creation, who has human-like attributes, who provides a moral compass, who has a sense of justice and intends that some form of resurrection and judgement will occur. As mere mortals we must remain ignorant of when this will be or what form it will take. All we can do is trust in our Creator with reverence and humility according to whichever of the great monotheistic faiths we find ourselves adopting.'

'But you are a Christian.'

'I am indeed. I believe it to be the most powerful way of relating to God. In our Lord Jesus Christ we have the human attribute of God. It may be that others, with different roles in the cosmic scheme, born in different cultures at different times, can best relate to God through different faiths. I believe that the Divine Light will eventually bring such people to the triune God.'

'What about Buddhism and Hinduism?'

'Buddhism does not involve a deity. There is no source of morality deriving from a personal God but it posits selfless behaviour which is in keeping with the moral codes emanating from the monotheistic religions. Hinduism is difficult to pin down, but predates the others by thousands of years and is not really monotheistic. Again, they have a place in the Lord's scheme which we cannot comprehend.'

Damien tried to absorb all this and resolved to study it further. He felt inspired to do so, and it was as a source of inspiration that Father James was sought and revered. Not so much for what he said but for what he was.

They finished their pancakes and set off again along the high horizontal track towards the Rydal Cave. Father James mentioned how it had been excavated as a slate mine and used up to about 1920. Since then it had become a minor tourist attraction until, a century later, many began to tire of visiting historical sites as space tourism progressively raised and widened their horizons.

When they reached the large, gaping mouth of the cave they found it deserted. Safety barriers, warning notices and statements denying legal responsibility for injury or damage abounded, all of them in a state of neglect and decay, even though people still visited the cave. The obsession with safety, which rose with the increasing secularisation of society in the early part of the twenty first century, had faded as trust and a sense of community began to grow with the resurgence of the classic religions, revitalised and brought into harmony by the Divine Light.

They sat on a large boulder near the entrance and looked back out over the valley with its two lakes connected by the River Rothay, bright in the glancing February sun. Father James reflected on how the 19th century poet William Wordsworth had spent some thirty years in the Grasmere and Rydal Water area.

'I've never heard of him and can hardly think of a single poet's name. I was trained as an engineer.'

'Forgive my preaching, but to go through life without taking in some poetry – and Wordsworth is hard to beat – is a sad thing for the soul. Scientists and engineers are in a strong position if they can complement their understanding of the material world with an appreciation of the qualitative aspects of life.'

Damien followed Father James as he set off on the return route. 'You must frequently go into space as a scoopship pilot. Does that not stir you in some way – the view?'

'People often ask me that – specially Isla. No, not really.'

'Not even the first time?'

'It was impressive, Father, that's all. There must be something different about me – every space goer I've met seems to get emotional over it.'

'It does normally have a profound effect. Many have been steered towards the Light as a result.'

'Isla says I need to be spiritually awakened. Pastor Wayne seemed to be making me feel spiritually alive for the first time. Now even that has gone.'

'Not all spirituality and transcendence is good. Fascists and serial killers feel the spiritual power of evil. They are not in themselves evil. Nobody is evil but some are influenced by evil because they have cut themselves off from the Divine Light, or its precursor in the religions, usually because they do not even know it exists. Pastor Wayne is not evil. He is simply misled and because he is a domino he unfortunately has the charisma to attract and so mislead others, with potentially disastrous results.'

'Is it possible to awake people spiritually to the Divine Light? Even those who seem totally resistant to it?'

'That is the job of a Hermit Sage.'

'Isla has mentioned them. Are there many?'

'Perhaps forty or so in all. There is one only a few miles from here.'

*   *   *   *

The footpath to the base of Helm Crag was broad enough at this stage for them to walk three abreast. They had walked on the granilite pavements through the middle of Grasmere village and seen the outline of the Lion and the Lamb rock formation at the top of the mountain, just visible in the far distance. Isla had remarked on the contrast between the dark red pavement material, flexible, tough, frost resistant, designed for optimum drainage in all weathers, and the rugged mountain landscape, flecked with rare traces of snow, that confronted them. Yet she thought it a pleasing juxtaposition, not an incongruous one.

Now they were on the pebble path winding up the lower slopes through the pine trees among which a light morning mist lingered. As the path narrowed they were brought closer together. Roscoe enjoyed just being beside Isla and treasured every word she uttered, every laugh, smile, glance or movement; but his pleasure in this was diminished when she responded to Eric. He had heard that women like men who can make them laugh and it was clear that Eric was either deliberately trying to amuse her or doing so, like he seemed to do everything, naturally and with ease.

As the path steepened and narrowed they had to walk in single file and Eric paced ahead. Roscoe normally did not like being in the rear when on a taxing group journey on foot: following rather than leading seemed to exhaust him more quickly. On this occasion he preferred to walk behind Isla, partly because it seemed polite, partly to avoid the embarrassment of not being able to keep up with Eric but mostly to enjoy the grace of her undulating body, revealed in contour by her green smartsuit, as she negotiated the pebble steps and, when her head was turned to one side, to see her auburn hair curling forward onto her cheeks

The path ahead bent sharply round and disappeared into a wall of bracken.

Isla stopped and looked up. 'Eric has got well ahead of us.'

Roscoe noted that she was breathing fairly heavily and he himself was beginning to flag. 'I can see a stone slab not far ahead. Perhaps we could rest for a while.'

'I realise I'm not as fit as I should be but I think we should press on, don't you?'

He hoped she was not trying to avoid being alone with him, that she did not want to catch up with Eric so that they could all three be together and enjoy Eric's amusing repartee. As they pushed on up the steep zig zagging gradient it became obvious that he was not going to stop and soon he was out of view.

By now she was out of breath and had to stop. 'Maybe we had better stop after all.' She sat on a small ledge overlooking the valley behind them, pointing out a brightly lit waterfall on the other side. They each blinked to reset their flexspecs to magnify the scene. As one who had spent much of his childhood in the vicinity he knew the name of it. 'Sour Milk Gill. The path beside it leads on to Easedale Tarn and then rises steeply to Codale Tarn. And beyond that is the stone hut of a Hermit Sage.'

'A Hermit Sage? There's one in this area? I have sometimes wondered if Damien should visit one. I saw him setting off this morning with Father James, although not in the direction of the waterfall.'

'No. Father James told me he was going to walk to the Rydal Cave and back this morning and that he intended to invite Damien to join him.'

Isla looked thoughtful. 'Can anyone consult a Hermit Sage?'

'In principle, yes, although there are procedures. Personally, I can't think of anyone who would not benefit from consulting one.'

'But what about you, Ros? Is it not a formal requirement for a Knight?' It was obvious she knew. Probably she had seen his records while working for Knightmaster Franklin. In any case she was a highly intuitive lady who would by now have detected his spiritual immaturity.

'I have discussed this with Father James. Yes, some time in the next year I must undergo an Enlightenment session with a Sage.'

Isla got up. 'I'm going to catch up with Eric. He must wonder what's happened to us. Coming?'

Reluctantly he got to his feet. He would like to have sat here all day talking but it was obvious she did not feel the same. After a few minutes they rounded a sharp bend and came across Eric lying comfortably on a slab of stone with his hands behind his head. There was a vague air of mock triumph about him. 'Sorry to get so far ahead. I was beginning to wonder if a wolf had got you.'

She laughed. 'We wanted to admire the view didn't we Ros? Why were you in such a hurry?'

'Just wanted some vigorous exercise. Which reminds me. There is a dance on in the village tonight.' Suddenly Roscoe felt deflated. He knew how much Isla would enjoy this and want to go.

'Oh? Is it in the village hall? I believe they have a genuine electric folk band performing in the style of a century ago, complete with holotributes.'

Mercifully no more was said and Roscoe set off ahead before Eric had a chance to take the lead again. He decided to set as fast a pace as possible to prevent them falling into conversation. All the time he felt ashamed at the selfish nature of his feelings for Isla and his inability to accept his limitations. Hopefully he would not feel this way after his Enlightenment but he had thought he already had some glimmering of an awareness of the Divine Light. Now even this was in doubt, despite conversations with Father James and possibly because of the influence of his father, a confirmed Atheist and denier of the divine.

It was an exhausting climb up the footpath but because he was more able to cope with the hardship when leading than when following he soon pulled ahead. On reaching the foot of the steep stony route to the top, a sheep grazed plateau with rocky outcrops, he stopped to rest and let them catch up. He could see them in the distance, walking side by side on the long grassy stretch to where he now sat. He focused his flexspecs with his eye muscles and saw their faces close up. Isla was laughing and Eric was looking happy. Why should their happiness make him so sad?

Isla and Eric caught up and sat next to him on roughly hewn steps, the lowest of a final steep path to the top. Like most mountain paths and steps for trekkers and pilgrims they were coated with Durafilm by a Robojobber to prevent erosion.

After resting in silence and recovering their breath Eric suggested they start climbing the last stretch. Roscoe went first, then Isla, with Eric close behind. One of the steps had crumbled away despite the Durafilm and left a small escarpment which Isla, being smaller, found difficult to negotiate and as Roscoe turned round to assist he saw that Eric was already giving slightly more help than chivalry demanded, and from her laughter it was clear she was enjoying it.

At the top they found an outcrop of rock and sat staring out over the slowly ascending valley known as Dunmail Rise, with a deserted thin track of crumbling tarmac along the bottom which once had been a road for the cars and lorries of a previous age. Transpods moved steadily through invisible trails in the sky, far apart. Some hovered or landed. Overall, there was no impression of crowding by vehicles to spoil the sense of beauty and grandeur. A small cluster of buildings further up the valley marked the Grasmere village.

'I can see the village hall from here, using my flexspecs,' said Isla.

Eric replied quickly. 'Which reminds me, why don't we all go to the folk band concert?'

Roscoe now had to make a choice. He strongly suspected that it would involve dancing, in which case he would once again have to display his ineptitude at this activity so loved by Isla and at which Eric was so skilful and adaptable. Alternatively, he could refuse to go. This would risk letting them fall into a bond of love and Isla would be lost to him. Yet if he went and remained aloof while they danced he would make himself unattractive to her and could equally well push them together. Eric must surely realise how painful this was for Roscoe; but if he felt as strongly attracted to her as he did then Eric could hardly be blamed for an element of ruthlessness, especially as Eric was even further from the Divine Light. Neither of them had yet undergone a spiritual induction with a Hermit Sage but Roscoe did at least have some awareness of it through his family connection with Father James.

'You two go and enjoy yourselves. I feel like staying in tonight.'

Isla and Eric looked concerned, and asked him if he was sure about this.

'Yes, please, go ahead. It's no sacrifice for me. There are things I need to do back in the house. In fact I would rather get back now than go on to the Gibson Knot.'

Slightly surprised by the alacrity with which they agreed he got up and led the way downward. Even though going downhill he felt heavier than going up.

CHAPTER 12

COUNSEL

The sun had not yet risen as the vertical white streaks of the waterfalls came into view. He had picked his way across the sheep-grazed grass, boggy peat and stones which formed the path upwards alongside the river as it found its noisy way down into the valley. Venus was bright in the east behind him.

He felt tired. Last night had been a disturbed one as he imagined Isla and Eric at the electric folk revival. Inevitably they would have danced closely together at some stage and the bond between them would have strengthened. Getting up early and walking into the mountains was the only way he could quieten his mind; but even this failed to quell his despair.

At the foot of the lowest cascade of Sour Milk Gill was a pool. He climbed down close to it, sat on a rock and stared into the churning water. It seemed to set off a stream of unconnected thoughts: the Knights, his future with them, the Hermit Sage of Codale Tarn, only a few miles further up into the mountains, the mission to impound a dominophile in Tripsino, the SSS and Damien, three centuries of life, and, inevitably, Damien's sister Isla. He could not avoid erotic thoughts and the turbulence of the pounded pool only seemed to encourage them. He remembered the teaching of Father James, deriving from both the Divine Light revelations and Christianity, which fully recognised the tumult of mind that accompanied male hormonal surges. The critical thing was to avoid dehumanising the girl of one's thoughts, to treat her gently, kindly and with sensitivity in one's imaginings, not to be the slave of one's own sensuality.

He got up suddenly and scrambled back to the higher path which led towards Easedale Tarn and, beyond, after a steep climb, to Codale Tarn. Not that he intended to go further than the first and larger of these. The sun was up and noticeably warmer by the time he reached the shore. He found a small rocky outcrop and rested against it, out of the cool wind and pleasantly absorbing the early sunshine as he gazed at the shifting patterns playing with the tarn's glassy surface, sporadically reflecting the mountains on the far side.

What did he feel for Isla? Was it just lust for a beautiful woman? Or did he really love her? Lust he could not deny. But did this exclude love? He certainly felt jealous of her obvious attraction to Eric. Was that because she seemed to prefer Eric to the exclusion of himself or was it just that he did not want to share her? But to want to possess her was not really love in the Divine Light sense. How did she feel towards him? He had no understanding of women, especially in a world where deep changes to the human psyche and society were underway. All the literature of the past was little guide to the new reality paradigm which was emerging.

Roscoe decided to meditate and try to invoke the Divine Light through prayer for the wisdom which he felt he was lacking, for understanding of Isla, and to ask for forgiveness at the possessiveness he felt towards her. Doing this did return him to a less troubled state of mind and gave him the will to focus on other problems than his own.

He remembered Damien. Surprisingly this did not remind him of Isla, even though she was quite close to her brother in a maternal way. How could anyone be so misled by the SSS? Presumably Pastor Wayne had a Q spectrum with strong spectral features corresponding to hatred and the desire to dominate. In addition he must have considerable charisma. How else could one account for the growth of an organisation based on one man's esoteric interpretation and modification of the Revelation book in the Holy Bible? It was not just a harmless cult but had spawned capable zealots backed by real destructive power and consumed with a mission to allow life on earth to be made extinct by a cosmic event.

The sound of a sheep nibbling at grass distracted him. Sheep grazing had been a rare sight in recent months because of the roundups by roboherders. His father had mentioned it. Periodically the Lakeland Ecotrust would remove grazing animals to restore biodiversity.

What Knightmaster Franklin had said about the SSS conference came back to him. If only he could be part of the envisaged impoundment mission that would surely impress Isla. Or would it? Could he really expect heroism to impress a woman of her stature and intellect? The chances of him actually participating in the mission were in any case almost non-existent. If any novice were to take part it was more likely to be Eric. He had already proved his abilities and heroism in Tripsino.

He turned back to make the return trip to the house and set off for the falls of Sour Milk Gill.

In the far distance was a small lone figure walking towards him and something deep within told him he knew the person. When the figure was close enough to reveal the colour of the hair and the gait of a female he knew at once that it was Isla. He noted that she was without Eric. Moreover, she at least had in common with Roscoe that she liked to go for lone walks in the mountains first thing in the morning.

'Hi, Ros. Looks like we had the same idea.' She smiled and looked pleased to see him.

'This has always been a favourite walk of mine.'

'I'm not surprised. It's beautiful.'

'How much further were you intending to go?'

'I'm not sure. What is there to see further along the path?'

'There's a fairly large tarn, that's a small lake. Only a few hundred metres on.' He looked back. 'Do you mind if I walk with you?'

'But you would be going back where you came from.' She appeared amused but in a way which seemed to indicate an attraction towards him.

'I don't mind. Did you enjoy the folk revival?' He walked beside her as she set off again, her smile indicating that she welcomed this.

'It was fun. Why didn't you join us?' He suspected she was teasing him. She knew he did not like, or rather was incapable of, dancing.

'Dancing isn't my forte, as you will have learned at the pre-mission ball.'

'Does it have to be? The point is to enjoy the event, rather than compete. Surely?'

'But even for that a certain natural competence, a sense of rhythm in the feet, is needed. I just don't have that.'

'Maybe you should try neuronic coaching. There are some excellent courses. Actually, I'm surprised that although you got through the Knight selection you lack rhythm in the feet. You must have good coordination and agility. It's amazing how complex the body is.'

He was walking close beside her and a throb of excitement welled up achingly in his body as her hand brushed against his. Was this all he felt for her? Lust? If so he was not free, just a product of the material world of atoms, no more free than a north pole of a magnet being attracted towards the south pole of another magnet. Yet no other girl had evoked passion like this. If destiny was bringing them together that did not rule out physical attraction. In the Christian theological model soul, mind and body were, in some unfathomable way, different aspects of the same essence. And it was becoming clear that she felt something for him, despite his clumsiness at the activity she liked most and his shortcomings alongside Eric.

Or was he imagining this? Maybe it was Eric she was destined to pair with, either in marriage or a Kinship Bond. He would have to use this opportunity to find how she really felt about Eric and himself; or at least start to uncover it.

They walked alongside the tarn and as they came to a stone ledge Roscoe suggested they sit down and enjoy the view of the lake. She looked at him full on. 'Thank you.'

'For what?'

'For arranging the meeting.'

For a moment he foolishly thought, in his optimism, that she meant their meeting on the path. But she was obviously referring to how he had brought about the meeting of Damien with Father James and so helped rescue him from the influence of the SSS. Was that the only reason why she seemed to like him? Because he had helped her brother? Helping her brother was only incidental to helping incapacitate the SSS, although when he had suggested to Knightmaster Franklin that he be invited to Grasmere he had thought that turning Damien from his path of self destruction would be a secondary result.

Isla qualified her thanks. 'I know that the main motivation was to get Damien's cooperation rather than to rescue him. Nevertheless, this has been the result.'

'Father James would have regarded both as equally important.'

She reflected for a moment and looked concerned. 'But how do you propose to make use of Damien's short time in the SSS? Does he know something that the KOP spies and hackers don't?'

'Not much of significance. The Knightmaster aims to use him in an infiltration. He will have to be actively on our side in aiding an impoundment raid. He will have to use his access to Pastor Wayne.'

'So he will have to deceive. Is that not alien to the Knights, except in actual combat to avoid the need for violence?'

'It is permissible when done for the right reason. I don't know the details but the proposed raid and the reasons for it will have to be judged acceptable by three hermit sages after a period of meditation.'

'He is not good at deception. He may be misguided but Damien is the most transparently honest person I know.'

'I could see that. But once this has been decided upon he will be thoroughly trained. The KOP and the Monastery have more advanced neuronic coaching techniques than any other organisation. I think you know this.'

'I do.' She became thoughtful. 'Who will be in the impoundment raid?'

'I don't know. So far all the planning is secret.'

'Do you think Eric will be involved? He certainly distinguished himself at Tripsino.'

Roscoe was shattered by what to him seemed a cruel remark, although it was true. It was not only at dancing that Eric outshone him. 'Perhaps. But on the other hand it could be merely that the right circumstances presented themselves.'

'You mean he was lucky. No, Ros. It was more than luck. Even I know that.' She laughed, good naturedly. 'Why does it bother you?'

He sighed. 'Isla, you know why.' He became angry. 'I have strong feelings for you, yet you seem to be always comparing me with him. I have only been in the Knights for a few months. Many years of active service lie ahead. I believe that future situations will give me a chance to prove myself.'

'Ros. Please calm down.'

They walked silently for what seemed to Roscoe a long time. Then she stopped by the waterfalls of Sour Milk Gill and faced him. 'I thought you would have realised. You have been trained in philosophy, you have conversed with Father James and through the Knights come into contact with the MDL.'

Inwardly he knew what she was leading up to. 'I know what the Divine Light and Christ teaches us. We must not compare ourselves to others. I understand that. But I feel for you, like never before.'

'And because you feel for me, you expect me to feel for you? Not only to feel for you but to never say anything complimentary about

Eric or enjoy myself with him because he happens to be good at what I like. That sounds like jealous, possessive infatuation.'

'So I'm nothing to you. I was mistaken. I thought a bond was growing.'

She turned and walked on quickly, looking irritated, but not fierce. He hurried to walk beside her, feeling foolish as well as dejected and rejected. They carried on walking down towards the bottom of the valley, where there was an old road that led back into Grasmere.

Isla stopped again and looked at him. 'Ros, please understand. I like both you and Eric. But we are in the age of the Divine Light. I cannot love you as long as there is so much possessiveness and biological desire. You should know this.'

'I do. But I also know how I feel.'

'Look, Ros, maybe later. When you have gone through the Enlightenment you may feel love for me, not lust, not possessiveness, not even one to one romantic love; but a new kind of male-female love.'

He knew she was right. There was no chance of them entering into an Oath of Bonding until he had learned how to cope with his physical desire for her. His sex-based 'love' needed not to be removed or replaced but to be absorbed into a new kind of love where body and soul were one, as revealed by the Divine Light and as Christianity taught. 'And what about Eric? Do you have generous, undemanding love for him?'

'He doesn't think the way you do, Ros. Maybe you did too much philosophy. I do have affection and respect for him, but that's all. It may never become any more than that. The type of love I'm seeking, and which I think you are seeking, has to grow slowly over time.'

'I'm not sure Eric is looking for that.'

'And are you? It is a question of "contemplating destiny". Have you heard that phrase from Father James?'

They walked the rest of the way in silence.

*   *   *   *

Father James stood next to a rowing boat beached on the shore of the Grasmere lake, which was dead calm now that the slight breeze of the morning had stilled. The sun was shining and it was comfortably warm. He sensed the divine everywhere: in the water, the sky, the pebbles underfoot and everything around. It seemed to unite with the divine within him. It was difficult to believe that he had once seen the world in a purely mechanistic sense. He recognised now that this had been an illusion, a product of obsessive reductionism.

A familiar voice, one he had known at intervals over forty years, interrupted his reverence for the natural order around him. 'Day dreaming again, James?' It was friendly enough, but there had always been a tendency for an edge of rebuke in Paul's voice since James the Atheist had announced his revelation, left Baroqo and set out on his ecumenical quest.

He gazed longingly at the sheet of water before him. 'It is some time since I rowed a boat.'

Paul looked out across the lake. 'Hardly a day goes by when I don't.'

The boat had water in it, left there to stop the wood drying out and contracting to make the hull less waterproof; so at Paul's instigation they turned it over, then tipped it back to the upright position. The floor and seats were wet. Paul wiped them dry with a rag which he had brought along and they dragged the boat down to the water, pushing it slowly in until it floated next to a small jetty. Paul picked up the oars which had been lying next to the boat and they each climbed aboard.

It seemed natural for Paul to take the first turn at rowing, to get them well clear of the shore, since it was his boat and he was well practised at it. After a few minutes he changed positions with Father James who then hesitantly started to pull at the oars, causing a large splash instead of cutting silently and powerfully into the water.

'You're out of practice, James. Take it slowly. It will come back to you soon enough.'

Father James grinned and took the advice with no hint of embarrassment, while Paul started off the kind of confrontational conversation they usually had on the rare occasions they got together. It was rare for anyone to evoke anything like annoyance since his experience of the Divine Light but Paul managed to do so almost every time they were in proximity for more than a day. 'Don't you long for those days in Baroqo?'

'A certain amount of nostalgia, perhaps. Nothing more.'

Paul looked mildly irritated. 'It was hedonistic heaven and would have continued for much longer if you hadn't broken up the band with your confounded hallucination.'

'Hallucinations have nothing to do with reality. What I saw has improved the world and people's lives, so it must, surely, have had some connection with the real world. Besides, I know the difference between a hallucination and an experience.'

'It may have improved things temporarily, yes. But I think it has put the world off its guard. You can't fight terror groups and malevolent people with non-violence and goodwill. You need guns and bullets to fight guns and bullets. The Knights and the Monastery are in denial.'

'No, Paul. You are in denial. You deny the truth of the Divine Light, of a divine creative source of all being, of the need to work in accord with Yahweh's will. You think the universe is a meaningless conglomeration of particles and force fields. Hardly an effective way of looking at the mystery of life.'

'This is metaphysics, James. Let's talk about something down to earth.'

'Like what?'

'Imagine two groups firing hot lead at each other, scattered in a forest, hell bent on killing. How do your "Knights of Peace" stop that without using force themselves? How do they stop it at all for that matter?'

'In a sense they will have failed if it even gets to that stage. Our main objectives are to remove all ordnance from the world and the will to use it.'

'Yes, very noble. But there are places outside the Global Federation jurisdiction where fighting happens all the time. Are the KOP going to give up on preventing those conflicts just because they can't have the weaponry needed to prevent them?'

'To yield to the temptation to use weapons would be to give up, to undermine the message of the Divine Light. Military organisations have used violence to achieve all kinds of objectives throughout history. Yet always violence begets more violence.'

'Sorry, James, but that's life.'

'No. It can't continue. With the technology now being developed it is no longer possible for humanity to survive without a spiritual transformation, one that, among other things, renounces violence. In the past such an ideal was seen as impracticable. Now it is essential. Either we remove the will to kill or we exterminate ourselves as a race.' He stopped rowing, letting them glide forward, the water gently slapping against the sides of the boat, and stared meaningfully at Paul. 'Now tell me which one of us is the realist.'

'You still haven't answered my question. How do you stop two armies or groups of thugs trying to kill each other?'

'And have you answered my question? Is fighting violence with violence ever going to defeat violence and can the world survive unless there is peace, given the destructive technology available and still being developed?'

Paul asked for the oars, took over the rowing and ignored the question.

Father James felt he had scored a point. 'However, since you insist, the KOP are well aware that interim measures are needed to stop acts of violence as they happen.'

'So they will arm themselves. They will be just like any other peace keeping force.'

'Not so. The KOP has new techniques for stopping battles which have already started. The details are secret but they come under the general heading SCIP.'

'Spare me. Not another acronym. What does it stand for?'

'I sympathise but this one is worth having. Stopping Conflict In Progress. The Knights put themselves in considerable danger but I have seen exercises and I can assure you the methods and equipment used are very impressive.'

'And they don't involve violence against the conflicting parties? Sounds like wishful thinking to me. Like God and the faeries.'

Father James continued rowing in silence for a while. 'And there is of course another method being used to prevent conflict, nothing to do with the KOP, which is to replace real fighting with virtual conflict in a Theatre of War. It is already being used to settle some arguments where the parties in dispute are both signatories to the Global Federation's directive on Virtual War for settling international disputes.'

'I don't see a flood of nations rushing to sign up.'

'The scheme has only been available for a year. It's being taken very seriously by a large number of nations and provinces reporting to the Global Federation, judging by the amount of diplomatic activity generated.'

Paul pondered this for a while, remaining uncharacteristically silent. 'Well, James, I have to admit it's worth trying.'

'But the schemes the KOP and the Monastery have in mind aren't. That seems to be your position. Could that be anything to do with your Atheism?'

'Of course. If the Divine Light is an illusion then the Knights and the MDL are pointless.'

'Quite. And if God does not exist, then you, I and everything in the universe are pointless.'

'Maybe they are.'

'Then what is the point in saying it is pointless?'

The conversation stopped and they carried on rowing in turns for another ten minutes before beaching the boat by the jetty next to the house.

*   *   *   *

After all of the party who had gathered at his parent's house had lunched indoors Roscoe and Eric went outside with Paul to help him dig up a large bush that had got out of control and was obscuring much of the flower bed which Tina had planted close to the front of the house.

Roscoe's parents had been wealthy since his childhood. His father had earned large amounts as a member of Baroqo as it performed around the world, thriving on an anti-establishment ethos and drawing large crowds of mostly young people. When the group broke up following James's vision he had tried to start his own band but it lacked the chemistry and self confidence of Baroqo. The music the public liked had really originated with James and when he not only gave up promoting Atheism but did what was seen as a complete *volte face* it not only affected the followers of his old band but the whole genre of iconoclastic, rock-baroque fusion lost its momentum.

Paul then started up a business using his artistic talents and sold paintings over the internet. He had their house built next to the Grasmere lake and it was here that Roscoe grew up. His childhood had been a happy one until at the age of thirteen he began to ask questions which neither Paul nor Tina could answer or to which they gave different answers. This led him to philosophy, a field in which everything is questioned.

Father James would come to their house occasionally to meet his old friend and Roscoe often heard them arguing. He liked Father James; there was an aura of both innocence and wisdom about him. He also attached great weight to much of what he said, both to him directly and to his father during their frequent arguments.

It was Father James who first alerted him to the Knights of Peace, something for which Paul never entirely forgave him. The chance to do something heroic and in as good a cause as anyone could imagine was as irresistible to him as to most people of his age, especially following the Cataclysm. Although Father James was not a Knight but the founder of the Monastery of Divine Light he had been instrumental in helping Knightmaster Franklin, as he became known, found the Order of the Knights of Peace, which Father James had conceived while meditating.

A terrace projected over the lake from the house and as the air was warm they all went to sit at the round table that stood there. A flask of ClearSpin stood in the middle. Roscoe and Eric sat either side of Isla, while Paul, Tina and Father James sat opposite.

After they had settled down they noticed that Damien was missing.

Isla seemed a little embarrassed by her brother's absence. 'He's in his room. He said he might come down later. He's still feeling a bit disoriented.'

'Understandable in the circumstances.' Father James spoke with kindness to Isla in particular. 'Who would not be disoriented? Certainty is something we all wish for – but never find - and by all accounts Pastor Wayne is charismatic and highly convincing in his deception. To have such certainty, or at least the promise of it, suddenly removed must be unsettling for your brother.'

'I know and it was me who did it.'

'You did what was necessary for his own good and if it results in Damien helping us with inside information it could enable us to stop the SSS doing something far more destructive.'

Paul looked doubtful. 'Certainly your brother needed to know. But as to whether the SSS really could be that dangerous, I have my doubts. Aren't they just another bunch of religious maniacs?'

Father James came back firmly. 'Religious maniacs, cut off from the Divine Light, yes. "Just another bunch," as you put it, they unfortunately are not. They even have their own R&D labs in India and China according to our KOP undercover Knights, and somehow they have acquired some gifted scientists and engineers, probably by hiding their true motives, as they did from Damien. They also appear to be wealthy enough to finance any operation or mission they desire. In summary, they need to be stopped. Not only stopped but dismantled as an organisation with its present objectives.'

'Fantasy.'

'Paul, we've all talked about the SSS often enough. You're just being difficult.' Tina looked at her husband reproachfully.

To anyone who knew these old friends it was clear that the conversation was going nowhere. After a few seconds of silence had elapsed Roscoe decided to change the subject with a question. 'Father James, recently I read that the GF is debating legislation on a new kind of extended family unit. Do you know anything about this? "Circle of Kinship" I think it's called.'

'A little. I looked into it when I realised it was close to getting passed in the Global Parliament. It seems to be a new way of coping with the problems thrown up by Life Extension treatment. Life spans of three hundred years will obviously create challenges for our society and for the individuals concerned.'

'Not necessarily.' Paul was determined to be argumentative. 'Life Extension will be an ongoing procedure. It only gives you another ten years at a time. You can elect to opt out at any stage.'

'True, but few would want to bring their life to a close while still enjoying it and having the potential to carry on.'

Eric interjected for the first time. 'How many people would be involved in this new family unit? I know zilch about this.'

'It would start with at least three people and like the old family unit would be based on the bond between male and female.' Father James looked as though he was glad the question had been asked and relished answering it. 'Also like the family it would be the means by which children were brought up in a stable, loving environment and taught to thrive in the world, as our Lord intends.'

Isla leaned forward to pour out some ClearSpin into the flasks around the table. 'Father, I think I read something about this. Is it called a Kinship Circle?'

'Yes. It was first put forward by a socio-economic think tank with members based in Stanford, Delhi and Beijing.'

Paul adopted a slightly mocking tone. 'James, you mean it wasn't suggested by the Divine Light?'

'As a matter of fact it was, in a sense. The instigator – Watson – at the Stanford Institute near San Francisco had gone to consult a Hermit Sage. Watson had been encouraged to pray to God and ask for guidance on the essence of the family and what might replace it in a world of extended life spans. He said he felt as though something external was clarifying his mind, then the idea just came to him.'

Paul scoffed and was reprimanded by Tina, who urged Father James to continue. 'Anyway, however you think he got the idea of the Kinship Circle it seems to make sense. Typically two male-female couples start the Circle. Any child born, whether fathered by one of the Kinship Circle men or from a spermbank, would be nurtured to maturity by the Circle. The four of them would swear before God to remain faithful to each other and to their children.'

'And would there be the option of expanding the Circle?' Isla gave the impression of knowing the answer already. It was a rhetorical question.

'Yes. Providing all had taken Enlightenment. If anyone in the Circle met any one outside the Circle and felt a love growing, they would be able to be sworn into the Circle by taking the Oath of Bonding. Providing no Circle member objected. In this way it would grow over the decades, more children would be born into a secure environment and all within would support each other.'

She responded thoughtfully. 'And each person would have a rich variety of relationships, relationships which would grow over the three centuries granted by Life Extensions.'

Isla looked as though this had just occurred to her and it sounded good.

CHAPTER 13

SERVANTS OF THE SEVEN SEALS

It was a small flint cottage of a kind common in north Norfolk. The front faced the main street of Burnham Thorpe. The rear had up to only a few decades ago backed onto the four miles of agricultural land that separated the building from the sea, but more recently it had become close to a broad salt water tidal creek as the rapidly melting ice of Greenland and the Antarctic had poured into the ocean, raising the sea level and countering the tendency of the old tidal creeks to silt up as local currents deposited sand and shingle.

The cottage was a few hundred metres from the reproduction fair. Both were used by the SSS. Pastor Wayne had chosen them as the most unlikely places one would expect to serve as the headquarters of an organisation destined to fulfil God's planned destiny for humankind, namely its complete demise; although this was a hidden objective differing markedly from the one presented to the public via the misleading blogzone which the Servants had released on the telepresnet in order to obfuscate their true objective and which revealed only their belief that they had been given a secret mission by God.

Pastor Wayne reflected on how this part of the world had been pivotal to the history of England in the early nineteenth century. Admiral Lord Nelson had been born here, had learned to sail as a boy in the nearby tidal inlet of Burnham Overy Staithe, and had fought the Battle of Trafalgar in 1805, a decisive sea battle during the Napoleonic Wars. Only a handful of people knew that this small village was about to play a much bigger role in the scheme of things and that he, Wayne, had been chosen by God to bring this about.

He stared out beyond the creek and the narrow stretch of salt marsh to the open sea and imagined it heaped high, churning and steaming and engulfing the land, the sky black as soot, following the impact of Bete Noire. Then he remembered with bitterness that no such apocalyptic scene would ensue without a change of plan.

Robson, a member of the inner sanctum of counsellors who directly advised and supported Wayne, waited for a suitable moment to interrupt. He knew that Wayne could react explosively at times and in view of the recent failure of the nanobot mission this could be one of those occasions.

'Pastor, there is a matter on which a decision has to be made.' Robson knew that it would inevitably have to be the Pastor who made the decision, because he was the one chosen to bring mankind to extinction and it was he who would always be correctly guided.

'Servant Robson, what are you referring to?' He asked the question politely but with a hint of expected confrontation

'The next Initiation is due on June 1st. The candidate Damien Hanson was initially approached by us to pilot the scoopship as part of the nanobot attack on the ADN antenna. If he asks to join the next Enrolment will this be allowed?'

'And why should it not?' There was a note of condescension in his manner and voice.

Servant Robson hesitated. He felt that Wayne would rebuke him whatever he answered unless he was sufficiently servile 'Pastor, I wondered if you had decided that his recruitment was dependent on his being required for the Omega mission. Now this mission is cancelled...'

'Cancelled? Correction, Servant Robson, Omega is not cancelled; only one particular attempt at it has been abandoned. There will be other chances to take the world to its Omega point. Why do you think we have laboratories in China, Brazil and India working on Omega technology? They don't know it, of course, but the technology they are developing will eventually permit another attempt to achieve our objective. And what objective is that, Servant Robson?'

'To end man's existence on earth, Pastor, as prophesied in the New Revelation.'

'Right.'

'So am I to take it that you still wish Damien Hanson to join the Servants at the next Enrolment in Holkham Hall?'

'Of course. Who knows what form a future Omega mission will take? We may still need to use the scoopship and, if so, we will need a pilot. I have consulted the Lord and he has told me that our order should never turn away potential recruits without a very good reason.' He looked round the room and then gazed reprovingly at Robson. 'I have said this before.'

'But we had wondered, Pastor, whether there might be a link between the theft of the nanobots and Hanson's recent interest in joining.'

'Nonsense! We approached him did we not?' Wayne looked at the other Servant in the room for support as he adopted a mocking stance. He could change mood or behaviour at will: charmingly supportive, friendly, hostile, angry, contemptuous, apparently sympathetic, cheerful, morose….whatever suited his aim of controlling those around him for what he had convinced himself was a higher purpose.

'Pastor, I should also point out that Hanson is not currently contactable. He seems to have disappeared from the surveillance net.'

'Well, wait until he comes back into the net then catch him.' Wayne laughed, clearly expecting the two Servants to acknowledge the humour in his remark and disappointed that they could manage no more than a trace of an awkward smile. Then he turned serious again. 'I think Hanson will serve us well, even if we don't need him as a scoopship pilot in the way we originally intended. Bring him to me when he is next seen or makes an approach. I want to talk to him.'

*   *   *   *

The transpod set down gently in the clearing of what until only decades ago had been a predominantly Scots pine forest but which now included a variety of trees suited to the higher nighttimes temperatures prevailing throughout East Anglia Province and the Britlandia land mass in general since the climate warming over the first half of the century, although winters remained cold due to melting ice pouring into the Arctic and North Atlantic. Damien had often played in the forest as a child and remained familiar with it even as the flora changed. It had been easy to point to the clearing, which was the same one that Roscoe had parked in when he raided the caravan.

Roscoe could see the apprehension in Damien's face. Not only would he have to deceive Pastor Wayne about the reason he had left the Cambridge area but also about his commitment to the SSS, commitment he now realised had been totally misplaced; and deception did not come easily to him. Yet when lives are at stake even the most transparently honest people can lie. And in this case all human life and most of the rest could hinge on his ability to deceive.

'When you get outside the transpod you will hear the fairground music I mentioned. Hopefully, when you meet them again and claim to be keen to enrol you will be taken straight to Wayne, probably blindfolded.'

'Suppose they don't. How am I going to get invited to the Enrolment?'

'You won't be able to in that case. Apparently people are never invited to Enrolments other than by Wayne himself.'

'So then do I have to get away?'

'Yes. As soon as you get a chance send me an encrypted flexcom message and I will pick you up at whatever point we agree on – probably this clearing.'

'And if I do get invited? How will I get away from them after meeting Pastor Wayne?'

'We will have to play that by ear. Just keep in touch whenever you get the chance. I or others at the KOP will be listening all the time. You will need to get the information about the Enrolment through to us without their knowledge. Isla's encryption software should be fine but if you can get out of Burnham while sending it all to the better.'

Damien was not convinced this would be possible but disembarked and immediately became aware of the distant music, whereupon the sliding door closed behind and Roscoe lifted the transpod gently upwards, steering it for a quick view of the open sea before heading back towards Cambridge.

He walked along a footpath which he suspected was in the direction of the music. He had a good sense of direction and hearing and since the music sounded as though it was getting closer it was obvious he had chosen the right path. From the edge of the forest he could see the caravan which Roscoe had raided and perhaps a hundred metres to one side was the reproduction roundabout, its model horses whirling round, smoothly rising and falling to the sound of the fairground music, the same roundabout by which he had first been approached by a member of the SSS.

He walked in towards the centre of the fair, then made his way outwards in order to approach the roundabout from a different direction. He waited next to the merry-go-round not far from where a knot of young men dressed in the attire of the middle classes of the early 1900s appeared to be lingering as though waiting for a friend. One of them was looking at him fleetingly and talking to another, who then walked towards him.

'Damien Hanson? We have not seen you for some time.'

'I have been visiting a friend's parents in the north west of Britlandia.' It was almost true, except it was his sister's friend.

'So why have you come to the meeting point? Are you still interested in joining us?'

Now the lying had to start. 'I thought about it while I was away.'

'And?'

'I've made up my mind. I want to join.'

'You want to commit?'

'Yes. What do I have to do?'

'You will have to talk to Pastor Wayne. We will arrange for you to visit him. Forgive us but you will need to be prepared for a somewhat "cloak and dagger" escapade.' He pointed to a café on a corner. 'Walk to the café, go inside and sit at a table next to the door.'

'What happens then?'

'Someone will walk into the café and sit at the table opposite you. When this happens you get up and walk into the men's toilets. A few minutes later two men will join you in the toilets. They will blindfold you and take you out of the café through a back exit. They will then put you into a transpod and take you to Pastor Wayne.'

'But why the secrecy? Who is the SSS hiding from?'

'An understandable question but the Pastor has good reason to take these precautions. He will explain.'

Would they be suspicious if he did not persevere with his questions? He decided it would be prudent not to give up too easily. 'But why does his location have to be kept so secret?'

'Nothing sinister, I assure you. Just a routine precaution. As I said, the Pastor will explain in due course.'

'I hope so.'

Damien did as instructed and walked towards the café. He sat down at the empty table immediately by the door and waited, wondering whether to select something from the menu display. It would depend how long he would have to wait. So far everything had gone well and his spirits had recovered from the low caused by his discovery of the true aims of the Servants. The danger that they might know he was working for the Knights was more exciting than frightening, although he was still concerned that he would not be able to keep up the pretence to Wayne, who had a strong personality and, despite his wrong-headed mission, was good at intimidation and spotting those who did not genuinely feel loyalty to him and the cause of the SSS. His pulse rate elevated as the realisation came to him of just how dangerous his situation could be if Wayne discovered that he was acting undercover for the Knights.

'Do you mind if I sit here?' The man was about middle aged and he realised that he was one of the group who had been standing near the roundabout. He gestured for the man to sit down. There did not seem to be any reason to wait long so he got up and went through the inner door that led to the toilet area.

He stood by the mosaic wall outside the men's toilet. The escorts arrived sooner than expected and he was totally surprised when one grabbed him roughly, thrusting his arm up behind his back while the other tied a black scarf gratuitously tight round his head. They hurriedly led him out to the transpod parked on a lawn at the back of the cafe and pushed him into a seat.

Damien just sat back but the fear in him was beginning to grow. If he had had any doubts about the dangerous nature of the SSS those doubts were now fading as he was transported in total darkness. However, it was only for a few minutes. The transpod landed and soon he was being led over a gravel path and then up some stairs and into a room.

The scarf was quickly removed. It had only been on a few minutes but he was finding it difficult to adjust to the light, relatively dim though this was, shining into the room through a small window of an old type, put in more than a century ago.

'Good morning, Mr Hanson. Can I use your first name?' The Pastor was effusive but he noted that there was no invitation to call Wayne by his first name.

'Yes, Pastor. Damien is my first name.'

'Indeed, I was aware of that. Welcome to the assessment. I see you are wondering what I mean by "assessment", is that so?'

'Yes, Pastor.'

'Well then, Damien, let me explain. I need to satisfy myself that you really want to join the SSS. Only then can I authorise your Enrolment on June 1st.' He had been looking friendly up to then but he suddenly adopted a pleading stance. 'The SSS, you realise, Damien, is on a mission. If anyone betrays us he could destroy that mission.'

'And what is that mission, Pastor?'

He brushed aside the question and resumed his flow of speech, but more quietly and with an air of mock modesty. 'I have had it revealed to me by God. He has also instructed me not to reveal the nature of the mission to those not fully committed to the Servants of the Seven Seals. The words came to me after reading the Revelation to St John and modifying the text which is in all the standard versions of the holy bible.' He turned to Damien in a challenging manner. 'You understand?'

'Yes, Pastor.'

'You don't wish to question me? You accept that the authority of God's will is in me?'

'I do.'

'Then you will swear on this holy book when the time comes.'

Damien was not a Christian or follower of any faith and had received no Enlightenment from the Divine Light. Yet he hesitated to agree to take such an oath. After meeting Father James he felt that there could after all be something divine in the scheme of things. It was something he was intending to investigate.

'You hesitate.'

'It is a big step for me to take Pastor.'

'Of course. But an important one. For you, for me, for the SSS and ultimately, as you will discover, for all mankind.'

'The book you are showing me – is it the one with the new Revelation text?'

'Yes, of course. Ah, I see why you hesitate. Yet I think I see your hesitation lessening. Am I right?'

Damien no longer felt he could offend against the true Christian God, who might, after all, really exist. But he could swear on what amounted to an adulterated version without offending against the sacred one. He was happy to lie to Pastor Wayne, but not to God, assuming there was one. 'You are right, Pastor. I will swear on the new book.'

'You are privileged, Damien. Few people in this world have access to the Servant's Bible. Now, all you have to do is attend our next Initiation on June 1ˢᵗ.'

'Where will it be held?'

'Holkham Hall on the north coast of the East Anglia Province. You will be given a module on the details. There will be a ceremony at which you will be asked, along with others from recruits around the world, to make the oath of fealty to the SSS. Our cause will later be divulged to you.'

He seemed pleased at Damien's response and called via his flexcom for some caffrosia to be brought in. They sat down on seats near the window and looked out on the marshes and the wide tidal creek. It occurred to him that the position of the cottage could possibly be guessed at from the view, although the Knights undercover team knew it already.

Wayne relaxed. 'Do you know how many Servants we have, worldwide? Several thousand. Many of them have special skills – you, for instance, are a scoopship pilot. The particular mission I had planned for you has been abandoned but I feel sure your piloting abilities will be needed at some stage. Or perhaps we can train you for something else.'

'I didn't realise the SSS attached so much importance to having a lot of skilled people. What sort of skills?'

'Well for instance we have several research laboratories in China, India and Brazil. To achieve the aim which God has set out for me we will need to use new technology. Few of those working in these laboratories are aware of how their research will be used. They are not committed members of the SSS. You, however, will become so after your Initiation on June 1st.'

'Why are the researchers not initiated?'

'Because if they were they would understand the use to which their technology might be put and there is a risk that they may not agree to do the work we need them to do. It is a somewhat sensitive matter. This will become clear after the Enrolment, when you have read the new Revelation text.'

A girl brought in two cups of caffrosia on a tray which she placed on a small table between them. Wayne picked up his cup and began to drink, savouring the coffee-like taste and smoky aroma. 'Where will you spend your time before June 1st?'

This was a question he had been fearing. It was one they had been bound to ask. He had already once disappeared from their surveillance since first expressing interest in the Servants and now he had been told the location of the next Initiation. After the Initiation he would be told the true mission of the SSS. He was becoming a potential security threat. The irony was he had already been told these things by Father James, Finley and Reed and it only remained to find out where they kept the flour at Holkham Hall. Once this had been established the Knights would be able to attempt a raid on the premises and insert QTCs in the flour. The Q-spectra emitted when these were ingested during the coming conference would identify the dominophiles.

'I would like to read some literature on the SSS, so I can learn more about it before the Initiation.'

'I asked where you will be, not what you want to do. And I should add that very little has been written that I've not told you already. After the enrolment you will be told much more.'

Wayne's tone indicated that he expected his question to be answered and Damien was concerned that a confrontational situation might be developing. He found it difficult to believe the contrast with how Wayne had been a few months previously. Then he had been welcoming and friendly, keen to nurture the interest of a potential new recruit who, as a scoopship pilot, could be valuable to the Servants. Now his egotism seemed to need to assert itself at the slightest hint of being questioned. There was also a complete antithesis between the two outwardly spiritual leaders who had come into his life: Pastor Wayne on the one hand, whose spirituality was centred on himself and Father James on the other, who somehow radiated wisdom, kindness and humility. It was clear that Damien had been badly deceived when the SSS had initially contacted him and he was thankful that Isla had put him in touch with the few people in the world who were aware of what the SSS stood for. It was an organisation built on power and submission to power. The power was almost as important to Pastor Wayne as his mission to bring about the end of humankind.

'I'm sorry, Pastor. I should have mentioned that I will be in Burnham Thorpe all the time.' This was the safest answer and appeared to satisfy him, although it raised the question of how he was going to inform the Knights that he would be attending the Initiation on June 1st. He felt certain that Wayne would order a close watch to be kept on his every movement, contact and communication. Strictly speaking, of course, he need not really contact the Knights again until after June 1st. Then, hopefully, he would be able to tell them where the flour supplies were kept. But if they lost contact with him they would not know whether to continue planning the envisaged Impoundment mission and he knew that Isla and her KOP friends would be concerned about his safety.

'Splendid. One of our Servants can escort you to Holkham when the time comes.' Pastor Wayne then called in two Servants via his flexcom to collect Damien. 'Escort Mr Hanson to his house in the village. Take the usual precautions and keep in close contact with him.' He spoke in a way which seemed warm while at the same time suggesting that his manner could change to aggression at the slightest perceived affront.

Damien was blindfolded and led out of the room.

*   *   *   *

Pastor Wayne sat alone staring out of the cottage window at the mud creek as the tide ebbed vigorously through it on a winding route across the salt marshes to the North Sea. It was only recently that this route had established itself. The sea level was still rising despite the measures to cut methane emissions largely from the thawing arctic tundra and previously frozen, methane-rich sea beds; measures which had been in place for decades. Yet the serious flooding in coastal and riverside metropolises around the globe was not going to give humankind the final destiny it deserved. Even if it did it would not please the Pastor because God would not have brought it about through him.

He turned away from the window and looked into the three-dimensional SSS website, the websphere, projected into the middle of the room. A small white globe spun slowly inside the website with various names printed in black on its surface. He focused his eyes on one and this caused the sphere to dissolve and be replaced by another in which a face appeared.

'Pastor, I have a message for you from our Novosibirsk group. They have been making good progress with the BH Generator and have reached a critical stage. The next stage could well be the only remaining one.'

'You mean it would achieve Omega.'

'Yes. The people working on this project have of course been under the impression that they are working for the Global Federation Security Labs. But some are beginning to question how a project of this kind can aid world security and think it is dangerous to go any further.'

'But we have the SSS Infiltration Team. Presumably they can bring the project to fruition if the main group is being difficult. After all, they may only have to do it once.'

'But, Pastor, if there is a technical problem the Infiltration Team may not be able to solve it. The technology is very delicate.'

'Alright. Presumably the project leader will be attending the Holkham Conference in September.'

'He will indeed, Pastor.'

He disengaged from the websphere without feeling any need to say goodbye, and noting inwardly that the black hole generator probably would not be needed. The nanobot mission to sabotage the ADN was far from finished.

CHAPTER 14

STONE ARTHUR

He walked up the disused road beside the beck, Greenhead Gill, which cut a deep trench on its way down from the mountains, then opened a small gate and continued on up a path beside a dry stone wall. Bracken was all around, the sky was clear and he was enjoying the ascent towards Stone Arthur in the fresh early morning air.

The nineteenth century poet William Wordsworth had described this little part of the Lake District in his poem *Michael,* about a shepherd. He had read this and felt that Wordsworth had experienced nature not as lifeless sculptures and forms but as part of the living logos of God.

The landscape was in some ways different from those times. There were more trees scattered along the stony path as it wound its way towards the rocky outcrop called Stone Arthur and at this particular time sheep had been temporarily removed as part of an ecological management programme. Also, although the world was changing, Roscoe had been brought up in a predominantly secular age, with his father strongly believing that there was no creator and gently mocking those who did, despite his wife's faith which he attempted, not always successfully, to at least appear to respect.

As he walked alone in the pale light of the just risen sun he sensed that there was more to the world around him than just matter and energy and this, he felt, came from the faith in Christ which was growing within him. This faith did not yet match that of Father James, or even Knightmaster Franklin, and he had not yet gone through the Enlightenment procedure which was a requisite for all those who had entered the Order, and which was known to strengthen faith in whatever classic religion one followed in seeking union with our Creator.

Bushes and trees grew less common as the path rose. Roscoe noticed how the grass was now a little longer than he was used to seeing it. There had been no sheep in the area for a month or so and it was not long before this showed in the less closely grazed slopes, ledges and plateaux, their normal smoothness giving way to a rougher texture.

On reaching his destination and having regained his breath he sat on a stone ledge looking out over the valley. Helm Crag was visible on the other side. Only a week before he had been sitting over there with Isla and Eric. He thought of the missions that lay ahead. One to plant QTCs in the flour supplies of Holkham Hall, the other to impound the dominophiles at the forthcoming SSS conference at that same place. Would he get a chance to demonstrate his abilities? Probably not. It was more likely to be Eric. Despite his conversations with Isla, which were beginning to become almost intimate, he realised that he still felt jealous of

Eric and how he attracted her. He realised with dismay how far he had to go spiritually.

It was mid morning and he still had plenty of time to get back down to the Grasmere house before lunch. As he descended towards the denser bushes and trees by the stream he suddenly stopped. He thought he had seen a movement through a thin patch of bramble. It could not really have been a sheep, unless the ecomanagers had missed one. It was too large in any case, unless it was an illusion. He edged forward very slowly to get a better view of whatever was behind the bramble bush; then he froze in amazement and fear as he became aware that a large cat-like creature was staring at him from the other side of the stream. It had been drinking but obviously thought that the sight of a lone human being warranted interrupting this basic survival activity.

Roscoe dare not make any move. He felt that the slightest motion could disturb the unstable equilibrium on which possibly his life might depend. He managed to activate his flexcom by pressing part of his smartsuit. It was a relief when his father answered almost immediately. Paul knew the fells and everything in them, albeit in a non-spiritual light, unlike his son or Wordsworth.

He whispered into the soundpad set in his smartsuit arm, raising it only slightly and slowly. 'Dad, I think I'm in danger. I am standing face to face with a large cat-like creature.'

'How large?'

'Much larger than a cat. Smaller than a leopard or lion.'

'I should have realised. Don't take your eyes off it and don't let it get behind you.'

'What is it?' He dare not move to activate his camera in case it provoked an attack.

'It's almost certainly a puma. Remember, if it moves, keep it in front of you, don't let it out of sight. It won't attack as long as it sees you looking at it. I'll be as quick as I can.'

What did his father mean by 'should have realised'? He continued to stand rigid but then the puma started to walk up the other side of the beck. Roscoe followed it, trying to avoid stumbling over boulders and rocks as he rooted his vision on the creature. Then a thick patch of bramble interrupted his view. He continued walking in the same direction hoping that the puma would appear at the next gap but when he reached it the puma was not visible. His pulse thumped and his forehead sweated as he quickly and intently stared up and down the stream. An unseen danger was much worse than a visible one. A vague awareness of movement arose in the periphery of his vision and as he swung round the puma appeared in the gap. It stopped, stared at him, then resumed its upward path, walking out of view again as it became hidden by more bushes.

At all costs he had to keep the creature in view. It had seemed safer to stay on the opposite side of the beck but he realised this was not really a protection. It was much more important to stop it getting behind him; so he stepped into the cold rushing water, waded across and climbed up onto the opposite bank. He saw it walking ahead, presumably unaware that a potential prey was behind him.

A message from his father was suddenly projected from a small oblong display built into the sleeve of his smartsuit. 'Is it still in front of you?'

'Yes. I'm following it – to keep it in sight, like you said. How long will you be?' Roscoe whispered into the flexor's soundpad.

'Minutes. Keep as quiet as you can and don't get too close. Is the wind blowing from you to the puma?'

'No. It's more or less at right angles to a line connecting us.'

His father replied by projected text. 'Good. You have to avoid it getting your scent. Ideally it would be blowing from the animal to you.'

He stopped momentarily to scan the sky to see if the transpod was approaching. It was not. Then as he turned back to keep his gaze on the puma he was shocked to find it had vanished. Again his fear level shot to a maximum. It must have crossed the beck. Would it carry on walking upstream? If so he would probably be safe. But if it was walking back downstream towards him on the other side, intermittently hidden, he would have to be doubly cautious. He stood as still as possible, looking quickly around in all directions, wishing he had an invisibility shield with him.

How did a puma get to be in this area? His father appeared to know, or at least thought he new. Then he remembered the absence of sheep. The few pumas which roamed on the fells normally survived by killing sheep and were very elusive. They must be short of food and so driven to a new mode of behaviour which included hunting anything edible, including humans, in places they would not normally have ventured to.

Suddenly, he could hear the hum of a transpod and instinctively turned towards where the sound was coming from. To his surprise it landed behind a clump of silver birch trees some way from where he was standing and several tens of metres from the edge of the stream, on the slopes that led down to it. He swung back round to face the most likely place where he thought the puma would be. But there was nothing. Then in one seemingly drawn out moment he was thrust savagely to the ground by a force from behind and two claws appeared either side of him. He was frozen with terror but soon became aware that this encounter was not solely between him and the puma. A third party was involved.

The next thing he remembered seeing was the puma scrambling and rolling over beside him with a human figure attached. His father's voice shouted. 'Eric, don't be foolish. Get clear so I can shoot it.' Then Eric went limp after being mauled and the puma was about to bite his neck when two loud pistol shots sounded and the puma leapt with the shock of a bullet entering its skull before collapsing in a heap.

Roscoe was bruised but otherwise unhurt. He got up and rushed over to Eric's prone, motionless form with his invisibility shield and a knife next to him on the stony ground. His father joined him. Somehow Roscoe knew Eric, unlike the puma, was still alive, although not from any biological signs. There was something indefinable about it which said plainly 'my eternal life still animates this body'.

Paul knelt down and took Eric's pulse. 'Are you hurt, Ros? I think
Eric's alright but he needs medical help and fast.'

'I'm fine, dad. You saved both our lives with that pistol.' Paul
placed a hand on his son's shoulder. He knew this had been a
difficult thing for Roscoe to say. The gun had been a subject of
many a bitter argument between them since the mere existence
of it was anathema to a Knight.

Roscoe looked up to see Isla approaching hurriedly with a small
first aid box. She must have been in the transpod with Eric and
his father. She descended gracefully to her knees and started
taking measurements, then tended to the deep scratch wounds
on his face and arms with healer strips. 'We need to get him to
the medical centre in Grasmere at once. Can you call them Ros?'

He took up his flexcom and summoned the Medical Hub.

Emotions welled up within him, competing for dominance. There
was deep concern for Eric, the friend who had possibly saved his
life and who had suffered serious injury in the process. There was
strengthened love for Isla as her magnetic femininity excelled in
her treatment, sympathy and concern for Eric.

And there was dejection.

*   *   *   *

Eric had been in an intensive care module for several days now.
His condition had stabilised but he was still unconscious and
Roscoe sensed the vulnerability of this friend who was normally so

confident and, unintentionally, intimidating. That this wounded and incapacitated Knight was a good person could not be doubted and this made him feel all the more shame at the thoughts which were once again entering his mind. Seeing how Isla had responded to his injury had evoked jealousy. Ironically, it was seeing her sympathy and compassion for Eric in his plight that made him love her all the more. Yet was it love if it was so possessive?

He wondered if after his Enlightenment he would be spiritually transformed. He already believed in Christ at some level and he also believed that the Divine Light had been a life changing experience for many. He had heard that after the experience of Enlightenment with a Hermit Sage one's original faith, be it Christianity, Islam, Judaism, Sikhism or Hinduism, was normally deepened and strengthened. In the case of the non-Christian faiths this meant the incorporation of the great commandment of Jesus Christ under the influence of the Holy Spirit as manifest in the Divine Light. All would eventually be in Christ except those who actively and knowingly rejected him.

Thinking in this way made him less self-obsessed as he looked down upon the passive face and shallow-breathing body. This was a being like him blessed with the gift of life, something which no one understood and which animated the intricately organised and ineffably complex hierarchy of biological systems of which any organism consisted. Once this life departed the body would descend into chaos, lose the power which integrated and controlled its hundreds of billions of cells into a person that experienced consciousness, thought, slept, loved, hated, desired, enjoyed, aspired, created, worked, played, ate, drank, expelled waste and appreciated beauty, truth and justice. The being that was Eric would be gone, totally absent from the material world around him; but gone to where, to what? He suddenly felt more intensely than ever that he wanted his friend to live. If he died he could never allow himself to love Isla after having thought of one of God's precious manifestations of life as a threat to his relationship to her. Only if he lived would it be possible to grow towards a spiritual equilibrium between the three of them.

He prayed inwardly that Eric would live and that he would cease to regard him as a threat. He prayed for the wisdom to evolve spiritually. His faith was not always strong enough to feel that he was in union with the Creator but on this occasion he felt closer to God than he had ever done.

As he emerged from the IC module the feeling of concern for Eric was already beginning to fade and give way to his wish to possess the love of Isla. He resolved to go to Father James for guidance. Perhaps he could be sent for Enlightenment earlier than scheduled. Fortunately he was still staying in the Finley household, having extended his visit in the hope of being able to talk to Eric if and when he regained consciousness.

Unless he could gain equanimity and peace of mind he would not be able to approach Isla with any hope of forming a Circle of Kinship that would last for centuries or taking an Oath of Bonding, which would mean a monogamous sexual relationship while rearing any children, preceded by six months of celibacy. He would remain immature and spiritually foolish. Nor would he be in a strong position to function as a Knight on active service.

He hoped he would find Father James on his own and as he approached the house after walking across several fields of rough grass was relieved to see him sitting on the bench by the lake.

'Any sign of improvement?'

'No. He just seems to be in a peaceful sleep. He's not in a coma. The doctor said he was stable.'

'He has a strong constitution. I think it will take more than a few nasty scratches from a mountain lion to take Eric's earthly life from us.'

'I hope so, Father, and believe so.'

He sat down next to him on the bench to contemplate the quietude of the lake, hoping that this would calm his soul, a hope that he soon realised was forlorn. The turmoil of confusion and uncertainty could not be dispelled so easily at this early stage of his spiritual growth. He had intended to wait until the normal year's anniversary of entry to the KOP for his session with Father James and a Hermit Sage but it was becoming clear that he would have to request at least some guidance sooner, even if this did not mean the full process of Enlightenment. He remembered that two days before the encounter with the puma Isla had suggested that he, she and Eric talk together. She had said the three of them needed to get together but had not really said why and he had not felt able to ask her. From the context it was probably something to do with forming, or, he feared, not forming, a Kinship Circle. Whatever it was that was in her mind he believed he would be able to talk more wisely after he had received spiritual guidance.

'Father. I am going through a difficult period and I believe you can help.'

'I take it that your soul is not like the lake as it is now but as it was during the storm two days ago.' He pointed to the small rowing boat floating nearby and tethered to a piece of stone close to the bench. 'Let's go for a row.' They walked over to the boat, clambered aboard and cast off. 'You take the first turn at rowing and start speaking when you have something to say. Then hopefully I can earn my passage by responding helpfully to whatever is troubling you.'

It was not until they had moved well towards the centre of the lake that Roscoe was able to formulate his thoughts and overcome the embarrassment of confessing his weaknesses, even to one so inspired with kindness and wisdom as this holy man of such unlikely origins. 'I am in love with Isla but in the wrong way.'

'The wrong way?'

'Yes. It is sensual and possessive.'

'And do you want to start a Circle of Kinship with her?'

'Yes.'

'Hardly a basis for a stable commitment, I agree.' He paused and looked round reflectively before continuing. 'But entirely understandable. She is a lovely lady. What else?'

'I am also jealous of her affection for Eric, who has been a good friend to me since we both entered the Order.'

'And do you want him to die because of this?'

'No.'

'Then you have little to worry about.' Was this all he had to say? It was not like him to be so dismissive and unhelpful, almost flippant. Was he taunting him? The oars felt heavy as his energy ebbed until at last his passenger continued talking. 'But you need some assistance in overcoming your present problems. Let me try to sum up your situation, Roscoe. You have undergone Life Extension and you are romantically, erotically in love with a girl who appears to have affection for your friend, to whom you probably owe your life. You would like to start a Kinship Circle with her. How do you think she feels about this?'

'I am not sure.'

'She is a female. As males we don't know how she feels at the visceral level. You would need to take an Oath of Bonding in order to form a Circle of Kinship. But the kind of love that is needed for a Bonding is more than visceral. It is more than romantic love.' He looked searchingly at Roscoe. 'Have you told her how you feel?' Roscoe confirmed that he had. 'How did she respond?'

'She said I wanted to possess her. And I do feel jealous about her obvious attraction to Eric.'

'She is right to be wary of someone at the mercy of his senses.'

'But how can I conquer my biological feelings? Why should I? They are natural. They are what living beings need to procreate.'

'True. But you are more than a living being. You are made in the image of the source of all existence, outside of time and space. Yahweh is also the source of agape love, not just romantic love. You need to unite with that source. When you do you will know – and she will know.'

He stopped rowing. 'Father, you are talking about God. But I don't understand why this creator of ten billion trillion stars should care about my love, or love at all for that matter. Forgive me, but looking at the misery in the world caring doesn't seem to be one of his priorities.'

'There are many who believe there must be a creator of the great cosmic system we live in but who cannot see why Yahweh should be concerned with love. It was a barrier to my own faith before the Divine Light. Your father mentioned it once while we were in Baroqo. We confirmed each other in our disbelief, or rather in our belief that there was no loving God, if indeed there was any God at all. Although looking back I don't think that deep down I was really an Atheist.'

He reached forward towards Roscoe, indicating he wanted to take the oars. They changed seats and Father James started to row, slowly and deliberately.

As he sat watching the oars rhythmically striking the water Roscoe realised that his own faith was not as strong as it needed to be. It was based more on a rational fear of the horrific consequences for humanity of a godless, chaos-driven cosmos together with the logical deduction that a meaningless universe would not create beings that sought meaning.

'Then I discovered that Love was what powered the universe, the whole spectrum of reality, "all things visible and invisible," as it says in the Nicene Creed.'

'How do you mean?' He felt a wave of anticipation that he was about to gain an insight that would change his perception of the world. Yet he had felt like this before and been disappointed.

'Is it not a reasonable supposition that the God of the classic religions – Zoroastrianism, Judaism, Islam, Christianity, Sikhism; even Hinduism and Buddhism in my view, if you look deeply into them – would want Yahweh's universe to bring forth life, beauty and order?'

'This seems to be what is happening when you look at history on a cosmic timescale. There may have been ups and downs over the ages but there is more life, beauty and order today, as far as we know, than, say, five thousand years ago. So yes, Father, it is reasonable.'

Father James rested the oars on the rowlocks and let the boat glide for a while in silence across the still lake. 'To generate and sustain life in the animal and plant kingdoms there must be love of a biological kind. Humans also need this. But they need something more because it is God's will that those made in God's image must emulate their maker in creativity and providence.'

'But how does spiritual love fit into this?'

He spoke gently, calmly, inviting correction or disagreement, with humility, in a non-didactic style. 'It fits in because it is necessary for the generation of "all things visible and invisible." God can be seen as a kind of spiritual engineer, if that helps. This higher form of love, unique to God and humankind, is as much a driver of creation as biological love. Love of knowledge, of beauty, of perfection, of justice, of one another – this is what drives forward humankind. And this makes humankind a potential cosmic force. The knowledge we gain of how nature works, our love of truth, our ability to cooperate but compete in a friendly way makes us able to create new technology with which to explore and transform the universe. The Creator has made us in the Creator's image so that we can be part of the Creator's plan. I'm not saying this is the whole picture. We can never know the full picture, spiritual evolution proceeds one step at a time on a tall ladder; but this is what has been revealed to me in the Divine Light vision.'

'How does higher, non-biological love between people bring forth life, beauty and order?'

'I need to add something before I try to answer that. This love between people can only be reached when we have union with the Creator, which we obtain through prayer or meditation or sometimes through revelation. We are connecting our minds, which are independent of space and time, with the source of the universe, which is similarly beyond space and time. There are also many who seem to have this union without even knowing it or having any help from an organised religion.'

'I have met such people. Even some who call themselves Atheists.

'So have I. Although I sometimes wonder if this is deceptive – we cannot see into a person's inner being.' He looked particularly thoughtful while saying this and interrupted his rowing. 'It is part of God's mystery that some are illuminated by the Divine Light without any attempt to seek it. They are born with it. Perhaps the Buddhist model of reincarnation is a way of looking at this – if you are repeatedly reincarnated you learn that union with God is all that matters and that can only be through Christ. We shall never know, unless God wills it.'

He started to pull on the oars again. 'But I haven't dealt with your question of how higher love generates order, beauty and truth. I'm not good at thinking up examples. Maybe you can help me.'

'Love of a higher kind between parents, whether in a nuclear family or a Kinship Circle, provides a stable and secure environment for the offspring which in turn helps them develop intellectually to solve the problems of life and to explore in the widest sense the world around them or beyond. This means more understanding of nature and more technology.'

'I can see that philosophy was a wise choice of study for you. That's a good one. Let me think of one now.' He stopped rowing and concentrated hard. 'Where there is love society functions more efficiently, unhampered by the bureaucracy and red tape that stem from mistrust.'

'I have another one, Father. Adults who love each other more than biologically support each other in whatever task they embark on. This allows love of science, beauty and art to thrive. And communication between people improves with love.'

'Just taking science alone. Think of the power that has been unlocked from the atomic nucleus. Now that it has been harnessed fully in finely controlled nuclear fusion we have the energy not only to transform our existence on Earth. With dark energy drives and Life Extension we have the means to colonise the planets, even those around other stars when we wish to. So you can see how love, especially its higher forms, really does make the world go round.'

'But how does this affect my relationship to Isla?'

'Isla, like many females, has an intuitive awareness of the presence or absence of this kind of creative and sustaining love, love which is part of God's scheme involving mankind. You and she are humans, you are in God's image. You need to get closer to God.'

'But as a man I have failings. My senses cut me off from the higher love, especially for Isla. She is so beautiful.'

'They don't need to. It is a matter of right attitude. When you lie awake thinking about a girl, any girl for that matter, you must hold in your mind the fact that she is, like you, a divine being, as are all men and women. If you need to make love to her in your imagination, do so while thinking of her deepest well being: your own gratification is just a by-product of physical relief. It is only sinful when you fail to concentrate on her rather than your own sensuality, when you allow sensual experience to blot out the higher love.'

'What is sin?'

'It is that which separates us from God. And if you do err, but sincerely ask Christ for forgiveness, it will be given. There is no need to be separated from him and from the eternal life by guilt. That is why he made the supreme sacrifice. That was his grace. And the more you accept his grace the more you will want to please God by good works.'

Suddenly they caught sight of the mauled body of a deer floating just ahead of the boat. It reminded Roscoe of the imperfections of the world which God had created and that his question about God's apparent lack of care had not been addressed. Father James held up his oars as it drifted by. 'Yes, Roscoe, God's world is far from perfect. It does not reflect his perfection. I don't know why there has to be so much suffering and death in this world. Yet how can we appreciate perfection without first knowing imperfection?'

'Yes, Father, but why do some have to suffer more, or die sooner, than others, regardless of behaviour or worth or belief?' He had often refrained from asking such a question of others for fear of upsetting their faith and he did not really expect a full answer this time.

'I'm not God. I don't know God's plan in which there is a purpose and a time for everything in the universe. But bear this in mind: our human existence is just a flash in time compared to Eternal Life and that faith in God gives you strength when faced with the darker reaches of this world. The kind of strength a sick or dying person gets when holding the hand of a loved one is a shadow of the strength that springs from God.'

He stopped rowing and swapped places with Roscoe, who then turned the boat round and headed for the mooring place near his parents' house.

CHAPTER 15

THE INITIATION

Damien stood in the reception area and tried to circulate among the twenty would-be initiates as they guardedly sipped caffrosia. He had no natural skill in starting or cultivating a conversation and in the past would have been regarded as somewhat autistic, rather than fulfilling a valuable role in the scheme of things. Yet he knew that the success of his mission might depend on eliciting information during conversation. And given the possibly critical importance of the mission he somehow had to overcome his natural aloofness.

Not that he was out of place. None of the people in the room seemed to be much animated with exploratory small talk or chatter about the organisation into which they would shortly be inaugurated. And this made it all the more difficult to break the ice without attracting attention or raising eyebrows.

He went over to the refreshment table and poured himself a beaker of hot caffrosia from a large jug. He noticed some warm doughy cakes which a girl in a smartsuit, set into the mode of a black dress, had just placed to one side of the jug. He picked one up, put it on a small plate, and decided to make another circuit of the room with the aim of starting a conversation. If he did not get into the habit of talking and listening to the new entrants or to the staff and adopt a generally proactive attitude he would not succeed in his mission. In a sense the survival of humanity might depend on him obtaining the answer to one apparently trivial question: where was the flour stored?

A large man with a red face, smoothed down black hair and his mode of attire adjusted to a grey tunic looked approachable, but it appeared from his stance and position that he was in some official capacity. So he continued to circulate among the recruits until he became aware that someone was talking to him, or more specifically, asking him a question.

'Hello. How did you come to be here?' It was a rather lanky youth with fair hair and a tendency to focus on some distant point to one side of whoever he was speaking to. Damien, like most people, found this disconcerting, but was also aware that he himself tended to look down and to one side when in conversation.

'I was on leave from my job and went along to an SSS meeting out of curiosity. One of their agents came up to me and we talked about the SSS. He said he would introduce me to the Pastor.'

'What do you think of them?'

He made an effort to remember how he had felt about the SSS before being approached by their recruiters and to judge how he was supposed to feel about them after his interactions with Pastor Wayne. 'I was relieved to see that there was an organisation which could give me a sense of purpose, which needed me to help it achieve its goals.'

'Goals. Yes, that's what I really wanted to ask you. They never made clear to me exactly what their goals are. I somehow got drawn in, feeling the SSS had a real sense of direction but never got a clear answer as to what they were headed for.'

He had to think hard about this. What exactly had they told him? In fact all they had said was that the Servants had a mission, a holy mission, and that this had been revealed to Pastor Wayne alone. The 'Lord' had told him that it had to be kept secret. Damien was amazed that the Pastor's hypnotic charisma had been enough to inspire trust and draw him in so far without any real understanding of what the SSS was trying to do. Had his flexcom not been intercepted by his sister he could easily have been here as a genuine potential Initiate.

Damien tried to sound convincing. 'I think that is what we are here for. As soon as we are initiated we will be told. Until then it is the Lord's will that the aims of the Servants be known only to existing Initiates.'

Just as the youth was about to ask a follow-up question a loud voice addressed the reception. It came from the red-faced man. 'Welcome to you all. No doubt you have questions to ask and I am happy to say that we are now ready to start our first presentation. So please leave your cups and plates here and take a seat in the adjacent room.'

The conference room was darkened and rigged for holodisplays and optical effects. A faint ethereal music was emanating from all directions as they filed in and placed themselves on comfortable upright chairs around a large oblong table. When everyone had settled down the music became a kind of strident fanfare and life-sized biblical figures were projected like suspended statues into the dark space above the table. A deep paternalistic voice then triumphantly announced: 'Our leader and prophet, Pastor Wayne.' The images faded as he made his theatrical entrance, his immaculate attire and grooming illuminated to a dazzling degree.

Damien was struck by how much this charismatic character, who he had last encountered in the cottage in Burnham Thorpe, could change his persona to suit the current purpose, which usually involved some form of manipulation. He was not at all sure that without the intervention of Isla and his involvement with the Knights of Peace, in particular with Father James, he would have been able to resist the personal power which even now threatened to draw him into this strange, dangerous army of the misguided.

The Pastor became quite pleasant. 'Good morning.' He waited for and got a responding greeting from the audience. 'I am so pleased you have decided to join us, to side with us in our battle to fulfil God's wish for humanity. Later I will tell you how this can happen, the exact way in which you can be part of the plan that has been revealed to me. Now no doubt you are wondering how I can be sure that the plan I have is not some illusion, that it is indeed from the Lord, delivered personally to me.' As he spoke he became less gentle and sympathetic in manner and voice, more didactic, more insistent, more righteous in tone. 'Well, I can assure you that before this period of Initiation is over you will understand and believe in me, as an instrument of the Lord, one hundred percent.' He settled back into a more gentle manner. 'But first, I ask you to sit back and enjoy this holodisplay, which will show the historical background to the Bible and explain the new Revelation which I have been favoured with and which builds on and updates the one given to St John on the island of Patmos, some two thousand years ago.'

Damien prepared himself for some persuasive dogma. No doubt it would be well argued and difficult to resist without much thought and study. He decided that it was best not even to listen but instead to think about other things, like how to find out where the flour was. The memory of the warm freshly baked cakes came back into his mind, fending off the domineering pseudo-biblical information and images being projected at him, pushing the Pastor's personal eschatological scheme. Then he thought of the girl in the silky black attire. Could she be the key to finding where the flour was kept? He had no idea how he would go about getting the information from her but he decided that, in the absence of any other strategy, talking to her would be the best option, difficult though this might be.

When finally the presentation ceased and they were all sent out for lunch he looked around but could see no sign of her. He would have to go to lunch with the others anyway. If he finished quickly he could look again before returning to the conference room for the afternoon session.

Lunch was difficult because he had not been listening to the presentation enough to be able to discuss it with the others. He just went along with what the majority seemed to be saying but now and then someone would ask what he thought about some specific point in the presentation to which he found the best reply was to say he was not sure and to ask the questioner what he thought. He pretended not to want any dessert and was therefore able to get back to the reception hall and conference room area earlier than he had expected.

Still she did not appear so he walked along a footpath close to the house. Maybe she would do the same at some point. It was worth a try.

After walking back and forth several times without catching sight of her he realised he would have to go back in to be a target for more attempted indoctrination. Then he remembered there would be a refreshment break. There was a good chance that she would bring in more caffrosia and cakes, although what he would say to her he still had little idea.

The afternoon session consisted mainly of Pastor Wayne talking about his vision. It was clear to Damien that this was totally different in nature from the one Father James had experienced as an Atheist music icon some thirty years previously. Not that he knew the details of this but from the Father's modest manner and his matter-of-fact, although occasionally slightly reverential, references to his Divine Light revelations it was apparent that it had been nothing like the over-colourful, stereotypically biblical and highly spectacular dream of the Pastor, which was strongly suggestive of a hallucination.

Again, Damien had not been listening carefully to the Pastor's words and so had no chance of being drawn in to the Servants of the Seven Seals. He did glean that somehow Pastor Wayne had come to believe that it was man's destiny to be exterminated except for a few people – that is, members of the SSS, who would be the instruments of the extermination. These people would be sent to paradise. The rest would go to some medieval concept of hell.

It was a relief to him when the afternoon break came, although the other candidates were no doubt becoming enraptured. Most of them, at least; but suppose some failed to succumb and so could not go through the initiation ceremony? It was quite possible some of them were not convinced of the veracity of the Pastor's arguments but were scared to resist, guessing that if their doubts were discovered and not corrected they would not be allowed to walk back into ordinary life.

He looked around the reception area and this time the girl did make an appearance. He approached the refreshment table as she was putting down a plate of cakes. Suddenly he knew what to do. Normally, small talk was the most difficult thing in the world for him but, probably because his subconscious had been working on the problem, or, as some would say, God's helping hand, he was confident that he would know how to start talking to her and get the information he needed. There was, of course, an element of deception involved. She would probably be flattered, thinking he was flirting, although given the idiosyncratic nature of SSS initiates, she may just be puzzled.

'These cakes…I had one this morning. They taste good.'

She looked him in the eye, slightly warily, and did not smile. 'You won't believe this but I've never tried one.'

'Not tried one? You ought to. Are they baked on the premises?'

'They are.'

'I happen to be a connoisseur and do some old-fashioned baking at home.' This was a complete lie but he did not flinch: so much was at stake. Even though he considered himself to be somewhere between Atheist and agnostic, he had an aversion to lying. Where did that come from? Social evolution? Anyway, he was lying to save humankind, although he could not fully disguise his nervousness. 'Could you possibly do me a favour?'

She looked incredulous that someone attending an SSS initiation, or any kind of SSS event, would have such a prosaic interest as baking cakes. She had a graceful figure and finely drawn features. Normally he would have been highly intimidated and never have considered making an approach to one who obviously attracted interest from males accomplished at flirtatious small talk. 'I wondered if someone could tell me about the flour. Could I possibly talk to the chef or catering officer?'

'I suppose I could ask. What do you want to know?'

'Really it would be best if I could just go into the kitchen with you. The afternoon session probably doesn't start for another five minutes. Presumably there is someone in there who knows about the flour.'

Reluctantly, but good naturedly, she beckoned him to follow her through a door into the kitchen. He looked intently all around and saw a large sack in the corner. 'Is that the flour?'

'No.'

'But presumably it is on the premises.'

'Oh yes. It's in the old ice house, which is locked most of the time. Obviously it's not used for storing ice any more. We keep a large supply of flour there. That's about all I can say. If you need to know any more you will have to wait till tomorrow - the chef and the catering director have gone home.'

'That's alright. What I'd really like to do is look at the actual flour and see how much I can tell about it. Then maybe someone here can test me. But suppose the ice house door is locked, will you be able to get the key?'

'Impossible. It's hidden away somewhere. She pointed to the clock on her arm display. 'Hadn't you better be getting back to the initiation?'

'You're right.' Damien felt elated. He had the information he wanted. Then as he returned to the reception hall he saw that it was empty and with a sudden wave of fear knew he would have to make an entrance to the conference room and explain why he was late. He did not want to have to deal with any questioning by Wayne and was glad to find the darkened room in expectant silence, free of conversation as they waited for another theatrical entrance.

*   *   *   *

It would not be enough. After the initial euphoria of finding out where the flour was stored he remembered as he was preparing to bed down for the night that for the Knights to be sure of getting access to the flour and implant the QTCs without leaving signs of entry they would either need to have a key or be sure that the ice house was not locked.

He rose early the next morning and walked up to the old brick building on the side of a grass hill running down to a lake, a winding ribbon of water which, up to two centuries ago, had been the source of ice for the ice house when frozen in the winter. The store was clearly visible from the main house and he had to assume he would be noticed; but since he had already feigned interest in examining the flour as a connoisseur this should not really be a problem.

The door was made of iron and it did not yield when he tried to push it. But had he pushed hard enough? The catering girl had said it was locked most of the time. He tried again, putting much more pressure on it, and to his surprise and relief it eventually budged. Inside there were several large bags of what presumably was flour lying on a wooden platform above the deep, wide well-like cavity where ice had originally been stored up to two centuries ago. The one nearest the door was open and half full. The others were sealed and he wondered how a Knight would get QTCs into the flour inside. Then he remembered that they had nanometric burrowing devices.

The original plan had been for him to complete the Initiation over several days, then let the Knights know where the flour was kept and, should they be needed, the location of any keys. The discovery that the door was locked some of the time, and that there was no way he could find out where the keys were without arousing suspicion, meant that the raid would have to be made when the door was unlocked. He would have to be on the premises shortly before so that he could signal this information to the Knights.

Should he wait until the Initiation was over? This would mean he would have to penetrate a strong security system. The only way to guide the Knights in for their covert implantation mission would be to do it very soon, providing that no one locked the door. He would have to risk contacting the Knights or at least someone he could trust to pass on the information. Isla would be the obvious person. If the SSS did detect that he had sent a message it would seem natural that he was communicating with his sister and if he used her quantum encrypted software they would have no way of knowing the content of the message, although what methods they might use to get this out of him physically did not bear thinking about.

Damien decided to walk round the lake. This would be a natural thing to do – he had seen other initiation candidates do it for relaxation. It was still light and he had his flexcom stored in his smartsuit arm. He set off through dew encrusted rough grass heading for a wooded area near the opposite end of the lake and once fairly well hidden pulled out his flexcom, locking in to Isla's identity code. He waited to see if she would answer and when she did not he spoke in a message to the encryption recorder.

'Isla, this is urgent. Please tell KOP they must send in a QTC operative as soon as possible – even tonight. The flour is in the ice house near one end of the lake but the keys are hidden. The door is unlocked at present but this is rare. It could be locked any time. Let me know when the Knights will go in so that I can help them find the ice house if necessary and escape with them after the implant. Contact by text only.'

He was beginning to feel hungry so he walked fast back to the house, guessing that the buffet breakfast would be underway. Fortunately, there was an empty table in the breakfast dining room close to a window which provided a good view of the ice house. There was no sign of any one approaching it so as of this moment, at least, it must still be unlocked. He would return this evening to check and hoped that some time today he would get a reply, although answering would be difficult since for most of the day he was unlikely to be alone.

'Excuse me.' He was interrupted in his thoughts by the voice of the catering girl. 'You wanted someone to tell you about the flour. The catering director will be here at the break this morning.'

'Thanks, but I'm not sure I'll be in the right frame of mind. Could we arrange this for another day?'

'He insists and is difficult to resist once he decides to do something.'

'Well, alright, I'll look out for him at the break time.' He tried to sound grateful.

This interview was not what he wanted. How was he going to hide his ignorance and avoid questions being asked about his interest in the flour?

This problem was on his mind throughout the next initiation session, given this time by one of the Pastor's inner circle and obviously intended to strengthen belief in the infallibility of the SSS's leader and prophet and his personal knowledge of God's plan. Why had he ever decided to request such an interview? Yet he had not actually asked for it. The girl had arranged it. Focusing on how to deal with the unwanted interview with the catering director helped prevent him being drawn into the initiation process, although at some point his lack of conviction was bound to be uncovered.

A slight massaging pressure on his arm indicated that a flexcom message had arrived. He would read it as soon as the session was over and before any interaction with the catering director. As they filed back into the reception area he could see him standing next to the refreshment table, obviously waiting for him. He made for the toilets and unfolded the flexcom. The message was clear: Roscoe Finley would land in a stealthpod tonight, at 2 a.m. in the wooded area next to the lake; and Damien would guide him to the ice house on foot, help with the QTC implanting and then return to the stealthpod for his escape.

A strategy for the rest of the day occurred to him. First, he had to avoid meeting the catering director. He could do this by staying in the toilet until the next session started, even if this risked the embarrassment of entering the conference room late again. Secondly he would have to attend all the remaining sessions that day so that he would avoid attracting attention by his absence until after the QTC implantation, by which time he would have escaped.

The first part of the strategy materialised smoothly. He sat in the darkened room again, with more strident proclamations by Pastor Wayne himself this time, all backed up with rhetorical questions and ready answers.

It was at the end of the session, just before lunch, that his plan was thwarted. Wayne announced that in the afternoon they would all be taken by two transpods to a hut several kilometres from the Holkham Estate where they would be subject to special instruction and prepared for the actual Initiation the next day. They were also told that they would not be returning to Holkham Hall until after the Initiation.

He had no choice. He would have to exit the Initiation before lunch. His absence would be noticed as soon as the party was transported and it would not be long before the SSS started searching.

As soon as the candidates started moving towards the dining room he positioned himself at the end of the queue, then as the last one entered in front of him he turned round and walked swiftly out of the main entrance. Outside, his first priority was to avoid being noticed. A robojobber was repairing the path down to the lake. Although it was, through necessity, moving painfully slowly it would serve to hide him from anyone looking out from the Hall in that direction. He walked to the left of it, shuffling carefully to ensure he did not move ahead and into view.

Bushes lined much of the water's edge so it was not too difficult to remain hidden once he had reached them. He had to be careful of the alligators which, for the last two decades had populated the lake, partly because global warming had made it possible and partly because, since the SSS had taken over Holkham Hall, deterrents to intruders had been a major consideration, although in general people had become less obsessed with eliminating risk as belief in eternal life beyond material death had become more widespread.

Not that Damien believed in eternal life. Even if it existed he certainly did not expect to have it. He was frightened, although he had not noticed that many religious believers were any less fearful when confronted with danger and wondered if deep down they really thought they were going to heaven.

After much dodging from tree to tree, from bush to bush, and looking intently around he reached the wood where Roscoe would be landing the stealthpod, but not until the early hours of tomorrow morning.

Here he was well hidden and could relax as long as he could find somewhere fairly comfortable to sit. He dragged a dead, fallen branch into a small clearing and set it against a tree trunk, the two together forming a seat, the back of which would stop anyone seeing him from behind. This would be a good place to sit until nightfall when he would contact Roscoe to see precisely where he had landed.

The days being so long in June he would have a long wait before it was dark enough to hide him from any SSS search party, although they would not be relying entirely on sight. Nevertheless, he felt easier and even began to reflect on things other than his immediate predicament.

He remembered his short walk to the Rydal Cave with Father James. There was something about this man which had affected him deeply. The evil nonsense of the SSS was already eclipsed and he knew that when this adventure was over he would want to find out more about the Divine Light to which an increasing proportion of the world were turning. Roscoe had told him he had chosen Jesus of Nazareth because he had his roots in the Christian culture and also he felt that the Almighty Creator had chosen this path for him.

Father James had asked him whether he had ever felt awe while viewing the earth and the universe from space. Why did he not feel this while so many others had? He knew that there had been other pilots on his training course who had not been moved by the celestial views they experienced as part of their work; but most people were awestruck and humbled before God, a God which Damien had doubted even existed.

Why did he rarely feel warmth towards others, even his own family? Presumably there was a physical defect in his brain. Pastor Wayne had ignited something in him with his charismatic rhetoric but this had proven to be so shallow, egotistical and spiritually wrong that it had taken only a short time with a truly holy man to dissolve it away and plant within him the seed of something good.

The sun was getting low and still he had heard no sign of an approaching search party. It was still, the silence punctuated only by intermittent birdsong.

An intricately made sliver of blood red cloud cut across the solar disc just above the top of some low conifers. Something stirred in his soul. It looked beautiful. Why would a meaningless, Godless universe, the type believed in by Roscoe's father, Paul, have conscious beings who experienced beauty? He had of course seen views of the earth from space which should have affected him more. So what was happening inside him? Had his meeting with Father James set off some kind of spiritual process?

As darkness came something disturbed his reverie. It was his flexcom and there was a message from Roscoe. 'Hi, Damien. I will land beside the lake close to where you are sitting now and at the time I said – 2 a.m. Please confirm this is OK with you.'

'The SSS people will be looking for me because I had to escape sooner than intended. Can you make it earlier – preferably much earlier?'

There was a long pause. 'I can't get there with the necessary equipment before 11.30 p.m. Can you hold out till then?'

'Looks like I have no choice.'

'See you then. Signing off now.'

The birds had stopped singing and there was a canopy of stars above the trees around him, the brightness of the stars slightly faded by moonlight. He heard various rustlings and stirrings. He was not normally a nature lover so did not realise these probably came from hedgehogs, although he was fairly sure that they were small mammals of some kind. Then he heard twigs breaking and his complacency left him. Something bigger than a small mammal was moving nearby. There was a crashing through the undergrowth and a deer, white in the moonlight, leapt into view, evidently in a panic as it bounded across the clearing, disappearing at once into another patch of undergrowth.

Initially he calmed down; but then it occurred to him that deer were very sensitive to far off scents and sounds. Why was it so frantic? Had it detected an approaching search party? He decided to take no chances and stood up, looking and listening intently in the direction the deer had come from. Should he move off? He could not go far because he needed to be near the rendezvous point. He decided to wait until he heard definite signs of people moving. When they got close he would hide himself in bushes close to the lake. But what if there were dogs or robosniffers? His scent would be easy to reference from that left behind in his room. They would detect him very quickly and he would be captured before the stealthpod arrived.

It was then that he saw lights flashing between distant trees and heard the whirring hum of a robosniffer. He felt mentally paralysed. It was still only just gone ten which meant it would be almost ninety minutes before Roscoe arrived. He walked down to the edge of the lake and got behind a bush. He considered walking into the water to hide his scent then remembered that there were alligators. It was dangerous enough standing where he was so he decided to go back to the tree in the clearing where he had been sitting and climbed up into the foliage. It was fortunate that there was enough light. He managed to get into a comfortable position, then called Roscoe on the flexcom.

'Things are getting desperate. I've got robosniffers on the prowl. Are you sure you can't get here earlier?'

'Impossible. My father is here. He has an idea about hiding in the lake to mask your scent.'

Damien was incredulous. 'But there are alligators. Are they active at night?'

'Hello, Damien. Yes, that's when they hunt for food. But there is a particular sound with a frequency spectrum that scares them off. It has only recently been discovered. I could download this onto your flexcom. If you lowered yourself into the water you could transmit the sound via one of your smartsuit piezoblasters. They work underwater and the alligators wouldn't go anywhere near it.'

Roscoe took over. 'Damien, my father may not belong to the KOP but he knows a lot about this kind of thing. He took up zoology after leaving Baroqo. I'm sure it would work; but we would understand if you don't want to risk it.'

'Well, I don't want to get caught by the SSS, now I'm on the wrong side of them. So you might as well download the sound and I'll give it a try.'

It was not long before he was back down beside the lake. He decided to test the effect of the sound on sighting an alligator in the moonlight, half submerged close to the shore. He turned it on and only had to wait a few seconds for the animal to start behaving strangely. It rolled from side to side then turned and swam off into the darkness.

He sat down on the grass and waited to see if the search party was getting any closer. The hum of the robosniffer was certainly much louder so he switched his smartsuit to waterproof, powered up the piezoblaster on his leg and walked into the water up to his neck, until he could not see the shore. Dogs barked at the same time as the humming. He would definitely have been caught by now since it sounded as though they had converged on the place he had been sitting and were sniffing around the base of the tree he had climbed. Then he became fearful when he realised they would soon track his scent to the water's edge.

The only solution was to swim to the other side, hoping the piezoblaster would protect him en route.

*   *   *   *

The sight of Cumbriana from three kilometres high, with its lakes and rivers sparkling in the moonlight, reminded Roscoe of old film he had seen of World War II night bombing raids. It had been a necessary war to stop evil. The pilots had been brave and it was tragic that so many civilians had died. Perhaps not all the raids had been necessary but it was easy to be self righteous in hindsight. As Jesus of Nazareth had said: 'judge not that ye be not judged.'

Now war was no longer a tenable option for humankind as it accumulated increasingly deadly and uncontrollable technology. Even evil could not be fought in the old way. It had to be stopped – but not by violence. He was grateful to be given this mission but it was becoming obvious that events were already getting out of hand and he knew that had Eric not been so badly injured he would have been the first choice after distinguishing himself so well in Ovoskotia.

Damien had not answered his last flexcom message. Presumably this meant he was in the water. The question now was would he be able to get out and meet up with him by the lake without the SSS search party spotting them.

Why had they chosen him and not a more experienced Knight? It could have been the short notice: there had not been time to find another Knight suitable for this operation. In any case, the KOP was a young organisation. And the fact that he had managed to procure the nanobots from the SSS, albeit without permission, showed his motivation. He was also recognised to be an above average stealthpod pilot where full manual control was essential.

He reached the North Sea and turned south, following the coastline southwards to East Anglia Province. The stealthpod slipped down easily to just a hundred metres above the fields near the east-west coast of what had been Norfolk and he could see the old stately home of Holkham Hall, built for the Coke family in the middle of the 18ᵗʰ century, looming up in the darkness, now only fifty metres from the sea after the global warming. He switched on the invisibility shield and headed over the forest towards the lake at low speed, with the finely controlled fusion engine quietened almost to silence, and dropping altitude.

As he touched down in the appointed place he could just see a boat rowing to the shore but there was, to his relief, no sign of any search party. He got out and looked round, then heard the sound of oars gently splashing on the water. Was it someone searching the lake for Damien? He kept well clear of the shore, since he did not have any protection from alligators. The splashing became louder and he realised the rower must be making for the shore.

Then an outline emerged from the thin moonlit mist which was forming over the lake and he recognised the voice hailing him from the boat.

When he had beached the boat Damien climbed out. 'I swam to the other side of the lake then came across this, which saved me having to swim back. It looks as though the SSS are out of the way for now at least. Did you see any sign of them as you came in?'

'No. So the next step is to get to the ice house. We'd better use the stealthpod and park it somewhere unobtrusive nearby.'

'Can't we take it right up to the ice house and leave the invisibility shield on?'

'No. It is not a hundred percent effective. We can't afford to take any chances. Nobody must have the slightest inkling that the flour has been tampered with.'

'Are there not individual invisibility shields you could use?'

'There are – but they can only maintain the necessary refraction power for ten seconds or so. They are also an encumbrance. We use them mainly for sudden strike impoundments.'

They entered the stealthpod and Roscoe edged it slowly to the other end of the long lake, parking it beneath a large oak tree which masked it from the moonlight and distracted the eye from any transitional visibility of the machine. Roscoe picked up a transponder station unit. 'First this needs to be hidden high in the tree. It receives Q-wave signals from the ingested QTCs, boosts the signal, then forwards it on to the Knight's HQ in Cambridge for analysis.'

'How does it identify which particular individuals are dominos?'

Roscoe had to think hard. He had learned about it during his training but had almost forgotten. 'Each package of transmitted Q-waves carries DNA data which the QTC picks up from a body cell along with the Q-waves. Almost everyone is tagged for DNA at birth so it's just a matter of matching up the signal to a database, which also has photographs and eye scans.'

'I'm surprised some people don't manage to avoid getting tagged.'

'The disincentive is high. Anyone not tagged finds it difficult to operate in the world – they can't buy food or healthcare; and if they are detected as not having a tag signal they are immediately arrested on suspicion of hiding their identity, wherever they are. Hiding your identity is an offence under GF law. Although some areas, like the Ovoskotia Reservation, are outside GF jurisdiction.'

'So how do you locate a domino if you only have his QTC signal?'

'We have to have two receivers of the transmitted signal from two different directions. This enables us to get a fix.'

'But we already know Wayne is a domino. I certainly do.'

'Yes, but there are bound to be other dominos at the conference. It's going to be a major international event. I don't know how this Pastor Wayne ever built up such an organisation. How can one misguided person mislead so many – including some of the cleverest brains in the world?'

'He is good at lying.'

They both felt comfortable sitting in the stealthpod and could have gone on talking much longer; but they realised that although a critical phase of the operation was behind them the main part of it was still waiting to be completed. Roscoe got out of the machine and felt around the tree for somewhere to climb, but it was clear that there was nowhere to get a purchase, so he dispatched an autoclimber to scale the trunk vertically, trailing a chain ladder which he could easily negotiate.

Having placed the transponder station deep inside the foliage he packed up the autoclimber and went back into the stealthpod to get the QTC technology pack. They both set off for the ice house, only some fifty metres away. Damien remembered that in daylight they would be visible from the main building; although it was unlikely they would be spotted, there was still considerable moonlight, so they crawled most of the way.

The door was indeed unlocked. Both were relieved that the mission was not going to be thwarted by a locked door but Damien had an extra reason to be relieved. It had occurred to him that the search party might decide to look in the ice house since he might have been seen examining it that morning and this might in turn cause them to have it locked by the catering director.

Roscoe went inside and set up a light. He opened the QTC technology box and extracted what looked like a short worm-like length of thick silver thread. At a signal from his flexcom it burrowed into the base of each sack of flour but the hole it left was barely visible even when you knew it was there. It was a burrowing device which disgorged into the flour in each sack an invisibly fine thread, only nanometres in diameter. This nanometric thread burrowed a network of tunnels in the flour. He placed a module of several thousand Q-wave transmitter chips over the mouth of the silver worm which then proceeded to implant a stream of QTCs into each sack of flour in turn.

They waited patiently until the last sack had been implanted and Roscoe tested that the QTCs were transmitting and that the transponder station was registering receipt of the signals. Then he invisibly sealed the tiny hole left in each sack. Now they had to get back to the stealthpod and this seemed an annoyingly slow process now that the main task was over. They were impatient to be out of the grounds of Holkham Hall and on their way back to the KOP base in Cambridge.

As they crawled across the dewy grass Damien felt a jolt in his leg and realised that Roscoe had grabbed it to get his attention. 'Look to your right, slowly.' He could see a light and two figures walking towards them, with a dog. Suddenly the dog barked and got excited then started to run towards them. With the energy and speed that only an urgent need to survive can generate they hurled themselves forward towards the stealthpod. The door seemed to take an eternity to open but they managed to get inside before the dog reached them.

Roscoe had the machine humming into the dark air in seconds.

Damien remarked with bitter disappointment that they had failed. The SSS would now become aware that the flour was being tampered with, but Roscoe said this was unlikely. The technology and methods used by the Knights were orders of magnitude more advanced than that of any other organisation and it was this which gave them a chance of forcing peace on a world in which a sizeable minority seemed not to want it or failed to recognise how precarious it was.

'Nevertheless, there is something we can do to throw up a layer of confusion.' Roscoe tilted the stealthpod towards the Hall and flew them rapidly towards it, then landed outside a large double glass door leading into the dining room. 'Quick, get out and help me smash the glass.'

They picked up some loose bricks and hurled them fiercely at the windows. They had been built during alterations made in the 2020s, so the glass was not of the more recent totally unbreakable kind and it was not difficult to shatter it and step into the room. 'Turn over the furniture and break the mirrors. Then steal anything that looks valuable.'

Before the search party could reach them they were back in the stealthpod and disappearing over the moonlit lake to the west.

CHAPTER 16

THE VALLEY
OF DEATH

The stealthpod hovered a kilometre above the floor of the steep valley, its refractor shield switched to invisibility mode. It was clear that the Ogrenians and Essonians below were in full killing euphoria.

This was only the second time that Roscoe had witnessed such depravity; the first time had been in Ovoskotia. He still felt unable to practise his Christian belief in loving one's enemy and was not really sure what 'love' meant in this context. It certainly could not mean the kind of love he felt for Isla. Father James had said it would not really become clear until he had experienced Enlightenment, just as the people fighting below would be doing in the Shanghai Monastery of Divine Light, although only a few of them were dominos.

Gun smoke puffed up from small clumps of bushes on the steep sides of the valley and men wielding machine guns were rushing with maniacal zeal from one firing position to another, aiming hot streams of lead at the fellow human beings they hated, exhilarated both by fear and the possible prize of death, either their own or their enemy's. Even from this height one could somehow tell that all the fighters were young.

Davies felt a deep sadness. As an enlightened Knight, seeking the Creator, he was sensitive to the presence of evil; or was it just the absence of spiritual light? Yet the sadness he felt could not be allowed to incapacitate him. Davies noted an outcrop of rock large enough to hide the stealthpod even without the invisibility field and also protect it from any bullets that might stray in that direction. He looked at Roscoe, indicating that they should start the attack and pointing to the outcrop. 'I say we should go down to ground level and park behind that. Agreed?'

Roscoe thought for a moment. 'It's going to be difficult to get the sleeper gas over all of them from that position.' He felt honoured that his opinion mattered to someone so capable and experienced as Combat Knight Harry Davies, who he had assisted on the Ovoskotia mission and who presumably had been pleased with his performance; although this feeling was slightly tempered by the thought that had it not been for the puma attack it would probably have been Eric on this mission. He momentarily thought of Isla and wondered how close she might be getting to Eric as he recovered.

'Indeed it is. There is a lot of hot lead flying about on that hillside. But "difficult" is the name of the game.'

'There's an alternative. If we could land higher up the hill behind that clump of fir trees I could move along at a higher level and we could both charge down from above. We could approach them from different directions simultaneously and with the advantage of height.'

'It would still be dangerous but we would have more speed and surprise. Let's do it your way. But whoever runs along the top is going to be in more danger so let's toss for it.' Coins were rarely used for anything besides making choices but Davies had one in a tunic pocket. 'Heads you go, tails I go.' Roscoe 'won' the toss. 'Are you sure you want to risk this? I have more combat experience.'

'All the more reason for you not to risk it. Your experience is valuable, Harry.'

'Well, we could argue all day.' Davies swooped the stealthpod down to the group of fir trees growing on a ledge on the steep side of the valley. As the door slid open they could hear the deafening cracks and thuds of ex-Soviet Kalashnikov submachine guns. These particular pieces of death technology were thought to be over eighty years old.

Roscoe took up his refractor shield and baton and moved along the rough stony path well above the conflict, holding his shield to hide himself from the combatants. He could go fast to minimise the chance of being hit by stray shot or slow to avoid losing his footing on the coarse gravel. A human scream of immense fear suddenly emanated from the battle below and made him wince. He guessed that someone had just lost a limb. He instinctively looked up and away from the carnage and saw that Davies had already released the camspheres. The battle and the gathering operation to stop it were being holofilmed for relay to the telepresnet. Hopefully, the world would witness another victory of life over death, of light over darkness.

He stopped to place a small hologenerator for use in the attack, then carried on walking until he found a tree at about the right position from which to gather himself. Davies's voice came through on the flexcom. 'Ready?'

Roscoe made some final adjustments to his baton and the second hologenerator. 'Ready.'

After counting down from five to zero they activated the three equally spaced hologenerators at the level of the path. Almost instantly a whole variety of solid looking holofigures materialised in attire ranging from that of local Ogrenians and Essonians to the tunics and mirror armour of the Knights of Peace. These strange manifestations moved in all directions, in varying modes and at different speeds, to the growing bewilderment of the combatants as they fought their bloody battle. Roscoe noticed that the gunfire was subsiding as each side became preoccupied with the holofigures. Instead of inflicting death on each other they stared in confusion at these multiple apparitions and even directed a few bursts of gunfire at them.

From their different positions Davies and Roscoe mingled into the swarms of holofigures and secreted miniature phials of sleeper gas. They moved between the confused fighters, dispersed as they were along the hillside, and released the phials carefully, so that each one clung to the clothing of just one person before discharging its gas. This was the most dangerous part. If one of the fighters spotted them as real people or if a stream of gunfire hit them accidentally they could die in seconds, because their mirror armour was not infallible.

Some of the combatants were wounded, a few very badly. The only way to deal with them was to spray-freeze the wounds as well as dispense sleeper gas so that they could be tended to in Shanghai after being collected by the stretcher party. It was not a pleasant task and it was clear that some of the victims were already dead while others were probably beyond help.

One cluster of combatants after another succumbed to the gas, its individuals staggering and falling into a coma. The plasma flumes into which the hologens were projected thinned and dispersed, and as they did so the images became ghostly and distorted. Davies twisted the end of his baton, causing a banner to unfurl and float above the deactivated battle, to proclaim its message of victory to the world, switching intermittently between Ogrenian, Essonian and English:

KNIGHTS OF PEACE
WAR ON WAR

They walked back to the stealthpod and called the HQ for ambulance pods and a stretcher party to take the sleeping would-be killers on to Shanghai for Q-wave analysis. Among the prostrate figures would be one or more dominophiles. Only by enlightening the dominophiles of the world could it become truly peaceful. Yet for any individual the process had to begin with an act of will – there could be no coercion.

Davies surveyed the scene with the aid of several camspheres and to his annoyance discovered that they had missed two of the Ogrenians. They were walking aimlessly among what to them appeared to be bodies, looking puzzled and suspicious. 'We can't leave them. They will be a danger to the stretcher party. I'm afraid this is not going to be easy. How do we give them a dose of sleeper without getting ourselves killed?'

They both stared at the display, feeling helpless. If they tried to get close in the stealthpod, even in maximum invisibility mode, they would be seen fleetingly and the Ogrenians would shoot. The vehicle could withstand the shot but it would not be possible to get out and get close enough to them to place the phials on their clothes before they were spotted. Invisibility shields only worked for short periods and even then would not make the whole body invisible to anyone looking intently in your direction. Davies had the germ of an idea. 'If one of us, or both of us, could get behind them and jump them we could plant the phials on their clothes in the struggle and get far enough away not to be affected by the gas.'

Roscoe could see that it was the only way but he could also see that it would be difficult to do, even if they moved the stealthpod to a different position. 'Would it be possible to use hologens again? Perhaps they could be used to distract the Ogrenians while we got behind them.'

'Possibly, Ros. But this time they won't be so easy to fool. They have already seen plenty of hologens.'

A plan began to form in Roscoe's mind. Not a foolproof one but maybe there were ways of removing its weaknesses. 'Sir, that outcrop of rock you pointed out initially. If we could draw them towards the base of the steep side then make them face away it would be fairly easy to jump down on them.'

'You mean park the stealthpod behind the outcrop then create a diversion? But there are three problems. First we have to get to the top of the outcrop without being seen; then we have to attract them to the base of the precipice; then we have to make them look away long enough for us to surprise them from above.' Davies reflected on this for a moment. 'Actually, only the middle one is a problem. How can we attract them towards the precipice?'

He felt awkward at proposing a solution which seemed to generate more problems than it solved, except that Davies had already solved two of them in his mind.

'We'll have to hurry, Ros. They might go away or start shooting at the bodies of Essonians for fun. So, how do we excite the Ogrenians' curiosity enough to make them move where we want them to go?'

'Harry, I may have an answer. These people lose all reason and caution when insulted by their enemies. If we could float a banner inciting their anger and guide this towards the rock face they would probably go there.'

'Eureka.' Davies considered for a short while what could be written to incite the wrath of the two Ogrenians. 'How about. "Glory to Essonia. Bags of shit to Ogrenia" ?'

Roscoe grinned. 'That should do nicely. But how do we get to the top of the rock without being seen?'

'That's easy. We just get them too close to the base to be able to see the top then we run up the slope on the other side, towards the plateau.'

'How do we get them to turn away as we prepare to jump?'

'Actually I don't think we need to jump. We can cocoon them from the top.'

'But we still need to distract them.'

'Well, this is where we have to be slightly non-conventional. I can arrange this but I suggest you look away so you have nothing to conceal from the Knights when we get back. I've turned off the camspheres.'

Roscoe's curiosity was aroused but he decided not to pursue the matter. He was confident that Davies would have a tactic ready which would get a result and if it meant breaking regulations, so be it.

Davies lifted the stealthpod upwards slightly, then down to the valley floor and along to the outcrop, where he parked on the slope. Roscoe spoke in the insulting banner message to the onboard message compiler and plugged his baton into it. Then he deployed a camsphere again, this time turning only its local transmission signal on. Davies went outside and released the banner from his baton together with three guider spheres from a gun-like tube.

Back inside they could see on the monitoring display the banner floating obtrusively near the Ogrenians and Davies steered it closer. As expected they looked both angry and mystified, and as it floated away from them towards the rock they followed it. This part of the plan was working perfectly.

'Now we walk up the slope. When we get to the top look away while I create the distraction. Then we fire a cocoon at each of them. The phials can be applied later and the cocoons removed.'

As they walked up the slope through the long grass Roscoe noticed the exuberant display of wild flowers and he thought of Isla. Why now, when danger was looming? Perhaps the red poppies reminded him of her hair.

On reaching the plateau they fell to the ground and crawled forward to the edge of the precipice. They could see that the two Ogrenians were talking together near the base of the cliff. Davies told Roscoe to look the other way and a second later there was an ear splitting bang and a flash. KOP regulations stated that weapons or munitions designed to kill or injure must not be used even in the cause of peace but Davies, being of a rebellious disposition, had decided that man-made laws, as opposed to God's laws, were not sacrosanct. Besides, in using this old hand grenade which he had inherited from his grandfather he was not using it as a weapon, merely a diversion to gain advantage for the purpose of promoting peace. It was, nevertheless, against KOP policy to use them on telepres broadcast missions. Any kind of explosive device would detract from the public image of the Knights and undermine their commitment to the elimination of all explosives.

The Ogrenians swung round to see where the explosion had come from. The two Knights rose to their feet and each aimed a cocoon gun at one of them. Davies's gun went off at once and his target was trapped immediately; but when Roscoe pressed the activator button nothing happened.

'What's up?'

'It's not working. These things might be easy to use but they aren't so reliable as batons.'

'We'll have to do it the hard way. It's only about three metres so *jump!*' They had to act quickly before the one who had not been cocooned saw them and took aim with his AK47. Both launched themselves over the edge.

Roscoe thudded into the ground and as he struggled to his feet he could see the Ogrenian drawing away slightly to take aim, while Davies seemed to have injured himself and was having difficulty getting up. This was where Roscoe's martial art derived training came into its own, allowing him to leap forward with almost supernatural speed and pull this man of large, muscular frame down in one rhythmic, integrated action. But they still needed to remove the machine gun from his grimly determined grip and to attach a gas phial.

Davies limped forward. 'Ros, hold one of his arms back. He can't fire with just one hand free. I'll see if I can prise the gun away but if I attach a phial it should release the sleeper gas in time to knock him out before he has a chance to break loose.' Davies gripped hard but was not able to overcome the Ogrenian's extraordinary physical strength so he let go and pulled out a phial from his tunic pocket, activated it and stuck it to the clothes of their struggling opponent.

Within seconds the sleeper gas took effect and the Ogrenian collapsed as Roscoe released his hold. But Davies could not get clear in time to avoid being similarly affected.

Roscoe now had to get his colleague back into the stealthpod since he was unlikely to regain consciousness for days but he was quite heavy and it would be impossible to lift him. He had one last look round the battle scene then boarded the stealthpod and sent a message to the stretcher party about his unconscious colleague.

It occurred to him that there might be Essonians or Ogrenians still conscious so he got out of the stealthpod and examined the area thoroughly on foot with a lifeforce detector. After several wide circuits of the area he was confident that Davies was in no danger of an attack from survivors of the carnage he had witnessed and climbed back on board.

As he took off and the mountains of Saukotia shrank below him he realised that he had completed another successful mission. The thought that Davies had to be left behind concerned him but he was nevertheless looking forward to getting back to Cambridge.

Father James had pointed out that pride was a sin, and all sin separated us from union with God. Was it so wrong to feel pride in what he had achieved and hope that it would impress Isla? Then on reflection he realised that it was not pride that he felt, but elation.

CHAPTER 17

THE HERMIT SAGE

It was dawn as the five of them walked up the damp stony path which was the final steep stretch towards the hut overlooking Codale Tarn.

A small stone building came into view. A nun-like figure in dark grey stood in the entrance, welcoming and composed in her demeanour. Her face had a few creases but shone with an indefinable radiance. Was it the Holy Spirit, or the Divine Light that dwelled in her? Roscoe decided they were more or less the same thing. There was no mistaking those who were filled with it.

On coming up to the hut Father James introduced her as 'Sister Agatha'. She was in fact a Sister of the Numinous, a Hermit Sage of the Monastery of Divine Light. She welcomed each one of them in turn with a friendly and dignified handshake then beckoned them in to the small stone hut. It reminded Roscoe of the one he had built during his trial as part of the entry test to the Knights of Peace, though this one was noticeably larger.

As they filed into the hut Roscoe was relieved to see that Eric, now almost recovered from the puma attack, was not accompanied by

Isla. She stayed close to her brother Damien, indicating no special privilege of affection for either Roscoe or Eric. There was an overwhelming sense of peace inside the hut, which seemed to calm Roscoe, and indeed all of them. Somehow this reminded him, through its contrast, of the barbaric battle between Ogrenians and Essonians he had witnessed only three days ago.

Sister Agatha announced that she was feeling rather hungry after her dawn stroll along the top of the valley overlooking Easedale and invited them to help themselves to bread, cheese and cakes, which she had placed on a small table, while she put the kettle on the stove, which burned logs from one of the large forest plantations covering parts of Cumbriana. Father James touched Sister Agatha on the arm and announced he would leave her to conduct the visit. He would go back as soon as he had had a cup of tea and one of her delicious cakes.

She brought over the kettle and poured hot water into a large teapot. Isla took charge of pouring the brewed tea into the mugs which Sister Agatha had placed on a small table and soon they were all sipping gratefully as a way of warming themselves up after walking in the cold mist of the early morning. They also ate pieces of bread and cheese, except Father James who eagerly finished his cake before leaving.

After a few minutes of eating and drinking Sister Agatha made clear her wish to address them. 'I believe that all four of you are interested in Enlightenment but have not yet had it. Am I right?'

They nodded assent, putting down their cups.

'The tour will, I hope, give you a basic understanding of the process so that, if and when you experience it, your mind and soul will be prepared.' She and Isla cleared the table, then Eric folded it up and put it in the corner

A white dome of very fine mesh material took shape above and around them as a black curtain dropped down to cover the door, casting the single room of the hut into deep darkness. Sister Agatha turned on a small dim lamp, then spoke in a gentle and reverent voice. 'Now remember, I'm here to answer any questions you may have. So please don't hesitate to stop me in my tracks.'

'You all have a Christian belief, I understand. Had you been, say, Moslems, or Jews or Buddhists, the spiritual journey inspired by the Divine Light would have been different. It might be instructive sometime for you to see the versions used for followers of other faiths. There is even a version for Atheists.

'But today let's sample the Christian version. Remember, the purpose is to show how your religion serves as a spiritual model for engaging with God. As you know, all the world's major faiths and mystical philosophies use the word 'light' to mean something which illuminates one spiritually and Father James was the first to receive what we call the Divine Light in a Holy vision. Under its inspiration he became a Christian and so able to heal the divisions between faiths.

'Now you've no doubt heard it said by followers of some religions that theirs is the only way to God and the truth. What the Divine Light shows us is that they are all right, in that each religion relates to a particular aspect of our Lord that God chooses to reveal to followers through a particular belief-system. We have discovered that the Creator is incomparably greater, more mysterious and more unfathomable than was thought at any time in history.'

Damien was an Atheist but had heard about Christians who would not admit of any route to God other than that of Jesus. Isla had told him that this was true from the human perspective but that Christ could bring people of all faiths into the Way of Jesus, although he was not sure what this meant.

Sister Agatha continued. 'Since the leaders of the world's classic religions have been illuminated by the Light they have recognised that we can relate to our Creator fully in only one way, which is through the Cross. It is only through this that the Creator of space, time, energy and life in all its magnificence entered into humanity. Yahweh surpasses all understanding. The Light teaches us that for any faith to believe itself to have a complete grasp of the true source of being is blasphemous. However, we Christians are right in saying we have exclusive access to human attributes of the Creator which Yahweh has chosen to reveal to us in his earthly Incarnation. In a sense the Holy Trinity encompasses the other monotheistic religions.'

Roscoe interjected. 'Sister, one thing has confused me for a long time and I don't know if you think it a fair question. How does the Divine Light relate to the Holy Spirit?'

'A good question. I have found the best way to look at it is this. The Divine Light is the work of the Holy Spirit. At this stage in our history God has chosen to reveal how our religions are necessary and complementary to each other, although this may be changing and the Holy Spirit is revealing this through the agency of the Light.' Sister Agatha paused to see if he wanted to follow up his question and her reply, then continued. 'Not that the Spirit and the Light are synonymous – the Spirit does other things than speak to us through the Light – it heals, confers gifts and yields fruit.'

'What fruit, Sister?' asked Damien.

'The nine fruits of the Holy Spirit are listed in the Bible, in the book of Galatians, chapter 5, verses 22-23. They are love, joy, peace, patience, kindness, goodness, faithfulness, gentleness and self-control. Humanity has in recent decades passed through an excessively dualist and reductionist period in history where such basic aspects of the Christian faith have been sidelined. Are any of you scientists or philosophers?'

Roscoe raised his hand 'I studied philosophy and I take an interest in science.' Isla hesitantly mentioned her mathematics degree and investigation of quantum encryption.

'Probably even those who have not followed science in depth will realise that in recent decades the strides made have been quite stupendous not only in explaining the previously inexplicable but in presenting to us new mysteries which make the universe so awe-inspiring, almost frightening, that the sense of a deity behind it is as great as it was at the time of the hunter gatherer, as he looked at the moon and stars, or witnessed thunder and lightning or the birth of a child.'

She turned the lamp off and there appeared a large holographic image suspended in the darkness. It was a still one of a wealthy man standing in front of a prostrate, undernourished man in rags.

'We are now in the first stage of a journey. Here the subject is taught that to go to the next stage he must understand the need for virtue. Without virtue it is impossible to reach truth because one is cut off from the divine source of reality, otherwise known as God. In a moment the image will become animated.'

The rich man appeared to come to life, although he was faint, as did the poor man, who was slightly less faint. The expression on the former's face was initially one of insolence but it gradually changed to a look of kindness. Then he knelt, touched the poor man gently on the head and gave him food and drink, at which both seemed to fill with light as a thin silver cord from the realm of God dangled in space and blended into their foreheads, . 'This is to show graphically and symbolically how a virtuous act brings us closer to union with God. And the closer we get to God, the more clearly will we see the reality of the world he created. During an actual Enlightenment process the pilgrim discusses the images with the Hermit Sage and is guided through the different levels. The Hermit Sage asks the pilgrim to meditate and pray as the journey proceeds. I will show you a few more images before we go to the next level.'

Now the dome appeared to become enormous, as big as a cathedral. A multiplicity of holographic scenes floated and slowly drifted throughout the seemingly huge space. A man was attacked by a vicious thug and refused to resist. Prostrate, he was kicked and punched in the face but refused to retaliate except with a look of loving pity, causing first his own body to glow with numinous light, then that of the attacker, whose face gradually lost its hardness. A man saw a lady being robbed by two thieves and intervened, in a kindly and firm way, causing all four people involved to glow. A man enslaved by pornographic images cast them angrily aside and became filled with light.

'These images and conversations with the Hermit Sage continue until the pilgrim has fully absorbed the message: that acts of goodness, rejection of evil, bring in the holy light and draw one closer to our Creator.'

The room went dark and a brightly lit spiral staircase that seemed to be made of stone appeared in one corner. 'At this stage the pilgrim climbs the stairs to the next level, which I invite you to do now.'

In single file they walked up the stairs and stopped at a platform in front of a sturdy wooden door of the type one sees in Gothic churches, marked 'Silent Space'.

'To open the door, just knock on it.' Eric was in front so he gave it three firm raps. They waited a few seconds and felt a slight trace of a sinking sensation, as though the platform was descending. Then the door swung slowly open and they filed through.

A seemingly limitless expanse of stars defined the hemispherical space above them and all was silent except for the chirp of crickets. The Sister whispered. 'Soon the sound of the crickets will fade and there will be complete silence. At this point the pilgrim just sits and meditates. At intervals the Hermit Sage enters and talks with him to guide him on the role of silence, which is principally to get you into a frame of mind, one in which you are open to the Light, to the truth of God.'

The chorus of chirps vanished into the starry nothingness around them. 'Now, to get a feel for what one experiences as the subject of the Enlightenment process, sit on the floor, listen to the silence for a few minutes and try to empty your mind.'

As they did so Roscoe remembered a poem, which Father James had drawn to his attention. It had been written by a Roman Catholic priest, Titus Brandsma, imprisoned in Dachau, a Nazi concentration camp in Poland, during World War II.

> *Leave me here freely all alone,*
> *In cell where never sunlight shone,*
> *should no one ever speak to me,*
> *This golden silence makes me free*

The silence was necessary in order to get closer to God and so feel liberated from what was known as 'sin'. The closer you got to God the more you shared in his divine plan and the less you were subject to the vagaries of the matter and energy surrounding you and which formed your material body, including the brain. Yet as a Knight it was not always easy to find the space and quietness needed to commune with God.

Sister Agatha seemed to read his mind and he felt she was addressing him personally. 'After passing through Enlightenment it becomes easier to commune with our Almighty God. Once you have related deeply to the Lord you will be able to regain this state with comparative ease. A short daily ritual, a prayer say, helps. Our Moslem friends in God may have something to teach us here. Devoutly observed procedures get us in the right frame of mind to feel the Creator's presence and let Yahweh illuminate our soul with love.'

A spiral stairway again appeared in a corner and they climbed to the next level. As before, there was a door and in this case the word 'Humility' was written on it. Sister Agatha opened it and as they assembled inside the room the image of a large figure of a smiling, self-assured looking man, proud and owing nothing to anybody, standing boldly on a smooth lawn with a montage of symbols of wealth and prestige around him – a yacht, a large house, an expensive looking transpod and a pile of gold bars. Then, the whole montage shrank and as it did so the curvature of the ground underneath tightened until the montage became a point on the surface of a large globe of the earth. This globe in turn contracted to a point next to a bright sphere depicting the sun, which itself decreased in size until it was one of billions of points of light forming a spiral galaxy. The galaxy then grew smaller until it became one of a cluster of innumerable galaxies. The cluster shrank to become a point of light lost among myriad points of light which remained static for a while. Then music began to play and the whole starry mass started to fly apart with increasing speed until eventually the individual galaxies became discernable as the space around them increased. It was at this stage that a small image of the man reappeared, this time near the bottom of this overwhelming cosmic spectacle, bowing before it in awe and humility.

'I think you will agree this very graphically shows the illusory nature of pride when set against our Lord's scheme of things. During an actual Enlightenment the subject experiences a number of such graphic displays which put his or her life in perspective. Some show the unimaginably rich, interconnected diversity of life on our planet, and how it seems to have originated and evolved by a guided process designed by the Creator. Others portray symbolically how space, time, energy, consciousness and love exploded out of total nothingness when the universe was created, and how love holds the universe in being and creates life. It all serves to put our own selves in perspective. Physically we are nothing yet spiritually we are the culmination of God's creation.'

The group remained silent for a while. Then Damien spoke in a chastened and reverent tone. 'I hadn't believed in God till now, Sister, even after orbiting the Earth. Yet I can't really see how all this could have come about by anything other than a Creator of some kind.'

Roscoe was surprised to hear Eric ask a question that had occurred to him frequently over the years. 'Sister, this reminds me that there is a God but how can such a being care about me, if I'm so small in Yahweh's scheme?'

'All of us care about each other and we care about God. The Abrahamic religions all believe that God made us in Yahweh's image. So God must care. How Yahweh can do so at an individual level is impossible to comprehend, but God is omnipotent, multi-dimensional and super-dimensional by definition.'

Eric looked uneasy as he replied. 'Impossible to comprehend.... difficult to credit.'

'It is indeed hard for us to credit but it is also difficult to believe that any kind of agency could bring this unbelievably vast, evolving, intricately organised cosmos into being with conscious life forms as its end point. Is it so difficult to believe that it could also have a means of focusing on billions of individuals simultaneously? God has the whole of eternity and the limitless resources of the heavenly realm to consider the prayers and problems of every individual simultaneously.' Sister Agatha paused a while and no one spoke into the silence, then she resumed in her gentle, kind manner. 'But we are digressing. In this introduction to the Enlightenment process we are concerned with the Divine Light. Having shown the physical smallness of man in the cosmic scheme – but not, as we have just discussed, in God's perception of us - we now proceed to the next level.'

The room went dark and as the illuminated staircase reappeared they climbed to the next level. The door this time had written on it 'God has many faces.'

They entered into an indeterminate greyness, almost like a fog. 'Here we focus on the real purpose of the Divine Light, which is to complete the Enlightenment process. What is that purpose? Have you any thoughts on this?' She looked at Roscoe, inviting him to respond but somehow without putting pressure on him.

Roscoe had been a student of philosophy and it was a friend of his father who had received the vision which was transforming the worldview of much of humanity. He felt he should be able to give some kind of answer. Yet he was confused. Why had the word 'Enlightenment' been used for what was a mystical, spiritual process? The Enlightenment in history had been a process of rationality displacing religion and authority. It had begun in the 18th century.

Isla stepped in. 'Is it to illuminate our minds and souls?'

'It is. It enables us to see more clearly, both at a rational and a mystical level. In fact perception drawing only on logic or only on mysticism is incomplete. Really, the Light fuses the two. It is one of the gifts of the Spirit as listed in chapter 12 of the first letter to the Corinthians. Not, incidentally, to be confused with the nine fruits of the Spirit listed in Galatians chapter 5.'

Roscoe then realised that she had answered his question and this was confirmed as she continued. 'You may wonder why the term Enlightenment has been used in association with the renaissance of religion when up to about half a century ago it meant the decline of religion in the face of reason.'

Eric interjected. 'Maybe it should be called the New Enlightenment?' Roscoe was surprised at his friend's sudden interest in philosophy. Was his close encounter with death responsible?

'A good point, Mr Reed. But in a sense the term "Enlightenment" as used more generally to denote our worldview, is really describing a continuation of the journey towards a true perception of God's creation. But you are right. "New Enlightenment" is a better term to use when talking about the historical process. I believe

I witnessed some scholars using this expression recently. It may well catch on and become established.'

Eric responded quickly. 'So we are still in the Enlightenment that started over three centuries ago?'

'Ironically, logic alone, although powerful, can be a self-destructive tyrant when it denies the divine source of reason, of the logos behind our universe and of our own being. It prevents us reaching the truth of our existence by denying its transcendental source, by attributing the existence of intelligence, love, truth, beauty and justice to mere chance events on a cosmic timescale. If we see the universe as without meaning or purpose then searching for further understanding of it becomes futile. On the other hand, religion without reason can also be tyrannical and negative in its effects. This is well known. It is why the original Enlightenment began. It was a necessary part of God's plan for humanity. I am indebted to a Sufi colleague of mine for this insight.'

She turned again to Roscoe. 'You all know Father James and... Mr Finley, I believe he is a friend of your father. Well, when he had his Divine Light epiphany it was telling him that reason and religion cannot be separated. They need to be fused into something more powerful than the sum of them if human progress towards its true destiny is to continue.'

'But Sister, I thought the Divine Light's main point was that different religions were to stop competing with each other.' Roscoe was convinced of this and Father James had said as much.

'That was indeed its main effect on human affairs in the short term. It followed as a consequence of the powerful revelation conferred on the world's spiritual leaders who became disciples of Father James.'

Damien spoke. 'How did it stop religious rivalry? It seems to me each religion thinks it has exclusive access to a Creator and regards all the others as misguided or heretical.'

'That is how it used to be. Some tried to pretend that there was more than one path to God but deep down they thought theirs was the only way and that their God was the only God. Then Father James was inspired by the Light to realise that there was undeniably only one God but that Yahweh was immeasurably greater, more fractal, more multidimensional than any one religion could conceive. To pretend otherwise was a kind of arrogance. Fortunately we have our Saviour, who took presence in humanity, to bridge the gap, to make God close - despite his power yet also because of it. And the Divine Light is a form of the Holy Spirit which now works through all the faiths, bringing them together in Christ.'

The Hermit Sage fell silent, almost tearful, and her voice almost quivered. 'Enough talking. Now to show the next sequence which expresses in a more powerful way what I've been trying to say. Also, we have to remember that the actual process goes on for days and involves a lot of silent meditation and prayer, as well as guidance from a Hermit Sage. And please bear in mind that all the images are metaphorical or symbolic. God has always spoken in this way.'

Myriads of reflecting, many-sided prisms gradually appeared out of the foggy greyness, growing progressively brighter as the greyness gave way to darkness. Emerging from the greyness was the vague but unmistakable form of a generic male face filled with loving kindness. This gave way to a similarly benevolent female face which then faded away to be replaced by the male face, a cycle which continued indefinitely. The prisms were small and arranged themselves into a formation - one large floating meta-prism with the same number of faces as each of the small prisms. Human figures appeared in similar numbers, forming a cloud around the meta-prism. Then a shaft of light suddenly shot out of one face of one small prism towards the image of a baby, causing the baby to glow with an inner luminance. Another small prism from the same face of the meta-prism, emitted from one of its many surfaces a beam towards a Benedictine monk and this too began to glow with an inner light.

Sister Agatha made a brief commentary. 'Each ray of light emitted from a face of a prism represents the Divine Light.'

The images faded and the stairs appeared again in the corner of the room. 'Now to the last level. This one seeks to convey the importance of combining one's intellectual powers with the sense of holy revelation and God's guidance.'

The images at the next level were more abstract. A large closed book, gilded in gold, was mounted vertically on an altar and a man was shown opening the book. The first page showed a jumbled array of geometric shapes, symbols, words and numbers. Then a prism appeared above the man and sent a ray of light into him. Then the disordered markings on the open page rearranged themselves into a clear structure of text, mathematics and diagrams. 'This is to show how the scholar's quest is in fact a process of revelation from God.'

When the presentation had finished the room returned to its normal state, with the stone walls showing. It was getting late. They would have to set off now if they were to walk back to the house of Roscoe's parents before dark. Although what they had experienced was only a demonstration and introduction to the Enlightenment process each of them now saw the world in a different way.

*　　*　　*　　*

That evening Roscoe sat in his bedroom at an old desk with a pen and a notebook which he used as a diary. He walked over to the window, pushed it open and looked out at the abundance of stars, with the Milky Way sprayed in a band across the jewelled firmament. It was difficult to understand how his father and Damien could be Atheists in the face of such splendid order, how they could imagine it all came out of nothing with no reason or purpose, that it created itself. How could they be so blinded by reductionism and analysis?

Just lifting the pen and holding it over the paper seemed to elicit thoughts worth recording and he knew that the act of writing would bring forth more thoughts.

7 July 2077, Grasmere, Cumbriana, Britlandia

…How can the Divine Light, as invoked in the Enlightenment process, cause an Atheist to believe in a transcendental source of being? Perhaps by exciting in him the powerful, objective perception, the fusion of reason and transcendence, free of pride and prejudice. This would automatically lead to an awareness of God and the desire to know him through some system of faith.

As he wrote this he realised that this was not original thinking. Father James had probably already told him years ago; but at that time he had not understood.

CHAPTER 18

AMELIA

The disused railway line slid beneath the transpod, occasionally marked by a small group of wind turbines, a relic from the days before abundant nuclear fusion technology was used to power most of the world. He was flying quite low and could see that the turbines, although not derelict, were obviously beginning to fade into dilapidation. In the distance, even from this low height, he could see a stretch of sea glinting in the sun and recalled that only a few decades ago there would have been dry land as far as the eye could see.

He had approached Cambridge from the north west having followed old motorways and main roads from Cumbriana, then picked up the rail line which skirted the city's northern and eastern boundaries. Before the line he was following reached the station, now converted into a museum of transport, he turned right and dropped the transpod into a parking area.

Parking space was limited. He had anticipated this because he knew that the Theatre of War would be a popular attraction, even with the reduced population, because transpod ownership was common and the availability of high capacity, three-dimensional routes across the country together with almost unlimited controlled fusion energy meant that owners used them even more than owners of automobiles in the old days of fossil fuels.

The population of Britlandia was down to only forty million after peaking at nearly seventy million before the birth rate declined, net emigration increased and the Plague took its toll. The average age had of course increased but the revolution in ageing research had enabled people to stay healthy, both physically and mentally, for much longer, even without Life Extension.

He walked along Trumpington Road. It was busy with throngs of pedestrians, many of whom he presumed were making for the same destination as he was. This was confirmed when he came to a grass expanse which had previously been a golf course and in which stood a large white canopy towards which moved a continuous stream of people. As he approached he could see a floating image above the entrance, three words with their silver letters revolving. Periodically the letters would stop rotating and the phrase 'THEATRE OF WAR' would be spelled out.

Inside was a large amphitheatre in which the battle would be conducted. Roscoe regretted that any type of battle was still necessary within GF jurisdiction. Yet if a battle had to be fought this was the only type acceptable in the modern world.

This was a symbolic battle. The Theatre of War was where disputes between ethnic groups or over geographical territories could be fought without carnage or destruction. Only countries within the Global Federation were culturally endowed to resolve quarrels in this way and it was unfortunate that there were still areas of the world, such as Ovoskotia, Essonia and Ogrenia, which did not belong to the GF and where ethnic tensions often erupted into violence.

Today's conflict would decide on a victor in a fight over water rights between Egypt and the Sudan, both countries through which the River Nile flowed with a diminishing volume of water. The two sides had not been able to negotiate an agreement and the only recourse they had as members of the Federation was to be represented by two small armies of life-sized robot soldiers equipped with a variety of weapons. Not weapons lethal to human beings. These were of course illegal under GF Law. They were designed to destroy only the simulated humans which fought in the Theatre of War, albeit in a realistic way which reminded the spectators of the wretchedness of real war. Knights occasionally liked to witness simulated battles since it strengthened their resolve to eliminate the technology which allowed real war to reap its harvest of death and offend against Yahweh.

Roscoe stood leaning against a waist high pillar, waiting for the first robot fighters to appear on the stage below. Then a gleaming red armoured figure appeared and walked around the large expanse of the stage. The audience applauded.

The robot held or had strapped to it a variety of lethal weapons, including a sheathed sword and a repeat action rifle. It managed to convey to the audience, in its stance, mannerisms and appearance, a sense of irony. All were about to witness the settlement of a real quarrel over resources yet no human being would die or be injured. It would be an entertaining spectacle, the battle would be skilfully executed, there would be finesse and skill in large measure; but above all it would convey the futility and inhumanity of war.

A large cascade of applause filled the arena.

A second robot walked calmly and with dignity into the stage area, this time from the right. It was equally well armed but dressed in a long purple cloak.

There was more applause.

Similar robot soldiers entered the arena, each dressed or designed in some way to be distinguishable to the crowd as an individual and each eliciting its own raucous applause, unheard by the humans who operated them from their control stations in Egypt or Sudan or, if they were hired from outside the two nations in dispute, other parts of the world. Despite the highly individualistic appearances the two sides were distinguishable by colour – red for the Egyptians, purple for the Sudanese.

When each side had seven fighters the applause stopped and the whole amphitheatre fell silent. The combatants moved and climbed into their starting positions on various boxes, high platforms and protrusions from pyramids around the arena. They all stood still and the lighting dimmed until they were barely visible. A solid gold ball descended slowly into the arena, coming to rest on a pedestal in the middle of the stage. A voice announced that the engagement was to be fought to agreed rules, that it was a war game, the object being to capture the ball. The rifles each had only ten bullets each. It was also emphasised that the outcome would have real consequences for the two countries involved.

A fanfare of trumpets sounded and the battle commenced.

A red soldier on a platform fired a burst from his rifle, the noise being loud enough to shock the audience, but narrowly missed the purple target standing on a ledge protruding from a pyramid. In fact there were no bullets but the outcome of each rifle firing would accurately reflect the actions of the humans who controlled the robots and puffs of blue smoke rose from the gun. The purple team took cover as best they could and a second shot was fired from a purple robot partly protected by the pyramid. It was aimed at a red robot which had stepped off its box and was running for the ball. The shot missed and a purple soldier leapt from its box onto the running robot, pulling it to the floor and clasping it from behind with one arm while pulling out a knife with its free hand. The knife was thrust into the side of the red robot which spurted blood and collapsed, its simulated biological circuitry and controlling computer calculating that such a wound would be fatal. Some in the audience gasped in horror at this spectacle, others seemed unconcerned but some cheered.

Roscoe found it difficult to comprehend how people could cheer even a simulated butchery. He hoped they who cheered were not Knights. Perhaps they applauded only because they wanted the purple team to win and, as regular spectators at the Theatre of War, were used to regarding the violence as harmless. Personally it disturbed him almost as much as what he had seen in Ovoskotia or Saukosia. But what disturbed him more was that some people seemed to find it entertaining and he recalled that public executions had been popular attractions up to the mid-nineteenth century. Spiritual evolution still had far to go.

Action from the red side, having suffered its first fatality, quickly escalated, evoking an equally busy response from the purple side. Shots and struggles erupted to the level where it was difficult to gauge who was winning. A compelling sword fight started in one corner of the stage and moved intermittently across to the opposite corner, arresting the attention of much of the audience until the death of the purple combatant brought it to an end. The red soldier then rushed for the ball but was blown in two by a high velocity round from a purple robot on the platform above, causing another robot from purple team, who was also running for the ball, to slide in the blood and fall off the front of the stage.

The conflict finished with the capture of the gold ball by the red side, of which only two were left operational, and the graceful acceptance of defeat by the purple side, with three still standing.

*   *   *   *

Roscoe walked out back across the grass onto Trumpington Road and made for the square in Cambridge still known as the Lion Yard. For many years this had consisted largely of market stalls but as the era of consumerism faded under the pressures of ecological stress these had given way to artists and story tellers. And around the square were various cafes, coffee houses and tea shops from previous eras used more as centres for informal meetings and discussions between scholars than for eating or drinking.

He went into an eighteenth century reproduction coffee house, the Graecian. Originally this had been an establishment situated in the Strand, in London, as Londonium had been called at that time, and used by intellectuals. He saw a table situated near the window with four people who appeared to be together and it seemed that they were about to leave. It would be a good place to sit and gaze out at the varied activities in the square. As they walked away from the table he noticed that a lady's handbag was left behind. He called to point this out but as he did so a girl turned round and said she was going to get some more coffee and would be coming back. Should he sit down or move to another table? Theft was virtually unheard of so to offer to keep a watch on her bag would not be appropriate. To sit opposite her place might make him seem over familiar; yet to move away would appear rude and at the same time forfeit the best position. He decided to sit.

The inside of the Graecian was as interesting to look at as the passers by outside as they perused the pictures displayed by artists. Gilt shelves displayed items that would have been purchased in the original establishment, such as pills, hair tonics, packets of snuff and cough lozenges. Near the far wall was a long wooden table with a pitcher and clay pipe on it. The rich aroma of freshly ground coffee mingled with smoke fumes from the stove on which stood a large blackened pot of brewing coffee. Every effort had been made to capture the ambience of such establishments and even the clientele somehow fell into the role of typical customers of the time as they discussed with relish the latest ideas, trends and fashions, although the faithfulness to the past did not extend to restricting access to males or dressing in eighteenth century attire.

The girl poured her coffee at a small table by the stove and he could not help being drawn to the femininity which revealed itself in her every movement and dress-covered contour. She was not starkly or crudely alluring but gently, subtly magnetic. He thanked God for letting such loveliness into the world. It was a soothing contrast to the metallic brutality of the Theatre of War.

He had found much of the military spectacle distasteful yet it had prevented a large amount of human misery, even for the loser. And being a member of the Global Federation the losing country of this resource war would receive help or compensation to deal with its water shortages.

As she put her coffee on the table she gave Roscoe what he interpreted as a maternal smile. Yet it was entirely kind and did not in any sense hint at a wish to control. 'I'm waiting for my tutorial. The others have gone to a lecture on Long Distance Bridge Design, which means nothing to me.'

'What subject are you studying, Ms…?'

'Mills. Music at Emmanuel College. And you?' She was calm and relaxed and gave the impression of being able to see into his soul.

'I'm working full time now. I used to study philosophy. My name is Finley.'

'Can I ask what work you are doing, Mr Finley?'

'I'm in the KOP.'

'A Knight! I'm impressed.'

'Only a novice.'

'Have you been on any missions?'

'Yes. Two. One in Ovoskotia and one in Saukotia.'

'I think I saw the last one on the telepres. Although as usual the identity of the Knights was hidden.'

They fell silent for a while, sipping their coffee, which was still too hot. Ms Mills continued. 'So what are you doing in Cambridge? Are you between missions?'

'Yes, although I've been spending most of my time with my parents in Cumbriana. My next mission is in September. I've just transpodded down here for the day to see the Theatre of War.' He noticed the miniature white circle on her forehead indicating that she had already had her life extended.

'But why would a Knight be interested in war, unless it was a war on war, which I believe is not the province of the Theatre of War?'

This was a difficult question to answer. The Knights of Peace were dedicated to eliminating war yet were encouraged to watch symbolically enacted battles involving graphic portrayals of violence. 'We need to keep reminding ourselves of what real war can mean to its participants. But the Theatre of War also risks impressing patterns of behaviour, so that people could become addicted to violence and oblivious to or even excited by violence.'

Ms Mills looked puzzled. 'So is this not a real danger? Even to Knights?'

'It would be were we not already devoted to stopping violence. And all of us, at some point, receive Enlightenment. The real danger is to those outside the Order. Many seem to regard it as entertainment. Some would say that the TOW should be banned. Yet the right to choose is precious.'

'It is fortunate that weapons are so hard to find – thanks to you Knights.' He decided she was not being patronising.

As their coffees cooled they drank more quickly and it was clear that Ms Mills was in a hurry. 'I must go to my tutorial now. Perhaps I will see you in Cambridge again.' She gathered her handbag and swept out of the Graecian.

It had been a spontaneous and enjoyable encounter of a type that Roscoe rarely experienced and he was disappointed by her sudden departure. She had not left any contact details or asked for any from him. He stared out at the street for a little longer, feeling slightly deflated, then got up himself.

He walked off in the direction of King's College chapel and came to a seat overlooking the expanse of drought-resistant cropped-clover lawn which led down to the river Cam. He touched his flexcom to retrieve the Holy Bible and began reading the book of Ephesians. It was one of his favourite passages because in it was the essence of Christ's message and role in God's cosmic scheme. He felt the need to pray and meditate, partly because of the still too vivid memory of the barbaric drama he had witnessed earlier, and partly because Ms Mills had stirred something inside him. So he walked over to the chapel.

Inside he strove to achieve an inner calm and union with the Creator, which he was sometimes able to do but on this occasion he was only partly successful. After a long session of contemplation he emerged and decided to spend a few more minutes on the bench before returning to the transpod and flying back to Grasmere.

In the distance he could see King's College Bridge, where Isla and he had started their morning walk to the Orchard studonium in Grantchester during which he had felt that a mutual attraction was germinating.

Why had she and Eric not wanted to come with him today? They had initially agreed but both made excuses only the night before. What were they doing now? He knew that there would be no physical intercourse no matter how strongly they were attracted. No Oath of Bonding had been made and in any case he was not convinced that the attraction between them was very strong, despite Eric's heroism and recovery from the resultant injury, two factors which might be expected to excite a woman's feelings towards a man. But they could be sharing a rowing boat on the lake, or climbing Helm Crag.... In which case any bond between them might strengthen. It often happened when people did things alone together.

He set off towards the transpod park, having decided to fly back to Grasmere without further delay rather than eat before leaving. He would only be staying there for a few more days; then he would be returning to the KOP base in Cambridge in preparation for the Holkham Hall attack. Knightmaster Franklin would have the latest information on the conference, including the ones which had been identified as dominophiles for impoundment along with Pastor Wayne.

Cyclists frequently passed by on the roads which had originally been built for cars, now an almost obsolete form of transport after the introduction of transpods. Urban streets were well maintained since cycling and taking rickshaws were the main ways of travelling in towns and cities, except for walking; whereas between the urban centres the roads were not normally maintained. He resolved that in future he would make more use of bicycles for getting around if only for the exercise.

As he walked back into Trumpington Road he heard a cyclist braking to a stop beside him. A girl dismounted and he saw that it was the one he had met in the Graecian coffee house. She looked flushed and happy as she spoke to him.

'Hi, we meet again. Mr Finley, isn't it?'

Surprisingly he could not recall her name at this moment, which embarrassed him. 'It's my pleasure. Was your tutorial successful?'

'It went quite well once the flexcom brought up the right support software. My tutor seemed at a bit of a loss without it.'

'My philosophy tutors relied a lot on support software.'

'Are you going back to, where was it, Cumbriana, right away?'

'Possibly. There's no particular hurry.' He noticed her long black hair glistening in the light of the setting sun and a small blemish in her face.

'Only I was going to the Wheel of Life for dinner. Do you know it?'

'It is a regular haunt of mine when I'm staying in Cambridge. Would you mind if I joined you?'

*   *   *   *

The large red sun was eclipsing itself below the horizon and enlivening the fingers of black cloud with crimson edges, while the buildings below ephemerally burned with red light. The restaurant capsule was in the highest sector of its vertical rotation and this fortuitously coincided with the most spectacular moments of sunset.

They had spoken freely and without thought of time. Neither Ms Mills nor Roscoe had been aware that a rapport was building rapidly. Then this transient scene presented itself and stopped the conversation.

Spontaneously Roscoe spoke. 'There is beauty therefore there is God.'

Ms Mills had read widely but had not encountered this aphorism. 'Is that a quotation? I have to admit I've not come across it. Sounds like one of your philosophers.'

He had not meant to say this out loud and, despite their growing rapport, felt slightly embarrassed since he now had to tell her it was his own observation without appearing proud. 'It just came out.'

'You mean it's your own expression. Why are you embarrassed?'

'Well, it could be that the last time I said it my father scoffed. He still clings to Atheism.'

'He's not alone.'

'You mean – you're an Atheist?'

'Not at all. I just meant there are still plenty of them left in the world. Or maybe I mean agnostics. There is a place for honest doubt in God's creation – it's so much better than wrong-headed certainty.'

They resumed their eating and drinking. Roscoe decided to risk appearing over intimate, while at the same time not having to avoid addressing her by a family name which still escaped him. 'My first name is Roscoe. Do you mind if I ask yours?'

'Amelia.' She looked searchingly at him. 'I see that we both have Life Extension.'

'Have you been Enlightened?'

'Yes.'

Roscoe now felt a dawning love for this woman that was very different from what he experienced with Isla. He hoped she was not already in a Bonding. From a rational point of view it would seem unlikely that such a lady would not have found herself bound to a man but, having already invaded her privacy with a personal question, he felt unable to ask her something so intimate. He hoped as he had never hoped before that she was free.

*   *   *   *

He took the transpod up to one kilometre and saw the sun setting a second time as he headed back towards Cumbriana. The shared meal with Amelia had left him elated and he wished they could have spent longer together but she had previously agreed to go to a college social event of some kind and although he was invited to join her he thought it best to decline in case it involved dancing, although from the conversation he had got the impression she was not so enthusiastic about dancing as Isla and saw it as something she was more or less expected to do. She was an altogether different kind of person. Besides he had to prepare for the Holkham Hall mission and time was running out.

There seemed to be within her a source of spiritual wisdom and maternal concern, a warm kindness, a graceful relaxed manner. She was not, like Isla, vivaciously attractive; nor was she classically beautiful. But her attractiveness to him, though more subtle and less physical, was unmistakable and more immediate than had been the case with Isla.

And this time he was sure from the start that she was drawn to him. She had given him her telepres address and asked when he would be returning to Cambridge. Whereas in the case of Isla, who he had known for nearly a year and been alone with several times, he was still uncertain and continued to suspect she was keener on Eric. She seemed wrapped in mystery. Amelia, too, had mystery about her but she did not seem to be tantalisingly

316

and deliberately hiding her true self and it was obvious from every nuance of face, body and motion that she was deeply enamoured.

Yet Isla still had a strong hold on him and he felt he would be devastated if she did not return his love. It was more visceral than for Amelia. She made him flush with hormones when she smiled or looked meaningfully at him, however fleetingly; while at the same time she was intellectually stimulating to talk to. He really needed to know how he stood with her.

But how could he complain about her indecision when he himself was now experiencing a growing love for two ladies simultaneously? Was this how Isla felt about him and Eric? Was this why she was so reluctant to reveal her true self? What he did in the next few months might determine the course of his whole life on earth as well as in that state of being beyond physical death.

What should he say to Isla when he got back to Grasmere? He might be foolish in assuming she had any feelings at all for him other than friendly affection. If that was the case he might as well find out sooner than later. At least he was confident that in Amelia he had found a lady who would return his love.

There could of course be no question of sexual fulfilment with either Amelia or Isla, without an Oath of Bonding. Such binding agreements applied to all sexually consummated relationships, whether in marriage or a Circle or neither, always entailed an initial period of celibacy, were always monogamous, even inside a Circle, and could only be terminated over a three month period. Any children born from the union would have to be reared and guided by the parents until the age of twenty five.

It was now dusk and he could see the dim relief of the Pennines drifting below, intermittently visible beneath wispy clouds lit from above by the crescent moon. Soon he would be over Cumbriana, ready to descend to Grasmere. He felt the presence of God in the near silence of the cabin.

*   *   *   *

The front door slid smoothly open, making only a faint humming sound to inform the occupants that a known visitor was entering. He walked through the hall to the large room from which, in daylight, the lake could be seen. Had his parents gone to bed? Were Isla and Eric in the house? He heard talking coming from the kitchen and realised it was his parents, so he opened the door to see them sitting either side of a table set against the far wall.

Tina joyfully greeted her son. 'Oh, Ros, you're back. I assumed it was just Isla and Eric coming in.'

His father seemed less obviously pleased to see him and was more jovial than friendly. 'Did you enjoy the war?' There was a mocking irony in his voice, reflecting how he had noted, while Roscoe was departing for Cambridge, the incongruity between the aims of the Knights of Peace and their recent habit of watching battles at the Theatre of War.

He ignored his father's taunt and poured himself some ClearSpin. Why did he have to joke or mock or be sarcastic about so many things? It seemed almost as though he was serious only when attacking something which Roscoe cherished, such as the abolition of war or belief in a Creator or in the reality of the Divine Light.

Yet he knew there was a father's love for his son behind it all and that, even for Atheists, where there was at least human love, God was not far away.

Roscoe decided not to rise to the bait. He had a more pressing question of his own which he directed at his mother. 'Are Isla and Eric in?'

Tina replied with a certain awkwardness and he was well aware that she understood his feelings and concerns about Isla and Eric, although even she, with her strong intuitions, could not yet know about Amelia. 'Well, there was another holotribute to a 1970s electric folk band in the village hall tonight. Jade I think. And you know how Isla likes dancing to all kinds of music and Eric seems to be good at that kind of thing.' Paul quietly left the kitchen, as though he would feel out of place in the discussion which was about to proceed and thought it best to leave Tina to find out what she could and give any advice, unhindered by his presence.

Roscoe sat down at the table where his father had been and replied heavily. 'I do indeed.'

'Ros, you are still very young for someone with Life Extension. There is plenty of time to find the right girl.' This concerned him. His mother was good at discerning a person's inner thoughts. Was she saying that Isla was not attracted to him, that he was wasting his time on her? Was she confirming his worst suspicions? 'You need to talk to her.'

'I have done. But she keeps me guessing, as though she wants my attentions but doesn't want to commit herself.'

'How do you think she feels about Eric?'

'I asked her and him separately. Isla is equally inscrutable on this. But I can't help concluding that with Eric's obvious attractions to females in general he is the more likely to have won her affections.'

'And Eric?'

'He claims to be no surer than I am about her feelings.'

'And how does he feel about Isla?'

'He loves her at least as much as I do and wants to start an Oath of Bonding as a preliminary to forming a Circle with her and me, but of course this is only possible if she feels towards me and Eric as we do towards her.'

'Have the three of you talked together?'

'No. I suppose each of us is afraid of hearing what we don't want to hear. But Mum, the situation has come to a head because of something that happened today in Cambridge.'

'In Cambridge?'

'I met a girl, Amelia, and found myself drawn to her – almost instantly. And the difference this time is that a girl feels the same about me. It is very different from Isla and me. This is love. With Isla it can only be infatuation unless and until she returns my feelings.'

Tina looked caringly, searchingly at her son. She satisfied herself in a few moments of feminine divination that he was not deluding himself. 'Yet you still want Isla and want her to love you, even though you are in love with this other girl?'

'Yes. Until now I had always wondered whether one could love two ladies at once. What I feel now, after even such a short time with Amelia, is that one can only love one at a time in a sexual way. If I form an Oath of Bonding with Amelia it will have to be monogamous. I want it that way and I'm sure she would want the same.'

'Ros, suppose Isla does love you as you had hoped until now?'

'After meeting Amelia I think I know what gender-based love really is. Isla is attractive to me and has affection for me. She does not love me as a man and love of that kind has to be two way. We can love each other in celibacy, even though she is attractive to me, as members of the same Circle of Kinship but I want to form a Bonding with Amelia.'

'And who else would be in the Circle? Eric?'

'Yes, I know he loves Isla and in his case I am fairly sure it is returned. They would also form a Bonding.'

'Do you really think a Circle would work? How do you know that after a period you would not find yourself tempted to break the Circle by having intercourse with Isla? Even if you remained faithful you might have to be tormented by temptation. And what about Eric, Isla and Amelia? This is all so …untried.'

'Father James said it was all part of God's scheme of spiritual evolution keeping in sync with our increasing life span and the need to form Circles of Kinship as the natural successor to the nuclear family, a new way of bringing children to maturity in a secure, loving environment and ensuring that they develop their full potential.'

Tina interrupted. 'James is a good man, Ros. Even your father admits that. But he has not had the experience of married life. He knew plenty of women casually or for short relationships when he was in Baroqo but that's not the same.'

'He is not an ordinary man, Mum. He experienced the Divine Light and later had his Christian visions. He divested himself of almost all his possessions. I believe he has derived truths directly from our Lord.' Roscoe got up from his chair and began to pace around the room. 'Maybe there will be temptation. But Father James says resisting temptation is an opportunity to grow spiritually.'

'Well, you may be right.' Tina sighed, wistfully, as if hoping that this was so but being afraid in case it was not.

'Only the transcendental love would be shared. This would be between all members of the Circle. The carnal aspect would have to be monogamous. The Bonding is a sexually consummated relationship within the wider platonic relationship of the Circle.'

'But a Circle of Kinship would be a huge commitment. Any child born to Isla or the other lady – Amelia? – would have to be looked after by the Circle until adulthood. Is that not so, Ros?'

Paul came back into the kitchen and sat down next to Tina as Roscoe continued.

'Are you saying that the new laws on Circles of Kinship and Oaths of Bonding which have been drafted by the Monastery of Divine Light and the Global Federation are not sound?'

'No, Ros. I'm just saying be careful. You've got nearly three hundred years of living ahead of you. It sounds as though you are saying that you want an Oath of Bonding with Amelia but want to be part of the same Circle of Kinship as Isla and Eric. Just think about it. And how do you know she is not already in a Bond? I suppose you didn't ask her.'

'No. She already has Life Extension and has been Enlightened. I know you might expect her already to have taken an Oath of Bonding with someone but I know inwardly she hasn't.'

'It is easy to comfort and deceive oneself with such intuitive feelings. I don't want you to be disappointed.'

Paul joined in. 'Your mother's right, Ros. I don't know what you've both been talking about exactly but with a three century journey ahead you can't afford to be even half a degree off course.'

The front door hummed open as Isla and Eric returned from the holotribute. They were laughing together.

CHAPTER 19

HOLKHAM BRIEFING

The forest was damp and cold. Pine trees were predominant but deciduous trees had become more common after the climate warming. Knightmaster Franklin enjoyed the freshness of the dawn before the start of his working day and often took a stroll around the wooden hut before starting work.

He stopped briefly in the clearing where he had noticed the two Cadet Knights – Reed and Finley - practising rapid cocooning techniques under the guidance of Tutor Knight Wang from the Shanghai KOP. It had been obvious to both him and Wang that each showed promise and, moreover, subsequent exercises had revealed that, once each of them had learned to curb their ego and competitiveness, together they generated an exceptional degree of synergy.

Before leaving the glade he spent a few minutes of prayer and meditation, asking God to give him the strength to cultivate the wisdom and judgement upon which so many lives depended. His decisions affected not only the Knights he sent on missions but the victims of the violence they sought to stop.

Today was when probably the most important mission of his career could be said to start. Upon its successful outcome depended the survival of humankind and a great deal of the planet's animal and plant life. He had of course spent a lot of time with Father James and others selecting a team and defining the mission. But in his mind an operation only really began as you assembled the team and outlined the plan of execution.

Inside the hut were five chairs facing the circular table at which he would be sitting to address the Knights selected for the raid. On it was a three dimensional-virtual model of the building where the dominophiles, along with a hundred or so other conference delegates, were known to be meeting on the day of the planned impoundment attack. He stared at it contemplatively. He had arranged for the Knights to arrive at intervals so that he could take them into the side room and talk to each one individually for a few minutes while at the same time the others would talk to each other round the table, thereby setting in motion a bonding process that would continue throughout the mission.

Four dominophiles were to be impounded; and this would have to be an incognito undertaking. To broadcast the mission on the telepresence network would be to endanger its success, since floating camspheres would have to be deployed around the building prior to capturing the dominophiles and this would risk alerting them, since the camspheres would have to be released inside the building prior to the impoundment. Had it been an outdoor operation the camspheres could have hovered unobtrusively. One had to balance the advantage of helping to mobilise the will of people throughout the world in fighting violence against the hampering of the mission at an immediate practical level.

One of the dominophiles, by far the most important target, was already known - Pastor Wayne. He wondered who the other three were. The Q-wave spectra relayed from Holkham Hall to the KOP Command Centre in Cambridge was accompanied by DNA identity information which could be checked against the Global Federation's database. This did not show their positions in the SSS or their present names, but it did show their history from birth up to joining the SSS, at which time they had disappeared from the records and, presumably, adopted different names. One had been a captain in a disbanded army regiment, the second had been an operative from the now-superseded CIA and the third a physicist at Cabal University who had proved to be gifted both as a theoretician and an experimentalist before vanishing from the Federation database not long after the SSS had started.

He could hear footsteps approaching along the gravel path and knew they were from Combat Knight Harry Davies. Often he gave the impression of being a little disdainful of regulations when trying to complete a mission but he always arrived on time when this had been agreed. The Knightmaster wondered how Davies would react to the news he was about to give him.

'Good morning, Harry, on time to the second as usual.'

'Predictable as ever, sir.' There was a slightly self mocking element in his tone, and Knightmaster Franklin smiled as he detected this.

'You speak as though you are slightly defensive about your punctuality.' He ushered him into the side room where there was a table with a camping gas stove, kettle and other tea making paraphernalia from the 1970s. 'Anyway, sit down. Tea?'

'As long as it's Afghan.'

'What else?' The Knightmaster filled the kettle with water, struck a match from a 1970s box of Swanvestas and lit the portable stove. He placed the kettle on the flaming ring. 'While we wait for that to boil I have some good news for you.'

'You've already captured Pastor Wayne?'

'Not quite as good as that but still news which I'm sure will be welcome to you; it certainly was to me when I first heard it. You will be the leader of this mission and I'm sure that comes as no surprise.' He spooned tea into a teapot and took the kettle off the stove as the water started to boil. 'Harry, some months ago, after the Ovoskotia raid, I requested that you be officially given the rank of Leading Combat Knight. Only three days ago I got official confirmation that you had indeed been granted this and in my view it's long overdue. So congratulations.'

'That's great, sir. Thanks.' Harry was pleased but there seemed to be no hint of pride at the news.

The Knightmaster, who had started his career as an army corporal seventy years ago, before helping found the Knights of Peace after leaving the army as a Brigadier only ten years ago, still had not adjusted to how little Knights cared about status, despite him having been instrumental in encouraging a disregard for prestige. Perhaps his surprise was at the degree to which the founders had been successful in instilling the values of the Divine Light. The Monastery had been instrumental in this. Not that Harry was indifferent to the promotion, especially as he was considerably older than most Combat Knights on active service; but the message his expression conveyed was 'good, now I can do my job more effectively – this is what I was cut out for' rather than 'I am a better, more important person than before the promotion,' or any bloating of ego.

They could hear the distant footsteps of someone else approaching the hut. 'Harry, later we will be discussing the mission in more detail but this morning I just wanted to outline it to you and the four others who will be taking part. The idea is to speak to each person privately for a couple of minutes before we all assemble with the others in half an hour. This will be your first chance to talk informally with your team. So if you would retire to the main room I can talk to Combat Knight Ryder alone – I believe he is arriving now.'

'He was with me on the Ovoskotia mission, as you know. See you later, sir.'

As the new arrival approached the round table the Knightmaster and Davies walked towards him to clasp arms, then Ryder and the Knightmaster retired to the side room. There was a kind of holiness about Ryder's eyes. It seemed to go with him having considered joining the Monastery before deciding upon the Knights. Nevertheless, all reports indicated he was not in the least unworldly and that he was highly competent at the practical tasks faced by Knights, with a special penchant for generating confusion using animated holofigs.

'Combat Knight Ryder, how do you feel about this mission?'

'It sounds challenging, sir.'

'And you like a challenge?'

'If the cause is good.'

'Well, I can assure you that is the case – if you think saving our planet and most of human life is a good cause.' He handed Ryder a cup of tea and noticed the mystified look on his face. 'I'll be explaining later, when I address the group as a whole. You will remember Combat Knight Davies?'

'Yes. We were together on the Ovoskotia mission.'

'He's just been made Leading Combat Knight and will be commanding the attack on Holkham Hall, or rather the capture of four dominos who will be attending a conference there in . September.'

'Will this be for arrest or impoundment, sir?'

'Impoundment in each case. As you will learn later the SSS is much more dangerous than they would like us to believe. And if you are agreeable I would like to make you second in command to Leading CK Davies. Is that alright with you?'

'It is. I enjoyed working with Harry on the Ovoskotia mission.'

A third Combat Knight entered the main room and sat at the round table with Davies, whereupon Ryder went out to call him in to the side room and take his place at the table. It was Combat Knight Max Hull, who, like all the Knights on this task, had participated in the Ovoskotia operation. He had been chosen primarily for his preternaturally fast reaction times and skill in handling a stealth craft where automatic control would be inadequate to the task.

After Knightmaster Franklin had again offered tea and had talked with Hull for a while the first of two cadet Knights arrived and, after a brief exchange with those sitting at the round table, entered the side room to take the place of Hull.

'Cadet Knight Reed. Good morning. Please take a seat. Tea … or caffrosia perhaps?'

'Thank you, sir. I would prefer caffrosia.' The Knightmaster could not conceal a slight disappointment at his choice.

'What do you know about this mission?'

Eric knew very little except that it was an impoundment rather than an arrest or destruction of munitions and that it involved the Servants of the Seven Seals. Roscoe had told him that it would be at Holkham Hall in September.

'I will say more about it when we assemble at the round table. You already know more than our friends in there. For the time being suffice it to say that it involves impounding the leader of the SSS, known as Pastor Wayne, and three others who have Q-spectra indicating them to be dominos. They will be assembled at a conference on the latest technology developed by SSS research and development teams in China, India, Russia and Brazil .'

'Why do we never hear about these? Why do the Knights keep it so secret?'

'The KOP has only known about them in the last few months, thanks both to Ms Isla Hanson's code breaking skills and to our intelligence network. Ms Hanson has been sworn to secrecy over this, incidentally, as are all of you on this task. On no account must the SSS be aware that we know about their R&D activities. The Holkham raid must be a total surprise.'

'I was aware that they have some crazy idea of destroying life on earth, believing this to be God's will.'

'More than an idea. You will know that your fellow cadet Knight, Roscoe Finley, recently stole some nanobots from the SSS. They had intended to use these to disable an ADN antenna in orbit as a way of sabotaging the GF's asteroid destruction operation being planned for early next year, when Bete Noire is expected to hit the earth.'

'But surely this has been prevented.'

'The nanobots have been removed and Ms Hanson's brother Damien, whose skills as a scoopship pilot they had intended to use, has, as you know, recently escaped being initiated into the SSS. But we are now aware that they have this global R&D organisation and it is only a matter of time before they come up with some equally nihilistic technology.'

'So we are talking about long term prevention.'

'Exactly.' They both finished their drinks. 'Cadet Reed, are you curious about why you were selected for this team?'

Reflecting on such things was not really in Eric's nature. He was happy to accept that he had certain abilities and characteristics which made him useful to the KOP but had not really thought about why he, still a relative novice, had been chosen in preference to many more experienced Knights.

'Is it because of my part in the Ovoskotia operation, sir?'

'Only partly. Although your performance was exemplary it is primarily because you and Cadet Finley do so well as a pair.'

'So he has been selected as well?'

'You joined at the same time as Cadet Finley. You have gone through much of your training together and been friends. Both of you are excellent at cocooning. But more than that. You have complementary attributes which make you particularly effective when working together. Cadet Finley has strong planning ability when confronted with unexpected tactical problems and a surprising maturity of judgement. He has also had experience of Holkham Hall and the SSS because of his mission to plant the QTC transponders in their flour supply. You, on the other hand, have both courage and initiative, and have shown quick thinking during combat. Moreover, you recently saved your friend's life. That can only have strengthened the bond between you.'

Eric felt slightly awkward. All that Knightmaster Franklin had said was true and made sense but he would not be aware of the friction between them over Isla.

In the few seconds of silence they could hear distant gravel being stirred as another member of the team approached the hut. The Knightmaster sat up from the more relaxed posture he had adopted. 'Talking of Cadet Finley I think I can hear him coming now. Which makes our team complete.'

*   *   *   *

As the five Knights stared at the holographic model of Holkham Hall it divided itself into two about a horizontal plane, the upper half sliding away to show the ground floor layout.

'Before I go any further let me name your leader for this mission. I believe you know him as Combat Knight Harry Davies. Today I was able to inform him that he is now officially a Leading Combat Knight.'

There was a general murmur of approval and all seemed happy to accept him as leader of the impoundment.

'We will launch our attack during the plenary session of the conference.' The Knightmaster pointed at the largest room with a twig from a pine branch he had picked up in the forest. 'This is the

Great Hall, close to the main entrance, where it is expected to be held. In all likelihood all four dominos will be present, although Wayne is the only one whose identity and appearance are known. The other three you will have to locate from the sources of the Q-waves once you are inside the building, and given that the place will be crowded that won't be easy. Now to back track. How do you get inside? Any guesses?'

No one answered, although several had ideas. It was clear he was going to pick someone out but such was the underlying kindness emanating from him nobody felt threatened. 'How about one of our cadets?'

Roscoe was fairly sure he knew the answer and having already completed the flour implantation at Holkham it only seemed natural for him to point out what most already knew. 'Sir, there are two open courtyards surrounded by state rooms, one of which is near the Great Hall.' He got up and pointed to them. 'Stealthpods could land in the larger courtyard with their invisibility shields on. This would be a way of getting close to the conference delegates.'

'Agreed. Thank you Cadet Finley. It will also be necessary to create a diversion because the invisibility shields are not perfect, as you know. This should not be a problem. How do we get inside?'

Looking at the virtual model of the building with its ground floor exposed there appeared to be only one door from the large courtyard into the building and it was possible this would be watched. Moreover, it led into the Great Drawing Room and would require an invading party to go through this and another large room now being used as a convening centre, as well as a corridor into the Great Hall where the conference delegates would be sitting, including the four dominos.

'I suspect nobody wants to say because it seems too obvious. It would not, I think you will agree, be wise to take the circuitous route from the courtyard via the main door to the Great Hall. And I'm glad to say we have an alternative route available thanks to a new piece of technology from the KOP labs in Shanghai. Basically, it involves silently, and almost instantaneously, making a hole in the brick wall close to the Great Hall entrance. A pity to damage such a splendid piece of architecture but I'm sure the Coke family who had it built would have forgiven us. The wall can be repaired in any case.'

Eric put up his hand. 'Sir, is there a name for this device?'

'Not yet. I'm sure the lab would be open to suggestions.'

The Knightmaster then made some hand signals which caused a red pathway to be displayed in the model. 'I have broadly defined your access into the building but nearer to the actual date Leading CK Davies, who I know would prefer to be known as Harry from now on, will be conducting a more detailed briefing and discussing contingency plans. That applies to the whole of the operation, not just this stage, but all the important stages: locating the dominos, immobilising them without injury and then getting them into the stealthpod without being prevented by SSS members.'

Ryder raised his hand. 'Sir, do you have any more information on Pastor Wayne? How did he come to start the SSS?'

'Very little is known about Wayne. He is good at secrecy. All we have found is that he started as a banker in London's financial centre, became aware of man's sinful nature and formed the idea that we did not deserve to survive as a species. Naturally, being a domino, he took it upon himself to ensure that humankind got its just dessert; and of course, as a domino, he would enjoy the exertion of power over others that this would entail. If you do manage to impound him, and if Valles Marineris monastery does manage a successful Enlightenment, he could be a big asset to the Knights. But that's assuming a great deal.'

Roscoe was puzzled about how they would actually locate the dominos after the Knights had entered Holkham Hall from the courtyard. It was a big building. All a QTC signal would tell them was the direction to go; it would not tell them in which room the source was located. Was this somehow obvious to the others or had they been told and he had not taken it in? Either way he would feel foolish asking such a question.

Then Eric stuck up his hand and raised this very point.

'A good question, Cadet Reed. The answer is that a dronepod will land in the second, smaller courtyard and this will also monitor the direction but from a different position. Where the two directions intersect will be the *approximate* position of the signal source, that is, our domino. You will have a plan of the building on your flexcom display and it will show where each domino is located.'

Hull also had a question. 'How accurate will the fixes be?'

'To within a few square metres.'

'There could be several delegates standing or moving in that area. How will we identify the domino or dominos among them?'

'Not straight-forward by any means, I agree. But I'm sure methods can be worked out based on the behavioural characteristics of dominos in confused situations.'

Davies interrupted supportively. 'And we can certainly guarantee it will be confused.'

The Knightmaster looked round the table to see if there were any more questions. 'That's all for now. Harry will be working out tactics with you in more detail over the next couple of weeks as we approach the mission date. I'm assuming you are all unreservedly behind this attack, one which could be highly dangerous, because Wayne can be violent and unpredictable. If not, and you would rather not participate, please say so now. It is essential that everyone be fully motivated. It would in no way prejudice your career if you decided to withdraw.'

Davies felt an ironic twinge. It was, of course, not quite true that nobody's career would be prejudiced by backing out of the most important KOP raid to date. It depended on how you looked at it. If you compared your career with what it could have been had you not disengaged you probably would be worse off. But refusing to take part would not make it worse than if you had not been offered the mission at all.

'Anyway, you have twenty four hours to decide. And I can now tell you the attack date – which turns out to be the autumn equinox, September twenty first, when day and night are of equal length.

Why the SSS chose that day for their plenary session will have to remain a mystery. Perhaps it is just a coincidence, if there really is such a thing.'

'Finally, I need hardly remind you that secrecy in advance of a Knight raid is even more important than it was for the military battles of the past. Since we cannot use violence surprise is our most powerful weapon.'

The Knightmaster looked around the table and decided it was time to bring the briefing to a close

CHAPTER 20

DEBRIS

The harshly brilliant sunlight illuminated one half of the orbiting scooper ship, leaving the rest in hard, absolute blackness. The full globe of the earth rotated below with imperceptible motion, like the hour hand of a clock, resplendent with its blue ocean, whirls, streaks and wisps of white cloud tantalisingly revealing glimpses of variously coloured land and the white polar caps of ice at the poles. And in all directions other than the earth or the sun the densely packed firmament of steadily shining stars, incomparable in majesty with the brightest night sky seen from any desert.

This cosmic panorama, were it being observed, would have stirred the soul. But the pilot of the scooper had only a few small darkened portholes through which to view the universe and he was preoccupied in any case with the task in hand. Much of the time he was glued to holodisplays and data readouts as he manipulated small levers and signalled with his hands to the visual input sensors.

That he was a fine pilot and engineer had been obvious to all since early on in his apprenticeship with Orbital Technologies. Had he stayed with the company he would have been destined to a rapidly advancing career; but there was in him a need for independence that outweighed the allurement of promotion within a corporate hierarchy. So instead of paying for Life Extension he used the money that the Global Federation Trust had accumulated on his behalf since birth to buy a second-hand scooper ship and set up his own one man enterprise offering the removal of space debris which might endanger craft launched into whatever orbit the client had chosen. Alternatively, the client could pay a smaller fee to obtain a report on exactly what discarded equipment or defunct satellites or abandoned space vehicles or products of explosions threatened any future artifice or captured meteoroid in a given orbit.

It had not taken long to accumulate enough money for Life Extension treatment. Not that he was sure he wanted this. It involved making pledges to observe certain moral codes which would curb his life style. What would he do with the time? He was not interested in exploration or discovery and would be quite happy with a short hedonistic life. Curiosity did not feature except where it was needed to solve some practical problem. What would he do with three hundred years of life?

His lack of curiosity extended to the job he was now doing. As long as he got the money and did what he was being paid for he was happy, although in this case the work was rather different.

The holodisplay showed a small piece of rock, irregular in shape and rotating slowly. It grew perceptibly as the scooper closed in. He guessed it was a meteoroid which had been captured by the earth's gravity. It could have stayed in orbit for a decade or for millions of years or even much longer. He did not really care. All he knew was that he had to scoop it up like any other piece of space junk.

He sent out the grabber arm from a recess in the ship and deployed the petals of the clutcher, which took hold of the rock and pulled it into the junk box under his control. After releasing the tethers which had kept him from drifting around the cabin he carefully floated towards the launcher bay and planted a small artifice into the ejector tube. It had been given to him by the client but what it was for he had no idea except that it was supposed to be part of some experiment. He had not even asked this much; the client, which called itself 'Near Space Environment Research', had volunteered this limited information. More importantly, as far as he was concerned, they had paid in advance.

It was similar in size to the meteoroid but was in the form of a cone with four protruding microthrusters and a small antenna. Once he was back in his seat and secured against drifting he hand signalled the launch command to the visual sensor and watched the cone slowly propel itself away from the launch tube. It was obviously highly stable and must have a gyro spinning inside so that the microthrusters could be controlled and directed in relation to a frame of reference.

All seemed to be working well and he congratulated himself on having got such a large payment in advance. He thought of the highly sexed girls in the brothel near his base on the outskirts of Kuala Lumpur, just outside of Global Federation jurisdiction, and decided it was time to return to earth; so he set the coordinates of the earth-to-orbit elevator terminal and waited for the scooper ship to guide itself inexorably towards its docking bay.

CHAPTER 21

QUADRANGLE

The need to practise for the Holkham Hall raid had become urgent. They were due to attack in only two weeks and the details of the operation had been finalised and imparted to the Knights only in the last two days.

Standing in the forest clearing which had been made next to Knightmaster Franklin's hut, Roscoe adjusted his smartsuit to a black tunic and trousers. Eric had set his attire to that of an SSS delegate, a suit with a roll necked sweater, and held a mock but heavy and lethal looking generic machine gun simulator. Earlier they had already had exercises with mock hand guns and in fact small firearms were more likely than machine guns or rifles to be used by a dominophile trying to resist impoundment.

'Eric, I'm going to use the hologen this time, rather than the blinder hood. The hologen is more versatile and much less obtrusive than a hood. We've got to carry our kit through the conference hall and the hood would be much more visible than the hologen unit.'

'You could be right. It will be tricky enough concealing the baton and we can't cocoon a domino without it.'

'Ready?'

Without further warning Eric picked up the mock weapon and rapidly shouldered it into firing position. Roscoe sensed this almost instantly, ducking behind Eric before he could pull the trigger. The movement was so fast it would have been impossible for an onlooker to tell which had come first, the raising of the firearm or Roscoe's evasion. The impression would have been one of simultaneity. Such a speed of reaction had only become possible after his intensive neuronic training programme, something undertaken by all Knights as a routine part of their induction into the Order.

Once behind Eric he with equal speed gripped his neck, knocked the gun to the ground and deployed a phantom replica of Eric from the hologen which then twirled in front of him while Roscoe wielded and manoeuvred his baton to eject the cocoon which spun a web to entrap and encase Eric, so that he was immobilised in seconds.

'Why did you use the hologen? Was it necessary?'

'No, not in this situation. But if there are SSS onlookers, and this is likely to be the case in practice, the more confusion and surprise we can generate the better.' There was a hint of indignation in his voice, as though he almost resented the implication that he was employing redundant tactics and unnecessarily using a technical device. He felt ashamed that he had allowed his voice to be modulated by such a petty emotion. It was standard practice to question one's colleague in training and one of the most important aspects of learning.

'OK, I get the point, Ros. Now can you get this stuff off me?'

Roscoe sliced through bunches of web strands with a laser knife. 'Sorry – I shouldn't be so touchy.' He grinned in self mockery. 'It comes with being a perfectionist.'

'Well I think it's your turn to be the domino and mine to be a perfectionist.' They reversed their smartsuit modes to mirror images of each other, so that Roscoe was now the SSS member and Eric was the Knight. Eric picked up the gun, pushed it towards Roscoe and picked up his baton. 'I'm going to close my eyes. Take aim the instant I open them. This will force me to expand my time perception and get behind you into the disabling position before you squeeze the trigger.'

Eric closed his eyes and Roscoe took aim with the gun; but as he did so, almost before then, Eric had managed with rapid precision to grab Roscoe's arm and apply a neurodynamic stimulator bracelet, which had the effect of loosening Roscoe's grip on the revolver and causing it to drop harmlessly to the ground.

The Knightmaster came out of his hut to give them encouragement; then he added, 'One thing I didn't mention at the introductory briefing – this mission is too important to risk failure in completing the main task, that is impounding Wayne and the other dominos, by diverting yourselves into subsidiary actions.'

'What kind of subsidiary action, sir?' asked Eric.

'I was thinking in particular of weapon disposal. There won't be time to deploy weapon digesting nanobots. Even stopping to pick up and carry a gun back to the stealthpod could be a distraction. Wayne has to be taken to a monastery for Enlightenment at all costs.'

'Does that mean restricting the impoundment to Wayne alone if necessary?' asked Roscoe.

'Of course. Wayne is the driving force behind the SSS. Get him to reform and the SSS itself can be considered finished.' He looked sternly at each of them and returned to the hut.

They continued with exercises for another hour, each time with the dominophile firing a different weapon, after which they began to feel tired and decided to sit on the wooden bench which the Knightmaster had erected himself, building it with saw, hammer and nails, using timber he had cut from a pine tree which he had felled from the forest with an axe instead of leaving it to a robojobber. It was the kind of activity which Knightmaster Franklin enjoyed and found conducive to spiritual balance, recommending it to all the novices who came under his supervision.

It was pleasant being able to relax after such intensive activity. They sat quietly enjoying their phials of ClearSpin; but after they had grown accustomed to the absence of physical and nervous stress the friends began to notice a gulf of silence between them – not an easy or even an awkward silence but one that seemed to express the presence of a barrier which had grown gradually over the months, although it had temporarily subsided after the Puma attack in which Eric had probably saved Roscoe's life at considerable risk to his own. Equally apparent to them was the reason for the barrier: Isla.

Eric had initially been unaware of any resentment at how close he and Isla were becoming; but increasingly he could not help noticing how a sadness and lack of spirit had been manifest in Roscoe whenever Isla and Eric were happy together. Ironically, Roscoe, recently having met Amelia, and, despite still feeling attracted to Isla, no longer felt the need to possess or impress her, a need which they both realised was something very different from love. And having experienced the kind of love which Amelia engendered and which he knew she returned he wanted this to be sanctified by an Oath of Bonding which would provide the love and security needed for the nurture of any child they may have. At the same time his obsession and sexual infatuation for Isla was beginning to evolve into something more spiritual.

Roscoe felt he should make the first move to break the awkward silence between them. 'Eric, I went to the Theatre of War in Cambridge recently.'

'So I understand. Anything particular about it?'

'No. Just another water war. But while I was in the town I went to the Graecian.'

'The Graecian?'

'It's a reproduction of an 18th century coffee house. You must have seen it, surely. In the Lion Yard area?'

'Can't say I've noticed it.'

'Well, I'm sure you've seen similar places.'

'Ros, can you come to the point? I don't think you are any more interested in coffee houses than I am.'

Now was his chance to set them onto a course of conversation which could resolve months of tension. 'You're right. It was someone I met in there that interests me. In fact more than interests me.'

'A girl?'

'Amelia. There was an almost instant mutual attraction between us.'

'Mutual? Are you sure?'

'Why is that so surprising? Not every woman is attracted by a man's dancing prowess. There are other qualities they go for.' Roscoe felt himself becoming hot with indignation. But he was not looking for an argument. Quite the reverse.

'Calm down. Of course, Ros, I know that.'

'Sorry. Anyway, there is a strong bond between us – strong enough for an Oath of Bonding.'

'Does she know this?'

'I've not asked yet but I'm as sure as it is possible to be that she would agree if I put it to her.'

Eric immediately saw the implication. 'Yet I thought you wanted to have a relationship with Isla, that you resented her interest in me?'

'So she really is interested in you?'

'Yes. I think so, anyway. I thought that you resented me for it.'

'Was it that obvious? Well, you are right. I did, and totally without justification. But not any more.'

'Because of Amelia?'

'Yes.'

'But you can't suddenly decide you don't love Isla just because you've come across another woman, surely. Do you mean you love them both? I know she still has feelings for you.'

'Yes, but in different ways. Isla still stirs me and had I not been bound by the Knight's Code or had we not both signed the condition for Life Extension and had she felt the same way about me, we probably would have had intercourse by now. There would have been no need for a Bonding Oath. And I still love her as a person. But the way I feel for her does not match my love for Amelia. It seems to me – and of course I can never prove it – that God has been keeping us for each other all this time.' He felt a little foolish. Only a philosopher would have considered it necessary to mention that he could not prove this. What he really meant was that he felt a deep conviction that Amelia reciprocated his love.

'So you intend to bond?'

'If she agrees and is not already bonded to someone else.'

'Does she have Life Extension?'

'Yes and also she's been Enlightened. I know you would think it highly probable that she must already have taken a Bonding Oath. But I don't think so.'

'Ros, hadn't you better find out before you start making plans? Or before I start making plans for that matter. If Amelia is free and agrees to take the Oath with you it would leave me free to bond with Isla.' He would of course be free to bond with her in any case but not without feeling that he was depriving his friend of the woman he loved. Yet Roscoe was now almost encouraging him and Isla to take an Oath of Bonding. But would Isla want this? How would she react to the idea of Roscoe being bound in love to another woman?

There were so many unanswered questions. They had arranged to meet Isla at the Orchard studonium for lunch, only a few minutes away by transpod, and this could be an opportunity to answer some of them. But Roscoe needed to be with Amelia alone.

'Eric, I'm going to flexcom Amelia.'

'What? Not to ask her about whether she's already bonded, surely? That would be a bit abrupt.'

'No. I'm inviting her to lunch with me.'

*   *   *   *

It was a rather dully lit assortment of college buildings beneath a cloudy and intermittently rainy sky that he looked out upon as he sat at an oval table for four in a transparent capsule of the slowly rotating Wheel of Life. It had clouded over since the morning exercise in the sunlit Thetford Forest. Eric, Isla and he had originally planned lunch in the open at the Orchard and this would not have been so pleasant without the late August sunshine. He knew Eric and Isla would not be depending on the weather to enjoy their lunch there without him. Moreover, they would be able to express how they felt about each other and about Roscoe more easily and fully. In particular, Eric might be able to sound out how Isla felt about a Bonding and tell her about Roscoe's new friendship with Amelia. He also agreed to raise the question of a Circle of Kinship and gauge her response.

He imagined Isla would be pleased that he was no longer clinging to her. She would be able to enter into a Bonding with Eric unfettered by the complication of him. But suppose Amelia did not want to go any further with him? Would he still want to forgo a Bonding with Isla and be left without a relationship with either woman?

Looking down at the main street he saw a girl on a bicycle pulling up outside the restaurant and realised it was Amelia. As she appeared on the other side of the revolving door he wondered whether this lady would indeed be joined to him in bondship, perhaps for three centuries, probably bearing children.

To his astonishment she walked straight up to him and as he stood up to greet her she rested her head on his shoulder and clasped her arms around him. That she did indeed reciprocate his love was no longer in doubt. What was difficult to believe was how quickly it had all happened. He stroked her long black hair tenderly. Then she drew back and sat at a chair opposite the one to which he now slowly returned.

They forgot all about the business of eating and just talked about what they had been doing until they suddenly realised how much time had passed. Looking at the menu displays built into the tabletop they each touched a small image of a pasta cone packed with noodles and protoveg globes, which immediately blinked to indicate that the order was being processed.

He felt no need to delay coming to the point. 'Amelia, I want you to know that I'm not in a Bonding. Are you?'

She smiled enigmatically. 'I've been waiting for the right person.'

He looked concerned and troubled. Had he after all been wrong in his conviction about Amelia?

Then he glowed and relaxed as she followed up her reply. 'God has brought us together.'

'So can we take the Oath of Bonding?'

Amelia, although certain about Roscoe, was not sure at this stage what an Oath of Bonding would entail. Nor was he. They searched the telepres site of the Monastery of Divine Light. First they would have to take a provisional Oath, known as an engagement. Then there would have to be a three month period of celibacy to prove that their love was not merely carnal before taking the final Oath, so that they could be as sure as possible that the Bonding would endure for the statutory minimum of three years in which no child was conceived. If their union produced a child they would be bound to each other until it reached the age of thirty years, after which they would have to decide whether to terminate the Bond or renew it.

Roscoe thought about the coming impoundment mission. It was due to take place in only two weeks and he was sworn to secrecy. Neither he nor Amelia wanted to arrange a Bonding consultation and a preliminary Oath without finding out a lot more about each other and preparing themselves mentally and spiritually.

Holkham Hall would demand his full attention and yet there was so much that needed to be considered. How would Isla react when she discovered his love for Amelia? Could it be that she was more attracted to him than he thought? He did not want to cause her any distress. Then there was the possibility of Eric, Isla, Amelia and himself forming a Circle of Kinship. He was considering talking this over with Father James. Maybe all five of them should meet and discuss it together.

But before any of this they needed to find out more about each other.

*   *   *   *

Beneath them was the green rectangular expanse of Hyde Park near the centre of Londonium, the largest metropolis in Englandia. In the distance they could see the sky plazas of Oxford Street projecting far above the surrounding buildings. The aptly named Serpentine lake was prominent, running vaguely north west through the middle of the park. At the south eastern end of the lake was a towering cylinder and the transpod gently homed down towards a temporary parking bay, one of many arranged radially around its axis, and with a gentle clunk docked into a robotic grabber claw which then placed the transpod in a permanent bay high up on one side of the tower.

They sat in the cabin of the parked transpod and held hands for a while, filling each other with their life force. Amelia smiled, asking what they were going to do next.

'Have you been to Londonium?'

'Not since it was London; and then only once and I was a child then.'

'Then I think Oxford Street is the place for us.'

They climbed out of the cabin and stepped towards the exit door. There were two moving spiral escalators behind the door and they got into the one descending. Emerging onto the close-cut clover which covered much of the park they walked alongside the north bank of the Serpentine, holding hands again. He asked her where she was born, where she grew up.

'Burnham Thorpe. I was born there. I was educated locally until entering Emmanuel College.'

He fell silent for a while, unable to respond. He had not intended to tell her about Isla until later but now he had no choice but to mention it. Not to do so would seem evasive in retrospect. 'This is an incredible coincidence. I know someone else in Cambridge, a mathematician, about the same age as you, who lived in Burnham Thorpe before going to King's College.' He could not at this stage bring himself to divulge the gender of this 'someone else'.

'Tell me the name and I'll see if it means anything to me.'

He steeled himself and decided to make as light of it as possible, although he was almost certain that she would be able to tell from his manner, facial expression and mode of voice that the person in question was not entirely a matter of romantic indifference to him. Nor would it be to her. 'Hanson, Ms Isla Hanson.'

The gentle grip of her hand suddenly relaxed and her face flushed. 'She won a prize in mathematics and was evidently attractive to the final year male pupils. Did you, do you, know her well?'

'In a sense.'

'What sense?' Her hand disengaged.

'We need to turn right and make our way across the clover lawn to Marble Arch, which you can see from here. It's at the end of Oxford Street. Unless you would like to walk along the lake a bit further.'

She seemed slightly irritated. Why did he always irritate any girl he had an interest in? 'It's up to you. I don't really care.'

'Amelia, I need to be as open with you as possible. Please don't misunderstand me. Isla is beautiful and clever, and I could not help liking her. I still do, even after meeting you.'

'And how did you meet her?'

'She was doing some admin work at the KOP selection centre. We've known each other for several months but there has never been any question in her mind of forming a Bond.'

'And in your mind, Ros. Did you want to form a Bond with her?'

Amelia had seemed so self-possessed, calm and understanding. Now she gave the impression of being as jealous and possessive as he had been towards Isla. Yet it was somehow different, as though these negative emotions were more superficial than those he had felt as he watched Eric and Isla growing closer together. 'I thought I did at one stage. But she recognised and so did I that I was infatuated and possessive.'

They stopped and looked at each other. Her eyes filled with tears.

'There was no real mutual love between us. What I feel for you is real, both gender based and transcendental. And I hope, no, I believe with all my heart, that you feel the same for me.' He reached for her hand but she declined to accept it. However, she appeared to grow less distressed and walked beside him in silence across the clover grass towards Marble Arch.

As they reached the Marble Arch monument they could see Oxford Street stretching before them into the distance, like a verdant canyon draped and covered in a rich tapestry of teeming life. It was a spectacle that never failed to startle him and he was pleased to sense the wonder in Amelia as she beheld it for the first time, despite her earlier distress. He too was healed by the sight, despite having seen it several times.

The sides of the canyon had previously been walls of concrete, plastic, brick and glass but these materials had been coated in vivofilm, a newly invented substance which when applied in layers prevented erosion or weathering of any kind and at the same time drained away any excess water from the layer of rich, nitrogenated humus sprayed onto the walls to support and nourish a rich variety of plants, ranging from the ornamental to the edible: flowers, shrubs, vegetable plants, fruit bushes and fruit trees of bewildering variety covered what had been arid towers of commerce. And what had been a street choked with automobiles only three decades ago was now a thoroughfare of life thriving in the fresh air.

Moving further along the street they encountered stalls selling fruit, flowers and vegetables grown locally on the vertical gardens either side and in the roof gardens above.

Amelia gazed around her. 'I had not realised there was such a place in Londonium. Or anywhere else for that matter.'

'There aren't many roads like this but I've heard that more are planned. Other cities are copying the idea. The Monastery of Divine Light conceived of them a few years ago and now the Global Federation funds their development.'

'I've heard the expression "the new face of the metropolis" recently. I suppose this must be it.' She was looking much happier now and he marvelled at her gracefulness of movement as she walked beside him.

Roscoe looked at her knowingly. 'It gets better.'

The stalls selling garden produce now gave way to a plethora of kiosks, platforms and tents with small individually sculpted buildings interspersed among them. There were also more stalls, this time displaying jewellery, hand crafted ornaments, musical instruments, books and antiques. Overall there was an impression of seething activity.

He noticed that one stall sold various string instruments and remembered that Amelia was studying music. 'Is your music course geared to any particular instrument?'

'Yes. The violin.'

'Look at these. I'm no expert but they seem exquisitely crafted.' They examined them more carefully under the friendly eye of the old man who looked after the stall. Some of the violins were made in Londonium but most seemed to have originated in Japan. Amelia focused on one from Tokyo and asked the stall holder if she could try it out. He cheerfully gave her a bow. She thanked him, smiling, then tucked the instrument under her chin and as she drew the bow across its strings a heavenly sound filled the space around her. Roscoe recognised the music. She carried on playing for several minutes and passers by began to gather around, some of them obviously entranced.

'Is it the Telemann concerto for trumpet and strings in C major?' he asked when she had topped playing.

'Yes. Well done. Not many people know the piece.'

'It is one of my favourites. Who adapted it for solo violin?'

'No one. I improvised.'

Roscoe gently placed one hand on her shoulder and held her slender arm with the other. 'Do you like this violin enough to let me buy it for you?' He knew it was expensive but it was affordable. He had already accumulated money from his pay as a Cadet Knight. Not that the pay was high but his tastes and interests hardly ever involved spending much.

She placed the violin back on the display stand and they moved around to the other side of the stall, out of sight of the old man. As Roscoe expected she put up a resistance. 'I already have a violin of course. And this one is rather expensive. Can you really afford it?'

'I know you like this instrument a lot and please, Amelia, let me buy it for you. I want to hear and watch you play it often. It would give me so much pleasure every time. And yes, I can afford it. A Cadet Knight is not so badly paid and my spending habits are modest.' He put as much insistence into his voice as he could muster without sounding desperate not to be disappointed by her refusal.

'I've always wanted a violin made in Tokyo.' She looked back towards the stand on which the violin was hanging. 'It has become famous for the making of string instruments just as it had for the playing of them by virtuosos since the Suzuki method of teaching the violin was proved so successful a century ago. And this one has a feel like no other I've tried. But...'

'Please. Let me give it to you.'

He walked up to the stall holder with resolve and signalled his wish to buy it before she could resist him further. The old man put it lovingly in a case with the bow and when Roscoe handed the case over to her the bond between them was restored almost to the intensity it had reached before their argument in Hyde Park.

They moved further along Oxford Street, past kiosks where craftsmen and artists demonstrated their proficiency in painting, drawing, sculpture, carving, engraving, woodwork, jewellery, knitting, needlework, crochet and lace making and past platforms on which entertainers did acrobatics, danced, juggled or told jokes. They strolled through tents in which fossils, rocks, archaeological finds and antiques were sold by recognised specialists without profit in mind, keen to explain their diverse wares and put them in context. Smaller tents housed spiritual counsellors willing to advise without payment on life decisions and how to relate more closely to God within different religions as well as Divine Light sages showing how different religions and cultures were all manifestations of God's eternal and ongoing Creation. They passed through the sculpted buildings, some of them museums with expert guidance on hand, both human and virtual; others were knowledge emporiums in which you could receive personal tuition and a study plan for almost any subject you could conceive in any field of human endeavour. There were large spheres and domes labelled with the names of different moons and planets. Inside these you could be fitted with sensors and experience other worlds in true virtual reality and interact with them through touch and sound as well as vision.

Roscoe was pleased and relieved to see that Amelia was impressed and obviously appreciated the wonder of it but was also concerned that, like him, she was beginning to feel fatigued by the competing demands on their attention as they walked through such a cornucopia of impressions and possibilities. 'How do you feel about all this?'

She smiled and quietly slipped her hand into his. 'It is more than I could have imagined.'

'There is so much to see but why don't we go inside the next place of interest we come across and experience it in more depth? Then we could have a rest and some refreshment in a sky plaza.'

'I'd like that.'

This plan did not quite materialise since the next building was a Knights of Peace recruitment centre. 'Not quite what I had in mind and I assume that goes for you,' he said and she concurred. They walked quickly past it towards a sculpted building with the name 'Temple of Cleansing and Recycling' displayed prominently outside.

Inside it was quiet and dimly lit. A small number of seats formed a circle near one end of an oval room. After being seated for a short while an authoritative sounding female voice permeated the room:

> *Our planet is a precious gift from the Creator. As God's appointed stewards of the ecosphere we must correct the sins of waste committed by our fathers and mothers.*

The room then appeared to fill with motion holograms of robot scavenger ships ploughing through large fields of floating and partly submerged garbage inherited from the waste generating economies that had predominated up to about 2015 AD. Most of it was plastic in every conceivable form: bottles, bags, cases, polystyrene foam, electrical insulation, wrappings, packaging and condoms.

> *Fortunately, the ocean currents have swept the garbage into known gyrating expanses of the Pacific and other oceans, so that roboscavengers can systematically draw in the waste and take it to the fusion powered incinerator and biodegradation plants at various points on the coast. This particular gyre was known colloquially in the early part of the century as the*

Great Pacific Garbage Patch and it reached an area
comparable in size to Africa.

The presentation then moved on to show the giant engineering
feats involved in the disposal of sewage and its conversion into
rich but disease-free fertiliser and compost as well as city drainage
systems. Scoopships collecting orbital debris or pushing it into
re-entry orbits which would cause it to burn up were also shown.
And the presentation ended with a prayer:

> *Lord our Creator and source of all being, all love and*
> *all truth, thank you for blessing our ancestors with*
> *the wisdom to abandon their wastefulness and create*
> *a new, sustainable world. Praise be to Almighty God.*
> *Amen.*

After the prayer they left the Temple and moved out into the
bright street. The entrance to a sky plaza was nearby and they
walked towards this. The door to the spiral escalator opened
automatically.

Amelia looked around and above her through the transparent
housing of the escalator 'How high do these go?'

'Something like a thousand metres. Those patches of cloud are
quite low and we should be above them; but they are very patchy
so they won't spoil the view.'

Emerging from the escalator tube at the top they moved into
a verdant terraced garden, partially hidden by a wisp of cloud.
A flower-strewn terrace of Tudor brick surrounded a close cut

lawn with a central pool and fountain with benches arranged around it. They were feeling slightly tired and found the garden so refreshing that they instinctively, as one, decided to rest. 'Shall we sit here for a while or go on to the viewing platform?'

'I like it here. The sound of water falling onto water is so life giving.'

'It makes me think of the water of life.'

'Christ said "whosoever drinketh of the water I shall give him shall never thirst but the water I shall give him shall be a well of water springing up into eternal life." He had just asked the Samarian woman to give him water from the well.'

'You've not told me much about yourself.'

'There was a reason I reacted so strongly when you mentioned Isla.'

'It was understandable. Anyway, I'm glad you care that much about my relationship to her – if you can call it a relationship and I don't think she would.'

'I first came into contact with Isla without realising it. We were christened in the same church in Burnham Thorpe. I didn't realise until my mother told me. When we were younger we were sometimes even in the same class at school but even then we never really came into contact and her name only stuck in my mind because of the maths prize she was awarded on Prize Day and because her beauty was sometimes remarked upon in playground chatter.' She stopped talking and became thoughtful.

'But you said there was a particular reason you reacted strongly.'

'It was Isla and I being baptised together and her coming into my life again while being part of your life. I feel it is not coincidence. I feel it is destiny and that the lives of all three of us are destined to be intertwined.'

'I have discussed destiny with someone you may have heard of: Father James.' He felt embarrassed in mentioning this name, as though he was claiming to be privileged and special.

'Really? That's incredible. How did you meet?'

'My father was in the same band, Baroqo, when he had his Divine Light epiphany.'

'Baroqo? I used to watch holorecordings of their concerts in the 2040s. So your father is Paul Finley!'

'That's right. Father James occasionally calls on our family but although my mother believes in the Divine Light and is a Christian my father remains a confirmed Atheist.'

'So what did Father James say about destiny?'

'He said he didn't know and that we are not meant to know. All he could be sure of was that there is some unfathomable pattern to events, that our lives do play a role in an unfolding scheme that encompasses the entire universe, which is evolving in some purposeful way.'

'And do you think he would agree that just now and then we get glimpses of this.'

'Not glimpses of the scheme itself. Only the Creator can perceive this. But occasionally things happen which show us that a pattern exists, that the universe is not a series of random events.'

'So do you think Isla is supposed to be part of our lives?'

'Father James would say we cannot know at an intellectual level. But if we seek communion with our Creator and receive Enlightenment we can sense whether certain juxtapositions of events have significance for us.'

'Do you want Isla to be part of our lives together?'

'There is a way. Have you heard of the Circle of Kinship?'

'Yes. I believe it is a new kind of extended family for those who have chosen Life Extension, meant to supersede the nuclear family.'

'One of my fellow Knights, Eric Reed, is a good friend. He met Isla shortly after me and from the start it was clear that they were mutually attracted. The more I think about it the more I feel they are meant to form an Oath. So if they do take the Oath, and if you and I also take the Oath, it would be possible for the four of us to make a Circle of Kinship.'

'Ros, that leaves a lot of questions unanswered. Like whether Isla feels the way you think she does about your friend – and about you for that matter. We need to meet together, maybe after the KOP mission you said was coming up – when was it, in two weeks?'

'Yes. That would be a good idea.' He was immensely relieved and his mind now felt at least temporarily released from these personal matters of the heart, so he would be able to concentrate solely on the Holkham Hall mission.·

A granilite path wound through the garden towards some stone steps which ascended the Tudor terrace. Above the terrace another path led to a panorama platform. Feeling refreshed they decided to follow the paths and view the whole of Londonium before making their way back through Oxford Street to the transpod and returning to Cambridge.

*   *   *   *

Being on time was something he prided himself on, despite his outward calmness when on a mission. Besides, it was often his job to be precisely on time: so many missions depended on people being at a particular point at a particular moment. He would have to walk a little faster although this was not a conscious decision. Officially he was at leisure and not on duty but his body somehow conspired to control his walking speed for punctuality without his higher self being aware.

The river Cam on his right did not interest him in any way. A passer by might have mistaken him for a scholar or academic, such was his attire and pre-occupied demeanour. In fact that was his default mode when not on duty as a Knight. He had always considered that one day he would take a long leave of absence from the Order and spend a decade or so pursuing one of his academic interests: the study of emergent systems and their role in guided evolution. Yet today he was focused on trying to plan for the most critical operation of his career in terms of its historical consequences, rather than solve any academic problems.

His attire was chosen digitally from his smartsuit wardrobe display. There were so many complete designs to choose from together with limitless permutations of garb it would be easy to spend more time getting dressed than in the days when this was a purely manual procedure. In his case it took only a few seconds because he selected from just a few standard outfits, including his Knight's uniforms. More often than not when off duty he chose a roll necked black pullover and grey trousers.

Leading Combat Knight Harry Davies had his faults but vanity was not one of them. In fact for a Knight who had not been Enlightened, and most Knights of fifty five had been, he had remarkably few faults, having imbued the ethics and moral code of the Order without the need to go through such a spiritual transformation. Some day, perhaps, he would. But for now, and, as one who had received Life Extension, he had plenty of time; he would spend his leisure as an amateur scholar, play the flute and have occasional casual relationships with women. He believed in one Creator but had not decided on the best way to relate to it. Buddhism and Islam had their attractions even though he was brought up in a western culture; but he felt he had not properly understood Christianity yet. Unless he died in action he had another two hundred and fifty years to sort this out. Meanwhile, when he wanted to pray, he would pray simply to God.

One of Harry's attributes was both a fault and a virtue, depending on context; but on balance it was more a virtue than a fault. He had a strong inclination to break the rules or depart from convention where he could see that more good than harm would come out of it.

There were unwritten rules and conventions in scholarship and fortunately, as an amateur, he was able to ignore the one which said you must not risk appearing foolish by proposing something which might make a lot of others look foolish. He had felt that certain deductions had been made in the field of evolutionary biology which were *non sequitur* but which were so widely accepted that the whole discipline was proceeding up a blind alley. So this was one convention he could happily override.

Harry's need to innovate was less easily accommodated in his professional life as a Knight. So often he would see a way of solving a problem which entailed breaking a rule; but at the same time he was well aware that for most situations the rule worked and allowed the Knights of Peace to operate smoothly.

He had discussed the Holkham Hall mission with Knightmaster Franklin repeatedly and the plan for impounding Pastor Wayne and the three other dominos they had hatched largely between them seemed good. Yet there was, he felt, room for improvement. This might be a case for breaking the rules.

*   *   *   *

It was not an ideal afternoon for drinking ClearSpin outside the Orchard studonium. It was cloudy and the wind periodically blew dust into their faces; but this was where they had agreed to meet Harry.

Eric put the glasses on the table and looked around him. 'Why do you think he wants to see us here, alone?'

'He has a reputation for being slightly eccentric. Some call him the Pied Piper because he sometimes plays his flute on missions, although not to lure rats, like the one in the fairy tale.'

'What does he lure then?'

'Not necessarily anything but on the Tripsina job I had to let some rats out of a cage in a busy street while he diverted the passers by with a tune.'

'Rats?'

'They excrete into explosives and there are explosive neutralising bacteria in the excreta.'

'Enough said.' Eric looked at his flexcom clock. 'He should be here in the next minute or so. Can you see him? I heard he likes surprises but how can that be if he is supposed to be so punctual?'

'Maybe because that in itself is a surprise.'

'Like this is a surprise.' A voice came from behind them as they stared out in the direction of the Cam and standing there holding a glass of ClearSpin was Leading Combat Knight Harry Davies, on time to within a few seconds. He must have gone into the studonium by another door and come out through the one behind them. He sat down, taking a sip from his glass, and Roscoe thought he saw a trace of embarrassment at what might be regarded as the childishness of surprising them in this way. 'Just my way of reminding you to expect the unexpected.'

'Only a week to go, Harry,' said Eric, to break the silence.

'When it gets this close it begins to concentrate the mind. I wanted to meet you both here off KOP premises because I want to arrange something that isn't strictly within the rules.'

It was what they had half expected and they knew they would have to agree unless it was something more important than the mission itself, and that was unlikely. Besides it was well known that Harry Davies could get away with transgressions like no one else and it was probably his ability to innovate that had caused him to be promoted to LCK at the age of only fifty five.

'If you had to sum up the tactics of the Knights in one word what would that be?'

They had been so involved in the details of the coming impoundment sweep that it was difficult to generalise. Eric ventured 'surprise.'

'You've got it. And there are two ways to achieve this: speed and confusion – confusion for our opponents that is. One way to confuse the SSS would be to depart from some well known practice of the KOP.'

Roscoe wondered whether Harry was going to go so far as to advocate resorting to violence. If so, he felt this would be too much of a price to pay. It would undermine the whole ethos and rationale of the Knights. 'What do you have in mind, Harry?'

'Don't worry. I've no intention of violating the non-violence code.'

Eric and Roscoe looked visibly relieved and Harry could not help being amused as well as slightly aggrieved that they would think him capable of such a desperate, and in a sense sacrilegious, measure. He quickly followed on: 'But some rules are more important than others. For instance, excluding females from missions is only a temporary expedient. The military forces of the past have had practical problems with mixed fighting units – problems of jealousy, hormonal stimulation, interference with concentration etc. etc. The Knightmaster assures me that one day there will be all female units and even, in special cases, mixed gender teams for special operations.'

Roscoe remembered Father James referring to this. 'I understand it's just a matter of working out the details. The Monastery has Hermit Sages communing with God in order to cultivate the wisdom required. They need to anticipate the problems and draft the rules accordingly.'

'You obviously know more about this than I do. Anyway, we don't have time to wait.'

They both looked puzzled. 'How do you mean?'

'We need a female on this team to help create a diversion and a distraction.' Davies looked at them alternately. 'I believe you have a female mutual friend. Is that so?'

'You mean Ms Isla Hanson?'

'I saw her at the ball before the Ovoskotia operation. She seems to have a natural talent. Can she dance solo?'

Eric responded at once. 'Yes. She's as good at that as she is at maths.'

Roscoe absently added an observation. 'In fact the mathematics seems to come out in her dancing the way it often comes out in musicians.'

'Now the Servants of the Seven Seals has some rather unusual bods in it - or rather they become unusual once they are in it. But I'm willing to bet that the sight of a gifted beautiful lady dancing on a stage would stir them and distract them as much as it would most males.' He looked at them to see if he had made his point. 'Imagine. If she could dance at the conference in the Marble Hall, unannounced at the end of one of the presentations and totally unknown to all present, that would create a lot of confusion.'

Eric interjected. 'But is that necessary Harry? Why can't we use a holofig?'

'We will of course be making good use of these but they do have their limitations. They only look real until you try to touch them or until you see one encounter a solid object. Like ghosts.'

'But the holofig would only need to dance in front of the audience.'

'Its steps and movements would be stilted and it would make no sound. Eric, it just wouldn't look real. Holofigs will be used a lot but we need to have some real people to serve as diversions.'

Eric protested. 'But she would need music.'

'Ideally, yes. And I'm coming to that. Do you think Ms Hanson would be willing to join us?'

Eric and Roscoe looked doubtful. Neither wanted her exposed to danger; but if she knew she had had the chance of refusal and that they had not given it to her she would resent this and with justification. 'Do you think these SSS people will be armed?'

'My guess is that Wayne at least will have some means of killing on his person. He is a domino and paranoid. As for the other three, who knows? One of them is a scientist, so probably he won't, but the remaining two could well be secondary leaders, so are more likely to be armed. But there is no reason for Ms Hanson to get caught up in the impoundment. She just needs to use her talents to create a diversion.'

Eric looked at Roscoe for approval before responding. 'Well, you've put the question, so I suppose we'll have to ask her.'

'No. That would be loading too much onto you. I'll ask her. Just give me her coordinates.' He fell silent and appeared to be mulling over something. 'Ideally, she would dance to some music. Do you know anyone who might play an instrument that would add to the distraction of Ms Hanson dancing? Preferably another lady, since most of the audience will be male and more likely to be distracted by a female.'

Eric racked his memory but could think of no females among the many he had known who would fit the role that the Leading Combat Knight had proposed. Roscoe, sadly, knew the ideal lady. And, like all those in the Order, he was intrinsically unable to lie to a fellow Knight.

CHAPTER 22

IMPOUNDMENT

From high over the coast the night vision display revealed a plan view of the Holkham Hall estate a little way inland beyond where the old coast road, now submerged, had run east-west, parallel to the shore.

The reason why Combat Knight Hull was notorious for his neuro-enhanced stealthpod piloting prowess became obvious to all on board. No automatic piloting could compete, even one harnessing the power of quantum computing. Suddenly he swooped the craft down to ground level. The scene changed at a dizzying rate and the g-forces pushed and pulled in all directions as the machine was hurled and steered through the darkness only a metre from the ground or the surface of the lake. After skirting the shore of the lake to the west of the main building he guided them across open parkland to the south and along narrow paths through the woods on the east side faster and more precisely than any robotic system could possibly have managed, then pulled them up vertically the moment the distinctive Palladian form of the Hall loomed in front.

Harry protested. 'Max, is this really necessary? Why can't you take us straight into the courtyard?'

He looked round, slightly affronted. 'I like to warm up, get a feel for the surrounding geography.'

'Well, I wasn't planning to tour the grounds tonight. But I guess you're right. We have to be ready for the unexpected. Anyway, here we are.'

Max put on the refraction shield as they hovered over the roofs of the west wing of the hall, moving slowly towards one of the two central courtyards, each entirely enclosed by walls of the building, before making the final silent, invisible descent to the gravel.

The cabin portholes had been switched to opaque mode so even with the lights on inside the whole form of the stealthpod would be undetectable in the dark. They could safely use the cabin as an operational base. A dronepod had already landed in the other courtyard and was relaying Q-wave and DNA data from QTC nanochips which had been ingested by Wayne and the other three dominos. Similar signals were coming into the stealthpod and from the two sets of signals the position of each domino was computed and projected onto a large cabin display as well as directly into the eyes of the five Knights.

Harry looked analytically at the display. 'So it seems that our friendly would-be destroyer of life on earth is in the Statue Gallery – not at the conference session. He's marked as X1 on the display. So for X1 read Wayne.'

Combat Knight Ian Ryder pointed out that this was not allowed for in the original plan.

'It was assumed that X1 would be in the Marble Hall, which is used as the main auditorium for conferences. So that's our first case of the unexpected. The one we think is the chief scientist, X2, is, this time as expected, chairing the main conference session and is situated in front of the audience, no doubt sitting at a table. The remaining two, X3 and X4, are sitting at the back of the audience. The Knightmaster suspects they are in a quasi-military role reporting directly to Wayne – probably what the SSS call 'Protectors'. Their Q-wave spectra certainly make them dominos and their DNA data match up to two people who were senior military officers until they disappeared from GF monitoring a few years ago. Any suggestions on our first move?'

Eric responded confidently. 'We need to release the spyflies so we can get visual information.'

Combat Knight Ian Ryder added that the spyflies would also gather data on the various modes of dress present and this would be fed into their smartsuit memories. The hologenerators would also quickly build up a library of images on which to construct holofigs with the highest camouflage factor.

'Sure. But then what?'

Silence. Then tentatively Ian volunteered an answer. 'Wayne, X1, is our first priority and he is also isolated from the rest. We should capture him first, while the element of surprise is strongest.'

'Good strategy. But how do we get into the Statue Gallery? The impounder team will first have to go through the State Sitting Room on the other side of the wall near where we are parked – once we've made a breach in it. Then they will have to go through the Marble Hall, then the North Dining Room, then into the Gallery.'

Harry looked around to check they had all understood. 'And anyway, there's another problem. Once we get inside our targets might move. The very first thing we have to do after deploying the spyflies is plant an identifier on each target: the QTC signals will only give us a rough fix at a given time. We need continuous real-time tracking.'

Roscoe had already thought of this and had to overcome a childish egotistical urge to broadcast the fact to all present. However, he was able to take advantage of his foresight by making an immediate suggestion. 'We need to act fast, in case any of the targets moves before we can even place identifiers on them. If, say, X1 moved to certain positions in the Gallery or elsewhere in the house the fixer beams would coincide and we would no longer be sure where he was, making it very difficult to attach identifiers.'

'Hundred per cent. Let's release the spyflies. Fortunately they can find their way into the building without us making a breach in the wall.' He made a hand signal to the video input which released into the night air twelve spyflies from a small module on the hull. They flew off in various directions and found their way into Holkham Hall through crevices and small openings then sped silently and unnoticed through the rooms, chambers, corridors and ventilation shafts. Eight of them deployed themselves throughout the building and relayed to the Knights a general picture of what was going on inside the building. The remaining four flew to positions close to each of the four dominos. Soon they had the information they required to start the mission, including the physical appearance of each target.

'Now we can think about attaching identifiers. This is where some very fast sleight of hand and a bit of musical diversion are needed. Are you ready Max?'

'If you've got your flute ready,' Combat Knight Max Hull replied, almost jovially. He set his smartsuit to the uniform of a conference steward.

'I have indeed. The pied piper strikes again.'

They turned off the lights and opened the stealthpod hatch. Harry, having set his smartsuit to simulate the coloured striped clothing of the medieval legend, stepped out into the darkness wielding a long wind instrument which he called a flute. Max held a rectangular furnace block against the wall of the North State Sitting Room. After applying the block in four adjacent positions the wall crumbled with almost surgical precision to provide a gap for them to walk through single file into the North State Dining Room, which, although brightly lit, was, as expected, totally unoccupied.

Max walked across the room and through a doorway which took him to outside the front of the building, then adopted a confident hurried stride as he re-entered via the Marble Hall. A steward in the reception area saw him only peripherally and did not challenge him. He stood behind the rows of delegates. They faced the speaker standing on a dais which had been erected in front of an impressive flight of steps leading up to the exit. Either side of the conference arena was a balcony with columns reminiscent of a Roman temple. Max stood at the back in a corner and looked carefully in the directions of two of the dominos indicated by the plan projected onto his cornea, the same one that had appeared on the large cabin display.

He recognised two of the dominos sitting in the back row. They had been tagged X3 and X4 on the display and were probably SSS Protectors. Somehow he had to plant identifiers on them and also on X2, the Chief Scientist, who was sitting at the conference chairman's table on the platform in front of the audience. X1, hopefully, was still in the Gallery of Statues but he could not be sure because his cornea image was not in real time and would not be until the identifiers had been planted.

Then there was a sound of pipes playing. The delegates looked around and up, trying to identify where this ethereal sound was coming from, until someone near the front pointed at the left hand balcony, where the pied piper figure was moving forward like a phantom, intermittently obscured by one of the Roman columns. Max noticed that X3 and X4 had got up out of their seats. They were looking serious and stood conversing together. He sidled up behind them with the deftness and expertise of a pickpocket and attached microscopic identifiers to their jackets before moving down the central aisle of the auditorium and up to the Chief Scientist who, not surprisingly, was looking puzzled and somewhat annoyed by this unscheduled turn of events.

'Sorry, sir. We appear to have an intruder. Do you want him removed?'

He replied with ill disguised irritation. 'Of course. Who is he, anyway?'

While in this disturbed state he did not notice Max planting an identifier on his jacket in the small of his back before climbing the steps towards where Harry, alias the pied piper, was now standing. He took hold of Harry and made a show of pleading with him to come quietly. The pair then walked down the steps, through the aisle and out of the main entrance to the building.

Harry quickly made his way back to the stealthpod via the still empty State Sitting Room while Max went back into the conference room, apologised to the Chief Scientist, walked up the step and around to the right hand balcony; then through the North Dining Room into the Gallery of Statues where Wayne should be sitting.

He walked officiously from one end of the Gallery to the other, passing statues and busts of Roman gods, emperors and empresses. Incongruously there was a particularly large statue of Pastor Wayne. This seemed doubly strange to Max, given that Wayne was planning to wipe out civilisation, in which case no-one would be left to witness this monument to his ego. But where was the real Wayne? He had assumed he would be sitting somewhere on the side of the Gallery.

Then Wayne came walking towards him, beckoning for his attention. 'I've just had contact with the conference chairman. He said there's been an intruder. Do you know anything about this?'

This was going to be difficult. He had to get Wayne to turn his back towards him, plant the identifier chip on him and walk away from the encounter without arousing suspicion.

'Yes, sir. A harmless eccentric who somehow got into the Marble Hall balcony. He's well known locally. Calls himself the pied piper of Holkham.'

Wayne gave a disparaging look. 'How did he get past security?'

'I think he must have been hiding somewhere on the premises since before the conference started. I just sent him on his way. He's probably wandering round the grounds playing his flute.'

'Well I'm not pleased. The SSS pays a lot for security.'

'Sorry sir. If you'd like to see him for yourself he might still be visible through the north window – the grounds are illuminated up to some distance from the house.'

Wayne resignedly followed him to the window then peered out: this was Max's chance to attach an identifier to his back. There was of course no sign of Harry. 'Sorry, he seems to have gone further afield – to the lake maybe.'

Max noted a questioning look on Wayne's face and realised why he had been able to create such a dangerous organisation. Not only was his personality hypnotic but he was remarkably awake to lies and deception, perhaps because he excelled at them himself.

'I'll have to go now sir. I'm wanted by the head steward. Will you be staying here? Perhaps there is something we could bring you.'

'Yes. I'll be here for some time. Bring me a glass of caffrosia.'

'Very well, sir.'

Relieved, but also concerned that Wayne was getting suspicious and would be on his guard, he turned away and retraced his route back to the stealthpod.

* * * *

Harry stared at the large display in the cabin. 'All of the targets have been tagged. So now we storm in with all guns blazing – if you'll forgive the metaphor.' He looked at Isla, then Amelia. 'Starting with diversionary dance and music. Is that alright with you, ladies?'

'I don't know about Amelia but I just want to get this over with.'

'I'm ready,' said Amelia, picking up her violin and bow. 'Shall I start with a Bach violin partita?'

'Is that the last one we practised with?'

'It is.' Isla turned towards Harry and gave a theatrical flourish, gently mocking. 'So please lead the way Mr Davies.'

Harry opened the hatch, beckoned them out of the cabin and led them across the courtyard through the slot in the wall and into the deserted but well lit State Sitting Room with its sofas, chairs and portraits. They reached an entrance to the empty balcony above the conference delegates. 'Just move along the balcony – there are no seats– then down the steps in front of the audience, then onto the platform near the steps. Treat it like a stage and start performing. Probably best to wait till this speaker has finished presenting his paper, so it seems like a natural break. It will make the Chief Scientist at least wonder whether its part of the proceedings, for a while anyway. And be more of a distraction, I guess.'

While they were waiting for the speaker to finish Harry sprayed an aerosol into the auditorium. Isla looked puzzled. 'What are you doing?'

'A KOP exclusive. This will disperse itself throughout the Hall in only a couple of minutes. Later, when we project the holofigs, it will be possible to animate them.'

The three of them stood looking down on the conference. Amelia wondered how so many intelligent people could be so wrong-headed, while recollecting that within the Nazi party of the 1930s and 1940s there had been great intellects who had departed equally far from the truth which originates with the source of all being, the Creator. She had discussed this with Roscoe. It had happened during the medieval Crusades and the Islamo-fascism of the early twenty first century. Was there an active force of evil or just an absence of spiritual light which caused such separations from God? Roscoe had said that most of the SSS were unaware of the full implications of Pastor Wayne's doctoring of the book of Revelation and the strange apocalyptic theology which he had constructed.

As the speaker finished answering questions from the audience Isla moved along the balcony and Amelia followed with her violin. It was as though they were in the wings of a theatre and about to go on stage, except that in this case the audience was not expecting entertainment but the presentation of a paper on how chaotic vibrations artificially induced in the planet's crust could be used to trigger earthquakes.

Facing the audience they descended the wide stairs side by side, bolstered with nervous energy. The delegates looked around and at each other, puzzled by the sudden appearance of these two beautiful ladies. Seeing the string instrument and having only recently experienced the surprise visit of the pied paper they anticipated some form of musical entertainment as Isla and Amelia stepped up onto the speaker's platform. The Chief Scientist looked bewildered but resigned himself to listen as Amelia started to play the third section of Bach's Partita Number 3, *Gavotte en Rondeau*.

Roscoe was transfixed as he watched the display in the cabin and listened to the playing, as relayed to the Knights by the spyflies hovering silently and unseen high in the Marble Hall. By what unfathomable, transcendental process had Amelia and Isla chosen this piece for their performance? Eric, too, not an aficionado of classical music, was startled by the choice.

'Ros, did you suggest this piece to them?'

'No. I haven't mentioned or played it to either of them.' For Roscoe it had always been a powerful expression of the harmony and mathematical elegance of nature and the universe, seen and unseen. He had repeatedly played a recording of it from an old vinyl album released in the 1970s to accompany the ancient TV series *Cosmos*, and more than once he had been exasperated by Eric's inability to be moved by it.

He could see that many in the audience were almost as spellbound as he. It was the last choice of music one would expect to be used for dancing. Yet somehow Isla had interpreted and internalised it and here she was expressing it with a graceful elegance in every step, ripple and gyration of her body while Amelia expressed it in the perfection of her playing.

'I have to say, Ros, this music does have something.'

Roscoe was pleased by his friend's belated appreciation of the partita but doubted whether he really liked it for the same reason. More likely it was Isla's erotic gracefulness of movement.

Harry spoke to Ian Ryder. 'You're the expert at generating confusion with holofigs. What have you prepared for us?'

'The Roman column images can be magnified and projected into the aisle and I can get an animated replica of Wayne to weave a path between them - hopping, skipping, walking and somersaulting in turn if you like.'

'Making Wayne look ridiculous certainly appeals to me. Has anyone any views on that?' Harry looked around the cabin. Roscoe and Eric pulled themselves away from the display of dancing as Harry turned down the sound.

'On the other hand it might make it more difficult for the delegates to suspend disbelief. Nevertheless, I think the strange antics would add to the surprise. I'll leave the details to you. But we need to act fast.'

Ian pulled out a small sphere from a pocket in his smartsuit, now in the form of a steward's uniform. There were sliding surfaces on the sphere which he would use to manipulate the illusionary events in the Marble Hall as monitored by the large cabin display and the personal one projected onto his cornea.

In the auditorium the delegates, the chief scientist who was acting as the chairman, the two protectors and the stewards continued to look bewildered, irritated and pleased by this unexpected entertainment while the next scheduled speaker was anxious to present his paper and was concerned that his time slot was being used up. Just as the chief scientist rose from his chair to speak to the stewards a row of solid looking pillars instantly appeared in the aisle. They were replicas of the Roman columns spaced around the balcony except that Combat Knight Ryder had increased their girth and extended them to reach up to the high ceiling of the Hall.

Isla and Amelia continued to perform and some of the audience suspected that in some inexplicable way the sudden materialisation of the pillars must be connected with this performance. Half the audience stood up, looking around in disbelief. Then a life sized image of Pastor Wayne walked sedately down the aisle from the back of the room, weaving between the holofig pillars with dignity until he broke the spell of gravitas by breaking into a gallop. But the gallop was short. He stopped and did a rapid pirouette, so fast his features were blurred. Then he skipped and somersaulted twice and stopped to bow as though expecting applause instead of puzzlement and disbelief.

Roscoe and Eric continued to be spellbound by the performance of Isla and Amelia; but Harry, Ian and Max were waiting for the real X1 to come into the Hall. Harry was looking slightly uncomfortable. 'I would have expected Wayne to call in on the scene by now. Instead he seems to be moving towards the Library.'

The chief scientist got up and the two Protectors, X3 and X4, moved towards the two ladies. Isla noticed them and stopped dancing. 'Amelia! I think they're coming to get us. I know it's only two against two but get ready to run.' They waited a few seconds, pretending to be discussing the next piece of music. 'Wait - I think they're going up the steps.' Soon it was obvious to the Knights in the stealthpod cabin that the Protectors, X3 and X4, had been called by X1 to join him in the library and the ladies continued their contribution to the chaos.

Harry frowned. 'X1, X3 and X4 are going to be difficult to catch. They're all together. Anyway, let's get X2 while we have the chance.'

Ian and Max left the cabin armed with a baton and a hologen. The chief scientist was fairly easy to cocoon and secure, being primarily a man of science rather than action, although like the other three dominos, he was successful at controlling others through intimidation and cunning, subtle though were his methods in dealing with fellow scientists and engineers of high intellect.

'So ...how are we going to separate Wayne from X3 and X4?' posed Harry.

'Can we use a thunderflash?' asked Eric.

'Yes – this is a covert mission. No telepres images to worry about. I hadn't thought this would be necessary but could you let one off in the south end of the Gallery of Statues? The Protectors are bound to investigate. If we are lucky X1 will stay put in the Library and this will give us a chance to impound him there without trouble from the Protectors.'

'Give me the tools, Harry, and I'll do the job.'

Harry slid open a small box from under the oval table and pulled out an explosive device the size of a pencil. 'This makes about as loud a noise as anyone could imagine so put your ear muffs in. There's nothing like a good old fashioned bang to disorient people for a short time, as long as it's unexpected. Just screw by one half turn, any direction, press the button at the end and throw.' He passed it to Eric.

As Eric skirted the Marble Hall via the east balcony he passed Isla and Amelia running back to the stealthpod. Isla told him to be careful since, despite the distractions, some of the delegates had seen the Chief Scientist being cocooned and whisked away. Instead of descending the steps into the conference hall he moved over to the west balcony, ran along it and out a side exit to the Dining Room which adjoined the north end of the Gallery of Statues. He got a flexcom alert from Harry telling him that Isla and Amelia would be doing another performance – this time in the north end of the Gallery.

While waiting Eric released a holofig aerosol. When they arrived they both put on ear muffs as he ran to the middle of the long Gallery and tossed the pencil device towards the south end, which was the end nearest the Library. The sound was painfully loud even through the ear muffs and there was no chance that Wayne and the two Protectors would not be disturbed by it, even though the Library was separated from the Gallery by two adjoining rooms: an Ante-Room and a Dressing Room. And although Wayne was obviously by now well aware that tricks were being used in an attack on the SSS he was unlikely to be able to resist ordering the Protectors to investigate.

Isla and Amelia resumed their performance, the stately melodic violin sounds echoing among the statues and busts. As each Protector emerged into the south end they cautiously made their way northwards, towards the women, keeping themselves intermittently hidden by the Greek and Roman statues. Isla could see that it was time to escape but was hoping for the next diversion to avoid being chased and possibly shot.

The diversion came when the north window behind them shattered and splintered with a metallic blast as the stealthpod nudged its way into the Gallery. Max was at the controls and Ian was next to him conjuring up a set of twelve holofigs generated from spyfly data, and these he remotely released from a compartment in the hull.

Max jumped into the Gallery and Ian lowered the entrance ramp like a trapdoor. Max shouted at Isla and Amelia to get on board as he saw the two Protectors recovering their wits after the initial shock, although the holofigs were certainly keeping them from being focused. He climbed in behind them and closed the ramp.

*   *   *   *

Roscoe and Eric listened intently for signs of activity from the Library but the thunderflash had dulled their sense of hearing. Numerous phantom images walked or glided out of the Library into the old Dressing Room in which they were now waiting: some of real people, including both Knights and dominophiles, while others were ancient statues of deities and emperors brought to life. Overall holofigs were a good idea but in this case they were making it difficult for the impounding team to keep their attention sharply focused, although the special glasses they were now wearing, designed to give a reddish hue to all holofig images, would enable them to pick out the real Pastor Wayne when he finally came into view. Or would one of the Protectors be next? Hopefully not. Max and Ian should be keeping them busy in the North Dining Room next to the northern end of the Gallery.

Harry joined them. 'He's definitely in there and it doesn't look as though he's going to come out. X3 has been impounded and is securely cocooned up in the stealthpod.'

Eric looked round to face him. 'What about X4?'

'We may have to let him go. He's ensconced himself in the north west wing - six interconnected bedchambers - and is armed. He's not worth the risk. Wayne is our number one priority. Ian is coming along to help out and Max is taking the pod round to the Gallery's south exit so we can haul Wayne aboard with less fuss.'

Roscoe assumed that Amelia and Isla would be aboard but felt unable to ask in case it seemed redundant or to question Harry's competence as the leader of the raid; but then Harry anticipated his query. 'And you'll be pleased to know that the girls are safely on board.'

Eric started. He had his glasses set to spyfly mode and could see the real Wayne walking towards the Library exit closest to them. 'He's coming!' The moment that Wayne entered the room Harry pulled a hologen from the holster in his tunic and fired off a holofig of a large grizzly bear while Roscoe set off the accompanying sound effects from a powerful miniature speaker. Predictably, Wayne was startled and distracted and actually began to take aim at what for a short time he thought was a real bear, unaware of the three Knights standing either side of the entrance. Eric jumped and grabbed him from behind while Harry clamped his arm with a neurodynamic brace, causing him to release his grip on the hand gun.

Roscoe leapt forward with his baton, ejecting from it a fibrous web which he manipulated into a cocoon which built up around Wayne, starting at the feet and working upwards. Then just before the top half of him was disabled Wayne pulled out another gun.

A powerful blast flung Roscoe violently to the ground. He seemed to be at the centre of an explosion and a blinding flash; but there was no pain. Then he felt weaker than at any time in his life and was conscious of Eric staring into his eyes as the darkness engulfed him.

CHAPTER 23

MARS

Pastor Wayne sat in the viewing bay of the *Confucius*. Although not an engineer he was inspired by the technology of the vehicle which now propelled him silently away from Earth and provided a comfortable environment, shielding him from the high energy radiation of the interplanetary vacuum and insulating him from the extremes of cold and heat as it moved out of the planet's shadow into the harshly strong sunlight.

For how long would he be kept in isolation from whoever else was aboard? Where was he being taken? What were 'they' trying to achieve? Who were 'they'? Was it the Global Federation, the Knights of Peace or the Monastery of Divine Light? He knew he had been 'impounded' by the KOP, who had invoked a new law passed by the GF; but where did the real impetus come from? The devil no doubt.

The view of his planet shocked him by its smallness. The *Confucius* was already far enough away to make Earth look no bigger than the Moon in the Earth's night sky. He knew, of course, intellectually that his home planet was tiny in the scheme of things; but to see it in reality was another matter. Not only was it small but it looked delicate and vulnerable. This pleased him in that it meant that the thin film of biosphere encasing the globe could be destroyed in accordance with God's wish, as a punishment for man's long cycle of sin. But God needed the Pastor to bring about his plan of annihilation, the final judgement. That was how he worked sometimes – through people: powerful, charismatic, gifted individuals like himself.

After the Cataclysm of 2045 the population had been greatly reduced by the HIV epidemic as the virus mutated into a form that could be communicated by droplet infection. The preceding decades of promiscuity had provided the ideal environment for the virus to experiment until it had eventually assumed a form which could spread uncontrollably. Yet there were still six billion humans inhabiting the fragile little world he now saw hanging in the blackness and until this voyage he had been one of them. How few of them realised how lucky they were to be living in such a haven. It was so precious. Why had disease not destroyed humanity entirely? How stupidly, sinfully they had acted to thwart God's plan for a new heaven and a new earth. How they had polluted and plundered their planet. Yet they thought they could go on as they were and that God would not become angry, as he had done repeatedly in the Old Testament.

The dark energy drive had already propelled the ship to ten earth radii. As the globe shrank in size the immensity of space increasingly impressed on him as did the unimaginably vast number of stars which moved through it, many with their own retinue of orbiting planets. He did not agree with the latest theory that the conditions for a thriving ecosphere were so vanishingly rare that the intelligent, conscious life of the Earth was probably unique. There were other places in the universe where God's plan would be fulfilled after being brought to an end here with Pastor Wayne as the Lord's agent.

The Pastor felt bitter towards his fellowman, except to those who bent to his will since they must be part of God's plan, albeit not such a big part as his. And there were plenty who unknowingly fell into his plan, who were deceived; such as most of the scientists and engineers he paid to do research which could lead to new forms of destruction. Even the chief scientist was only dimly aware of the ultimate aim which Wayne had in mind for their discoveries and inventions. He was indeed a master of deception; but it was in God's cause.

The door behind him opened like the shutter of a mechanical camera and a slight, bearded man in a tunic stepped into the room. It was a loosely hanging tunic of real cotton, not a smartsuit simulation. 'My name is Aalim. Peace be upon you.'

Wayne did not respond to the warmth and kindness which emanated from this man. It did not even register since it was not in his nature to feel such emanations, although he understood the words and knew that the smile signified either friendliness or a desire to at least appear friendly.

'Can you tell me why I am here please?' There was a hostile offhandedness about Wayne's reply and question.

'Of course. You have been removed temporarily from the world for your protection, and, ultimately, your Enlightenment, as an alternative to arrest.' Aalim said no more but sat next to him, gazing out of the viewing bay window at the receding Earth hanging in a tapestry of stars.

'What right have you to arrest me anyway?'

'We have sufficient evidence of your plans and preparations to sabotage the mission to destroy Bete Noire. It is an impoundment under the Global Federation Impoundment Act of 2076. That is all I can tell you at present, except that after six months, possibly less, you will be released with generous compensation. We are on our way to Mars where we will be taken to the Monastery of Divine Light at the Valles Marineris and I will introduce you to the Hermit Sage there.'

'I will of course be taking legal action when I am released. This is outrageous.'

'As you wish, Pastor. But we are on a pre-programmed transit orbit to Mars and since there is nothing you or I can do to secure your release may I suggest you just go along with us until we have returned to Earth. What have you to lose? All we ask is that you listen. At the very least your stay with us will be more pleasant and interesting than if you close your mind – or should I say soul?'

'Evidently I have no choice. Why do I have to be taken to Mars, anyway. Surely you could have imprisoned – sorry, impounded – me in Shanghai.'

'Correct. But we feel that taking impoundees away from the earth increases the chance of a successful Enlightenment.'

'I assure you that I will not be one of your successes.'

'Please, do not close your mind Pastor.'

They sat in silence for several minutes. Aalim thought of his father, a Moslem televangelist, and how pleased he would have been to see his son working under the inspiration of the Divine Light. Then Pastor Wayne asked how long the journey to Mars would take.

'Only six weeks on our continuous power trajectory. For much of the time you will be left alone in your cabin. Gravity should be no problem because the ship is constantly accelerating or changing direction and the living quarters are automatically rotated in three dimensions to give you between one third and two thirds of the Earth's ground level gravity. However, you are free to come here when you wish and I will be happy to talk with you or answer any questions I can.'

'So I'm a prisoner.'

'Pastor, by the end of your impoundment I hope you will not look upon it as a period of captivity but as a route to freedom.'

'Freedom? Freedom from what?'

'From the material world. You will be illuminated by the Divine Light and so in union with our Creator. You will no longer feel bound to destroy it or dominate your fellow man; nor will the particles and energy fields of the material world be the sole governors of your behaviour.'

'This is nonsense. I will be free of the world when I or my organisation, the Servants of the Seven Seals, have destroyed it. God will take me into heaven.'

Aalim considered this. 'God made us in his own image. True?'

'So many claim.'

'He is the Creator – he brought the universe, including humankind, into being. And he holds it in being and infuses it with intelligence and direction.' Aalim looked pleadingly at him. 'Would it not seem reasonable for our Creator to wish us to imitate him by creating, albeit on a tiny scale, rather than destroying?'

Wayne scoffed. 'Can I go to my quarters?' Aalim complied. He led him through the viewing bay exit, along the tubular corridor and into Wayne's cabin, then disappeared.

*   *   *   *

Every effort had been made to make his room comfortable, relaxing and interesting. His meals were of fresh vegetables and protix, appetisingly prepared and cooked with sauces, his bed was of medium hardness, there was a small exercise machine designed to keep him fit in a prolonged low gravity environment, the humidity and temperature were optimum, a world knowledge robot moved modestly around the cabin to provide information or training or guided learning in any field imaginable and all the while the view through the window made it impossible for him to forget both where he was and how infinitesimally small was his place in the created order.

One facility in his cabin he had not yet tried. Resting invitingly on the desk was a hologame console. Wayne usually played games only if he knew they would enhance his ego in some way or give him the sense of power over others, and this device was, in these and other respects, an unknown quantity.

As his hand strayed near to it the console suddenly came to life and numerous diaphanous cubes hovered in front of him, rotating sedately in three dimensions. At first they were placed at random, then they multiplied in number and arranged themselves into concentric circles around one cube at the centre.

The central cube stopped rotating, then became more solid as words appeared on its nearest face: 'World of Good and Evil'. A faint animation occupied each face of each of the rotating cubes which encircled it. He stared at the array of shifting scenes with a mixture of puzzlement at the theme and grudging admiration of the technology.

Was he being manipulated, observed, indoctrinated? Perhaps. But his curiosity and the paucity of other diversions in his cabin caused him to look for a pattern.

The central cube intensified in brightness as the title of the game faded to be replaced by the words 'Spreading of the Light' giving way in turn to the vivid depiction of a charitable act in which an old man had dropped his wallet. A small girl picked it up and gave it to him with both earnestness and trepidation. The old man smiled. Then cubes in the first circle lit up. One showed the old man now sitting on a bench looking defensively, coldly, at a passer-by until a faint beam emanating from the central cube entered his world and his face transformed into open friendliness. Another cube in the first circle showed him indifferently passing a mother with a toddler until another beam from the central cube caused him to stop, smile at the child and talk. Then there was a third cube showing him sitting morosely at a table in a restaurant when another ray from the centre caused his face to melt into one of relaxed warmth. Other cubes in the inner circle showed the girl being similarly affected by beams from the centre. One had her watching a group of children bullying a small boy. As they left him crying she approached and, on receiving a beam from the centre, comforted him until his sobs subsided. In another first circle scene she sat in a classroom with a very nervous young man evidently having just joined the school. A beam touched her and her smile strengthened the teacher's heart.

The positive events of this nature in the cubes of the first circle each sent out rays to the second concentric arrangement of scenes, which then generated positive emanations to seed the third circle. In this way the entire cabin was filled with illuminated circles of loving kindness.

For just a moment Pastor Wayne looked pleased, but rapidly resumed an air of cynical detachment.

Then the central cube faded and a ripple of fading spread outwards, until all the cubes had faded into blankness. He was puzzled to see that the window had become opaque, without him noticing, while the cabin was filled with light. He became puzzled. What was the point of all this?

The central cube lit up and one of its faces again showed the scene with the old man dropping his wallet; but this time the girl kept the wallet, flashed it in front of him insolently, kicked him in the balls and ran off. He shouted obscenities with hate and despair in his trembling voice. The cube went dull red.

The first circle of cubes illuminated and showed the same animations as before. Dull red rays emanated from the central cube and each one caused a very different transformation of the scene it touched. The old man watched the passer by with a mixture of fear and malice. He leered lustfully at the mother with the toddler. He sat cringing and defensive at the restaurant table. Each time a red ray touched a cube in the first circle the scene on its face changed from neutral to evil and the brightness subsided to a dull red glow. The girl joined the bullies in taunting the small boy. She made wounding, insolent remarks to the young teacher. And as before the influence spread out to the second, third and subsequent circles until it filled the room with a dark, dull redness, which then turned to blackness.

But this time the window was not opaque. Starlight flooded into the room. He could almost feel the frightening immensity of space, sense the celestial splendour beyond the window of the cabin, and for the first time in his life, for just a few moments, he experienced smallness; but not humility. He comforted himself by recalling his superiority of charisma and intellect over everyone he chose to meet, qualities conferred on him by God and to be used by God.

The lights came on and as the cabin door slid open Aalim stepped inside, smiling pleasantly. 'Peace be upon you.'

'I am disappointed.' Some of the dismissive hostility had gone from his voice and manner, though he was still far from friendly. 'I was expecting an interactive game, not a lesson in morality.'

'Your disappointment is unfounded, Pastor. There will indeed be a game and I'm here to explain it.' Aalim extracted a small cap, like a Moslem prayer cap, from a pocket in his tunic. 'We are not expecting you to become a Moslem but to play this game you must wear it.'

'Why should I, a Christian, want to wear this?'

'I am a Sufi under the Divine Light; but, I suggest, no-one would call you a Christian. You do not love God because you despise your fellow man. Let me quote from the New Testament, from the first letter of John, chapter four, verse sixteen. *God is love; he who dwells in love is dwelling in God and God in him.*'

Wayne grew angry. 'But I am doing God's will.'

'But Pastor, you are not absorbing the essence of Christ's message. If you do not love your fellow man you cannot love God.'

'How can you, a Sufi, tell me about God's purpose?'

'Like Father James and many Hermit Sages from all belief systems I have experienced the Divine Light. It has revealed to me that our loving Creator surpasses all understanding; he searches us out and invites us into his realm of being by different faiths and different paths within each faith. Previously the Christians have understood most closely and clearly the means by which Yahweh seeks us – the Holy Spirit. But now we all know it as the Divine Light, as first presented to Father James in his vision.'

Wayne showed supercilious exasperation. 'The world is fooling itself. Religion is about the wrath of God, not just love. The Lord has chosen me to help him punish the fallen humanity he created.'

'Are you saying you do not love your creator?'

'Of course not. You are putting words into my mouth. It is because of my love for God that he has chosen me to end the wickedness of man by wiping him from the face of the earth.'

'You are bitter. Do you love your fellow man?'

'I have every reason to be bitter. How can I love this human race which has done so much evil. Humanity has no right to survive. It has refused to comply with God's laws as written in the scriptures.'

'Pastor, let me quote another verse from John. *We love because he loved us first. But if a man says "I love God" while hating his brother, he is a liar. If he does not love the brother whom he has seen, it cannot be that he loves God whom he has not seen.* So I repeat: if you hate man, how can you love God?'

'I thought you were going to show me how to play this game. I need to do something to pass the time. Why do I need to put the prayer cap on? Surely you don't expect me to pray to Allah?'

'It is not actually a prayer cap, although perhaps one day you will come to realise it has a spiritual purpose in the context of this game.'

'Can you get to the point?'

'The cap has been specially developed in the Shanghai Monastery laboratories and has a neuronic interface with the game logic entities. It is an extraordinary technical achievement and one can only see in it the hand of Allah, the same Creator who in past ages inspired us to construct mosques, temples and cathedrals. And the game is not meaningful or fruitful without wearing it.'

'Very well, let me put it on.'

Aalim handed him the hat. 'You will be given a simple didactic task: to teach an illiterate man with learning difficulties to read.'

A life-sized holographic figure of a middle aged man sat on a chair at a table between him and Pastor Wayne. There was sadness and fear in his face.

'How do I get the highest score? By teaching him as quickly as possible I suppose.'

'Not at all. The object is to teach him to read without inflicting mental pain.'

'You can't learn anything without pain.'

'I disagree. Effort and hard work, yes. But pain? No. In this game whenever you cause the pupil to suffer your score will be reduced.'

'Hardly a reflection of reality.' There was derision in his voice and face.

'In a sense I agree. That is not how the world works or has worked for many thousands of years. Results are what count – not how you get them. But the world is changing, Pastor. It started with Father James's vision. A new reality – God's reality – is evolving in our midst like a growing and spreading light in the darkness. And in this reality it matters very much how results are accomplished.'

'I don't know what you're talking about. Just let me get on with it. What's the game called, incidentally?'

'The E-game.'

'Not exactly original.'

'Perhaps. Except that in this case "E" stands for "Enlightenment," not for "electronic."'

'Nonsensical though the concept of Enlightenment is you do not really expect me to believe that a computer game could ever induce it. Or rather, if you think it can that convinces me totally that there is no such phenomenon as Enlightenment.'

'You are right. All the computer game does is prepare you for the actual process, which is personally conducted by a Hermit Sage.' Aalim waited for a response and when none came he continued.

'Perhaps I should leave you now. The instructions are built in and you will learn these soon enough. But a word of warning: it might be painful.'

*　　*　　*　　*

The avatar pupil had been given the name 'Henry' and he waited with simulated trepidation on his face, as if expecting his human tutor to chastise or humiliate him as he failed to progress.

Pastor Wayne considered his strategy. Henry, he was told, had learning difficulties; so he would have to start with something not too ambitious.

What exactly was the objective? He asked for text on this and it appeared in front of the holographic avatar. He had to get the pupil to read just one page of writing – and to pronounce ten words from it selected at random. The sooner this was achieved the higher would be his score. He guessed that Henry could learn to pronounce just the first five letters of the alphabet in a short time, despite his slowness. The next step would be to show him words made up entirely of these letters and get him to voice them.

'Henry, I want you to repeat after me each letter I show you. I am going to show you the first five letters of the English alphabet.'

A searing pain engulfed Wayne . He realised it must have been transmitted from the simulated student to his own brain via the neurocap. He saw Henry's thoughts floating as disembodied sentences above his head. *What is the alphabet'? What are letters? Why do I have to learn them? What happens next? Five is too many letters for me to memorise in one go. What will he do if I can't remember them? Will he get cross? Will he shout at me? Will he punish me? He doesn't respect me. My mind is seizing up.*

The pain subsided and Wayne was undecided what to do next, his indecision eating up valuable time which would subtract from his score. It was already minus 50 points because of the suffering, fear and uncertainty he had engendered in Henry. All these doubts and questions. Aalim had said that he could be called in at any time to discuss how to proceed and no points would be lost: the clock would be stopped. The Pastor decided to avail himself of this help and so summoned Aalim to join him.

'How can you possibly build up points if fifty are deducted for just telling the pupil what to do?'

Aalim smiled. 'Pastor, you saw yourself the plethora of questions which are in Henry's mind. Would you not feel afraid if such questions entered your mind? And would your learning process not be hampered?'

'But such questions would not come into my mind.'

'Exactly. Because you are blessed with a quick retentive brain. People like Henry have so often been tested and found wanting and the memory of these bad experiences causes these questions to come into their minds and make it even more difficult for them to learn than it would be with their innate learning impediment.'

'But I can't do anything about that.'

'You can remove the need for the pupil to ask himself such questions.'

'How can I do that? If he is scared of me I can't help it.'

'Henry must have your complete trust. You must reassure him that you will let him progress at his own speed.'

'His own speed? My score depends on my rate of progress and this is going to be far too slow with a retarded pupil to teach.'

'Not as slow as if your pupil is paralysed with fear and uncertainty. If he were a real person you would have to, indeed want to, love him as God intended you to do. Granted, Henry is only a simulation and love cannot be measured; but what the game is looking for is the kind of behaviour that goes with love.'

'How do I know...'

'Exactly, Pastor. You must learn loving behaviour. That is what the E-game is trying to teach you. Only by loving behaviour will you get a high score and avoid being jolted by pain every time you err into the behaviour which would distress or disturb the pupil. On this voyage you will have many hours in which to up your score by loving behaviour towards this and other avatars.'

'So how would I deal with the present situation?'

'I can only give you an example or two.'

'Of course. I can easily extrapolate from those.'

'Not so easily, I suggest. Loving behaviour has to be learned and practised if you do not have love – agape love, the love of God, the love that is willed - within you. You have to get into the habit of looking at the world from someone else's viewpoint. For example, Henry has to understand what the alphabet is. So explain it to him. Tell him why it's important. How central it is in learning to read and also why learning to read is such a liberating experience. You also have to dispel his fear of how you might react if he fails to make the progress you expect.'

'How can I remove fear? We are dealing with a simulation, a mathematical model.'

'The model at least recognises patterns of loving behaviour through the words you use. So think hard on these words.'

'This is not the kind of thing one expects from a computer game. It's going to be difficult.'

'Pastor, when you have learned loving behaviour the hard way, through the E-Game, you will be closer to union with God, you will be more able to summon the will to love, to sense Yahweh's holy presence. But before you can attain this union you will need to visit a Hermit Sage.'

'Just leave me to get on with the game.'

For an instant Wayne felt inadequate; not mentally but spiritually. Aalim sensed this: 'Certainly; but I think, despite yourself, you are already beginning to see the light.'

* * * *

The *Confucius* crept imperceptibly towards Phobos, its irregular, far from spherical form progressively filling the window of Wayne's cabin until eventually all he could see was the floor and inner rim of Phobos's large impact crater, etched with intricate, metallic patterns and pocked with a brilliantly shining but much smaller crater in one quarter of the large one. He had heard that Phobos was thought to be an asteroid captured into orbit by the gravity of Mars long ago and drawn into its present orbit some three thousand miles above the Martian surface. It reminded him of the asteroid which was now heading for Earth, and which, like almost all asteroids, would not be guided by the laws of celestial mechanics into such an orbit but instead was on an impact trajectory and so had the potential to destroy all of humankind living in its delicately balanced biosphere, as the Lord had intended.

Aalim appeared at the door to his cabin. 'A magnificent sight, do you agree?'

'Perhaps. But why are we tethered to it so closely? We appear to be right inside the crater walls.'

'Indeed we are. It is to protect the ship from interplanetary debris while we are on the surface.'

'How will we get to the surface?'

'In the Mars Descent Transpod. If you are ready we will be entering the transfer module in two hours. This will take us into the MDT which will fly us down to Iani Chaos, one of the warmest parts of the planet. It reaches the temperature of an early autumn summer's day prior to global warming. That is at noon. It drops to minus forty degrees at night.'

Wayne was eager to pick holes. 'Forty what degrees?'

'Fahrenheit and Celsius are the same at minus forty.'

He looked momentarily sheepish then quickly resumed his more assertive stance. 'But after my impoundment and debriefing in the Shanghai KOP they told me and my fellow captive that we were going to the Monastery of Divine Light, as they call it – he to the monastery near Shanghai and I to the one recently constructed on Mars in the Valles Marineris.'

'That is indeed your final destination. But the main operational base is at Iani Chaos. There you will meet the Hermit Sage who will escort you to the monastery.' He walked back towards the door.

'Why did you separate me from my first protector and why were we selected for "impounding" as you call it?'

'You are both dominophiles, as was the second protector who escaped.'

'Dominophiles?'

'Certain individuals amongst us have a natural tendency to dominate others.'

'But anyone who is stronger in intellect, personality and physique will naturally have dominance over someone weaker. In my case God had chosen me to bring about man's nemesis.'

'In a sense; but the dominophile *seeks* to dominate, regardless of his innate strength. He or she wants power for its own sake. They are identified by their Q-spectra, as were you and your two protectors. We can also analyse the sociodynamics of a group of people and by combining the characteristics of the group with the Q-spectra of individuals within it we can identify critical situations, ones which are likely to lead to conflict or social breakdown. In your case we already knew you were dangerous because we had discovered your desire to destroy humanity; in particular your scheme to prevent the deflection of Bete Noire. Fortunately, we have already thwarted this scheme by acquiring the nanobots you intended to use as a means of sabotage. But we also know you have the will and the possible ability to find some other means of destruction.'

Wayne's heart thumped strongly.

'So, Pastor, I will be returning in about ninety minutes and then we will be on our way.'

Wayne was disappointed. There seemed to be no departure from the original plan to subject him to Enlightenment. He had hoped that after numerous arguments with Aalim and his cynical attitude to the E-Game they would by now have given up on this. He had always had the option of refusing Enlightenment but he felt this would be seen as a weakness, implying that he did not have the spiritual confidence to withstand the gentlest persuasion and guidance of a Hermit Sage. It was obvious now that they still felt fully confident that he would succumb to the Divine Light and thought that his belief in a God that wished to destroy his own creation could be changed.

His conviction that God wished humankind to be destroyed and that he had been chosen to be instrumental in this, continued; yet within him there were other feelings. He had sensed with stark clarity the majesty of the Creator's works in a way he had never done while trapped on the earth's surface. From the windows of the *Confucius* he had seen his minuscule home planet as a precious point of refuge for intelligent, self conscious life in a cosmos which, to date, had shown no sign of it anywhere else. Wayne, like most intelligent people, had always assumed that there must be other planets with advanced life forms on them, rare and widely scattered but, in a universe of ten billion trillion stars each with attendant planets, nevertheless numerous, and that these would reveal themselves as the technology of exploration and communication evolved; but it was increasingly looking as though mankind might actually be alone in a bleak and arid universe. And for the Pastor the presence of other sentient beings in the universe had been more than a working assumption: it had been a belief about which he felt increasingly defensive and which he clung to because it was one of the pillars upon which he had constructed his apocalyptic doctrine of a forced Omega point, a belief that as humanity was deservedly destroyed by God's judgement other more deserving civilisations would prosper.

But what would it mean if indeed earth was the only abode of life in the entire cosmos? What if the sterile glittering rock of this crater, hanging beyond the window of his cabin, devoid of a single bacterium, was the story throughout the universe? He quickly dispelled the idea from his mind, praying that God would free him from such heresy. In any case, human history had been one of relentless evil. Its continuation could not be justified in God's eyes, or at least in Pastor Wayne's.

Why was there so much talk about God's love? People had far too sentimental a view of the Lord since the New Testament. Did they really think they could count on his love to save them from judgement? Could they not see his wrath and his power? It was written about all through the Old Testament and in Revelation, especially the parts he had altered at the Lord's request.

He began to feel nauseous. Since the ship had stopped accelerating he had been weightless and had to get used to being moved around the cabin by the force of recoil every time he touched or pushed against a solid, anchored object. He harnessed himself to his bed and waited for Aalim to return.

*   *   *   *

Outside the MDT window the star pierced blackness of the Martian night gave way to the pale pink of dawn, its progression accelerated by their hypersonic motion eastward and they could make out the rapidly changing landscape as it slipped silently toward and beneath them, although at this speed and height they could not see individual features other than the largest chasms, ravines and craters highlighted and deeply shadowed by the low sun ahead.

Aalim indicated the ground beneath them. 'You can't see it now but directly below us is the monastery to which you will be taken later, and at much slower speed, after we have landed at Iani Chaos.'

'So is that the Valles Marineris beneath us?' Wayne found it impossible to conceal his awe at the scale of a valley in which the Grand Canyon would be lost as a minor sub-feature. 'Exactly what is the Iani Chaos?'

'It is a depressed area near the eastern end of the Valles, strewn with all shapes and sizes of boulders. The equator has the highest average temperature on Mars and inside the Iani Chaos it can reach nearly thirty degrees Celsius at noon.'

The MDT slowed down from its headlong hurl eastward then hovered above the Martian base. Aalim remarked on a surface feature etched in the red, rocky expanse. 'Does it remind you of a tadpole?'

'In my fanciful moments only.'

'I fear this chance resemblance of an areological feature to a tadpole is the nearest you will get to experiencing life on Mars. No trace of a living organism has been found here or anywhere else in the solar system other than on earth. Yet, like the earth, it has been around for five billion years.' Aalim looked resolutely at Wayne. 'So you see Pastor, life is incredibly rare and precious in the universe, more so than was ever envisaged a few decades ago. The SSS should bear this in mind, do you not think?'

Wayne looked supercilious, defiant and deceptively serene as he relished the thought of man's destruction. He maintained a scornful silence.

As their height dropped they could make out a square cluster of four transparent domes which was the main Martian colony and they landed in the middle.

So how had God brought him to this? Here he was, sitting on another planet with a turmoil of concealed doubt churning his innermost being.

Aalim started to put on a self pressurising sensor suit and handed one to Wayne who did the same. The door of the transpod cabin opened to form a ramp which they walked down, then across the red dust towards an airlock door in the side of one of the domes. Wayne could feel the texture and warmth of the summer soil beneath his shoes; and he wondered how the sensor suit conveyed through transducers, pressure points and the microclimate control system, a feel for the environment outside the suit. As soon as they had entered the airlock it quickly re-pressurised and the inner door slid open to reveal the person that Wayne had been transported fifty million miles to meet.

CHAPTER 24

AWAKENING

A cross, which seemed to be made of wood and yet somehow glowed with spiritual light, floated in the dark greyness before him, then faded and gave way to the image of Christ in a robe. Love emanated from the whole figure, not just the face, and appeared to strengthen his own will to love. He knew the vision was nearly over; it always ended this way. Yes, it had finished; he felt relaxed but drained of energy in a pleasant way and decided to continue seated in the cell for a while, reflecting the truths that had revealed themselves to him today and on the progress that had been made with the Enlightenment process.

It had been a disappointing exercise so far. The Pastor's resistance had been unprecedented over the last ten days. He had resisted every conceivable effort to bring him, gently and voluntarily – for there was no other way - to the Divine Light. Was there indeed such a force as evil that kept some people away from the Light? It was easy to imagine how the priests of biblical times had pictured evil in terms of devils.

Yet he felt he had come close to success. It was clear that Wayne was yielding, though progress was painfully slow.

The holomonitor showed that Wayne had gone outside in his pressurised Envirosensor smartsuit. Why this late? It was getting close to sunset and the temperature would fall steeply as soon as the sun dropped. The suit would be heated enough to keep him alive for an hour or so after sunset but he would nevertheless feel bitterly cold within minutes of the sky turning black.

Once outside the airlock he could either admire the view or make his way down the hundred metre stairway that had been carved into the rock below where the monastery had been built into the side of the cliff and from which it jutted out further than would be possible with a similar structure on earth, where the gravity was three times stronger. Now Wayne was half way down and appeared to have stopped. Perhaps he was admiring the view, although this seemed out of character and looking down on him from this height it was impossible to detect any clues of stance. If he carried on descending it might be necessary to warn him to get back before nightfall.

The cell had a music option, although a Hermit Sage used it sparingly: silence was often the most powerful way of being in the presence of the Creator. Nevertheless, music had its place and would serve to fill in a couple of minutes before he decided whether to contact the Pastor. He might even have to go after him.

He had for a long time been wondering how he might now react to the sound of Baroqo, so he blinked a signal to turn on the recording of his last stage performance. It was arresting, powerful, mathematical; but not inspiring. He had written the music himself, over thirty years ago. The recording was live and included the sound of the audience, clapping and chanting in exuberance, thinking they were Atheists; but in reality he felt that at some level God had been present since natural law had been written in their hearts by their unacknowledged Creator. He now believed that the most soul elevating and beautiful music was invariably written by believers in a Creator. Handel had written the Messiah as a strong believer in Yahweh as expressed in Christ. Baroqo's music was paltry by comparison. He wondered whether he should try composing again, now that God dwelt in his being; but somehow he felt this would be in conflict with his present role in the divine scheme and that he should leave it to others.

After a few minutes he blinked the music away and walked over to the observation canopy. Wayne was now quite close to the floor of the canyon, a tiny speck.

*   *   *   *

It was disconcerting, this feeling that was welling up in him. The Pastor felt stronger yet more humble at the same time. What was causing it? Through the thin boots of his Envirosensor smartsuit the ground felt almost like shingle on a beach back on earth. He was facing the other side of a canyon three kilometres wide and seven kilometres high and along the length of the canyon to his left he could see the small pale disc of the sun only a little above the horizon. Tall spinning pillars of dust and ethereal wisps moved deliberately in the wind that swept along the valley, occasionally dimming or even blotting out the sun in the cold pastel pink of the sky. A crescent, Phobos, much smaller and fainter than the solar disc, hung above him, deceptively stationary but in fact almost visibly moving, like the minute hand of an analogue clock. He was beginning to feel chilly even in the heated smartsuit.

He turned to see the faintly stratified towering wall of sand behind him, rising several kilometres sheer. Had there really been so much water on this planet? It was generally agreed that deep torrents and leaping mountains of water had swept through this canyon at various times over the aeons. The very sand which formed the sides of the canyon had been deposited on the floors of ancient oceans.

But if so much time, so much water, why no life? Mars had been bombarded with organic molecules from comets, the so called building blocks of life, for as long as the earth.

A familiar voice interrupted his reverie: 'Pastor, it is getting late. You need to get back inside.'

'Yes, of course. I know how cold it gets.'

'And it also gets very dark. You won't get much light from Phobos.'

'I've got a torch. Stop fussing.' He switched off the flexcom, but with only a slight sense of irritation.

The sun now touched the horizon and shot out a uniquely Martian configuration of ever changing light beams as it slid slowly out of sight. Then the sky turned instantly black and was sprayed with astonishingly bright, steadily shining stars, except for small patches where the sunlight from below the horizon still caught high suspended cloudlets of dust scudding rapidly above. It was so dark where he stood, slightly unsteady in the low gravity, and so quiet except for a faint shrill whistle of the thin fast moving air around the contours of the smartsuit, that he almost felt suspended in nothingness.

The temperature was falling fast and he switched on the torch. It clearly illuminated a way to the winding rocky stairway that led up to the monastery. He calculated that he should be back inside within half an hour. It would get cold, but not deathly cold.

Why was he feeling lighter, as though a burden had been lifted? He began the ascent and was looking forward to meeting Father James again. He had something to tell him.

Then the torch failed and he was engulfed in darkness.

* * * *

Father James looked down from the observation canopy and noticed that the trace of a beam which had been moving ahead of the Pastor had disappeared. It would not be necessary to go down to escort him up the steps, since although he would be in pitch darkness and no safety rail had yet been erected on the left hand side, he could stay safe by feeling the rock face on his right. Nevertheless he was concerned not to have heard anything over the flexcom for several minutes and when he decided to call there was an ominous silence before Wayne replied. 'I'm making excellent progress; the steps are getting less steep but...'

A wave of terror abruptly swept through Father James. He had forgotten that a section of the path was not flanked by the cliff face and there was no rail on either side. It was perfectly safe in daylight and in such a low gravity field. If the path was levelling out he must be getting close.

'Pastor – be very careful. The stairway turns into a ridge and there is no rail or cliff face either side. I'm coming down with a torch.'

'But the temperature is dropping fast. I'll freeze to death if I don't get back in the next half hour.'

'You can't possibly cross the ridge path in darkness. Just move forward very slowly and stop as soon as the cliff finishes. Then stay absolutely still until I light up the path.'

'Absolutely still? I will freeze more quickly.'

'Well, just move about on the spot to keep your circulation going. But stay in one place in case you step over the precipice.'

Wayne realised that if he did fall off the ridge it would in fact mean the end of human history.

*　　*　　*　　*

Father James had put on a pressurised smartsuit with a more than usually powerful heater yet he still felt cold as he emerged into the Martian night and began the slow, careful descent, gripping his torch. He tried clamping the torch to his headgear but because of his movements this failed to reliably light the ground closest in front and although the hand rail helped it was not sufficient to avoid a serious risk of tripping over a discontinuity or a piece of stony or sandy debris; and such a fall might even toss him over the precipice. Even with the gravity being only one third terrestrial strength he would still hit the valley floor as hard as from a height of thirty metres back on earth.

He could not afford to proceed as slowly as he would like: Wayne might freeze fatally before he could be brought back to the warmth of the monastery. Part of him thought it was not worth risking his life unduly to save a dominophile who, if not enlightened before his release back on earth might once again enthuse the SSS and bring humanity to the risk of extinction. Yet if Wayne lived and was enlightened his example could eventually cause his followers also to embrace the Divine Light. Besides, it was unholy to allow through inaction the demise of any human being, and despite himself he had come to feel a sense of respect for this man, misguided and egotistical though he was. And of course as a Christian he had to cultivate the will to love, in the agape sense, even his enemies.

As the descent became shallower the path eventually levelled out, with the unfenced ridge ahead and Wayne standing at the other end.

'Pastor, can you hear me? Please, answer.'

There was a long pause, then a tired reply. 'Yes…of course.' Wayne was beginning to lose consciousness but was still aware of the implications if he died before letting Father James know the piece of information in his head. He knew that he had lost the battle against Enlightenment, otherwise he would not be thinking this way. 'Father, I have something to tell…you.'

'Never mind that now. I'm lighting up the path so follow it, as fast as possible. Please be quick.'

Wayne moved unsteadily forward along the ridge, which fortunately was not as narrow as he remembered, religiously following the patch of ground illuminated by the torch. He began to speed up and it did not take long to get over the dangerous unfenced section.

'Right, now all you have to do is get in front of me and walk upwards as I shine the torch. Then we will be truly on the home stretch.'

'Father...I'm not sure...' Then he collapsed.

It was fortunate that the gravity was so weak. Father James managed to contort himself into lifting the dormant domino onto his shoulder and staggered falteringly forward, focusing all his attention on reaching the monastery door above, calculating that he would get there in fifteen minutes. It was going to be close. And having to control the torch with one hand made the operation doubly difficult.

His foot caught a loose stone and he stumbled, causing the Pastor to shoot forward, his arms flung in front of him and his head crashing slowly to the ground.

The jolt must have temporarily revived him and he tried to speak. Wayne, aching with the intense coldness, remembered the importance of what he had to say. 'Listen to me, please, Father...' His speech faded away and Father James lifted him onto his shoulder, then resumed his staggering course back to the monastery.

*   *   *   *

All he could do now was wait for the revival chamber to either do its work or alert him that it had not been successful. What did he mean, 'I have something to tell you'? Something inside Father James told him that he must at all costs find out what the Pastor was trying to tell him. But what more could he do than wait? The revival machine would have no concern for the outcome, no will to summon up extra effort, no awareness of the consequences of life or death. It made no difference to an inanimate system. One set of life signatures was as significant as another. Not that a machine could even experience significance.

Aalim's voice came into the flexcom. 'Father, how is he?'

'The revival display is showing a critical time of eleven minutes. After that he will either start to regain consciousness or fade away quickly.'

'How did he respond to Enlightenment?'

'Very slowly. He seems to be showing signs of losing commitment to his SSS mission but I'm not sure he will go as far as opening up to the DL. His ego is so strong, even as he becomes aware of the self-deception that has plagued him all his life. But I'm not without hope. You could have said that about me thirty years ago.'

'But you did not wish the world harm, even when you were an Atheist.'

'True. My self deception was to ignore the real me and think I was nothing but matter and energy. It did not cause me to set up in competition to God, because I did not believe there was one.'

'Nothing buttery, it was called by some at the time. Nothing but particles and energy. Of course, the Pastor will swear he is only doing God's will.'

'He is calling his own will God's will. He can only find God's will when he has recognised his humility.'

'Well, let's pray that he lives and that his brush with death will have helped him discover his real self, which can only be found through Yahweh.'

Father James wondered what had happened with the other domino impounded on the Holkham mission, one of the two protectors of the Pastor. He knew he was being given the opportunity to receive Enlightenment in the Shanghai MDL.

'Aalim, have you got news from earth about the other impoundee?'

'I heard he has submitted. It might help you encourage Wayne to make the final commitment. On the other hand it might do the complete opposite. Well, Father, I must say goodbye now, unless there is anything else you want to discuss?'

'No. I'll let you know as soon as he recovers, assuming he does. God's peace to you.'

He blinked the flexcom into silence and sat quietly with his hands cupped upwards on his lap, his eyes closed, praying that Yahweh's love and mercy and the grace through Christ would enter into his being and into Wayne and the spiritual space around them, and that it would steer the Pastor towards life. Not just physical life but eternal life, that which transcended soul and body, that which was common to soul and body and of which the two were but aspects of a greater transcendent self, united in the kingdom of an unknowable God.

It was of course impossible ever to know Yahweh. Even Father James's most intense of the Divine Light visions, which had awoken him from Atheism, only gave him an awareness that there was a God and that Yahweh was unknowable and that the source of Yahweh's loving kindness was powerful beyond human imagination and the truth of God was also beyond our understanding. Thomas Aquinas had, through God's grace, discovered this in the thirteenth century, saying that whatever one said about God was untrue as soon as one had said it. If only God would choose to impart his unknowability and glorious splendour to the Pastor – then, indeed, he would be transformed. But to question Yahweh's purpose, except in the deepest humility and in a spirit of reverently desiring to know, was not our place in the order of the universe. Achieving the Enlightenment of one so egotistical and intellectually gifted as Pastor Wayne would have to be a painstaking process.

A gentle undulating hum began to pervade the room. It was coming from the revival chamber, the cocoon-like structure in which the Pastor was lying. He walked over and peered into the transparent upper segment. The life display had indicated a definite improvement in the parameters of his material existence and it was clear he was gaining consciousness.

The cocoon opened and the Pastor stirred, his eyelids flicking open with an abruptness which was almost startling. 'How do you feel, Pastor?'

'Groggy but alive would sum it up.'

'It was certainly touch and go at one stage. But I believe you have something to tell me. Is that so?'

'Do I?'

'Just before you passed out you started to tell me something.'

Wayne had appeared calm as he emerged into consciousness but now seemed worried and disturbed. This was not the look of someone transformed by Enlightenment. 'Sorry, Father, I am not ready to submit to your "Divine Light" as you call it. However, I have grown doubtful about my own beliefs.' He found the strength to sit upright. 'What I have come to realise on this journey is that life is precious. Seeing the desolateness of this planet has given me an awareness of how extraordinarily rare life is. I could even believe that humans are the only intelligent, sentient beings in all Creation. Intellectually, of course, it was already somewhere in the back of my mind – the astrolife searches have been yielding nothing all this century. I had not fully admitted to myself the real possibility of such a lonely universe. There may not be anyone else out there at all. In which case there would be no one to take our place in God's scheme.'

'Yes, Pastor. I agree. The circumstances that led to humankind evolving in the ecofilm of our home planet are incredibly rare. It almost looks as though God made the universe for us alone – to see and perhaps to explore. Certainly not to destroy. I am not one for quoting the scriptures, but please allow me to point you to Isaiah 45: 18.' Father James opened the bible at the cited verse and handed it over. Perhaps you could read it out.'

Wayne looked thoughtfully at the text. 'Very well. *For this is what the Lord says: he who created the heavens, he is God; he who fashioned and made the earth he founded it; he did not create it to be empty but formed it to be inhabited.* If I recall correctly Isaiah was saying this around 700 BC.'

'So can you believe that Yahweh would wish to destroy Yahweh's people? Is it not more likely that Yahweh would want them to inhabit not only the earth but the entire material universe? To Isaiah at the time it was conceptually impossible to see the cosmos as anything other than the earth.'

The Pastor sighed and showed humility, then looked troubled again. 'You are right, Father. Now I need to tell you what I started to say before losing consciousness. You are of course aware of the ADN project to destroy Bete Noire.'

'The Asteroid Defence Network. Yes. It is about to send a missile towards Bete Noire to deflect it from its collision course. You nearly succeeded in thwarting the mission with a nanobot swarm, to be deployed in orbit close to a guidance antenna, but one of our Knights managed to steal the nanobots from your operatives in Burnham Thorpe. You no doubt remember the episode.'

'Fortunately for us at the time we had a duplicate nanobot swarm ready to be deployed from an orbiting vehicle.'

Father James quickly restored himself to a calm state after the initial shock of hearing this. He considered the situation. 'Is the deployment likely to go ahead with you impounded?'

'Quite likely. I had left a plan to be implemented by either one of my two protectors. Since only the First Protector was impounded that leaves the Second Protector to carry out the plan.'

'How can we stop him? The interception missile has to be fired off in only ten days.'

'I will do my best to cooperate. Can the Bete Noire mission be delayed to give us more time?'

'Time is not on our side, Pastor. The missile has to be launched to explode a certain distance and direction from the asteroid, so the launch time is critical.'

'Ten days may not be sufficient. This is not going to be easy.'

Father James had not thought anything could be more important than guiding a domino through to Enlightenment; but stopping the sabotage of the ADN mission was just that.

He hailed Aalim on his flexcom.

CHAPTER 25

RECOVERY

Oblivion turned into darkness which then gave way to light. Sounds could be heard – the raucous squawk of a crow, and in stark contrast the soft melody of two girls conversing. The voices seemed to care deeply about him, welcoming him to the conscious state as shapes gradually became clear and meaningful: a window, partly open with sunlight streaming in; a cabinet at the end of his bed; a face looking down at him, another slightly behind. By degrees the faces became first familiar, then known, as did the voices.

His hand was gently clasped by the warm, compliant palms of a lady. 'Ros, it's Amelia. And Isla is here with me.' She spoke with a slightly doubtful tone, wondering whether he had recognised them; but from his expression she had no doubt.

He felt peaceful and remembered that he too had a voice; but where he was and how he had got there he could not recall. 'Amelia? Isla? What happened? Where am I?'

'You are in the KOP hospital in Cambridge. Do you know what those initials mean?'

He tried hard to remember.

'Roscoe, they stand for "Knights of Peace". You were shot by Pastor Wayne while trying to impound him. The bullet went through your brain but it has not done permanent damage. Stem cells were used for neuro-regeneration and the nerve patterns needed for you to function restored themselves.'

The word 'Knight' immediately brought everything back to him. The raids in Tripsino and Saukotia, the Burnham Thorpe nanobot snatch, his friendship with Eric, with Father James, the long infatuation with Isla, the frustration, the jealousy, the short deep interaction with Amelia, the Holkham raid, the gunshot from Wayne. Then he recalled the trial, Knightmaster Franklin and his first months as a Knight. His face showed comprehension, that he was fully engaged with past and present.

'What happened to Wayne and the other dominos, Wayne's so-called protectors, were they impounded in the end?'

Isla spoke. 'The First Protector was impounded and taken to the Shanghai MDL, the other escaped. As for Pastor Wayne he was taken to the monastery on Mars.'

'Why to Mars?'

Isla got up and began to walk round the room as she talked. 'I asked the Knightmaster the same question. Apparently it had been Father James's idea. He thought it would help shock him into realising the wrongness of the SSS's mission and make him more susceptible to the Divine Light.'

Roscoe gazed out of the window then back towards Isla. Her expressive face, auburn hair and graceful profile still excited him at a visceral level and even as he was still emerging into full awareness he was careful not to let this be detected by Amelia – spiritually advanced though she was, there resided within her the natural emotions of jealousy and passion, much subdued, but nevertheless present at some deep primeval level. Not that there was any real doubt: Amelia was his destiny and he was hiding his feelings for Isla not out of betrayal but to spare her any pain that might be caused by a misinterpretation of them. 'I think it will depend more on the skills and wisdom of the Hermit Sage, whoever that may be, and the grace of God.'

'Another surprise for you, Ros,' said Isla. 'A committee of monks and KOP officials decided that the Enlightenment of Wayne was so important that Father James himself should be the Hermit Sage.'

'Father James? On Mars? And has he succeeded?'

Amelia leaned forward. 'I spoke to him a few days ago; but you know what these interplanetary conversations are like. It was difficult to converse with a delay of ten minutes between asking a question and getting an answer. The Pastor certainly hasn't reached Enlightenment yet but I did get the distinct impression that progress is being made. There are still a few weeks before he has to be returned to earth for release.'

Isla got a message on her flexcom. 'It's from Knightmaster Franklin. He wants me in his office and from the tone of his voice it sounds as though it's something important.' She gave them an anxious smile. 'He says it's urgent so I'll have to go now. See you both later.'

Roscoe and Amelia were glad to be alone together.

* * * *

The Knightmaster ushered her into the room quickly and asked her to sit. She had frequently acted as his secretary during her quantum computing studies at Cambridge and she was confirmed in her sense that this was not going to be an ordinary visit.

He began before she had even sat down. 'There is no time to waste so I will get straight to the point. You know Father James, I believe?'

'I have met him a few times.'

'Well, I've just received a message from him. You recall that Cadet Knight Roscoe Finley recently managed to "steal" a swarm of nanobots from the SSS?'

'At Burnham Thorpe wasn't it?'

'Correct. Well the news from Mars is not good, even though it is from Father James. Apparently, Finley's raid was not the end of the story. The SSS domino known as Pastor Wayne has renounced his belief in his mission to destroy the earth.'

He paused and was about to continue but Isla interjected. 'But that's good news isn't it sir?'

'As far as it goes, yes. But he hasn't, I'm afraid, proceeded to Enlightenment. Much worse - he has told us that the nanobots taken by Cadet Knight Finley were backed up and that a sleeper plan has been set in motion to place another swarm close to one of the ADN antennas. Unless we can stop that plan unfolding, or it goes wrong in some way, humankind is likely to suffer the same fate as the dinosaurs.'

She tried to absorb what she had heard. 'Surely there must be something we can do, sir.'

'We can't do anything until we know who was delegated by the Second Protector to enact the plan. Which is why I've called you in? You have considerable decoding skills and may be able to locate the person or at least get information that leads us in that direction.'

'I'm fortunate to have learned quantum computing and to have the use of the Cavendish facilities. Do you have a name I can use as a key?'

'Apparently the Pastor thinks the person carrying out the plan was someone called "Cosmo". That was all he found out before he was impounded. From then on the Second Protector was responsible and we don't even know his name – nor does the Pastor it seems; but he did know that he was sometimes called "Jonathan". Do you think there is any chance you can get somewhere with this information?'

'It's possible, sir.'

'How soon can you start?'

'As soon as I can get back to my quantum decoding set –up.'

'How long do you think it will be before you know whether you are going to succeed? Or is that a daft question?'

'From past experience I either succeed very quickly with this sort of decoding problem or it takes weeks or it never gets solved at all.'

'Anyway, I don't have to emphasise how important this is. I will ask our Shanghai team to work on it at the same time.'

'I'm ready to see if I can beat them.'

'You have a head start. Don't let me detain you a moment longer. Good luck, Isla.'

*   *   *   *

Damien could see his sister sitting in the staff restaurant of the Cavendish as he walked towards the door past the large oval-shaped window. He could see why she attracted so much attention from men and as Eric strolled cheerfully toward him, also making for the door, he could understand how she would be drawn to one so relaxed, confident and traditionally dashing – the complete opposite of himself.

Characteristically Eric greeted him in an open and friendly way. 'Hi there Damien. This can't be coincidence. Did Isla call you?'

'Yes. She wants the three of us to have lunch. Apparently she has been working on an urgent problem and feels the need to share it with us.'

'Did she tell you how urgent?'

'No.'

'She will when we sit down.'

They had already ordered lunch from the rob waiter and after settling down together at a table by the window Isla and Eric told Damien the nature of the decoding problem she had and the reason why she, or the Shanghai MDL lab, had to succeed. Then came the admission that so far she had got nowhere with the information at her disposal.

'It's difficult to see how Shanghai could do any better with the same key word,' said Eric.

'The only response I get is coded references to the SSS team which is trying to prove there is advanced biological life in other star systems.'

The robowaitress approached them quietly with almost graceful gait and placed three glasses of ClearSpin on the table.

Eric was frustrated on Isla's behalf. 'You must have been given the wrong keyword by the Knightmaster. I know he is about as reliable a source as you can get and he got the word 'Cosmo' from Father James. But did Pastor Wayne give him the right name? It could be a decoy to fool us.'

'I had wondered myself,' said Isla.

Damien suddenly looked thoughtful and about to engage with his sister and Eric, something which was still not natural to him. Memories began to work their way to the surface of his mind. The word intended to be a keyword for breaking an SSS code instead was setting off recollections of his training as a scoopship pilot. 'Wait. Did you say "Cosmo"?'

The robowaitress brought their meals. An atmosphere of promise and a resolve to cooperate in the collective solution of a problem were being generated by the three of them and this eclipsed any thoughts or comments about the delicious food that had been laid out before them.

'That's the word I've been using.'

Damien became animated. 'Cosmo? I remember someone of that name. He made a big impression on us at our scoopship training course, mainly because he was so good at intercepting simulated orbital debris. His scoopship piloting skills were also exceptional.'

Isla looked puzzled. 'That suggests the name was right. He is just the sort of person you'd need to place a nanobot swarm in orbit. So why do my searches draw a blank?'

Isla was going to ask if Cosmo had been a friend of his then remembered how difficult her brother found it to make friends. In fact as far as she knew there was nobody who could be described as his friend. But then her brother volunteered that there had been an unlikely rapport between him and Cosmo.

Eric leaned forward putting his plate to one side. 'Maybe we should talk about this more, Damien. If this man Cosmo is the same one that Wayne referred to then the more you can tell us about him the more chance we may have of getting a lead.'

'He was a strange person – even stranger than me you could say. He was popular but at the same time did not fit in.'

Isla interrupted in a sympathetic voice. 'Maybe that's what you had in common. Neither of you fitted in.'

'Yeah, that's probably right. He just talked about his plan to set up in business. He said he was going to buy a second-hand scoopship when his GF trustee fund became available, although at the time he was working for Orbital Technologies.'

'Wait, that could be a lead. I can use my flexcom for a straightforward search on OT.' Damien watched Isla enter the phrase 'orbital technologies' with her eye movements. Then she entered 'cosmo'.

'No! His name was spelt "Kosmo".'

Eric looked at Isla. 'So that's why you've been drawing a blank.'

Isla got up immediately. 'I'm going back to the lab now.'

*   *   *   *

Decoding the SSS's messages was never easy even with the power of a quantum deciphering module at her fingertips. She had cracked the coding this morning but now she was locked out again since the SSS automatically reset its encoding scheme every few hours. It took several hours of hard work, even following up inspired guesses and decoding strategies with notes and diagrams manually pencilled onto a piece of paper. She was thankful that the use of computer technology had been forbidden to her, as it had been to many, before she reached the age of 20, so that a full understanding of the principles of mathematics, physics and engineering could be obtained without distraction or ignorance of the foundations on which these fields of endeavour were built.

Eventually one of her deciphering strategies worked and she was ready to enter the keyword 'kosmo' instead of 'cosmo'. She decided to use the keyboard this time. Yes, it was obviously making sense to the system she had penetrated. Now to enter 'orbital technologies' and combine it with 'kosmo'. More activity. Now the information was flowing. She did not normally think in this way but it almost felt as if Yahweh was making things happen to save his creation.

'Hello, Ms Hanson. Any progress? The Shanghai team say they are stuck.' It was the Knightmaster over the flexcom. He had a habit of changing his form of address to his part-time secretary between her first name and a formal title.

'Yes, but first you must let Shanghai know that the keyword you gave me is spelt with a "k", not a "c". And there is more information they should know but I need to talk to the team directly if they are to have any chance of building on what I've already uncovered. For instance, my brother Damien was on the same training course as Kosmo.'

'This sounds promising. What else, Isla?'

'It appears that Kosmo is now working near Kuala Lumpur as an independent scoopship pilot. He was hired by the SSS to replace an orbiting meteoroid, one large enough to be monitored by our GF tracking system, with a modified version that looks sufficiently similar not to show up as anything unexpected.'

'Modified in what way?'

'By packing a swarm of nanobots inside. Microthrusters were added to steer it – presumably towards the ADN antenna.'

'Wonderful work, Isla. So now we know in principle what needs to be done. It's a matter of getting hold of the meteoroid or disabling it in some way. And that means finding Kosmo and asking him. Do you have anything on his whereabouts?'

'Only that he operates from an office at a known address in Kuala Lumpur.'

'But will he help? Is he ideologically committed to the SSS?'

'Damien doesn't think so, sir. He is a neutral hedonist who works for money and doesn't ask questions. Damien's guess is that once he discovers the purpose of the stuff he has planted in orbit he will do all he can to help us. He's selfish but not, as far as my brother recalls, evil.'

'Well, let's find him. I just hope he is at the address you have turned up.

It is of course possible that more information on Kosmo's current location can be found. How likely is that, given the progress you are currently making?'

'Not very, actually. I could hand over what we know to the Shanghai team. They might be able to build on it and get more information by a different route and approach.'

'Yes, please send them what you know. Meanwhile, let's call in your – what shall we say, friend – Cadet Knight Reed. We need to formulate a plan of action at once.'

As he started to make contacts and arrangements Isla ventured a suggestion. 'Sir, you may have heard that Cadet Knight Finley is recovering fast. He would, I know, having procured the original batch of nanobots like to be involved in capturing the ones now in orbit.'

'I appreciate your concern, Isla, but you must realise that if Cadet Finley's condition slows us down in any way it would not be acceptable to include him in the operation.'

'I was only expecting that we would discuss the plan with him.' She thought about why she wanted to include Roscoe and decided she had been hasty. It would put him under a strain, possibly marring his recovery, and there was no real reason why he could be expected to help in planning a raid in which he would not be able to participate. Maybe part of her could not let go of him romantically. Was she harbouring some deep-down resentment that Amelia was alone with him, despite her own attachment to Eric? Probably not. 'He is strongly motivated to come up with ideas because he doesn't want his original Burnham Thorpe raid to have been in vain. But I guess you're right, sir. We should leave him undisturbed.'

'Is there anyone else who ought to be in on this?'

Eric had come into the room and was sitting next to Isla. He joined in the discussion over her flexcom. 'Damien, Isla's brother, would be a possibility, sir.'

'You may well have a point there, Cadet Reed. He knows the character of our friend Kosmo better than any of us. He is not in the Knights of course but considering what is at stake we are justified in bending the rules. What do you say, Isla?'

'It would please him to participate and he could be very helpful. After lunch he was going over to the library so he is probably still nearby. Shall I call him?'

'Yes. Let's all meet in my room in the town centre as soon as Mr Hanson can manage and see if we can hatch a plan to save the world. That may sound dramatic but it is nevertheless true.'

*   *   *   *

Roscoe was feeling well, although slightly weak, as he rested, alone with Amelia after first Isla, then Eric had left the recovery room. They were totally at ease with each other and felt closer now than before they had last been alone together before the Holkham raid. He had previously wondered whether he should ask her to take an Oath of Bonding at some agreed date but had feared rejection, even though he was quite certain she felt the same way. Why should he fear rejection? Father James had explained to him how pointless it was. God is truth. If one is rejected in love, or one's friendship is declined, one has found truth, since the illusion that one has been in a mutually giving and fulfilling relationship has been shattered. And every step towards truth is also a step closer to Yahweh.

Because he was still rather weak they had not spoken much; but the silence between them was an easy, relaxed one, with no tension or embarrassment. This in itself was how sure he was that Amelia would agree to become engaged.

'What's the weather like? Maybe we could go outside. I'm sure the doctor would agree.'

She went over to the window and looked out onto a courtyard of flowering white acacias. 'I think he would. Shall I speak to him?'

He gestured his agreement as she picked up her flexcom. It was a pleasure just to sit and watch her doing things for him. As expected the doctor thought it would 'do him good' to get outside. It was strange to hear such an expression three quarters of the way into the twenty first century but it reflected the fact that there was still no reductive, scientific explanation of the benefits of a pleasant environment on one's health, just as the placebo effect and the power of positive thinking were real phenomena beyond analysis. As indeed were the Holy Scriptures and the events poetically portrayed in them.

Amelia supported him as he climbed tentatively out of the bed, his muscles weakened by lack of use during his long coma and guided him gently outside onto the square of lawn surrounded on three sides by acacias. They sat at a small round table.

'Lia, before the Holkham attack we had discussed getting engaged as a commitment to a later Oath of Bonding.'

'Ros, I don't think you should be thinking of this now. You need to concentrate on getting better.'

'You mean you are not so sure about this as me.'

'No – I am sure. But we agreed that we needed to discuss it with Eric and Isla.'

'Why? Surely this is just between us. It doesn't affect them.'

'But it does, Ros. Surely you can see that. Isla and Eric want an Oath of Bonding and we have discussed forming a Circle of Kinship with them if they also become bonded. You have previously been involved with Isla and Eric is your friend. We all need to talk about this together.'

'Perhaps we could call them over now.'

A robin hopped onto the back of the vacant chair beside the table.

Amelia looked exasperated. 'Not now. We need to think more about this first. And so do they. This affects our whole future.'

'Only for thirty three years, assuming children are involved. That's only a bit more than a tenth of a lifetime for one with Life Extension. Without children we would only be bound for three years.'

Although she thought her reply was entirely justifiable per se there was another reason for delaying a meeting. Secretly she had received a message from Isla about the second lot of nanobots and in no way did she want Roscoe to know about it until he was fully well again.

She placed her hand on his. 'Just wait, Ros. I do want to get engaged, definitely. I just want to do it at the right time, in the right way.'

*   *   *   *

It was almost like a rain forest. Fronds, verdant growths and towering festoons of rich flora glided beneath and around them as the transglobal approached the cityscape. Here and there were mosques covered in Islamic art and they had to twist and turn around the tops of skyscrapers protruding triumphantly above the greenery in which they were predominantly shrouded. The twin towers of Petronas also stood even more clear of the jungle-like mass. They had been doubled in height to a kilometre during the new materials revolution, the same revolution which had made feasible the Global Federation elevator to orbit. Its distant cables were barely visible as thin grey lines rising into the heavy thunder clouds from the equatorial terminal station.

'Is that really a city?' Damien was commenting rather than asking a question.

'It's Kuala Lumpur, the world's greenest metropolis. Somewhere in this tangle is our friend Kosmo with a K.' Eric was looking for a landing place not too far from Kosmo's coordinates.

Isla read the thermometer and saw that it was over forty degrees Celsius even though it was only April. Hopefully, the greening of the city would have been designed to make it more comfortable down there than in a normal city at that temperature but it would nevertheless be oppressive.

As the transglobal locked onto the coordinates which Isla had obtained for Kosmo's address it took them down in a gentle spiral to a clearing in the foliage which was the nearest they would be able to get without walking.

Standing on the grass next to the transglobal they felt uncomfortable in the hot humid air. A granilite path appeared to lead into an orchard of mango trees and from their flexcom maps it should take them to the place they wanted. It occurred to Eric that it would be better if just Damien and Isla tried to contact him initially. Three of them might raise questions and put him on guard. He would recognise Damien and know he had a sister, who he would no doubt find attractive. Probably this was an unnecessary precaution but he felt that just the two of them would seem more friendly and more likely to get his cooperation. They could always call him if he was needed later for any reason.

It had been a long time since Damien and Isla had done anything together as brother and sister. Not since their childhood adventures. They set off along the path and soon were among the mango trees. Some fruits were hanging sufficiently low to grab so Damien reached up and picked one for each of them. They were juicy and it was difficult to avoid getting sticky as they ate them. He felt foolish at being so impulsive but she rebuked him for feeling this way, thinking that one of Damien's faults was not to be impulsive enough. They found a small fountain and used leaves to wash their hands. It was also refreshing to splash running water over their faces.

After resuming their path a small rectangular building with an ornate twisted spire at each corner came into view. This was where Kosmo lived according to the coordinates Isla had obtained. Nearby were several small huts which according to the travel information served as brothels. Damien guessed that Kosmo would be no stranger to such places and that he had deliberately chosen to live close to them.

Isla looked around. 'I've heard that there are gangs in this area associated with the brothels. Do you think it likely that your old friend would get involved with them?'

'Indirectly, perhaps. He was a law unto himself. I don't really know.'

A seductively dressed girl sitting on a seat under one of the mango trees and smoking something, probably a spacing out drug of some kind, eyed them with detached interest. Then as they walked towards the door of Kosmo's residence a tall powerfully built Malaysian man got up from a seat and moved towards them. From his gait and expression it was clear that he regarded them with suspicion. That Kosmo would have a bodyguard was totally unexpected although given the nature of the neighbourhood they realised they should not have been surprised.

He said something to them in Malaysian. Isla's flexcom identified the language at once and translated it into English almost in real time. The machine voice sounded a lot more friendly than the Malaysian's: 'What do you want?'

Damien replied. 'I'm Damien Hanson, an old friend of Kosmo who we think lives here. We need to see him urgently.'

'What about? Is the girl for his pleasure? He is not expecting you.'

Isla felt deeply insulted. 'I am Damien's sister, Isla Hanson. I'm a mathematician.' They would never be able to explain why they were here and had not thought it would be necessary to make up some credible excuse for meeting him. 'Just tell him who we are and he will know that we are his friends.'

'You are not expected. You cannot speak to him now.' He spoke in a threatening way and obviously not in a mood to be persuaded.

They made a quick retreat and walked along the granilite path until well out of sight of the bodyguard. Then Isla called Eric on the flexcom. 'Trouble. Eric, you'd better join us since it appears your skills will be needed to get a meeting with Kosmo. We've encountered a somewhat unfriendly bodyguard who doesn't seem to like the unexpected.'

'In which case I can get you past him; but can you open the door? It's probably locked with a security code.'

'I've got remote access to some of the quantum computing system at the Cavendish. It shouldn't be too difficult.'

'I'll be with you in ten minutes or so.'

They sat down, preparing for a wait of at least twenty minutes, given Eric's propensity to be less than precise in keeping appointments. As they sat there Damien wondered why his old friend would want a bodyguard at all. Had he become involved with the SSS on more than a one-off contractual basis? When he put this to Isla she was non-committal but did not seem to want to talk about any alternative theories. Somehow he thought she was hiding something, as she had often done as a big sister even during adulthood. He wondered whether she was like this with Eric and how it would be if and when they entered an Oath of Bonding.

What really mattered now was that they find the orbiting artifice with its secreted nanobots and remotely steered microthrusters before the ADN antenna was destroyed, and with it possibly the whole of human civilisation. Which meant they had to speak to Kosmo and get his cooperation. A lot depended on Eric's non-violent combat skills as a Knight of Peace. Isla wondered why the Knightmaster had not sent a bigger more senior team to accomplish the mission. Yet she knew he was always ready to take calculated risks and must have quickly considered the situation from all angles.

'Over here.'

It was Eric calling from among the trees, well away from the path. Slightly puzzled they got up and moved over to join him. His smartsuit had adjusted to local attire for a man of his age in Kuala Lumpur and with one hand he held a black, cloth-covered box by its handle.

'The pied piper gave it to me to use on this mission.'

Isla laughed. 'What are you talking about? Who is the pied paper? This is a serious mission.'

'Let me explain. You've already met him as Leading Combat Knight Harry Davies. He earned this name by sometimes playing pipes in the street to distract passers by when on certain kinds of mission.'

'So what's inside?'

'You might call it a box of tricks. I intend to use it to get the bodyguard away from the door. Just follow me but keep well back so he doesn't see any connection between us. Watch me from among the trees and as soon as he is out of sight you can start trying to get through the door.' He walked on ahead and as he got close to the bodyguard Damien and Isla moved further away from the path and hid among the trees.

Eric stopped close to the bodyguard, who looked suspicious and uncertain, and placed the box on the path. He pulled up the lid and made a show of looking inside, pulling out a long flute-like wind instrument and began to play a simple tune which Harry had taught him. As the bodyguard came up to protest a huge fountain of fire appeared to rise out of the box, rotating and twisting like a tornado and, as expected, he looked fearful and cautious. Then Eric released a solid looking holofig of a samurai warrior wielding a rotating sword which he inserted into the pillar of fire until it seemed to glow red hot. He held the sword against the trunk of a tree which then seemed to smoulder with the heat and Eric could not begin to fathom how this particular piece of deception technology worked but it had a marked effect on his adversary. The sword by its appearance and motion terrified the bodyguard and he ran out of sight within only a few seconds.

'Now's your chance, Isla. I'll keep a watch in case he comes back, which he may well do when he realises the holofig has disappeared. It can only stay in form for fifty metres or so; then it literally vanishes. In any case people usually figure it's an illusion eventually, even if they've never heard of KOP deception technology.'

They ran up to the door and Isla pulled out her flexcom from her smartdress. Within seconds alphanumeric symbols raced across the display and Damien attached a feed to the lock which sent digital pulses generated from the Cavendish computer. Isla looked frustrated. 'It would help if we knew how many characters make up the combination. It's going to slow things down if I have to keep trying sequences for different code lengths.'

Isla had exhausted the possibilities of a four character code and had just started running sequences of five when Eric, from his vantage point in the foliage of a tree, saw the bodyguard approaching. This time it would be more difficult to repel him. 'Keep trying. I've got some more technology.' He jumped down from the low branch where he had perched himself and reached inside the box again. He released another holofig but this time it was a mirror image of the Malaysian, dressed in exactly the same way. But instead of walking head on to the bodyguard it approached from behind and tapped him on the shoulder. He turned round and screamed in startled terror then ran off into the mango grove. 'That's a first field trial for a tactile holofig, fresh from the Shanghai lab. It seems to work. Still, I hate to frighten anyone that much.'

The door at last swung open. 'Eric, we are going in now. Will you keep a watch?'

'I'm ready for him but somehow I don't think he'll be back in these parts for a while; nevertheless, I recommend closing the door behind you.'

They walked into a small vestibule decorated sumptuously, wondering how to make their presence known. They could hear a girl laughing from a room upstairs. There was something erotic about her tone and Damien guessed she was one of Kosmo's 'guests of pleasure', an expression he remembered from the training school days. They climbed to the landing and heard talking from inside the room and Damien immediately recognised the voice of Kosmo.

Isla spoke quietly to her brother. 'D, I think you will have to call to him. It would look even worse if he finds us in his house unexpectedly.'

Damien had already decided there was no alternative and so spoke loudly through the closed door to the bedroom. 'Hi, Kosmo, it's me, Damien. Remember?' They stopped laughing and talking, and a short silence ensued.

'It's *who?*'

'Damien Hanson. We were on the OT course together. About five years ago.'

'I do remember but how in the name of hell did you even find me, let alone get in the house past my bodyguard?'

'It's a long story. I'll explain later.'

Isla could not resist interrupting. 'Please, this is urgent. You've no idea how urgent. I'm Isla, Damien's brother.'

'She works in quantum computing and specialises in decryption. It enabled us to break into the SSS network and to break the lock code.'

'Too much intelligence in a woman is not normally to my liking but for a lady with a voice like that I would do anything. Just give me a couple of minutes.'

They could hear indignant and incredulous noises from Kosmo's 'guest of pleasure'. The building was old in structure and design so that the floorboards creaked as they moved about in efforts to cover themselves. Eventually the door opened and a girl came out in a pink robe, looking embarrassed. Isla recognised her as the one who earlier that day had been sitting smoking on a seat near the granilite path. She ran down the stairs and disappeared through a side door. The hiss of a shower followed soon after.

Kosmo strode onto the landing, almost as though he was making a theatrical entrance and there was a slightly self-mocking air about him.

'I must excuse my friend outside the front door. I don't know how you got past him but congratulations anyway.'

He had always lived a hedonistic life and took nothing seriously. Either because of this or despite it he had been liked by most people, including Damien who could not be more unlike him. However, the situation they now faced was too serious to warrant flippancy or humorous dismissal. Would he understand?

Isla spoke in as grave a tone as she could muster. 'Please, listen to us. Could we go and sit down somewhere?'

He began to grow sombre. Was it just Isla's loveliness that was getting through to him? Was he just trying to please her? Or did it mean he somehow sensed the gravity of their mission? He was a businessman as well as a superb scoopship pilot, and so he must have a good grip on reality at some level.

He motioned them into a room where they could all relax and drink ClearSpin, or in his case strong whiskey.

'I can't imagine what this is about. So go ahead.'

Damien began in earnest. 'A few months back you took on a contract from an organisation that calls itself the SSS. Your brief was to locate a rock with particular orbital dynamics within a narrow range and to replace it with a device of similar size.'

'I had no idea what the real name of the organisation was but they didn't call themselves that.'

Isla remembered that the SSS had contacted Kosmo under the cover of the name Near Space Environment Research.

'So why the secrecy? Why didn't they use their real name?'

'The real name is Servants of the Seven Seals.'

'Aren't they just harmless cranks? The name alone suggests that.'

Isla corrected him. 'Cranks, yes. Harmless, no. The leader has exceptional abilities to help him to, as he sees it, bring about God's judgement.'

'Which is?'

'To kill us all off for disobeying him. To finish us all off in one final nemesis.'

'Well, if there was a God I wouldn't blame him and there wouldn't be anything we could do to stop him. But since there isn't, I think we should do our best to stay alive. It's called survival instinct.'

Damien was irritated by this off-hand dogmatism. He himself had been sceptical about the existence of God yet after meeting Father James he was inclined to believe in the reality of some transcendental source of love and being. But this was no time for rumination.

Kosmo continued. 'Anyway, how do I fit into this?'

Damien replied with deliberation. 'The object you placed in orbit was not a scientific instrument but a destructive device.'

He raised his eyebrows. 'You are not going to tell me that a small metal cone in orbit is going to wipe out the human race?'

'Indirectly, yes.'

Isla asked whether he was aware of the Bete Noire threat. She could well have believed that in his day-to-day pleasure seeking he had not really taken it in.

'The ADN should take care of that surely. I certainly couldn't do it with my scoopship.'

Damien retorted that his policy of 'no questions asked' had backfired. 'You and your scoopship may have prevented the ADN from deflecting the asteroid. The device you placed in orbit was packed with a swarm of nanobots and remotely controllable. The ADN missiles must be released if Bete Noire is to be deflected. And this requires all three guidance antennas to be working; but the nanobot swarm is programmed to disable one of them.'

The implications of what he had done, albeit in innocence, took away his confident stance. He put down his whiskey and grew dejected. Isla could not help feeling sympathetic at the burden he must be feeling as the import of his actions of a few months ago sank in. 'But you can put things right, if we act fast. You can get back to your scoopship and recapture the nanobots.'

'I assume we have plenty of time...' Kosmo stopped in mid sentence as he realised that although Bete Noire was not due to hit the earth for at least six months the interception missiles would have to be launched very soon. 'How long do we have?'

'Five days' said Damien.

'Five days? But can't they send out something else to intercept it?'

Damien, despite his autistic nature, felt that Kosmo was deeply concerned and troubled, for all his bravado about the transience and meaningless of a human existence where all we could do was survive and enjoy ourselves. Isla also sensed this. She had spoken to Roscoe about such people and knew that in this situation he would have asked why, if that was all Kosmo believed, should it matter that humanity was going to become extinct because of his actions?

'No. Bete Noire is thirty kilometres in diameter. It needs some very specialised technology to deflect a mass that big.'

Kosmo remained silent for a while, cradled his head in his hands then looked up at them in despair. Damien pleaded that all he had to do was board his scoopship, enter the location data module into his navigation system and destroy or retrieve the nanobots.

'I'm afraid that's where you're wrong, D. My scoopship is out of commission and I don't have the location module. They insisted on keeping it.'

It took a while for them to fully accept the reality of the implications of what Kosmo had just said; and when they did they each felt like one who has just discovered that a loved one has a fatal illness.

CHAPTER 26

REVELATION

The irony did not escape him as he stood on the ledge, facing the dizzy vastness of the Valles Marineris canyon.

He had brought the Pastor close to Enlightenment and now it looked as though they, his friend Aalim and a few others at the main base, would be the last humans alive. Water was available here, frozen and dirty but able to be extracted and purified. Oxygen could be manufactured by electrolysis of the water or breaking down the iron oxides in the reddish soil. The regolith and rocks contained nitrogen and other nutrients needed to sustain life. But Mars Base 1 did not have the technology to extract these or provide the artificial ecosystem needed to grow them properly. And there were no females to start a new generation. Earth was still like an umbilical cord to human existence on this stark planet. If only this collision had threatened us at a later stage in human history.

He almost wondered if Pastor Wayne had been right. Maybe God did plan that we would become extinct. Otherwise he would not have let this happen. But the collision had not occurred yet; there was still time, still hope.

The old question of free will surfaced. If God knew we would exterminate ourselves why did he create us in the first place with the free will to do it? Yet it was perfectly possible for God in Yahweh's kingdom, in Yahweh's greater reality beyond our laws of physics and causality, a state of being to which human concepts cannot be applied, to know our destiny and yet give us what in our lesser reality is understood as freedom of the will. Just as energy could be a wave and a particle at the same time, the two seemingly contradictory ideas could be reconciled. A professor of philosophy had once put it to him that the contradiction between free will and God's foreknowledge was illusory. He recalled that Roscoe had told him about the Molinists of the seventeenth century. They had shown by logic how an event, even a thought, could generate foreknowledge in an omniscient Creator, outside of time and space, without this affecting the person's free will.

A towering twisting pillar of dust zigzagged across the plain. He calculated it must be about a kilometre high and the way it moved seemed to suggest intelligence and purpose, and perhaps, in a sense, there was a purpose to each movement, but one not fathomable to us. After all, an ant in a nest has no idea that it has a purpose which any human observer can clearly see. Or does it?

His body tensed as he distanced himself from such reflections. It was futile to speculate on Yahweh's ways. God was beyond our conception and even the notion of a motive could barely be ascribed to our holy Creator. All he knew was that the Lord was real and that it was in Christ that God had chosen to reveal Yahweh's grace, love, truth and justice to him. And it was through the Divine Light, created by the Holy Spirit, that he could be in harmony with those following other faiths because the same Light was illuminating them.

He lamented his days as an Atheist, as a follower of the creed of 'nothing buttery', of greedy reductionism, where everything and every human condition and every thought and every concept was nothing but the product of chance, particles and energy governed by the laws of nature which had existed for ever and never been created.

Pastor Wayne came alongside to share the view. He had changed, definitely. He at last showed humility, but still had not reached Enlightenment. 'It's strange, Father. Like everyone else I always had access to the mounting evidence that we were probably alone in the observable universe. But it's only seeing this place and interplanetary space, how it contrasts with our world, packed with life and intelligence, that has moved me to wonder if humankind does indeed have a role in bringing life to the cosmos.'

'Pastor, I'm afraid I have some unwelcome news.'

'Unwelcome? To whom?'

'To everyone. Although a team has managed to find the individual who planted the nanobot swarm in orbit he does not have the data needed to locate it.'

'Why not?' The Pastor was genuinely alarmed.

'I asked the same question. It appears he had to return the data as part of his contract. This was insurance to prevent people like us getting hold of the data and blocking the sabotage.'

Wayne released an exasperated sigh. 'Of course, I should have realised.' He had entirely lost his air of superiority and a heavy sadness was manifest in his voice. They headed back along the top of the canyon towards the monastery. 'I need to pray for forgiveness. Father, can you help me attain Enlightenment in these last days?'

'I'll do my best and hope that God is with me and with our friends back on Earth. And considering what's at stake I think that's quite likely.'

*　　*　　*　　*

He lay awake on top of his bed, his arms folded behind his head. He had just surfaced from a deep sleep and he felt calm and at peace for the first time in his life. Images were in his mind, memories not of dreams but of some kind of transcendental experience of a truth from outside of space and time.

All his life he had professed not only to be in contact with God but to be the means by which Yahweh enacted the plan to bring to an end the race that Yahweh had created. The whole of human history was being brought to its conclusion through him, the Pastor, bestowing on him an importance and uniqueness comparable to that of Christ, to the extent that he had felt able to correct the book of Revelation as instructed by God. Now he realised that what he had thought was a divine epiphany was simply a desire to assert his control over his fellow humans. Father James had led him to believe, without preaching or didactic forcing, that the messages he appeared to have been receiving over the decades could not have been from Yahweh but were either from his own mind or from some numinous agency of evil. They certainly bore no resemblance to the Divine Light visions as described by Father James. Nor did they resemble in any way the classic revelations described by the great Christian mystics, such as St Julian of Norwich or the one spoken of by the theological philosopher Thomas Aquinas, who in the thirteenth century had received a theophany so startling that he was struck speechless for days afterwards.

Recently there had been a scientific development which Father James had been able to cite and which had finally broken down the barrier which had been keeping the Pastor from Enlightenment. Neurologists had recently detected the difference between patterns of brain activity accompanying those subjective experiences caused by internally generated stimuli and those coming from some external, transcendental source. The Pastor could resist no longer.

He stared around the small monastic cell and felt relaxed as his gaze focused on the plain white ceiling. Why did he feel so calm? Unless something miraculous happened humanity would reach its omega point and it would have been his doing. The quietness of soul began to give way to overwhelming guilt and torment. His body began to writhe and his head sweated. His fists and toes clenched and unclenched. It was as though his body could not accommodate any more agony or anguish and he cried out, as though appealing in desperation to the Creator. Then he tugged at his hair as the blasphemous comparison with Christ invaded his mind.

Father James heard the cry and quickly made his way to its source. He laid his hand on Wayne's forehead. 'Be at peace in Christ, my friend.'

The Pastor had never been open to such loving kindness and the experience almost filled him with tears. 'I have stretched Yahweh's forgiveness beyond all limits. The whole race is going to suffer.'

At times like this Father James' voice assumed a certain quality that somehow derived its authority from both sympathy and humility. 'There are no limits to the mercy of our Creator and Yahweh's grace through our Lord Jesus Christ. Whatever happens, it will have been a part of God's divine scheme. Anyway, rest, Pastor, there is nothing more we can do for the present.'

He moved away from the bedside and through the small cell window contemplated the arid, starkly beautiful Martian landscape, then said a short prayer: '*Lord, I know you will save us and that such places as this are for us to bless with life. Amen.*'

Never had the Divine Light caused such pain. He waited patiently for the Pastor to calm down, then, seeing his eyes close, returned to his own cell.

* * * *

He sat up with great suddenness from a short period of fitful rest on the verge of sleep. A name filled his conscious mind, a name he was not sure that he had known before. Where did it come from? Dimly perceived associations began to surround the name. A memory of a meeting in a small room with the First Protector and someone else. The name was not the First Protector's but someone with whom they had both had important business and at this moment he could not recall what that business had been.

Wayne got up and paced around his cell, frustrated at the feeling that this name was the key to so much but unless he could remember in what connection it would be useless data.

CHAPTER 27

REDEMPTION

He stopped rowing for a minute and let the boat glide towards the King's College Bridge, the water lapping gently against the hull. He remembered meeting Isla there that morning, how she had come up behind him. The image of her still excited him viscerally; but there was no sense of betrayal on his part or hers. The love between him and Amelia, now sitting opposite him, was of a different order and Isla was now fully committed to Eric.

'I suppose this is a strange thing to do – go for a row on the Cam when humanity is approaching Omega, thanks to Pastor Wayne.' His voice echoed as they floated through the tunnel of darkness under the bridge.

'Why? There is nothing we can do to stop it.'

'Are you sure you've recovered enough, Ros?'

He felt a warm sense of gratification at her concern. 'I checked with the doctor. I just need to be careful.' He pulled on the oars just enough to propel the boat forward and they continued without speaking for a number of strokes before letting it glide again.

Amelia broke the silence. 'I suppose it's pointless to think about what might have happened, but I can't help reflecting on how life might have been for us – not just you and me, but Eric and Isla. We were on the path to a Circle of four.'

'Five possibly. Damien has become very receptive to the idea of joining. As well as being Isla's brother he seems to get on remarkably well with Eric, considering how different they are.'

'True. I'm also surprised how well he seems to have gelled with Kosmo, who sounds about as different from him as one could imagine. You can never tell how two people are going to relate to each other – it's beyond chemistry.'

'Would you have wanted children? I mean, if Bete Noire had missed us.'

'Yes, at some time probably. I'm not really sure; but there are so many studies I want to pursue that would not have been possible before Life Extension.'

'It's so difficult to take in. Is this really the end of humankind? I can't believe it, deep-down. Can you Lia?'

'No. It may be totally irrational but I think something will prevent it. Call it faith.'

'Do you think human history is pre-ordained?'

'That's not a fair question! You know Father James fairly well. What does he think?'

'He says much has to be taken as a mystery.'

'That doesn't stop one having theories, though, does it?' Amelia smiled sympathetically.

'Well, he is not one to hold back from speculating. He seems to have two thoughts on this. One is that the structure of causality and space-time make it possible that what appears as coming from free will in our reality is in fact pre-ordained in God's greater reality, the one we enter when we get eternal life. The other way of looking at it is that even if the structures in God's greater reality correspond to ours it could be that only certain events are pre-ordained to be part of a divine plan. A limitless number of events can lead up to the next preset nodal event and all these are the result of free decisions which may or may not be in accordance with God's will.'

'Does it make a difference whether the decisions match God's will?'

'If they do, then the route to the next pre-ordained event is smooth and painless. If they don't then there is pain and misery before the next pre-ordained node can be attained.'

Amelia reflected on this. 'Could this be what we call judgement?'

'It makes sense to me, Lia. God has set up a moral universe in parallel to the physical one. If we ignore laws in the physical world – for instance if we step off a cliff we ignore the law of gravity – things go wrong. It's just the same if we try to break the laws of the moral universe, say by gratuitously harming another person. It's bad not only for the victim but for the perpetrator and for many others, directly or indirectly.'

'So that's what sin is. If the SSS are right, and we are about to terminate humankind, it just means we have violated too many of the universe's moral laws, as placed there by God.'

'Yes. But Yahweh has mercy and grace through Christ. Yahweh wants us to thrive, not be exterminated. I think Yahweh will help us help ourselves. I also think God wants us to colonise the rest of Yahweh's Creation, to bring spiritual life to it. Only where there is biological life can there be spiritual life.' Part of Roscoe wondered whether he should be presuming to think what God wanted but Father James's view was that since we were made in God's image he expected us to be creative in some way and constantly seeking the truth, as long as we recognised that the final answer would always be beyond our grasp.

A bend appeared in the river and Roscoe continued to row until they had got round it, when a small landing stage could be seen in front of them. They could see a patch of grass near the jetty and as they found each other's eyes they both thought it would be pleasant, if not more than pleasant, to lie on it, perhaps touching each other.

'Ros, I think it's time you had a rest. Shall we pull up here for a while?'

He steered the boat in until it thudded gently against one of the posts which held up the low wooden landing stage, then threw the mooring rope around a small bollard and helped Amelia step out of the boat. Holding her hand sent desire through his bowels and body as he led her to the small expanse of warm luxuriant grass. But although his body ached for her it felt different from how it had with Isla. The difference could not be put into words. The attraction he felt to Amelia was both stronger and yet, inexplicably, easier to resist, as though something in her was giving him the strength to control carnal desire. Or was it God giving him this strength through his faith? Or could it be that God was reaching him through her? He thought how much more difficult it had been for young men and women of previous generations, in a predominantly secular world where the media or their peers constantly urged them to be a slave to their passions of the moment, to do what made them feel good with little thought of the consequences.

As they stood on the grass he cradled her head tenderly in his hands. 'This is our test. If we can withstand the temptation to make love physically until six months after being engaged to be bonded then we can take the Oath of Bonding together.'

Amelia laughed gently. 'Then we'd better not lie down, Ros. And we'd better not waste any more time getting engaged.'

A feeling of gloom and foolishness dispelled their euphoria as they remembered Bete Noire and they sat beside each other. What were they waiting for, if the world was going to end in any case?

'Ros, could this really be the end of hundreds of thousands of years of human evolution? It just doesn't seem likely.'

'No. We have been in dialogue with the source of creation since hunter gatherer times, searching for the truth, developing spiritually in dialogue with our Creator. Much of the Bible is devoted to it. We have a long way to go.'

She watched a duck that had been swimming towards the opposite bank climb out of the water. 'If it is the end, then I feel that as a race we have been the precursor to something greater. Maybe just as an individual moves into eternal life, when brought into contact with God, either before or after physical death, the human race is about to move to some higher form of existence. Like a baby emerging from the womb into the light and the wholly different experience of the outside world.'

Roscoe recalled that Father James had used the same analogy, the baby being born, to illustrate how we enter into eternal life as individuals. 'So in a sense it would not be the end, just a metamorphosis. In any case, it appears that even Pastor Wayne no longer believes in a plan for our extinction.'

Remembering that they had arranged to meet Eric, Isla and Damien at the Orchard they got back into the boat and cast off.

*   *   *   *

Eric put down his ClearSpin. It seemed an incongruous thing to be doing, drinking and talking in the gardens of the Orchard. Unless something very critical could be done in the next three days this whole pleasant environment would become a lifeless inferno. He looked over at Isla. 'Exactly how long before the impact, assuming that nasty piece of rock is not deflected?'

'I don't know the exact date.' She touched Damien's arm. 'I left a file on your flexcom. It's called something obvious – like "impact estimate"?'

Damien picked up his flexcom and digitally fingered through the files. 'There's nothing that obvious. Wait, this must be it. "BN intercept trajectory."' She nodded and he scanned through the file summary. 'April 10.' Isla did a quick mental calculation. 'Which is in just over seven months.'

Isla looked at her brother with a blend of delight and sympathy. He had emerged from his withdrawn, guarded self since being involved with the KOP and she knew that he would so much like to have taken Life Extension, bonded with a woman and joined the Kinship Circle which she and Eric would have formed with Ros and Lia. In fact, he had indicated he would probably want to join the Circle even as a single person.

She had reminded herself that they still had at least seven months of life together. If, as now seemed inevitable, the SSS sabotage of the ADN mission could not be forestalled they could all live together in a sort of unofficial Circle. There would be no point in the two couples waiting for sexual union: the period of abstinence was meant to test their resolve and self control in preparation for a long period of living together. But it could be awkward. Damien would feel lonely.

The mournful hooting of wild geese gently interrupted the peaceful afternoon as a small flock flew overhead. Roscoe thought this flock had probably just arrived from Iceland. He had always been especially fascinated by migrating birds, how they seemed to confirm the intelligence and interconnectedness in an ecosphere in which every creature, bacterium and virus in the web of life had its own role in the scheme of things, its every action having to be at a certain place and a certain time in order that an unimaginably complex system should fulfil its destiny. Perhaps it was not just animate matter that was part of the system. Maybe every particle in the universe had an assigned role.

Amelia and Isla had walked over to look at a rose bush on the other side of the garden.

Eric glanced at them intermittently as they bent down to savour the scent. Roscoe imagined that his fellow Knight was wondering whether he should have picked one for Isla and presented it to her in a spirit of chivalry. Such a gesture would have been regarded as ridiculous for much of the century but in recent years, since the Knights of Peace had gained prominence throughout most of the world, it had become almost a standard part of the courting which led up to an Oath of Bonding, although he knew that it would not happen this way with himself and Amelia. It was just one small example of the cyclic sweep of history, a history which, since his baptism and confirmation in Christ, he had increasingly come to realise was reflected both metaphorically and literally in the Bible.

'Ros, do you and Lia have any plans for the next few days?'

'None. We can't really take in what's happening. I suppose we'll just go on from day to day. After the nanobot swarm has done its work all our fates will be sealed. What we will do then who knows? What about you and Isla?'

'Likewise regarding the next three days; but as for further ahead she often talks about us all living together somewhere for the seven months, presumably instead of waiting for an Oath of Bonding …Hey, wait. What's Isla doing?'

Roscoe looked up and could see she was looking intently at her flexcom and they could hear her referring to 'KF'. Amelia came over, leaving Isla deep in conversation. 'Isla has just had a contact from the Knightmaster, as you call him. I don't know the details but it seems Pastor Wayne has divulged some more information.'

Isla rolled up her flexcom and walked over. 'I've got something more to go on. Another name – Hexton, quite an unusual one fortunately. It seems that Wayne could not initially remember why this name had come into his mind after he had recovered but it has. Can you get me back to the Cavendish really fast?'

Eric hailed a transpod from the nearest rank and it appeared within a minute, landing quickly and silently on the grass near their table, lowering a ramp at the same time. There was room only for two in the cabin and Isla asked Damien to come. 'Eric, I'll explain later. But Damien needs to be with me.'

The transpod disappeared into the hazy blue of the afternoon leaving Roscoe and Eric mystified and full of questions.

*　　*　　*　　*

A morass of data engulfed her as she touched, prodded and blinked at the quantum decryption interface. She needed to work out the metacode, the system of rules which governed the daily changes in the encryption code. The metacode had itself morphed since her last session. She would have to enter as much known data as possible and match this to the apparently chaotic expanse of symbols and characters in which she was beginning to feel submerged. She had tried inputting 'Kosmo' and 'Hexton' but with no result. Could it be that there was no record of 'Hexton' on the SSS network? Kosmo could not of course know one way or the other – he would not have divulged his identity.

She sat back in her chair, looking dejected. 'I feel we are so close. If there was just one more piece of information we could feed in to crack the metacode....'

Damien interrupted. 'Would it be any use guessing the year in which Kosmo and Hexton negotiated over the locator data? The MODEL I think it was called?'

Isla slapped her forehead. 'Of course! What year would you think is most likely?'

'2076, I'd say. But we could ask Kosmo directly.'

'Yes, D, we could; but time is ticking away so let me just go with 2076 now.'

'I could try to contact Kosmo in case it doesn't work.'

'Yes, yes, please, do that D.' She frantically touched and spoke to the interface, trying all manner of inspired guesses and making full use of the extraordinary computer power at her disposal. Still there was no result. When she looked up she saw that her brother had gone – no doubt outside to get some fresh air while trying to contact Kosmo. She decided to try feeding in '2077'.

This allowed the quantum decrypter to perform its magic. The amorphous streams of data crystallised into intelligible information. But there was so much of it. She needed just one file.

Damien came back into the room.

'D, I've cracked the metacode and this has allowed me to break into today's encrypted info.'

'That's just as well. I can't get a response from Kosmo. So can you find the MODEL?' Just at that moment Eric, Roscoe and Amelia came in to join them.

Isla sat back in her seat again and folded her arms. 'There is an overwhelming amount of info here.'

'But as far as we are concerned, no knowledge,' observed Amelia with sympathy.

'I still need to find the file, the one containing the location module. What could it be called?' She looked around pleadingly at her friends. 'Any guesses?'

Damien half heartedly explained that it was known by the acronym MODEL, standing for Module for Orbital Debris Location, well aware that the SSS were unlikely to use this as a name for the file, since it was such a common abbreviation and in any case debris location packages were common.

Eric motioned Roscoe and Damien over to a corner while Amelia tried to console Isla in her stressful predicament. 'Look, we may be missing an angle here. Presumably this Kosmo must have negotiated with someone from the SSS when he gave them the MODEL data he had produced for locating the nanobot capsule.'

'The SSS would have provided an anonymous contact in Kuala Lumpur,' suggested Roscoe. 'D, has Isla tried "Kuala Lumpur" as a file name?'

'Yes, with no result.' Damien thought for a moment. 'But you've given me an idea. Another possible name for the file could be the name of the SSS contact.'

'But he would have been anonymous,' responded Eric. 'Or it could have been a she.'

Roscoe qualified this. 'In a sense anonymous, but he or she would more likely have used a false name.'

Damien pointed out that since the SSS would have studied Kosmo's lifestyle carefully before making contact they would probably have known his weakness for Pleasure Girls and realised that he would have given in fairly easily to feminine powers of persuasion. The name used by this female contact could have been used as the name of the file.'

Eric looked at each of them in turn. 'A long shot, maybe; but worth a try.'

Roscoe agreed. 'D, have you left a message for Kosmo to come back to you?'

'Yes, but with so much at stake we can't leave to chance whether he replies or even reads the message.'

'Let's get the Knightmaster to help.' Roscoe appealed to Eric, then to Isla. 'He has a lot of influence with the GF and should be able to broadcast a general telepresnet message.'

*   *   *   *

Damien could not help feeling at a loss as the two couples began to talk among themselves, unwittingly leaving him out of the conversation as their bonding to each other strengthened with the threat of the approaching black finale to bio-evolution on Earth, possibly even within the observable universe.

He went to his apartment in the centre of Cambridge and lay head upward on his bed, staring at the wall and wondering what the chances were that Kosmo would remember the name of the Pleasure Girl and even if he could, would this be the file name used by the SSS? Or supposing it was indeed the name. Would this necessarily allow his sister to decipher the code and hence get the MODEL data into a form which could be fed into a scoopship guidance and control system? But these questions paled alongside another one. Who, beside himself, would be in a position to use this navigation module at such short notice? Surely he could not be expected to do so himself, as one who had recently left Orbital Technologies and who had been very junior in the company. He did not even have his scoopship to use.

The sound of crickets filled the room and he realised his flexcom was hailing him from somewhere on the other side of the globe. He recognised the voice instantly, even before the face appeared. 'Hi, D. I just heard the telepres broadcast.'

Damien was amazed that Kosmo should contact him directly. 'Hi, but shouldn't you be going straight to the Knightmaster?'

'I thought you were short of time. Anyway, if I had gone to him it might have led to the GF bureaucracy becoming involved and I would rather they didn't know where I am. They can make life difficult if you don't play the rules.'

'So what have you got to tell me?'

'What do you want to know? All the announcement says is that I may be able to provide the KOP or the World Fed with information of critical importance to the coming Bete Noire mission.'

'You remember my sister Isla?'

'The lady who accompanied you to Kuala Lumpur? I certainly do.'

'Well, she is an expert code breaker using the latest quantum computing technology from the Cavendish. She is trying to break into the SSS network to find the name of the file containing the MODEL navigation data which you obtained while placing the nanobot capsule in orbit.'

'Unintentionally, I might add.'

'Of course. But if we had the data we could in principle load it into the guidance system of a scoopship and retrieve the nanobots.'

'We? Who's we? I've already said that my machine is out of action, tethered in the servicing bay 35,000 clicks above the Pacific.'

'Yes, I know. But as to who would do this…that I don't know.'

'Well I think I do. You were as good as anyone else I know at raking in the orbital debris.'

'But I'm on sabbatical from Orbital Technologies. How would I get permission? It's a lengthy procedure. The GF would have to override OT's Chief Entrepreneur and bypass global regulations to give me access to the fusion drive scoopship I was using.'

'Look, I've heard of this Knightmaster Franklin. He's known for cutting through bureaucracy when it has to be done. And everyone, even the whole of the GF, will act fast when they know the score. So brace yourself, D, for being the saviour of the world.'

'But I'm just a junior.'

'A junior in the right place at the right time. Or should I say in the wrong place at the wrong time, as far as you are concerned.'

It was becoming clear that Kosmo was right. He could well have to do this job himself and convince the Knightmaster there was no other way.

'Anyway, Kos, you need to give me the name of the SSS contact, otherwise it could all be academic. Isla can't guarantee a successful decryption even with the name. It's just that it's the only chance she has.'

'Well, D, the name is Sabrina. In retrospect she turns out to have been the most expensive Pleasure Girl in all history.' Damien sensed that, uncharacteristically, he was not being flippant.

*　　*　　*　　*

The morning twilight backlit the Illawarra Flame tree. It was two days before the launch window of the projectiles to be used for intercepting and diverting the incoming asteroid Bete Noire, which otherwise would strike the planet in seven months. Brother and sister walked towards Damien's parked scoopship. Unlike Kosmo's it was ground based rather than attached to the upper level of the ground-to-orbit elevator which Kosmo used to get into orbit.

'Things have certainly moved fast….for me to be in this situation.'

Isla shrugged. 'I've worked with the Knightmaster on and off ever since my Cavendish course started so it doesn't really surprise me. I know his powers of persuasion. That plus the respect in which most people, including the GF staff, hold the Knights of Peace.'

'Maybe if I can do this they would let me join?'

Isla looked doubtful for an instant but then said cheerfully. 'Yes, D, I think you would have a good chance.'

'Even with my low empathy scores? Autism is not a normal characteristic of Knights.'

'New ways of overcoming this are close to being available. Besides, if ever there was a case for making an exception this is it.'

'Or would be, if I succeed.'

'If you don't the question will be academic. But you will. I feel it.'

They briefly embraced before he climbed in through the open hatch of the transpod-type scoopship. After closing the hatch he ran through a check of his guidance system and confirmed that the MODEL had been properly loaded. It seemed to be functioning without the glitches one might expect after the data had been decrypted so there was no reason to delay taking the scoopship off the ground and raising her upward out of the atmosphere using the relativistic magnetron lifter, then pushing her forward with fusion power until she reached orbital velocity.

Despite Damien's autism and failure to be much impressed by views of the earth from space which most found overwhelming or soul stirring, he did marvel at the extraordinary silent power of the RM lifter against the gravity and he became aware that the gravity had been there since the planet was created as a lifeless ball of partly molten rock from the clouds of primeval matter that had enveloped the sun. And for the first time he did indeed feel in awe of the earth's delicate beauty as it hung motionless, a living globe in the star-filled blackness. This could not come to an end. He now believed that Father James was right when he had told him that man's destiny included spreading life throughout the universe, from the ecofilm which surrounded the globe which filled the observation port to the limitless expanse beyond.

Nevertheless, as he had also learned from Father James, he could not ask God to do the job he now had to do. Even if he had full-blown faith the Lord would not expect him to pray for direct help. Only when help coincided with the unfolding of Yahweh's cosmic plan would he get help, and there was no way any person could know that. That was how it seemed to him. He had to trust in his holy Creator to give him strength and calm, yes; but it was his duty to do his utmost to succeed by his own effort and will.

The fusion engine controlled by the MODEL data injected him into the correct orbit. He would also have to use the MODEL data to guide him towards the pseudo meteoroid. Then he had to get in close and release the engulfer. The engulfer would cause the meteoroid to disintegrate and at the same time surround it with a net to ensure no debris escaped. Why had he been so worried? It was largely an automated operation, quite unlike the alternative method of removing debris with a grabber arm. That was ruled out. The Pastor had told Father James that the nanobot capsule inside the meteoroid was primed to explode since it was probable that the target was booby trapped to cause the destruction of whoever or whatever got close enough to use a grabber. You could fire a missile carrying an engulfer from several kilometres and escape any explosion triggered by this.

The biggest uncertainty was one of timing. How soon before the ADN deflector missiles were fired towards Bete Noire would the nanobot swarm be sent in to attack one of the ADN antennas? Probably any time now. Hopefully they would not be launched until as close to the deflector missile launch as possible – this would make it impossible for the guidance antenna to be replaced by an ADN repair team. But suppose Hexton and his SSS associates had found out about what Damien was doing on behalf of the Knights of Peace, the Global Federation and the whole of humankind? They would almost certainly decide on an earlier attack time, which could be before the engulfer-carrying missile was launched.

He thought it very unlikely that the SSS would have found out about his mission to sabotage a sabotage, but nevertheless was inclined to complete the mission sooner rather than later. He was now only six kilometres from the target. One more kilometre and he would be close enough. He had already checked the control streams but decided to do so one more time. After all, in this situation it was best to keep busy.

Damien flicked his right eye twice and this initiated a test sequence. Streams of digits and symbols glided and rotated in front of his eyes. All were green. But then a red symbol showed up. Just one. How critical was this? It could well indicate something very minor, such as a back-up circuit malfunctioning, in which case there was no need to worry. In any case there was nothing he could do at this stage, although he would have to alert Orbital Technologies as well as the emergency control team comprising leaders from the GF, KOP and ADN. He touched the built-in flexcom to select a channel to the mission coordinator and pointed out the error symbol.

'Can you relay the d-stream to us? There is an engineer here who might be able to diagnose the error.'

'Yes. I think so.' He blinked an instruction into the flexcom interface and waited for confirmation of receipt. Then there was a long wait while the team digested the data and tried to deduce what was causing the red error signal.

He stared through the large front observation port. There was the usual expanse of blackness punctuated by a limitless number of stars, some bright and isolated, some forming luminous cloudy patches and ribbons, but all of them glowing steadily, free of twinkling, in clear colours. It all seemed more meaningful now, after his long discussions with Father James, and later with Roscoe, Eric and Isla, and the neurohealing sessions they had recommended. Why had he not appreciated its significance, its beauty and its terror? Perhaps his previous indifference had been a consequence not only of his autism but his association with Kosmo while training as a scoopship pilot. He and Kosmo had probably been as different as any two humans could be yet they had one thing in common: indifference to the transcendent grandeur of the universe despite having the opportunity to sense it more than most. Damien had been lost in his own world, which included the removal of orbital junk; while Kosmo had been lost in the pursuit of sensual satisfaction and the enjoyment of the admiration, sometimes adulation, of his peers because of his piloting skills, his social confidence and his success with beautiful women. And somehow Damien had sensed a liking and respect from Kosmo which had not come from anyone else. Even his sister Isla had seemed to feel sympathy for him rather than respect. But was indifference to the rest of the universe enough to account for the friendship? Perhaps it was that in a sense they both felt cut off from their colleagues, unable to share the normal to and fro of social interaction, albeit for very different reasons.

Now, whenever he went into space, there was no question of him feeling unmoved. Yet at this moment he was concerned with practicalities while at the same time being fully aware of the consequences of failing in his mission. As he gazed at the starry firmament in front of him he felt immense impatience. The pseudo meteoroid was only two hundred metres away. He could discern its shape with the unaided eye. At any moment a puff of gas could escape from the nozzle of the small propulsion engine strapped to it and it would move off towards the ADN antenna with cruel finality.

A pinpoint of light moved into the edge of his field of vision and he wondered whether this might be a stray satellite. Then the flexcom clicked into life and the mission coordinator's resigned voice came through. 'The engineers can't sort out what this signal means. At least not in the time we have available. It looks as though you will just have to try the launch system and see what happens. The chances are it's something trivial.'

'But if it's not, if the launcher fails? What shall I do?'

'We'll just have to discuss that if it happens. So try the launch now, without further delay. Every second we delay increases the probability of the nanobots setting off.'

Damien knew what he would have to do if the launcher failed and tried to put it out of his mind. He opened the code file and blinked in the firing code.

Nothing happened. Had he made a mistake. He was not prone to errors of this kind but he had to try again. Still nothing. He spoke into the flexcom again. 'No result, I'm afraid. Does this mean I have to go outside?'

'I'm sorry Damien. There is no alternative. The chances of this kind of error are almost infinitesimal but it's happened and there is no way we can fix this problem in the time left. Have you spacewalked before?'

'I had some simulations and have practised remote mechanical handling in a zero G environment. But no, I've never had to spacewalk; but since I don't have the equipment or the time for anything else I will just have to learn fast.'

'Remember to keep yourself tethered. We are praying, Damien. God be with you.'

Until recently such a statement would have seemed as silly to him as it would have done to Kosmo. Maybe that was what made them click together. They had both been Atheists. Now, at Isla's instigation, after talking with Father James and the Hermit Sage, Sister Agatha of Easedale, he no longer felt so certain about the absence of a Creator. In fact, he actually prayed for the strength to succeed.

He released a panel in the wall and pulled out his helmet and gloves. Then he removed the belt from his trousers and placed this inside the helmet. It took twenty minutes of fumbling to get everything properly fitted and working before he was ready to move into the inner airlock. Another five minutes passed before the air had been sucked out of the airlock and he could open the outer door without being pushed into the vacuum by the pressure differential.

It was a totally new experience drifting on a thin tether through nothingness with what seemed like the entire universe around him. He wished the circumstances had allowed him to savour it; but the meteoroid was now so close he had to act fast, so he unclipped his right hand thruster gun from his thigh and fired one short burst which caused him to slowly drift towards the target. It seemed to be approaching him too fast and his heart thumped. He fired the gun for as short a burst as was possible and fortunately this slowed him down enough to be able to get a purchase on the meteoroid as he clumped against it. Holding on as tight as possible – which was tighter than necessary – he moved his legs around until he had straddled it and was riding it like a horse, which but for Damien's lack of humour might have caused a momentary smile, even in a situation this critical.

He untied the belt which he had strapped around the arm of his spacesuit, placed the thruster back in its holster and in a series of clumsy, painfully slow contortions managed to wrap the belt around the meteoroid, leaving a small amount of slack. He pulled out the thruster again and inserted it under the smartbelt which then tightened itself until the thruster was secure.

At this point Damien was immensely relieved. Although the job was not done he had got past the most difficult part for one who was not naturally agile physically. Now he was floating alongside the meteoroid, detached from it and reaching for the mounted thuster's trigger which he was able to push fairly easily and click into the locked position, causing it to emit a gas stream which began to move the meteoroid away from him. All he had to do now was get back to the scooper ship which he could easily do by pulling himself along on the tether.

As he got to the airlock door he decided to look back, partly for the satisfaction of seeing the meteor-shaped artifice, packed with nanobots, being propelled away from a start position that would have allowed it to sabotage the ADN interception project. He also wanted to enjoy the universe while relatively relaxed and with his newly evolving sense of wonder.

Just as a sense of peace – was this the peace of God?– was beginning to rise he became aware that the meteoroid was no longer moving away on a trajectory determined by the gas gun he had attached to it. Instead it was beginning to veer as though correcting for the gun's thrust.

Already alarmed he was startled when the flexcom in his spacesuit came to life. Nobody on earth should be able to reach him at this position since neither the earth nor any orbiting relay transmitter was in view and the signal would be cut off by the scoopship's hull. Somehow he connected the voice with the point of light that had entered his field of vision earlier and which he could now see had gained in size and was moving slowly towards him.

'Mr Hanson, I presume.'

'But…is that Kosmo?' was the only reply he could manage.

'That's me. And you are wondering how I got here. There's no time to explain. You've no doubt noticed the disobedient demon.'

Then his tone became serious, more deeply serious than Damien had ever known in one who was normally so playful. 'I know that neither of us believe in God but I'm asking you for God's sake to get inside, *now*. And set an escape trajectory for yourself, quick as a wink. Only then can I stop the meteoroid.'

Kosmo had always been full of tricks. Damien's experience was that they always worked and there was no alternative but to trust to whatever scheme was hatching inside his enigmatic skull. Not to do so would mean the certain end of the ADN mission; but to trust him would mean there was at least a chance. So he pulled himself in through the outer door, closed it and re-pressurised the airlock. As he discarded his helmet he could see through the window Kosmo's spacepod tourer – not a scoopship – closing in on the meteoroid. But the spacepod had no grappler arms or other means of doing anything to the meteoroid. So what was the plan?

'D, have you set your escape trajectory?'

'No.'

'Then do it and activate. I can only beg you to trust me in this. Do it now, please.'

Damien was conscious that he should be consulting the mission coordinator but felt this was a case where rules were made to be broken. He did as his old friend had asked.

As the scoopship began to accelerate he saw the tourer do the same as it headed in a doomed straight path for the meteoroid. There was no doubting what would happen next but he did not look away. How could he look away? How could he not face the truth? The truth that one person's life was about to be sacrificed for the sake of humankind's future. The least he could do would be to witness the act of heroic martyrdom from this most unlikely of heroes. As the two objects moved out of view he turned his head to look out of the side porthole and there, in one moment, he saw the tourer spacepod crunch into the pseudo meteoroid and disintegrate in deathly silence, its myriad spinning fragments, along with the space-suited body, drifting rapidly away.

Kosmo's last trick had worked.

CHAPTER 28

REBIRTH

Roscoe sat opposite his father in the viewing room overlooking Grasmere. The midday May sun glittered off the small choppy waves and sheep were grazing on grass mounds near the shingle shore. There was a comfortable silence apart from the enthusiastic chatter coming from Amelia and his mother in the kitchen. He and his father had not felt so easy in each other's presence since he was a child but the two great events – the thwarting of the SSS sabotage mission and the impending engagement to make an Oath of Bonding – had lifted the gloom which shrouded most people and replaced it with the brightness of hope.

'You've struck gold there, Ros. They get on well together, Lia and your mother. Early this morning before you and the Knightmaster arrived they were out picking mushrooms for the casserole.'

'Casserole? Done traditionally? I thought I could smell something good.'

'It's a long time since she's done this – you or Lia or the occasion must have inspired her.'

'They certainly seem happy in there.'

The holodisplay on the wall suddenly showed a thick-set figure approaching. Roscoe recognised the face and bearing of Knightmaster Franklin as he walked towards the front door, left ajar, and stepped into the atrium on his way to the vista room where they were sitting. 'Father James told me about the view from here.'

'It certainly stops us moving anywhere. Tina and I more or less chose the house because of it.' Paul then disappeared into the kitchen to perform some trivial task allocated to him by Tina, so that he could feel he was contributing to the preparations.

'Lunch is on the table,' announced Tina as she entered with Father James and Amelia, leaving Paul to continue with his token task. 'Father J has been walking around the lake and has just come in through the kitchen.'

'To be greeted by a delicious looking casserole tended by two equally delicious ladies.' There was kindness in the Father's voice.

Tina then returned to supervise and dispense in the kitchen while Roscoe and the three guests made their way into the dining room. Roscoe stayed close to Amelia and they sat down next to each other, with her at one end of the oval table, their legs intermittently touching so that he sensed her femininity. The Knightmaster sat at the far end from Amelia, while Father James sat next to Roscoe.

After Tina and Paul had put the casserole pot, six plates, a flask of ClearSpin and six glasses on the table they sat down, with Paul opposite Father James. Roscoe had become aware of how this usually happened when Father James and his father were at the same meal table and wondered if it reflected their strongly opposing views on so many things. No doubt this would come out as the lunch progressed but he hoped that neither would lose their equanimity, something which even Father J sometimes came close to doing when in discourse with his old friend and adversary. For now, at least, all was calm and pleasant; and perhaps the presence of the Knightmaster and Amelia would change the chemistry to something less potentially explosive.

'As a rule Tina prefers me to keep out of the kitchen,' said Paul, jovially. 'She says I get in the way. Can you imagine that?'

Tina let out a token dismissive laugh and nobody answered; but glancing momentarily to his left Roscoe could not help reading Father James's normally non-judgemental expression, which appeared to portray that he could well imagine that his old friend and adversary could make a nuisance of himself in a place which at this stage of social evolution was often seen as a woman's domain, though now through choice and inclination rather than any tendency to male dominance.

The Knightmaster was the first to break the pleasant silence. 'Well I must say this is as good a way to celebrate as one could wish for. I sometimes brew a cup of tea on a century old camping stove but to have traditional food traditionally cooked, and in such good company.... a rare treat indeed.'

Paul was quick to reply diplomatically, although Roscoe, Tina and Father James could not help wondering if there was a touch of irony or sarcasm in it given his views on the Knights of Peace and the Monastery of Divine Light. 'We are fortunate to have you both here – and honoured. I have many questions about the KOP and the MDL.'

Tina interjected, looking towards Amelia. 'And of course we must not forget that our main purpose is to celebrate Amelia's engagement to our son Roscoe.'

Father James asked when their actual Oath of Bonding would take place.

'That's in six months. Amelia and I thought that shortly after the Bete Noire deflection would seem a good date.'

'Splendid.' Father James said this thoughtfully, not mechanically. 'Now before we eat would you mind if I said a word of prayer? I know we are not all believers but...'

Paul could not refrain from a patronising response as he looked appealingly round the table, smiling. 'If this makes you feel better, James, I'm sure nobody would object.'

Roscoe responded with ill-disguised irritation. 'Dad, when will you realise it is nonsense to hold on to the idea of an eternal meaningless existence. If it was meaningless you would not even know it was meaningless.'

Paul laughed dismissively, then looked around with incredulity as his five fellow diners bowed their heads in prayer.

> *Merciful and gracious Lord, fractal and holy, accept our thanks for our place in your scheme, the sustenance of our soul and for the food we are about to eat. And stir up within us a sense of your glory and sustaining love. In the name of our Saviour. Amen.*

He still could hardly believe that the popular musician who had started Baroqo had become in a sense the spiritual leader of the world's religions and, in particular, had brought Christianity to the next phase of its spiritual evolution, transforming the world's religions through the Divine Light.

As the business of eating got underway conversation started with pleasant trivialities about the food before them, then progressed to the weather, and it was this which led to considerations of higher things.

Father James addressed the table cheerfully. 'I perhaps should have included in the prayer gratitude to our Creator for allowing us to be here to enjoy the weather with the threat of Bete Noire removed thanks to the work of the KOP and the heroic actions of Kosmo Kingsley.'

'Not bad, for an Atheist, would you say? Saving the world?'

Paul could not resist the jibe. And Father James could not, despite his usual calmness and self restraint, help responding with incredulity, although he did manage to retain at least an outward expression of goodwill towards his antagonist. 'How do we know he was an Atheist in those last few hours? How do we know that God did not deliberately choose an Atheist to avoid divisions in the world religions that could not be healed even by the Divine Light? In any case, the Holy Bible abounds with examples of God bringing about his plan through non-believers.'

'Nonsense....' retorted Paul, his anger not so well suppressed. 'Pure speculation.'

'Indeed, but rational none the less.'

Knightmaster Franklin quickly rose to his feet. 'Please, friends, I suggest we talk about something less theological on this occasion, something less likely to promote strong feelings in the presence of these two young people. After all, we are here to celebrate their engagement as well as our survival as a species.'

Paul and Father James agreed to switch subjects for the sake of the occasion. Roscoe decided to take this opportunity to elicit from the Knightmaster information about the plans and proposals of the Knights of Peace.

'Sir, I heard that the KOP's Inner Chamber are considering new strategies for tackling No Hope Reservations.'

'A Global Federation term.' The Knightmaster looked apologetically at Father James. 'Not an expression I would have chosen.'

'One born out of frustration, I suppose. They are also known as Hate Reserves. But I agree it does give the impression that trying to reform such communities is a futile task.'

'More than an impression I would say.' Paul showed ill-suppressed exasperation as he stirred the casserole around on his plate and Tina gave him an admonishing glance. 'Especially as such communities are riddled with religion and superstition.'

Father James almost rose to the bait but the Knightmaster responded before he had a chance. 'According to our sociodynamics team such factors are secondary. It is craving for power which is the main impulse to war. Those who instigate and thrive in conflict exploit whatever gets people to follow them – ideologies like Marxism or Nazism, dynastic loyalties such as the Wars of the Roses in 15th Century England, class wars as in the French Revolution or patriotism as in the Napoleonic Wars.'

Partly to console his old adversary the Father admitted that the present conflict zones in the Reservations did tend to use religious and ethnic divisions to fan conflicts over resources but then proceeded to brush this aside by observing that the main reason people fought each other to the death was that they were able temporarily to lose their humanity by concentrating on some 'greater' cause. A cause other than the one true God, for there could only be one.

'And humanity is a greater cause than God,' said Paul, almost triumphantly, 'because God does not even exist.'

'Humanity is God, in a sense. That is why Christ came to us, to sanctify humanity; and His resurrection gave us hope, it was the triumph of life over death.'

Paul gave a mocking look. 'James, I think that's enough preaching for one night.'

Tina decided it was time to intervene. 'Paul, will you stop being adversarial?' She tried to say it with good humour. 'Knightmaster, perhaps you could carry on where you left off?'

Amelia supported her. 'Yes, you were talking about the Inner Chamber. I know both Roscoe and I would like to hear about anything they were considering.'

'Well, they have come up with a possible new line for the KOP Council to vote on. They are essentially a think tank but their latest proposal seems to me to have great promise. As you know there are still numerous No Hope Reservations around the world, areas where conflict or the potential for conflict is so embedded that all one can do is try to remove and enlighten the dominophiles.'

Amelia looked slightly puzzled. 'Roscoe has mentioned dominophiles but I'm not sure what this means. I know I played a small part in removing one – Pastor Wayne – from Holkham Hall. But I'm not sure what it really means.'

Paul could not refrain from making an aside remark about religious maniacs being the main kind of dominophile. Father James ignored the remark as irrelevant.

The Knightmaster continued. 'Dominophiles are those who like power for its own sake.'

Roscoe expanded on this. 'They either deliberately ferment conflict or, alternatively, become instrumental in the growth or continuation of conflict once it has arisen. In either case it helps them acquire power. The twentieth century novel by George Orwell, *1984*, talks about such individuals who derive pleasure from exerting power over others.'

'Well, Cadet Knight Finley has probably told you that the Knights of Peace have until now concentrated on removing dominophiles from populations where they are likely to be instrumental in the eruption of violence. We have developed quite a powerful method of modelling societies and groups in which social dynamics suggest a strong likelihood of conflict.'

'We call them Social Instability Zones,' said Roscoe.

'Moreover we have found ways of identifying dominophiles and impounding them. After that we hand them over to the Monastery of Divine Light, where a Hermit Sage tries to give them Enlightenment.'

Paul scoffed. 'Sounds like the Inquisition all over again.'

Father James insisted that an impounded Dominophile was not in any way coerced. It was legally essential under GF rules that no enforcement was used. The process of Enlightenment does not work if force is used. Non-violence, even at a mental level, is intrinsic to it, as it is to the KOP.

'The impoundment and Enlightenment processes have worked fairly well in the past and many conflicts have been stopped or avoided.' The Knightmaster resumed his discourse. 'However, it is a constant battle to prevent battles starting. Now the Inner Chamber has worked out ways to avoid whole No Hope populations being influenced by dominophiles.'

'Prevention rather than cure,' reflected Roscoe, who had heard rumours.

'Very much so. Until now we have concentrated our resources on removing dangerous dominophiles from unstable sociodynamic systems and, where possible, Enlightening them. However, there is in principle no reason we can't Enlighten whole populations.'

'But there are still about half a billion living on Hate Reserves,' said Paul. 'Besides, what right have we to "Enlighten" them, may I ask, Knightmaster?'

Father James responded in defence, but remained calm and congenial. 'What right have Hate Reserves to stay as they are when they threaten the well-being of the bulk of the world's population? And what right have we to ignore the miserable plight of those born into them, starved of material security and human dignity, of all hope?'

Roscoe looked critically at his father, as did Tina, and he appeared to have resigned himself to being in a minority and keeping quiet. 'Alright, Knightmaster, I'm sorry to be argumentative. I am a host after all. Please, carry on. Whatever differences we may have I know the KOP is a major player in the world and it would be stupid of me to pass over this opportunity to hear what it plans.'

An inaudible sigh of relief emanated from the other five diners and the tension in Paul himself seemed to dissolve.

'Please, Mr Finley, I am well aware that the KOP as it is today is somewhat limited in its efficacy. However, the Inner Chamber has some firm proposals that promise a major advance in our efforts to transform the world.'

'And Paul, you are right.' Father James was at his most conciliatory. 'There has to be some departure from the principle of equal rights for all, one of the ideals on which the most prosperous and socially just regions of the world are founded. Just accept this for the moment and see if you agree the price is worth paying.'

The Knightmaster continued. 'It is lasting peace we want. Our aim is that the Knights of Peace will make itself redundant because our aim is to change human nature itself. That is what the Bible means by redemption. Impossible? What do you say, Father?'

'Dostoevsky, the Russian author of the 19th century, was concerned that without God anything is permissible. The wretched outcome of Nietzsche, Nazism, Stalinism, social Darwinism, nihilism and populist Atheist diatribes against religion led to horrors we are all only too aware of. In his grace God has now revealed to us that if we let him into our inner being human nature can be as Christ wanted it to be when he sacrificed himself 2000 years ago after some hundred millennia of human evolution - spiritual and biological.'

'So, at a more practical level, how do we transform a No Hope Zone into one with hope and a decent life for its people?' The Knightmaster, with his rhetorical question, was obviously gearing up for an exposition.

'Let me start by restating our present focus in the cause of peace. The KOP has demonstrated its ability to identify and impound dominophiles, ones who love to dominate. We identify the dominophiles by inserting microscopic chips into the food of suspected populations and using these to monitor brain activity. The brain activity patterns are relayed to our quantum computer systems which allow us to diagnose social instability and the incidence of people – dominophiles – who are likely to initiate or perpetuate violent conflict. We then impound those individuals for Enlightenment. You look puzzled Cadet Knight Finley.'

'There is much about the KOP and the MDL which puzzles me, Knightmaster. Leaving aside questions of human liberty, if these brain waves indicate anti-social behaviour would it not be logical to treat the brains with drugs until they cease to be a threat?'

'It would,' replied Father James, 'if the brain activity were really the cause of the behaviour. But neurological research has shown that although there are some correlations between brain activity patterns and behaviour they are just symptoms of something much deeper, something transcendental which causes both the behaviour and the brain activity.'

Paul gave the impression of distancing himself from the discussion and adopted a condescending air. He was vaguely aware that such ideas were emerging from neurophysicists but did not realise that they had become so widely accepted. The other five diners looked surprised by his adherence to the old idea that physical processes in the brain were the root cause of all decisions rather than an effect.

Amelia filled the ensuing silence. 'Knightmaster, I also have a question. How does Pastor Wayne fit into this? It seems there was no sociodynamic instability around him; so how did the KOP become alerted to him as a threat?'

'The Servants of the Seven Seals and their doctrine of deserved nemesis were well known. Only when a few individuals managed to escape SSS indoctrination did our KOP Social Monitors discover the seriousness of their plans and the resolve of Pastor Wayne to enact them.'

Amelia asked whether the Pastor was in fact a dominophile.

'Very much so, very much so. He enjoyed dominating others and had the kind of personality to do it, although in his defence he genuinely believed in mankind's deserved nemesis.'

In the memory of Father James was Wayne's recent Enlightenment on Mars and he felt impelled to come further to his defence. 'The Pastor was of course guilty of being judgemental, a sin we are all prone to and which would distance us from God were it not for his grace through Christ, which is open to those who accept it. But ultimately he showed humility in receiving the Divine Light.'

Roscoe, addressing Amelia, added that as a result of Enlightenment the Pastor would no longer find pleasure purely in exerting power over others. He would still be a strong leader, but one working in accord with God's will and so helping others realise their potential.

'Indeed,' the Knightmaster concurred. 'Now, subject to a favourable vote by the Global Federation Parliament, we are about to embark on a new strategy, one which concentrates on the prevention of whole communities or tribes becoming dangerously unstable rather than removing dominos from populations which have already fallen into such a state. In fact, more than that. We want to turn Hate Reserves into sources of creativity, growth and love.'

'A tall order if I may say so,' observed Paul.

'But not one we can turn our backs on,' retorted Father James.

The Knightmaster raised his arm in emphasis. 'Difficult it will be. But I see no choice. The destructive power of the technology now at our disposal will not allow us to survive as a race unless the nature of every man and woman on the planet is transformed. Our Creator has given us the means to do this through the Divine Light, is that not so Father?'

Father James nodded assent and Paul sat back in resignation.

'The most important part of our strategy is its modular nature. There are still half a billion people living in No Hope Zones so we have to convert them piecemeal and bring them into the GF one by one.

'Having decided on a particular region, call it Zone X, the first step is to identify the leaders by impregnating the food with QTCs and analysing the signals from the individuals who've ingested them.'

'What's the difference between a leader and a dominophile?' asked Paul.

Roscoe looked at his father in exasperation. 'The leader leads by inspiration, by the releasing of a person's potential. He or she enjoys seeing people realise and put to good use the talents the Lord has given them. The dominophile crushes human potential, intimidates and forces people to obey him and takes pleasure in doing this. Not all leaders are perfect, of course, but they are in general better than dominos.'

The Knightmaster continued. 'The leaders we need to get on our side – the side of peace- will be in schools, training colleges, universities and churches, synagogues, temples or mosques. We have formed a KOP unit to set up pleasant conference centres in remote locations, to which the impoundees will be transferred. At these centres there will be intensive sessions to teach them the value of democracy, integrity, justice, creativity and the seeking of knowledge. It took most of the GF regions - e.g. Europe and North America - centuries to learn the value of these virtues.'

'This sounds impressive,' said Amelia, 'but haven't such things been tried by missionaries in the past?'

'They have but not on such a thorough, methodical basis as we are planning. And without the knowledge of the personal mentality of each person that technology is now beginning to provide. There will be one person teaching each leader in an interactive, non-confrontational style. While the teachers are learning about the kind of society they can have and that the GF is willing to help them achieve it we will be giving the same message to the population at large. Health and Wealth Mercy Teams will be dispatched to offer support to whoever needs it. The KOP will be inviting people to join it and help with its peace missions. Free communication and computer technology will be distributed and classes on how to use it will be free to attend. In fact we may even pay people to attend the first few lessons.'

Roscoe wondered whether the present policy of impounding dominos would continue in the targeted region.

'Quite possibly, as long as this does not risk interfering with the long- term solution of winning the support of the locals and bringing them into the GF. Impounding dominos is not usually popular with the local population. Nevertheless, a few reformed dominos make all the difference.'

Paul objected that there could be resentment at being manipulated.

'Possibly; but to help offset this we propose giving Peace prizes to local people able to suggest tactics for preventing or resolving conflicts. The No Hope Zone would of course have to get to a certain stage of development before this became a possibility, although there are bound to be a few talented people who will get the message quickly and see the potential for social harmony and have the imagination to see how fulfilling life could be without hatred and distrust.'

Tina excused herself from the table and went to fetch the dessert, which was a crumble made from the apples which Paul had picked from the tree in their garden last September, when the Holkham Hall raid had taken place. They had been frozen. Home made food still had a uniqueness about it which could not be defined, something beyond scientific analysis and she was pleased that her home-cooked casserole had been enjoyed so much. She wished Paul would not be so confrontational; but perhaps this was an inevitable consequence of his anachronistic Atheism which put him in a minority in any group of people he was likely to be part of.

Amelia ventured half apologetically into the kitchen. 'Can I help?'

'Thanks – perhaps you could take these two into the Knightmaster and Father James while I get the rest ready?'

She took the plates into the dining room and returned while Tina was still dishing out the four remaining crumbles. Looking up at Amelia she asked her if she liked cooking or did she prefer to rely on synthetic culinary systems.

'I have not felt any urge to cook so far but I have often wondered whether I might look into it. I suppose I'm bound to with so much life ahead in the Circle.'

'He's so pleased to be sharing his destiny with you. How do you feel about committing yourself for so long?'

'I know we have to be together. We both feel it is within God's scheme.'

'And I'm sure Isla and Eric feel the same. The four of you will make a wonderful Circle.'

The rest of the meal was quieter and more harmonious. While Tina and Amelia had been in the kitchen Paul sensed that he had gone too far with his arguments and that as a host, and in deference to Tina, who was particularly averse to any kind of confrontation, he should seek to promote harmony rather than sow discord, although he felt that Father James was more suited to such a role, a feeling that was confirmed when the latter spoke.

'I understand that Eric and Isla are to join us later.'

Roscoe confirmed that although they had been unable to arrive in time for lunch they would be here for the evening and that the four of them were to go to the holotribute in the village.

'Won't that be a first for you, Ros?' asked Tina.

'And for me, I'm afraid,' interjected Amelia. 'Neither of us are keen on dancing but it seems our fellow Circle couple enjoy these events so much we had better at least try to make an effort to understand what they see in them.'

'Who is being "holotributed" tonight?' asked the Knightmaster, making it clear from his manner that he was not familiar with this form of entertainment.

'Jefferson Airplane. They were an anti-war folk rock psychedelic band of the late 1960s.' Roscoe suspected that this would be a less dance oriented event than most holotributes. The band had been something of a social phenomenon, tied up with the rise of a counter culture and protest against the Vietnam War of that time.

Father James pointed out that although they were often associated with hallucinogenic drugs these were principally a symptom and symbol of their disillusionment with the prevailing society, naive though they were in thinking they could fill the spiritual vacuum with drugs, since the illusions engendered by these only separated them further from their Creator.

'However, is it not true, Father, that the world "hit" *You need somebody to love* has been seen by scholars of the Monastery as a kind of foreshadowing of the Divine Light, along with another song of those times by the Beatles, a group from England which was popular globally.'

'*All you need is love,* exactly so Roscoe,' responded Father James, 'in a sense these two songs summed up the essential message of God, although few at the time would have realised what was happening. In retrospect they seem to have been part of our Creator's divine scheme. Who knows?'

Paul was about to make some protest when the holodisplay in the corner of the room showed that Isla and Eric had arrived and were standing by the door in the light of a reddening sun as nightfall approached.

*   *   *   *

The music was strange and full of contradiction. Drums played a flamenco rhythm with military precision, the electric guitar was both disciplined and anarchic and the attractive, colourfully dressed girl singer had a richly feminine, yet slightly hard, voice to which there was a sinister undertone. Surreal holofigures of white rabbits, mushrooms and doctored depictions of scenes from a twentieth century cartoon of a nineteenth century book called *Alice in Wonderland* moved in three dimensions around the auditorium mingling with the audience, who were dancing freely, amid these bizarre projections. Roscoe reflected that all this was from a unique episode in human history, an era of unprecedented change which was still in progress, though now more truly creative and in harmony with the divine scheme, no longer made rootless by worshipping the created order rather than its creator.

The music now changed from the iconoclastic surrealism of *White rabbit* to one which conveyed a message which had never died even in the darkest, apparently Godless eras of man's spiritual evolution: *You need somebody to love.* Roscoe enjoyed the power of the music and for the first time in his life found himself dancing with abandon: no discipline of footwork was demanded, the beat was strong and, most important of all, he felt at one with Amelia. He even felt an affinity with Isla and Eric, though he could not fail to be aware that even in this slightly anarchic dancing milieu they stepped and gyrated more adroitly than either he or Amelia could manage.

Although it was enjoyable and cathartic Roscoe was relieved when Eric, also slightly breathless, suggested they take a break.

As they ascended the spiral staircase to the Night Dome he was reminded of that evening before the Ovoskotia operation when Isla, Eric and he had attended the pre-mission ball. It had not been an entirely enjoyable night: his lack of dancing agility, his frustrated infatuation with Isla and his jealousy towards Eric as he gave pleasure to Isla through his easy command of the steps and movements needed in a pavane, were unpleasant memories. Yet there had been enjoyable aspects. While they had watched the Dance of Life performance and during the break he had been able to enjoy Isla's electrifying presence, although even this was, in retrospect, a less than fulfilling experience, undermined by anxiety and the uncertainty of any relationship he could imagine himself to have with such a beautiful and intelligent woman.

The Night Dome was a refuge of tranquillity and complete silence. The acoustics were such that only those sitting at the same table could hear each other at all and the stars outside on this cold May night, together with wisps of slowly drifting cloud, were projected into the dome with such realism that, apart from the comfortable temperature, you felt yourself to be in the open. Eric pointed out that if you stared at any one nebula, star or planet for more than thirty seconds it would be magnified until it became a three-dimensional object.

'Then if you blink three times it replays its history, right back to when it was forming from interstellar dust and gas - if it is a star that is, and not a planet,' added Isla.

Amelia was about to suggest they focus on an object now but it appeared someone at another table had already done so, for just as their ClearSpins arrived a spiral galaxy grew out of a speck in the sky, then, as time reversed, it expanded to fill the whole dome with a more or less homogeneous mass of stars which, as time went forward again, drifted slowly towards a point, forming into a spiral structure at the centre of which a black hole came into existence. Stars fell into it and were absorbed while others formed in the ring of hot gas surrounding the small sphere of black darkness.

After they had witnessed this display of celestial physics in action for a few minutes Roscoe could not help noticing how Isla's hair and delicately sculptured eyes, nose and mouth, caught stray traces of light as she moved her head. Although it stirred him he did not feel guilt. He could now appreciate a lady's loveliness, even viscerally, without being driven by passion to act, 'a slave to sin and death' as it says somewhere in the New Testament. He was now free to be righteous through his relationship to God. His love for Amelia was both one of will and one of emotion alloyed with sexual attraction: nothing could take it away, so he could be safe in experiencing the attraction of other women.

Eric wondered who the girl singer had been in the holotribute.

'We'd probably have to ask Father James,' said Roscoe. 'Or my own father Paul. They were both musicians and interested in the twentieth century roots of their own genre of music.'

'If you are talking about the original artist, and not the girl who was doing the live performance tonight, I think it was Grace Slick.' Amelia registered Roscoe's surprise at her knowledge and continued. 'I studied the history of popular music in the twentieth century as a social phenomenon before concentrating on the violin at Emmanuel College.'

'Were they connected with the ant-war movement?' asked Roscoe.

'Yes. There had been a general revolt against war in most western countries. War in the sense of large mechanised forces fighting each other, as in the American Civil War and the two World Wars.'

'Then terrorism and ethnic conflicts started and grew in number as dominophiles learned how to exploit the vulnerability of democracy: freedom of expression and legally enforced human rights.'

Eric wondered why such societies could not have suspended these privileges. 'The trouble makers could then have been defeated and the rights restored afterwards.'

Roscoe was doubtful. 'This would have destroyed democracy, the very thing which these dominos hated.'

'Not necessarily Ros,' said Amelia. 'For instance, such rights were suspended in World War II when fighting fascism but they were brought back afterwards.'

'But then there was a clear end to the war. With terrorism the threat continues indefinitely. For as long as there are people in the world wishing to change it by force.'

'So that's where we come in,' said Eric. 'We stop people wanting to change the world by force.' He looked around and saw that most people were returning to the auditorium. 'Are we all ready to go?'

They got up from the table and moved to the spiral staircase, descending and rejoining the audience as two couples. More people were participating now, as heavy rhythmic beats and soaring guitars dominated the music and this further allowed Roscoe to lose his self-consciousness to the extent that he enjoyed himself, as did Amelia, even when they moved separately. The holofigures were now absent. Eric and Isla were consummately expert as always and sometimes Roscoe and Isla moved together as did Eric and Amelia, so by the end of the evening the four of them felt truly in unison, all previous awkwardness between them having dissolved.

*   *   *   *

Walking back to the house they skirted the shore of the lake. It was a cold night but their smartsuits self adjusted to keep them comfortably warm except for their heads and the sharpness of the air on their faces was invigorating after the hot humidity of the auditorium. The moon was full and the lake was just still enough for its reflected image to be discernible as a sphere rather than a smudge of illumination.

Standing on the jetty near the house they looked at the stars, the silence punctuated by the lapping of water. Amelia wondered whether humankind could really be alone in the universe. Roscoe had noted that up to only a few decades ago it had been confidently expected that there must by now be millions of other civilisations in a universe of ten billion trillion stars. As the possibility dawned that humanity could be unique, or at least so rare that it would never encounter any intelligent life form other than those which abounded in our own ecosphere, a sense of loneliness, almost terror, had seemed to engulf humanity's thinkers and visionaries, while at the same time there was a growing certainty that the universe was there for a purpose, intricately designed for humans and that this lifeless cosmic expanse was waiting to be explored and colonised.

Then Eric asked from which direction the asteroid was approaching. Roscoe pointed out the star Spica, suspended above the outline of the fells on the southern side of the lake. 'It will be travelling towards us until it is deflected in October, when the ADN missiles are scheduled to reach it.'

'I suppose this will definitely happen. Is there anything that could go wrong? Could the ADN missiles miss?' Amelia looked at Roscoe.

'It is as certain as the sun rising tomorrow. Both are subject to the same laws of celestial mechanics. The only possible thing that can go wrong now is the deflection explosion system but this has several backup systems, although nothing is ever one hundred per cent failsafe.'

They felt a sense of hope, of the future but also of the unknown. It seemed as though the whole human species was about to metamorphize in some way, to fulfil some destiny beyond its imagination.

'We've all had Life Extension,' said Eric. 'If the world changes in the next three centuries the way it has in the last ....'

Isla held his arm. 'I can't begin to imagine but I know we will be together, as a Circle.'

Amelia agreed and added: 'With children, with new members, new relationships.'

'But I feel God is with us,' said Roscoe. Without consciously intending to do so they linked arms as they looked out over the lake. 'Shall we pray?'

Epilogue

Paul sat in the viewing bay of the *Confucius*. In a few hours he would be entering the descent vehicle and bound for the MDL monastery, built into one side of the Valles Marineris. What was this intense loneliness, this desolation, he felt? It had grown over the forty days of his journey, starting as he left Earth orbit and seeming to get worse every time he looked out and saw his home planet appearing a little smaller. Now it was just a bright blue point.

Father James had warned him of this. It was not just that he missed the actual richness of experience of a biosphere seething with life and so benign to humans and full of beauty to the human eye. The panoramic views of the untwinkling stars of outer space had initially been fascinating and breath-taking but, unlike the lakes, mountains, trees, flowers and sky of Cumbria they were the same all the time, harshly cold and constant, telling a story of total lifelessness. Or was life just very rare? Either way the prospects of finding biologically-based sentient beings seemed virtually nil.

Back home he knew there were people around, even when walking alone across the fells where nature itself was like a living companion. Now, although there were fellow passengers and crew members, he felt he was in a tiny bubble floating through an arid infinitude of vacuum and dead matter. Yet he knew that not everyone felt this way.

The vessel had rotated and the viewing bay was now filled with the red globe of Mars. Soon the gravity simulation would be turned off as the *Confucius* was prepared for orbital capture manoeuvres and docking with the Mars descent transpod. He decided to get up and experience normal weight for this last hour or so before landing. In less than a day he would be inside the monastery - strictly as a tourist, of course – and living under a gravity pull less than half the Earth's.

Apparently this feeling of cosmic loneliness was greatest among those who denied the living God. He was one such person and yet did not want to be part of a lonely species. But if there were no extraterrestrials, what? He thought it must be comforting to believe in God, especially the one that many believed had assumed human form 2000 years ago, but he could not base his worldview on what was comfortable. It had to be true. Yet without God what was truth? Why did it matter? If all was illusion why not cultivate the illusion of God? But if truth did not exist what would that mean for science and reason?

Walking across the viewing bay deck his back felt warm, a blinding light suddenly filled his eyes and his legs collapsed under him. He fell to the floor, wholly helpless. It was no illusion.

*   *   *   *

His sight had not returned. It had been a sudden plunge into darkness without sleep. The world which had been there moments before now seemed more real because of its absence. Father James had often referred to a song from 1970 by Joni Mitchell, 'Big Yellow Taxi', which had the line 'You don't know what you've got till it's gone.' Only when you lose something do you realise what you had.

The MDT pilot needed to guide him to the monastery entrance, almost carry him, despite the low gravity. Aalim had greeted him and led him to the guest area. Was he blinded forever? He had travelled 40 million miles to see Mars and now he saw nothing. He had already been feeling space loneliness; now he felt utterly helpless and very afraid. Afraid of being blind for the rest of his life? Somehow he felt he was going to recover but he was nonetheless fearful of something and still a black emptiness resided within him.

'My name is Aalim. You may have heard of me.'

'Father James mentioned you as a part of the Enlightenment team on board the *Confucius*.'

'Yes. I know him well, or have done at various times. At present I am in my capacity as a Hermit Sage and have been asked to show you the monastery while you are on Mars. I have of course called the doctor.' Aalim touched him on the shoulder. 'Paul, I know you may think this strange but you must not fear what is happening. God is with you.'

'How do you mean? I've just been struck blind. Why should I not be afraid? Has James not told you I don't believe in God. Even if I did how would that change anything?'

'It would change everything, Paul. You would no longer feel alone and you would be confident that in the end all would be well, whatever your present state. There would be nothing to fear. It was said in one of the letters to the apostles: "Perfect love drives out all fear." And the gospel of John said that love is God and God is love.'

'How can love or God stop you feeling frightened?'

'It dissolves your ego, takes away your pride. You have nothing to lose when you have lost all pride. Yet having lost it you are able to gain truth and live in God.'

'What about pain or blindness or deafness? Should we not fear these?'

'Surprisingly, no. We would rather not experience them and we can even take steps to prevent them; but we do not fear them. If they happen the true believer has faith that they are for a purpose and puts himself or herself into union with God with no loss of dignity because there is no dignity to lose, no struggle to engage in. Ultimately, whatever calamity engulfs us we are in God's hands through Christ. In faith we are indestructible. We are absorbed into his being in the life which continues through physical death and is everlasting.

'Eternal life? Are you saying eternal life starts before we die physically?'

'Yes. You get it when your pride and ego die. This is what the prayer of St Francis means when it says "For it is in dying that we are born to eternal life." Only when your worldly self dies is God able to help you and draw you into his being.'

'And dementia? Does this not show that our minds are just the product of biologically produced brains?'

'What do you mean when you say "I think *with my* brain"?' You are referring to something beyond the brain. One yogic teacher said of meditation: 'I am watching myself think.' Leading philosophers have reached the conclusion that the brain and body are the means by which the soul interacts with the material world and learns from it. When the body or brain malfunctions the soul struggles and learns until released by the physical death of the body-brain system. After the struggle the soul is wiser.'

Paul felt vulnerable. His Atheist faith was under threat. His old friend and adversary Father James had been trying to convert him since Baroqo disbanded decades ago and he had always resisted. Had this been set up? James had a lot of influence with the monastery on Mars. Had he arranged for Paul to be temporarily blinded by a drug just to make him receptive to Aalim's persuasion? No. It did not feel like that and in any case James would not work that way. That was always a rule when Enlightening dominophiles. Free will was sacrosanct since without it one could not achieve Enlightenment. This much he had learned about the Knights of

Peace. It was considered better for Enlightenment to fail than to resort to any form of coercion, no matter how gentle.

Strangely, despite his absence of sight he did not feel especially frightened or anxious. Yet he still felt uneasy with the whole situation.

'Paul, why do you resist so much?'

'I don't want to be fooled by something fictitious. I want truth.'

'There is no truth without a transcendent deity as a source and absolute reference point. So you really do believe in a God, albeit an impersonal one. Would that not be fair to say? Otherwise reality is just a hall of mirrors, a maze with no centre.'

Paul had never gone as far as conceding this in his arguments with James but always managed to bluff his way out of the dilemma. Somehow the blindness and the fact that Aalim was not an old friend made him less resistant to this difficult question. The blindness had reduced his pride and so removed an obstacle to truth. 'OK, I suppose there must be some kind of causative agency that created reality and holds it together.' He realised he was using the very words James had uttered years ago but that he had refused to accept.

He sensed a glimmer of light. Gradually his sight was returning and as it did so a vague image of Christ began to form in his brain. Or was it in his soul?

*　　*　　*　　*

Paul and Aalim walked across the floor of the Valles Marineris beneath the noon sun. The dusty ground was reddish and the towering canyon walls framed a pinkish sky. Their pressurised smartsuits were the latest technology for walking on Martian soil, ultra comfortable and allowing one to sense the texture and relief almost as much as with bare feet.

'The air temperature is quite comfortable at around midday so our smartsuits don't need to provide heat, only pressure and oxygen. So what you are feeling now is the warmth of the Martian noon at the equator during summer.'

'I believe that is quite exceptional for Mars.'

'It is indeed, Paul. Exceptionally life friendly not only for Mars but for anywhere in the solar system or any exoplanet discovered to date. Even at this spot the temperature tonight will be tens of degrees below zero. Cosmic and solar radiation is also a problem anywhere other than on Earth.' Aalim stopped, looked up and around. 'Biological life is not the only life. All of Creation is alive in God, in some indefinable way, when we observe it.'

They walked in silence for several minutes then Paul started speaking. 'It is difficult for me, you must understand, to accept so many of the biblical events. The whole bible story seems ridiculous when compared with science.' It was more through habit he said this. Inwardly a transformation had taken place since the temporary blindness and he had not yet accepted this.

Aalim's sonorous voice in his helmet sounded sympathetic. 'You have been steeped in scientific materialism, which fails to capture reality other than at a functional and limited level. What you have to realise is that reality is multidimensional. The battle between good and evil, order and disorder is happening outside of time, before the Earth was formed, now and in the future. In fact before space, time, matter and energy were created. The physical world we see around us, the observable universe, is only a tiny part of a huge story that encompasses both the spiritual and the material. There is a whole heavenly realm. Angels are real beings in another dimension.'

'Are you saying that some of the more bizarre events of the Old Testament happened literally?'

'The truths conveyed by the supernatural events described in the Bible– and they are quite rare, by the way - are much more important than the events themselves. What is really important, and part of the greater reality, is what they mean, the essential truth behind them and the story of human perception of God that has been unfolding through history. Modern physics shows that our world is not solid but pure energy reflecting something real and solid beyond our four dimensional world. Evolution is now definitely accepted as purposeful and teleological. So you can see that the Holy Bible must rely on imagery to a great extent to convey its truths within our limited reality. Some things occurred literally and it is clear from the biblical text and cultural context when this was definitely the case. The Resurrection, in particular, was a literally, objectively true event that changed the course of human history. This was every bit as real as the Big Bang creation of the universe *ex nihilio*. Both are supernatural in that they originate from beyond space and time. When He appeared after physical death it was as a substance otherwise unknown, a new state of being.'

'How? Could He not have been a ghost or a hallucination?'

'No. The witnesses themselves knew the difference between a hallucination and an experience. They actually emphasized that it was not a ghost. They also were able to touch Jesus, as did the disciple Thomas, for instance. And yet, though solid to the touch, he was able to appear out of nowhere in our four dimensional world and vanish back into it, pass into the realm of God, which is outside any dimensional reality since God himself created the multiple dimensions invoked by string theory to explain quantum phenomena and elementary particles.'

'What about the Holy Spirit?'

'A major influence on world history since the Pentecost, when it became ubiquitous, common to all nations, races and religions. Ever since it descended on humanity after the Ascension of Christ violence in the world has, on average, despite advances in killing technology, decreased. Recent history may seem violent but compared to the world before the Pentecost it is a great improvement. Had today's weapons been available before Christ humankind would have become extinct. Death by violence before the first civilisations was the norm, whether in fighting between individuals, constant warfare between small groups, ritual sacrifice of children, gender selection by infanticide or the killing of the sick or disabled or elderly infirm. Violent death was almost the norm. The first civilizations, like the Sumerians, introduced order which diminished violence in society and concentrated it in battles by armies over city states and with other civilizations. Rome maintained a brutal order.

'Then came Jesus Christ and the Pentecost, causing the Holy Spirit to influence all nations and religions. Healing of the sick, care for the poor, In faith we are indestructible, educating the illiterate and searching for truth pervaded society.'

'But what about the wars of Christian nations?'

'It was a departure from the commandments of Jesus that caused these. Christian nations had their share of unjust rulers and power hungry individuals, encouraged partly by the Viking and Islamic invasions to resort to war; and once the culture of war had invaded the Christian countries they even fought each other. But the fighters and monarchies were greatly outnumbered by those actively promoting the commands of Jesus Christ in the Sermon on the Mount. Healing of the sick, feeding of the poor, loving even one's enemy, educating the underprivileged and searching for truth – these were practised by hundreds of thousands under the influence of the Spirit. Great institutions rose up – hospitals, charities and universities. Even some of the armies were permeated by values based on Christ's commands, as is our own Knights of Peace today. Then came the move to abolish the age old practice of slavery, exploitation of women and racial discrimination. All this started in Christendom and gradually spread to other parts of the world.'

The sun was getting low and the temperature was dropping rapidly. Soon their smartsuit heaters would not be able to cope. They headed back towards the monastery and decided to negotiate a small hill on the floor of the Valeris Marineris since this was the shortest route. Their boots kicked up the red dust into smoky twirling patterns which blotted out the Sun before dispersing.

Paul began to see everything differently. Not so much because of what Aalim had said but through his sudden loss of sight and physical collapse while still on board the *Confucius*. His ego, pride and prejudice had been dissolved away. The obstacles to perception of truth had vanished. Then the vague form of Christ had appeared in his soul. He felt that the material world, the universe, was just a stage which had emerged from a greater, spiritual, multidimensional reality. One on which we all played a part.

Of course the Resurrection was real. It had changed the direction of history over two millennia against the strongest resistance by vested interests and even misuse or neglect by people within the church institutions. Just three years of itinerant ministry had generated thousands of manuscripts within decades of the Crucifixion. Paul Finley now accepted it as a real miraculous event, like the creation of the universe in the Big Bang. It had rippled through history and caused those who followed Christ truly to forgive without limit, to love our enemies, to repay bad treatment with good treatment, to help the poor, the sick and the outsider. Archaeological and other extra-biblical evidence had been accumulating through the 21st century but he had previously heard about each nugget in isolation and concentrated on listening to desperate debunking arguments which, though weak, distracted him from awareness of the overall case for the reality of a supernatural event two thousand years ago.

A spiritual power was mounting within him. He felt the need to announce his submission to the living God and said calmly without theatrics: 'Christ is risen.'

Aalim smiled but said nothing. There was still a mile to go and they had to hurry before the intense cold blackness of the Martian night overtook them.

* * * *

The observatory in the monastery gave a night view of the stars and planets not unlike that from the *Confucius*. It was a sparse room but comfortable. They were drinking ClearSpin and had been sitting in comfortable silence for a while.

Questions flooded into Paul's mind; but they were questions which sought answers, not rhetorical questions or questions designed to win an argument. He sensed that this Hermit Sage would be able to answer the questions as well as anyone and better than most. Father James could have answered them equally well but he was an old friend who he had known before the subjugation of his ego. One rarely regards the words of a friend as authoritative.

'I still have questions.'

'Of course. But I suspect they will be of a different kind. And some will be unanswerable but by all means try me.'

'As a Christian, how do you view the exploration of space? I can't see how this fits into God's plan. There does not appear to be anything like conscious life here or anywhere else apart from Earth. So why don't we just stay on Earth?'

'This monastery is one reason. Taking dominophiles here for Enlightenment works better than taking them to the one in Shanghai, the other MDL monastery. We think it helps reduce their sense of self importance, their pride. As I said before, pride is the biggest sin for all of us, not just dominos. Enlightenment is essential if lasting peace is to be achieved, so that we do not have to rely on the Knights to keep the world in peace. Only through spiritual peace can there be true peace on Earth, the peace that would please the Lord.'

'Yes. But I thought a monastery on the moon would serve just as well; or one in orbit. Either would be cheaper.'

'True. But not much. The economics of spaceflight changed radically with the dark energy drive. And certain aspects of Mars, such as the day being only 37 minutes longer than on Earth, the possession of at least some air to soften the sunlight and evidence of past water in large amounts, somehow accentuates the contrast between the two planets in most other ways.'

'But apart from the monastery what real reason has there been to go into space?'

'In a sense, it is simple to answer this. It is God's will. But from humankind's perspective it seems entirely reasonable that we should exploit the mineral resources of the solar system's countless asteroids rather then further damage the life-filled environment of Earth, a gift from God.

'The urge to explore both intellectually and physically reflects the creativity of the Creator, in whose image we are made. In exploring we uncover evidence of God's exuberance, playfulness and joy in making and developing the natural order for us, His children.'

Aalim recalled that Father James had posed another possible reason for the outward urge, as some science fiction writers and space visionaries had called it. He said it was to prevent the formation of a monolithic world government on Earth, as was likely to happen with the Global Federation. Humanity would migrate and learn to set up self-sustaining colonies, as we are already doing on Mars and the Moon. With the growing power of technology and our ability to copy and learn from God's natural order it could even become possible to terraform some planets.'

'Is there a biblical precedent for this outward urge?'

'Genesis chapter 11 talks about the world speaking only one language at the time they were constructing a tower on a plain in Babylonia, one so tall it would reach the sky.'

'The Tower of Babel?'

'Yes. God said that too much progress was being made, that soon men would be able to do anything. Evidently this was not part of his plan so he scattered them all over the Earth and mixed up their languages. Could this be happening again now?'

Paul conceded. 'We certainly have the technology to spread out over the solar system and eventually further. And in doing so our language and culture could again diversify. A fascinating thought.'

'Perhaps faith in the Creator will be increased as humans spread out, colonise and transform the universe. There will be a revived awareness of reality. From the Enlightenment up to the New Enlightenment of today civilisation has been protected from it, and able to live in an illusory bubble. Especially the growing number of people entrapped in urban areas and cut off from the greater reality.'

'So do you think I may feel differently on my return trip to Earth?'

'Quite possibly. You are more likely to sense the presence of God instead of feeling totally alone. But you will need to pray and meditate frequently.'

'My son Roscoe is a Knight. You may have heard about him from Father James.'

'I have indeed. He was involved in the impoundment of Pastor Wayne for Enlightenment here in this monastery, I recall. A great success story for the Knights and for the Monastery of Divine Light. Previously the Knights have been confined to destroying ordnance and arresting dominophiles by non-violent methods dependent largely on deception technology.'

'Just now you mentioned the New Enlightenment. As well as telling me about Enlightenment as a spiritual programme for reforming dominos Roscoe sometimes referred to the New Enlightenment as a recent historical epoch.'

'Yes, Paul. We at the Monastery of Divine Light coined the expression. It has not yet gained general usage. The New Enlightenment supersedes the intellectual one that took place after the Renaissance and which started in France around 1650. It was initially called the French Enlightenment and essentially it was the rise of reason at the expense of union with God and led ultimately to a departure from reality, with tragic consequences in the twentieth century, such as totalitarianism, when 100 million died and many more lives were cruelly disrupted. Logic in science proved so powerful that men in white coats became the new priests. However, as the 21st century advanced it became apparent that science was dealing with only a small fragment of reality, the one that fitted into the framework of empirical reductionism. Anything outside that framework did not exist for these priests. Numerous phenomena, including miracles, were ignored or denied because they did not fit into their conceptual framework. The western nations ignored the power of evil from those who denied Christ and who filled the spiritual vacuum with evil religions like Nazism. Yet by the second decade of the 21st century there was a growing awareness by western society that scientists were presenting much too narrow a view of life and the universe, useful though it was for practical purposes. Reason itself actually showed by logic and theoretical physics that reality was much larger and stranger than could be investigated by reason alone.

'The New Enlightenment incorporates the traditional one. Reason and science are still very much part of it. The difference now is that they are recognised as limited to only a small part of reality – a very important part from a practical viewpoint and even intellectually. But the New Enlightenment includes the transcendental awareness of the numinous nature of reality and this means submitting ourselves to the triune God.'

'Why not some other concept of God?'

'The Resurrection happened. What Jesus said is true not only at a social but at a divine cosmic level. The early Church Fathers, 150 years before the conversion of Constantine, interpreted the sayings of Christ and did their best to devise a spiritual model which described the reality he represented. We call it the Holy Trinity.'

'Are you saying Christianity is exclusive?'

'In a sense yes. It is exclusively inclusive. It is able to accommodate other monotheistic faiths but no other faith can accommodate Christ because He brings humanity uniquely into communion with the godhead. It is either true or not true. We know it is true, just like the Theory of Relativity is true and the idea of the Earth being round, not flat, is true. We cannot pretend reality is other than it is.'

'But Father James said you had been a Sufi.'

'In a very real sense I still am. Much of the preternatural truth about God which was revealed to me is now incorporated into my faith in God through Christ. However, had I been a true Christian to begin with I would not have been able to switch to Sufism without a contraction of my worldview to something smaller and less personal and denying the foundation of the progressive social change that has occurred as a result of belief in the Resurrected Christ. The same goes for Judaism, Hinduism, Buddhism and any other religion. Converting to any of these from the way of Christ would be to shrink one's perception of reality, to be denied the fullness of God.'

'Is that not rather arrogant?'

'Is it arrogant to believe that the Earth is round not flat? But don't mistake me, Paul. Christians in the modern world have much to learn or re-learn from other faiths. Sufism, for instance, has been defined as a science whose objective is the reparation of the heart and turning it away from all else but God; and the practice of meditation or contemplation in Buddhism is easily applied to prayer. Some of the mysticism of other religions was in fact practiced by the earliest Christians, such as the Desert Fathers, who were hermits, ascetics and monks in the Egyptian desert in the third century. The covenant of Jesus Christ has been very imperfectly practiced but nevertheless it has resulted in huge strides forward in science, technology and social justice.'

'How did Christianity allow scientific progress?'

'From the sixteenth century it provided the conceptual framework for peer reviewed science, especially in Protestant Europe. Not only was truth sacrosanct there was faith in a rational, creative, monotheistic God in whose image man was created. If it had not done so we would not be here on Mars.'

'Why Protestantism in particular?'

'The important point here is that, unlike the Catholicism of that time, it set the precedent for questioning authority in searching for truth. This and the Gutenberg printing press led to the publication of scientific papers and peer reviewing of these in the great Christian universities. Truth, not authority, was sacrosanct. Order in nature was expected from a rational God and was found. The Greeks, for instance, did not have a tradition of peer reviewed scholarship so that even though brilliant ideas and insights were born by thinkers such as Plato and Aristotle they did not evolve or get refined or applied or tested or rejected in a systematic way. Ideas could not thrive and evolve.'

'But Lemaitre conceived the Big Bang model of cosmology and he was a Catholic priest.'

'Very true, my friend. But by the early 20th century the phenomenon of peer reviewed science had proved so powerful that it engulfed the entire western world. Knowledge grew exponentially. It was safe to propose revolutionary ideas for critical examination. Today such scholarship is universal in all fields susceptible to logical investigation. And this has led to enormous advances in technology and Transhumanism. One of the aims of the Monastery of Divine Light is to pray and meditate on what humankind should do with the power it now has to change the physical nature of a human being for good or evil. It is not possible to answer such questions by logic or science alone. Only by connecting with the divine source of our being and eclipsing our pride and reflecting on the Holy Scriptures can we hope to get guidance from God.'

'Now for a question you won't be able to answer.'

'There are many questions that cannot be answered by any worldview, even that of Christianity.'

'The Holy Trinity I accept is a mystery but how can belief in a triune God be called monotheism? How can three Gods be one God?'

'God the Father, God the Son and God the Holy Spirit are different attributes of a single source of being, the godhead, having personhood. The Bible shows how this God relates to humanity, indeed to the universe. Each attribute is best understood and related to as being a person. They are collectively eternal, an uncaused first cause, the source of reality and we are made in the image of the godhead. We thirst to merge with it through love, grace, truth, justice and creativity. Trying to form an image of the Trinity is impossible because it originates outside our dimensions. It is like a flatlander living in two dimensions trying to understand a three dimensional being which interacts with him or her. All the flatlander can do is see how the 3D being manifests itself in 2D and construct an image embodying the nature of the manifestation. That is about the best I can do.'

'Well – I didn't really expect much more.'

'I need to sleep now. Probably you have had enough theology for the time being. Tomorrow we can watch the Martian sunrise.'

*   *   *   *

Dawn broke suddenly. There were strange auroral effects and they could see the Martian moon Phobos hanging in the sky, in half phase, visible before and after daylight.

Aalim said he would like to say something more about the Trinity. He bent down and drew a circle in the red sand with a piece of rock he had picked up. Then he dug three narrow trenches radiating like a star from the central circle. He wrote 'God' inside the circle, 'Father' at the end of one trench, 'Spirit' at the end of the second and 'Son' at the end of the third.

'As I said last night: God the Father, God the Son and God the Holy Spirit. It is all one God with personhood but the Father, the Son and the Holy Spirit are three different persons who are also the one God, albeit a different aspect of His personhood. The three different persons are all absorbed in one eternal Being from which the reality we experience emerges. They are in a dynamic relationship which generates spiritual divine love, the essence of the triune God. It flows into our being. It is free and unearned – grace. It is available to every person born, independent of their deeds; but to receive it you have to be in the right spiritual state. Otherwise not even God can make it work.'

'Which is?'

'Freedom from pride - a state of humility, a complete emptying of your worldly ego, a recognition that everything about you and around you comes from God. This is why pride is the greatest sin. It makes you unable to receive the grace of God through Jesus Christ and even fail to accept that reason and logic are gifts from God.'

'Where does the Divine Light fit into this?'

'It is really another name for the Holy Spirit. Or rather a manifestation of the Spirit which illuminates people of all faiths with an awareness of the reality of the Trinity. Father James in his early ecumenical days used this expression rather than Holy Spirit in order to help break down the prejudice against Christianity that had arisen, largely over the last century or so, partly through non-Christian or even anti-Christian behaviour by people within the church institutions. And it undoubtedly helped bring many from non-Christian faiths, including Atheism, as well as nominal Christians, into relationship with Christ.'

Paul reflected. He felt he was emerging from the darkness into the new reality. His past existence seemed like a dream. This was real.

'You have probably had enough questions for one day but here is another one - again it is probably unanswerable.'

'It's what I'm here for. I am an evangelist.'

'Why does an all loving all powerful God allow so much suffering and evil?'

'At one level we can't answer this. Beware. We are just pin pricks in the vastness of space and time created by this omnipotent being that exists outside our four space-time dimensions. We must be careful not to judge God. Pride gets in the way again. Nevertheless, we can try to imagine things from God's point of view by extrapolating from our human experience.'

'How?'

'In our ordinary so-called "secular" lives.' He paused for emphasis. 'By the way there is no such thing as a secular life. Everything, every atom, every organism and every person, comes from Christ, outside of space and time, before the Big Bang.'

He gave Paul time to take this in. This was not a lesson in theology. This was real. 'Nevertheless, it is a word one can use to mean ordinary day-to-day life in which we forget about the bigger picture.

'Most learning comes from things going wrong, which usually means suffering of some kind. If you slip over and injure yourself you learn to be more careful, thereby reducing the chance of a greater accident. Others around you are affected. They have the opportunity to help you and develop spiritually. You witness the gift of natural healing. When a loved one dies physically while in a spiritual state favoured by God that person will be resurrected in Christ while those close to that person learn and are strengthened while still biologically alive.'

'What do you mean by "favoured by God"? Does this not mean being in Christ?'

'One who is truly in Christ will indeed be favoured. It requires you to have faith in Him. Then you will receive grace. Some may not have heard the gospel but still be favoured because God knows how they have responded to the amount of revelation to which they have been subject through the Divine Light, which is the Holy Spirit. The fruits of the Spirit will be visible in such people even though they have not heard the Good News via human preachers.'

'What about those who have persistently defied Christ? Do they go to hell?'

'Yes, if God looks into their heart and finds only pride and darkness. Possibly they get a second chance before they enter fully into the afterlife awaiting Resurrection in Christ. But we cannot know. This life may be the only one where we have a choice.'

'Hell. What is hell?'

'As I have said reality is multidimensional; and that includes hell. It is beyond imagining. It is the place and state of existence in which those who consciously reject Christ congregate. It is a confluence of evil souls. Imagine spending eternity with such beings unrestrained by the presence of love and peer pressure. A terrifying thought.'

'It scares me that I came so close to it.'

'Perhaps you were not so close to rejecting the Lord. I personally believe that God has a special place for those who genuinely seek truth rather than fill themselves with pride in themselves. It may occur during the dying process. You would be shown two paths very clearly – one of light, one of darkness. If you choose the light you have eternal life and are resurrected in the Lord. Only if you chose darkness would you lose it. But this is merely a view. People should not let it govern their spiritual conduct. Some Christians believe that God's infinite love and mercy eventually drowns out

542

all evil in this world or the afterlife. But why not just concentrate on loving Christ as our saviour? The rest is human speculation.'

'One more question. This has always been a barrier to belief and still confuses me. How is the burden of sin removed by grace? How could God do this by consigning his son to crucifixion? Why could he not just have forgiven us?'

'First, let me observe something Paul. The fact that you have all these questions means you must have been thirsting for the Word over a long period. It is a real delight to God that you have overcome your pride after such a long struggle and that truth is so important to you.'

Aalim stood still, looked skyward and bowed his head momentarily in silent prayer. Then he looked up to address Paul's questions.

'When you unlock the door and let Christ in you will be able to develop faith. When you have faith you receive the gift of grace and all your pride melts away so that you no longer feel everything depends on you. It is all in God's hands. His infinite love wipes away all tears, banishes fear and destroys all guilt. You therefore wish to thank, praise, glorify and serve God through the people you encounter or those you seek out.'

'But why the Crucifixion and the Resurrection?'

'There are different ways of looking at this. He needed to make clear that the sacrifices which were universally made at that time, by pagans and Jews, were not needed. No more burnt offerings by Jews or killing of children by pagans. That was a stage humankind had to move beyond. Jesus made a sacrifice to end all sacrifices except the Christian sacrifice of loving service to God through people.

'At the same time God needed to experience the human condition and perspective. As an extradimensiional entity he was able to do this and to die as a human while remaining alive in his realm. Hence the Incarnation in which he experienced temptation and the limitations of humans. He also needed to give hope to all by conquering death through the Resurrection. And it was only by coming into humanity and leaving it that he could bring the healing and transforming power of the Holy Spirit into humanity.

'It is too easy to get weighed down by theology. I would advise you not to worry too much about it, once you have fully submitted to God. Just believe in the Lord, trust in him and let yourself be filled to the brim with the Holy Spirit and the loving kindness of the Father. Have you said a prayer before, Paul?'

'No. Never.'

'Well let's say one now. This is very simple and I find it anchors me down to the essence of Christianity, expelling all dogmatism, sectarianism, imperialism, culturalism, egotism. It was a prayer Father James taught me when I first submitted myself to Jesus Christ. When you pray this deeply and appeal to the Holy Spirit, it has a truly transforming effect. If everyone followed it and lived it then war would truly be finished. The Knights of Peace would no longer be needed.'

'And my son Roscoe would have to change his career.'

'I fear it could be some time ahead, Paul. Possibly even beyond the three hundred year generation that is now common with Life Extension. Or it could be very soon, if that is the time for a New Heaven and a New Earth.

'Remember that we bow our heads to show humility, the most important and neglected of Christian virtues. Say this repeatedly throughout the day and it will bring you ever closer to the grace of the Lord Jesus Christ. Say it with me now, Paul, aloud.'

Aalim transmitted the text to Paul's flexcom set into the right arm of his pressurised smartsuit so that he could read it out.

They stood facing the Martian sunrise and bowed their heads.

Lord, make me an instrument of your peace
Where there is hatred, let me sow Love
Where there is despair, hope
Where there is darkness, light
Where there is doubt, faith
And where there is sadness, joy.

Divine Master, let me seek not so much to be consoled, as to console
To be understood, as to understand
To be loved, as to love
For it is in giving that we receive
In pardoning that we are pardoned
And in dying that we are born to eternal life

The End

Lightning Source UK Ltd.
Milton Keynes UK
UKOW02f0639031014

239525UK00001B/37/P